PRAISE FOR MERCY

This cozy gothic angel romance is sizzling but tender. Funny. Passionate. Tense. Heartbreaking. A beautiful portrayal of intimacy as reverence. Be prepared to savor every word.

— MORGAN DANTE, AUTHOR OF
PROVIDENCE GIRLS

Haramaki blends forbidden romance, religious iconography, and dark ritualism in this perfect Paranormal Fantasy. For fans of Lucien Burr and V.E. Schwab, MERCY is bold, queer, captivating, and adventurous.

— FREYDÍS MOON BESTSELLING AUTHOR
OF HEART, HAUNT, HAVOC

A compelling tale of romance and healing, MERCY lures you into a world rich with history and mythology.

— K. M. ENRIGHT, AUTHOR OF MISTRESS
OF LIES

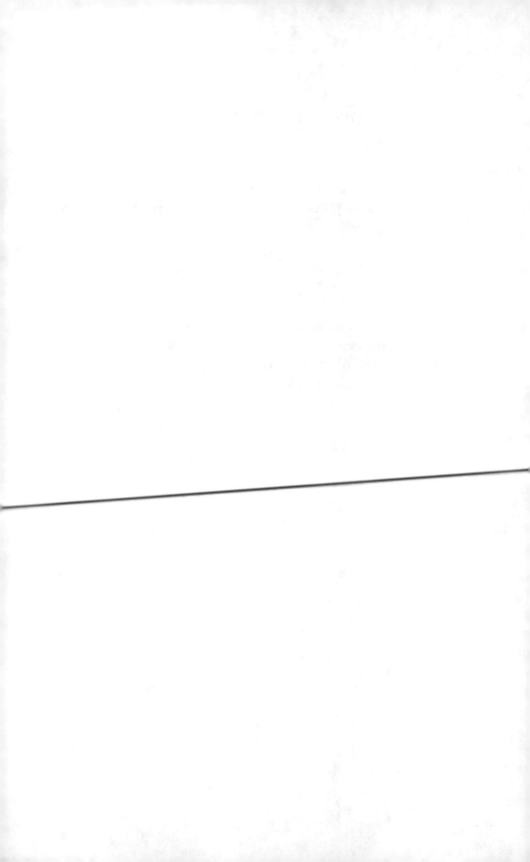

MERCY

Contact: ian@cometkins.com

Cover Art: Soren Häxen (www.etsy.com/shop/corpsehaus)

Editor: Quinton Li (www.quintonli.com)

To my Wranglers, Loons, and Eli for supporting me through the ups and downs of this writing journey.
Eli gets singled out because I've known him for like 20 years okay.

CONTENT WARNINGS

This book contains content that may be triggering or otherwise unpleasant for certain readers. Please read the following warnings and proceed with discretion.

- Explicit sexual content
- Suicidal ideation *(mild)*
- Abusive parental figures *(mother)*
- Alcoholic parental figures *(mother)*
- Deceased parental figures *(father, cancer)*
- Parental violence *(mother)*
- Homophobia
- Death of a romantic partner *(not main couple)*
- Physical assault *(no sexual assault of any kind)*
- Sexual harassment of a main character
- Abusive church dynamics

PART I

NIGHT

1

September 12th, 1927

To call it a body was perhaps beyond the point of useful description. Father Ilya Pavlovich Sokolov kneeled to examine the bloated pile on the nave floor, the horrific stench making his eyes water as he got close. He held one side of his hood across his nose to block it, fighting the urge to gag. Blessedly, it had been raining the past few days; the ones they'd found in the heat were a nightmare.

It was the same as the others. Flesh tattered and falling away from bleached white bone, scored and pitted from teeth. Ilya tilted the head to examine the skull cavity, finding it open and half full of ooze and flies. Most of the limbs were missing, ripped out of their sockets. What muscle remained was pale and swollen from the downpours. There was also the matter of the acrid, black slime seeping from every wound, clinging on in spite of the weather. There were no doubts; this was the doing of the drekavac that had terrorized Velak for months.

It was a creature from the Realm of Eternal Night. Any living victims had simply been faster than the friend or family it got to first. He'd heard it described as enormous, black-furred, and covered in thousands of red eyes. It had a pale fleshless face, as if to mock their Great Father, the Moon. It smelled of death, and it left black ink in its wake.

Ilya was not beloved in Velak, and the tides were turning ever harder against him. The people already believed him to be useless since his predecessor passed, but his supposed inaction on the drekavac had them in a quiet fury. The Church Hunters had ignored all of his pleas for help thus far, determining Velak too small to bother with; it would have to be a personal matter for Ilya.

The woman who had brought the body wailed, "What are you going to do about this? How many more of us must die, Ilya?"

Ilya looked up at her. They never dignified him with his title.

Tears stained the woman's cheeks, her modestly embroidered dress dingy with mud, blood, and sinew. A pang of guilt lanced through his chest, seeing the simple clothes she wore, contrasted with the finery the Church gave him: vestments of black with traces of ivory and gold. A circular cutout sat in the center of his chest, surrounded by the pattern of a Sun. Golden medallions strung with pearls held his hood together and sat around his waist as a belt. He was a shining, immodest spectacle.

Both of them were exhausted, angry, and at their limit, much like everybody else in town. Ilya had spent weeks researching answers; he was just a priest, this wasn't his jurisdiction. The paltry church library had supplied little in the way of information. He'd learned almost nothing about what a drekavac *was*, let alone how to fight one. His training was in healing and holding ceremonies, not combat, thus he was woefully unequipped to handle this. This is what the damned Hunters were *for!*

He dragged a hand down his face. She might as well have been driving daggers into his skull for how she looked at him.

"I've told you all a thousand times the Hunters won't return my letters and my telephone isn't working to call the Capital. I have *nothing* I can do. Perhaps the rest of you could help me—"

The woman clenched her fists and slammed them against her thighs. "Enough of your excuses. My son is dead! Stepan is gone and that beast left me nothing but *scraps!* There's been over a dozen dead so far! We're all dying! *Do something* you *useless* man! Do it yourself for all the good you bring!"

All Ilya could manage was an exasperated sigh. He got to his feet and threw his hands up in frustration. "And what would you have me do? Throw myself to the beast as a willing meal? Then you'll have no priest and as many monsters as before!"

"Better than having a useless murderer continue sitting in this holy place."

She spat at his feet and stormed out of the church, leaving him alone with the mass of meat that had once been the aforementioned Stepan. He stared down at the body and sighed again. He supposed it was time to do more dirty work.

Ilya was not a strong man. The graves took hours to dig and ended up a fair bit more shallow than they should, but he had neither the stamina nor will to make them properly. The old grave-keeper had died shortly after Ilya's father, and since then nobody had bothered to take up the mantle. As ever, his priestly duties extended well beyond what they were meant to.

Ilya dug until his body threatened to give out, using the last of his strength to claw at the sparse grass and haul himself out. He was filthy, damp earth coating his skin. Every speck of dirt on his skin made him itch and filled him with immeasurable anguish. Visions of trash mountains and bottle fields in his mother's home flashed in his mind. He roughly scratched at his arms in a feeble attempt to soothe himself.

The soil around the church had a nasty habit of being *mud*. Grass *tried* to grow, but its success was debatable. Ilya could never get clean because of it, and even after over two decades enduring, he still hated it. He was shocked the church hadn't slid down the hill and crashed into the town square yet.

Ilya washed up inside the rectory. He changed into the gold vestments for last rites, silk brocade with delicate embroidery made from metallic thread. Unfortunately, Stepan would become the latest victim of both the drekavac and the town's irrational behavior. For all they screamed and shouted at him, the people of Velak never came for their loved ones' funerals. They hated him so much, clung so hard to the lies they told themselves about him, they couldn't be around for their last rites. It baffled the mind.

He lit his spiked golden censer, swayed it from side to side, and whispered a prayer to their Mother Sun. He asked for the deceased's safe travels into the Realm of Eternal Light and to find peace in death. The smoke from the incense filled the air. Ilya breathed it all in. He closed his eyes, silent for a beat before moving the soil back over the body. It would be many months until the ground settled enough for all the new graves to have headstones, so he drove in a wooden stake to mark it temporarily.

Ilya was putting his shovel away when numerous voices rose in the air from further down the muddy hill. Making his way around the church to the front, his body heated and prickled as his anxiety rose. He froze when he came upon the rabble, suddenly finding over a dozen eyes on him. There was a lack of torches and pitchforks, but there were more people at his church than there had been in all his years of service. The message was clear.

He swallowed hard as Mayor Ivan marched up to him, shoving a thick finger into Ilya's sternum. The mayor's face was scrunched and red, fury clear even through the wiry gray beard covering his face. Ilya braced himself and waited.

"I've had enough of you, Sokolov," Ivan hissed, jamming his finger against Ilya's chest with greater force, "You're going to go out there and *kill it*, or die trying."

Ilya glanced from the mayor to the rest of the townsfolk behind him. The heat of their eyes bore holes into him. This wasn't all the people of Velak, but there were far more than he could ever attempt to fight off. If the drekavac didn't tear him to shreds, these people would.

He couldn't decide which was worse.

"You know I'm not trained in combat, Mayor Ivan." Ilya kept his tone careful, tiptoeing around the mayor's anger.

An older man from the back of the crowd shouted, "I shot it last night! Stupid thing ran off my farm before I could finish it! Figure it out!"

Ilya managed to stifle a groan of contempt. So *they* could shoot it, but *he* had to finish the job? Nothing these people did surprised him anymore, and they had become even more nonsensical of late.

He swallowed hard as they surrounded him. His only hope to get out of this was to kill it, then. He had no idea how. No matter how many times he told the people he was a healer and his magic wasn't capable of doing harm, they wouldn't listen.

He should've abandoned his post ages ago — excommunication be damned.

Ilya held up a hand in an attempt to quiet the angry murmurs among the crowd. He hoped they couldn't see how it shook. "All right! All right. But if I die, know that you'll have to fix this your-selves! Now get out of my sight!"

Ilya broke out from the group and marched through the door to the sacristy to gather his things. Once out of sight his body began to shake so violently his shoulders ached from tension. He couldn't get his breathing under control and he had to use every bit of his strength to keep from screaming.

At least the drekavac would be fast when it killed him.

Probably.

Eventually he pulled himself together long enough to prepare for his demise. He gathered his specially synthesized bricks of incense, placing one into his censer for later. They could paralyze anything that breathed in the smoke, and perhaps it would be advantage enough. He packed extra herbs, a lantern, and tied a dense cloth over his mouth and nose. Ilya had to pray the incense could finish it off. More likely he'd become the next pile of flesh left amongst the pine needles and birch leaves.

He slumped against the wall and tried to collect himself again, asking the air how he got here. Could he have avoided this? Why did it have to be him? He'd wanted to be a priest like his father, but now all he could do was curse his name. It seemed the Sokolov men were destined to die young.

He stepped out into the graveyard once more. He overheard a

few of the townsfolk whisper they were shocked he hadn't run out the back. It hadn't occurred to him he could escape, but he was sure he'd run into the drekavac if he did anyway. They were surrounded by miles and miles of dense woods and rocky outcroppings with plenty of places for a terrifying beast to hide.

Ivan crossed his arms across his chest, watching Ilya make his way to the muddy path down the hill before giving him a solemn nod. "We do want you to succeed," he called out, "Even if it doesn't seem like it!"

Ilya rolled his eyes once he was on the path, huffing to himself. The evening air had settled in and the chill enveloped him. His breath hung around his face in a fog, even in spite of his covering. He stumbled down the slick path and pulled his hood up as an icy drizzle began to fall. He scowled as his vestments began to absorb the late summer rain; one more box to check on the list of things making Ilya's day dreadful.

NIGHT HAD SETTLED in by the time he made it to the part of the woods the attacks had been reported. The rain was coming down in a light trickle and Ilya was grateful it wasn't yet a downpour. His censer would never work if it was too wet, and he'd also like to be *a little* less miserable while being eaten.

Ilya fumbled around in his pockets until he found a match. He used his cloak to shield his censer from the wind long enough to light it, replacing the top in haste. He watched the sickly yellow smoke tumble out of the sun shaped openings and gather around his feet, an aura of toxins to protect him. He struggled with his lantern next, relieved when it too managed to light.

A great scarlet light hit the trees. The shadows of the woods grew darker against it, dancing as the flame shifted inside of its glass case. It fought against the breeze threatening to snuff it out; Ilya gritting his teeth in the hope it would stay alight. The evening glow behind the mountains had faded only moments ago. Darkness bloomed and left him a beacon in the middle of an ocean of dark conifers and ghostly birch trees.

Ilya tightened his grip on the lantern and began marching forward. He took care to be as silent as he could manage, dread filling him with every snapped twig or crushed leaf.

The further he traveled the more baffled he became that the drekavac had found any of them in the first place. He had to be several miles away from town now, nothing but trees in any direction. All he could hear was underbrush beneath his feet and rain pattering against his hood. His hands ached from the cold leaching into his bones, every breath like fire as he walked. His censer had long burned out, his lantern was starting to wane, and more and more, Ilya felt like a pig up for slaughter.

He swore under his breath and packed spare herbs into his censer. He wasn't sure why he bothered, perhaps to finally draw the drekavac out in the hopes it would put him out of his misery. He wished he could run back home, but that would surely draw its attention faster.

The scent of juniper, cinnamon, and sage wafted about him. Ilya untied the cloth around his face to breathe it in, one last comfort preceding his death. He swung his censer back and forth on its heavy chain to spread the smoke as far as he could.

There was a glint out of the corner of his eye. A sharp, penetrating smell hit his nostrils and overpowered the botanicals he was burning. Ilya froze. He cursed himself as the chain of his censer rattled in his terror.

He strained to look out of his peripherals, revealing nothing.

Lovely. It was behind him then.

Ilya whirled around as the gooey form lunged at him. It swiped at the air with bony claws covered in pitch. The creature had long black fur slicked through with oil oozing off its body, the sun-bleached, eyeless skull of a wolf jutting out from the mess of darkness. It towered over Ilya, hundreds of glowing red eyes embedded in its skin staring at him, tiny arms lining its belly flexing in anticipation.

Ilya caught a glimpse of the single red eye in its mouth, side stepping out of the way, heart beginning to pound. The drekavac snarled at him with a gaping maw, barely held together by strings of sinewy muscle stretched with the movement. Ilya held tight to the chain of his censer as he sent the metal pot spiraling at the beast. The spiked metal cracked against the bone and it cried out in pain. The sound was high pitched and garbled and it thrashed, sending ink everywhere as it stumbled back and whimpered.

Ilya's breath came in rapid, short bursts as he took the creature in. Its right back paw dangled limp and useless under its body, clearly shattered in several places. So that farmer had injured it after all.

The beast stared him down and Ilya swung out his censer once more. The drekavac leaped out of the way, twisting its unnaturally long body and lunging at Ilya from his side. Ilya had no time to turn away. Teeth sank into his left shoulder, bone scratching bone echoing in his ears. Blood burst from flesh and splattered hot on his cheek, the pain too great for Ilya to make a sound. The drekavac smelled like acid, his wound burning as black slime oozed into it. His heart was pounding so hard his blood rushed in his ears.

Ilya used his uninjured arm to slam his censer against the drekavac, heavy metal pot cracking against a thin front leg. It howled in pain and released him from its death grip, limping backwards from him. The leg had snapped and was clearly not fit for use. Hope flickered in his chest as the drekavac turned tail and ran back into the woods.

He took a moment to catch his breath, adrenaline taking over and making him follow. Ilya gripped at his injured shoulder, cursing his oath to the Sun. Her acolytes weren't allowed to use their healing magics for themselves, thus he was forced to live with this excruciating pain. He couldn't think beyond his singular task, following after the beast as it limped along. He was determined to finish the job.

The creature was fast, but the frequency of inky black puddles left in its wake told him it was slowing down. Hours passed as he followed it, the pain of his arm dulling to a throb he could shove to the back of his mind. His throat was raw from how long he'd been jogging after the creature, drool gathering in his mouth from the exertion. His lungs burned and he'd been on the verge of collapse ages ago, but he couldn't let it go now.

His father once told him a tale of how humans used to hunt the great megafauna of the past by following them for hours on end, not letting up until the animal grew too exhausted to fight back. Ilya hoped his ancient ancestors were proud of him for employing the same tactics.

The indigo light of dawn began its slow creep into the woods as the drekavac rushed into the mouth of a nearby cavern nestled into the side of the mountains. It swallowed the creature whole, enveloping it in darkness. Ilya pressed on, leaning against the mouth of the cave to catch his breath. Sweat poured down his back and soaked through his curly hair, sticking to his face as he stumbled forward.

The growing dawn light revealed the cavern was shallow, a few feet deep at most. Finally, the furry, inky form collapsed on its side and heaved desperate breaths. Ilya loomed over the drekavac, watching it curiously, bleached bone mask staring at him. It let out a mournful whine before it laid flat, resigned to its fate.

Indigo turned purple behind Ilya as the light began to grow, and it allowed him to properly take the creature in. It was very thin, the bulk of its form coming from its soaked fur. He glanced at both injured legs and spotted bone sticking out of the back one. That man from town had done a serious number for how mangled it was.

Ilya felt sorry for this animal. Despite terrorizing Velak for months, laid out in front of him, literally on its last limb, he couldn't muster enough anger. Every breath it took came out as a whimper, and even in its weakened state it was inching away from the coming sunlight.

He heaved a deep sigh. Mayor Ivan would have his head if he knew what Ilya was about to do.

Ilya stepped close to the drekavac and ignored its soft growl. He kneeled next to it and placed a hand on its shoulder. It flinched at the touch but could do nothing to respond. Ilya let his fingers sink into the inky fur, rubbing against bone covered by paper thin flesh beneath. He caressed the creature's body, moving to the injured leg.

The drekavac lifted its head and snarled when he touched it. Ilya clucked his tongue and shook his head. "If you keep hissing at me I'll never be able to fix it, you know."

The creature stared back at him with its hollowed eyes, while the single red eye in its mouth seemed to constantly be looking in every direction. The lack of further snapping suggested it was listening to him.

Ilya rested a careful hand against the fracture. A glowing symbol of the Sun formed in the air around his wrist, golden light leaking from his palm. Bone cracked as it shifted back into place, flesh stitching over it once more. The drekavac whined at first, then sighed in relief as it relaxed, slumping against the rocks.

Ilya jumped back when the body began letting off noxious smoke. He pulled his hood across the lower half of his face to avoid breathing it in and watched in shock as the oil-slicked fur began to slough off the body. The bony mask fell away in shards, the body began to shrink, and a new, more human form took shape.

Ilya hesitated as he kneeled next to the body again and pulled clumps of fur away. He gasped as his pale hand revealed warm, tawny colored skin covered in even darker freckles. The remaining slime burned his hands as he forced his way through and at last revealed the body of a man.

Any traces of ink smoked and burned away as the red light of dawn blazed behind them. Ilya touched a hand to the man's cheek, barely a caress. He moved his thumb across the man's face, more intimate than he intended as he took in the sight.

The man's face was sharp and handsome, cheeks rosy with warmth. His face was dusted with more freckles and his long black hair fell across his forehead in delicate strands. Ilya brushed it back, taking it all in.

All this time, the beast was simply a man cursed to kill. All that was needed to reverse it was for someone to take a chance.

Fresh guilt welled up in his chest, working its way down to his stomach to tie it into knots. He could've saved this man so long ago, could've prevented so many deaths. If he were better at his job, maybe he could've made it all go away.

Ilya removed his cloak and covered his mystery man to save his dignity. For now he'd wait until his charge woke up.

Then they'd figure out how to get back home.

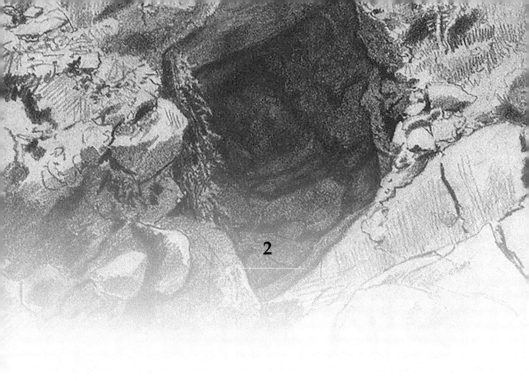

2

September 13th, 1927

Ilya attempted to doze against the mouth of the cave and ignore how much pain he was in while waiting for the man to wake. He jumped when the mystery man gasped. Ilya went still and watched him, lips parted in anticipation.

The man grumbled and pushed himself up, using his bad hand to shield his eyes from the bright noon light. He first glanced at his surroundings, dark brown eyes settling next on Ilya. Ilya gave him a half-hearted wave.

"Who... the fuck are you?" the man asked.

Ilya frowned at the language. "I could ask you the same thing. I'm Father Ilya Pavlovich Sokolov. What do you remember?"

The mystery man sat up and gripped his head. He hissed in pain and took a moment to collect himself. There was a drawn-out pause while he stared at the ground, finally rubbing his temples and shaking his head.

"Not jack nor shit," the man replied.

"That's helpful," Ilya sighed.

"Who asked you anyway?"

Ilya's cloak was beginning to slide off of the man's shoulders, exposing thick, toned muscle. Ilya's throat went dry as his eyes roamed over the man's skin, trying to count the freckles. He shook his head and blinked as he got to his feet, holding his hand out for the man.

"Well, we have a long way home, so I suppose there's plenty of time to tell you what I know. With any luck it'll jog a memory or two," Ilya said.

The man hesitated and then took Ilya's hand, hauling himself to his feet. Ilya glanced up and down his body for the briefest of moments, admiring the strength that lay under the lithe muscle. When he caught himself he turned around, crossed his arms, and cleared his throat.

There was a soft, husky laugh from behind Ilya that made heat crawl up his neck and straight to his ears. His skin was burning hot and he couldn't bear to turn around. His normal complexion was comparable to a corpse, he'd be far too obvious right now. He wouldn't expose himself like this.

"It's free to look you know," the man said, "but I hear a photograph lasts longer."

Ilya guffawed and marched forward, waving this *insufferable* man along with him. This man couldn't even remember his own name, but could remember to be an obnoxious, flirty pest? Ridiculous.

THEY MADE decent time on the walk back to Velak. Ilya took his time explaining what had been happening with the drekavac, doing his best to tread carefully. The man's irritating demeanor grew somber as he was informed of what he'd been made to do all these weeks. Ilya couldn't help but sympathize. Nobody wanted to end a life without knowing, especially when they weren't themselves. It must be hard to cope with.

"You know," the man said, "I remembered something while you were talking... I'm Danya."

Ilya glanced over at the mystery man; Danya, he supposed.

"Well, that makes things easier, Danya. Now I know who to yell at when you can't keep your behavior in check."

Danya huffed at him. "Ilya, right? You're kind of a dick, you know that?"

Ilya snorted. "I can take my cloak back and make you walk around town naked if you think so highly of me."

Danya glared back at him. "Sure you'd like that, fucking pervert."

Ilya ground his teeth together but refused to sink to Danya's level. It never did any good to argue with people who were determined to hate you.

They moved in complete silence save for the sounds of the woods around them. Ilya assumed Danya was trying to conjure up more about his life, perhaps contemplating his actions as a monster. It seemed like a lot to have on your mind; so much death, so little memory.

The silence was broken when Danya asked, "So... what's with the outfit?"

Ilya blinked. What a strange question.

"I'm a Sun priest of the Church of the Eclipse," he replied. "You don't remember this? I suppose if you can hardly remember your name you're not going to remember much about religion."

"I... think I kind of know it, maybe. But you look way over-dressed and undressed at the same time. You're basically drowning in all that shit." Danya frowned and pointed at Ilya's chest. "And what's with the boob window?"

Ilya guffawed, confused by words he'd never heard in his life. What in Sun's name was a "boob window"? Danya couldn't be from this country if he used such strange, vulgar language like that. Regardless, Ilya didn't need comments about his uniform. "I don't have a choice in what I wear, Danya. I like it. Nobody needs to see me anyway."

"Doesn't explain the boob window," he replied.

"It's to expose my heart to the light of the Sun, our great Mother above. Shouldn't you be excited about me exposing myself anyway?"

Danya scoffed. "No. Your uniform's weird. And why haven't you healed yourself? That gash is gonna get infected."

"Because I can't and if I get an infection it'll be your fault anyway," Ilya snapped.

Danya clamped his mouth shut and glared at Ilya, turning his eyes ahead to avoid looking at him.

Fine then.

They were back to strained silence as Velak came into view once more. As they made their way to the edge of the woods, Ilya gave pause. The townsfolk would be suspicious of both of them. Ilya very much not dead, and with a strange naked man in tow. Frankly the nudity would be enough reason to avoid town directly. Tensions were high and he wasn't interested in tempting fate.

"Why don't we go around— I'll take you to the church so the others don't see you. You're indecent anyway," Ilya said, jerking his head to direct Danya where to go.

Ilya spotted Danya's cheeks go a bit red. Danya nodded and said, "Yeah… I don't really feel like flashing everybody. Already got their priest."

Ilya snorted in good nature and led the way back to the church. The hill was an even bigger sloppy, muddy nightmare than yesterday. Danya struggled with his bare feet and Ilya clenched his jaw as mud splashed onto his clothes.

"This fucking blows," said Danya.

"Indeed," Ilya replied.

They had almost reached the top when Danya slipped hard in the mud. He grabbed a puffy sleeve, dragging Ilya down as he fell. Ilya shouted as mud splashed around them, seeping into the back of his vestments, into his hair, into the still open wound on his shoulder. Danya laughed and Ilya snapped his head up to glare at him with all the fury he could muster.

"Why in *Sun's name* did you do that?" he hissed.

Danya's laughter devolved into a fit of giggles. He covered his mouth in a feeble attempt to hide it. "Sorry— It was a reflex."

Ilya got on his feet and stumbled up the rest of the hill as fast as his legs would carry him, leaving Danya lying in the mud. If he didn't change this instant he would *scream*.

Ilya threw open the door to the rectory and grabbed at his injured shoulder from the strain. He made his way to the kitchen and started to peel his muddy top from his body, setting it in the sink. Even this one thing brought him immense relief. He couldn't help but to sigh.

Ilya jolted when he heard Danya snort, turning to see him in the doorway smirking. Ilya panicked and lifted his shirt up, cheeks going hot in shame.

"No, please keep going," Danya crooned.

Ilya set his shirt aside again and snapped, "Why is it that you've only *just* remembered your name, but you can recall enough to make a mess of me and act like a complete and utter pig? Enough of this!"

Danya held up his hands in defense, sighing after a moment. "I'm sorry! You saved my ass and I'm being one for no reason. I don't want to think too much..."

Ilya sagged at Danya's confession, heat sapped out of his mood in an instant. He was frustrated, but he wasn't unsympathetic to what Danya was dealing with. Still, he was being very, very annoying.

"Yes, well. Get it together while I start the bath. The rectory just had a water heater installed, so you're in for a treat," Ilya said.

Danya hummed and sat at the kitchen table. Ilya took that as his sign to leave, first moving to the room in the corner to grab his spare clothes, then making his way back to the bathroom. He adjusted the taps and waited until it was the perfect temperature, rubbing a wet hand over his face. His skin prickled all over with his disgust. It was hard to tell if it was Danya's flirting, how filthy he was, or both.

Upsetting either way.

He got in the tub and leaned back to stare at the ceiling. Being killed by the drekavac would make his life complicated, but in reality, being dead would be so much more simple, wouldn't it? Now he had an insufferable man to look after who kept mocking him. It was insulting, even if deep down he enjoyed the attention.

Velak was too small and too closed-minded for him to ever have a romantic relationship. He'd come to grips with that long ago. He'd die alone and unloved, taking his secret to the grave.

Thus was the fate of Ilya Pavlovich Sokolov.

He tried to not dwell on it as he scrubbed his curls free of mud. He felt human, being clean. He'd rubbed his skin raw with the soap to find a modicum of relief. He cleaned out his wound, grateful that it looked worse than it was. It would scar, and likely his arm would ache for a while, but it wouldn't need stitches.

Once he finished he got out, drained the muddy, soapy water, and then refilled it for Danya. He took care to bandage his shoulder, relief washing over him as every last speck of dirt and blood was finally off of him. He could be calm now.

He stepped out of the bathroom once he'd redressed in casual clothing, spotting Danya staring out the window at the setting sun. Ilya rubbed his eyes, unsure if he was seeing things; he could swear that Danya's eyes looked lighter than earlier.

"Tub's ready," Ilya said. "I'll see if I can't find something spare for you to wear."

Danya gave him a solemn nod and headed into the bathroom. He shut the door quietly, leaving Ilya alone. Ilya let out a beleaguered sigh and walked back to the kitchen sink, starting to scrub out his vestments. He was relieved nothing had stained the lighter parts, and glad they were mostly black anyway. If he'd missed anything he didn't have to know.

It was too damp outside to dry his things, so he hung them above the fireplace, directly across from the kitchen. He got a small flame going to help the drying process and warm the main room, stepping back into his bedroom to find things for Danya. Danya was a fair bit taller than him and certainly more bulky, but he hoped a few of these things might be suitable temporarily. He set them in front of the bathroom and dragged himself to the couch.

He was leafing through all the paperwork for the recent death records when the bathroom door opened a fraction. Ilya spotted a tawny colored hand swipe the clothes off the floor before slamming it shut again. He couldn't help but laugh; perhaps Danya seemed to have found his dignity again.

A brief moment passed and Danya came out of the bathroom, giving Ilya an incredulous look. While Ilya normally swam in his clothes, Danya was a tight fit. He could see muscle shift under the gray sweater as Danya moved, Ilya drawn to it. Ilya met Danya's eyes when he cleared his throat.

"You must look like a skeleton under there if these barely fit," Danya said. The soft fabric was tight across his chest, straining to be contained. "What the fuck is this?"

Ilya snorted. "I think you're just big."

"Are you calling me fat?"

"If you want."

Danya rolled his eyes and swiped Ilya's papers out of his hands, examining them closely. He frowned as he read them, going still.

"Find anything interesting?" Ilya asked.

Danya gave him a sheepish look and handed the papers back.

"I wanted to see if something would jog my memory," Danya whispered.

Ilya supposed he preferred Danya contemplative more than annoying. He was much easier to be around.

"You know, I am a healer... Not a good one, but I am. I don't know of any specific memory magic, but maybe I can try something?"

Danya met his gaze and Ilya had his suspicions confirmed. Danya's eyes were definitely a lighter color, more like a dark honey than the black they'd been earlier. They were stunning. Ilya found he couldn't look away, holding his breath.

"I'd appreciate that if you're willing," Danya replied. "Everything feels like it's on the tip of my tongue. I can just reach out and touch it but it slips away right as it's in my grasp."

"I'll see what I can do. Sit."

Danya did so, tilting his head toward Ilya. Ilya set his hands against Danya's temples, rubbing his thumbs into his forehead. Danya closed his eyes, taking a deep breath. Ilya let his fingers dig into the long locks of hair falling down Danya's head, pressing his palms firm against him. He poured all of his focus into his hands, the thrum of his magic extending out from his chest, down his arms, through to his fingertips. They prickled with power, every ounce he could muster. The symbol of the Sun encircled his wrists, warm light emanating from his palms once again.

Ilya transferred everything he could to heal Danya's mind, grimacing with the exertion. He wasn't a strong healer by any means, but he also wasn't sure memory was fixable this way. The mind was a mysterious, jumbled thing where any small change could set off its balance. Ilya worried he might make things worse.

Alas, there was nothing. When he healed an injury the warmth of the Sun flowed in his hands; right now it was just making his palms sweat.

The glow died down after a moment, Ilya pulling his hands away. Danya's eyes fluttered open, a deep frown on his face.

"Nothing," Danya sighed.

"I suspected as much, unfortunately. Perhaps you just need time to recover, find the right triggers. You were attacking Velak for months, but who knows how long you'd been transformed. Seems like a long time to be trapped as a beast."

There was a mournful expression on Danya's face. Ilya bit his lip as a pang of sympathy lanced through his chest. Everybody hated hearing that time was the best medicine, but it was the truth. Ilya swore to help and to heal when he'd made his oath and burned his eyes out long ago, so he would help Danya however that took shape.

Ilya smacked his thighs and got to his feet. "Well, it's time we ate. I don't suppose you remember any food you enjoy?"

Danya was sinking into both the couch and himself, head turned toward the floor. Finally, he replied, "I don't know."

Now Ilya couldn't decide if he preferred Danya when he was a flirtatious pest. He expected he'd have to help Danya work through a lot of mood swings in the coming days. He reached to pat Danya's shoulder, a brief and gentle touch to show he was there. He stepped away towards the kitchen, rummaging through the icebox to see what he had that might be quick. His stomach had been growling at him for hours.

He cobbled together a few sandwiches and set their plates on the big oak table, glancing at the couch to check on Danya. Who, notably, was missing.

Panic bubbled up in the pit of his stomach. He rushed to check the bathroom, the chapel, and the attic. With no signs of him, Ilya rushed outside.

"Danya?" Ilya called.

"Here," Danya called back.

Ilya deflated in his relief, following Danya's voice to the grave-yard. Danya was sitting in the dirt, knees held to his chest and staring at all the fresh graves.

"This was me?"

Ilya watched Danya, hesitating to answer. Would it do any good to be honest? Would Danya do something drastic if he said yes, fragile as he was right now? Danya had spiraled so quickly since they'd come home.

"Does it matter?"

Danya cast a frigid glare at Ilya. "Of course it matters. I killed people, Ilya!"

"But it wasn't you, was it?" Ilya kneeled next to Danya, nudging him with his shoulder. Ilya knew he was far from perfect. He wasn't going to judge Danya for any of this.

"But it was! It... It was all me," Danya sobbed, pressing the heels of his palms against his eyes. "All I remember is being so *hungry*."

Danya continued to cry, burying his face against his knees. Ilya lifted his hand, hesitated, and then placed it on Danya's shoulder. He dug the pads of his fingers in, enough to show he was present.

"I begged for help from the Church and tried to do my own research, but I couldn't find anything to help the town. I'm not a fighter... Had I known what it would take..."

Danya seemed too preoccupied to respond to him. Ilya waited, keeping his hand on the anguished man. He could heal physical wounds, but mental ones were another beast. If he knew how to fix those, he'd be the best healer in the world.

Another moment passed until Danya wiped at his eyes with the edge of his sleeve, clearing his throat. Ilya took his hand off of him then.

"Sounds like you're a shitty priest."

Ilya huffed a laugh. "You're not the only one who thinks so. People have refused to even come for funerals…"

Another long silence passed between them, the Sun sinking lower in the sky as evening approached. It was warm compared to the previous night; a welcome break as they sat in the dirt.

Danya refused to take his eyes off of the new graves. Ilya could see his eyes roaming over all the wooden stakes, counting them out. Ilya had tried to not think too much about the number. His guilt had been eating him alive, the lack of answers leaving him utterly powerless.

And yet here they were. The drekavac's reign of terror had come to an end. All this time, and all he'd needed to do was his job: heal.

He couldn't even heal his own father from his illness. His skills were so lacking the townsfolk relied on traditional medicine instead. To heal a murderous creature like the drekavac, to show it such mercy? It shocked him. It had been pure instinct, a primal need to make it better. Maybe the spirit of the Eclipse used him to enact its light, managing to make him useful. He couldn't say.

He'd just known he had to help.

"You're right, Danya. I am a shitty priest. I don't even know if I'm a good person," Ilya whispered. "Everybody in town would agree with that. But they're not much better, to be honest… How many of them would have my head if they knew you were here, or what I'm really like."

Danya looked over at him, red highlight from the setting sun outlining his silhouette. Even with the evening shadows, Ilya swore he could see the faint golden color of Danya's eyes.

Danya asked, "What are you saying?"

Ilya gave him a wry smile. "Only that we're all terrible in our own special ways. I know there's people in town who abuse their children, their spouses, who steal and lie and cheat their neighbors. I wouldn't be surprised if there's anybody who's killed too. And they all *knew* when they were doing it!"

Danya scowled at him. "What's your point?"

"My point is, Velak is an awful place, and you'll fit in fine here. Perhaps in time you'll remember who you are, where you came from, how you were cursed. Who's to say how one comes upon such a terrible fate?"

Danya stared at him, taking a moment to let the words sink in. His brows knit as he stared at the ground. "What if I was a killer before this?"

"Well, you don't have to be one now. We'll cross that bridge when we come to it. Now, come eat dinner. It's a bit meager, but I'm sure you'll live."

Danya scoffed. "How appealing."

"I change my mind, go back to brooding and being silent."

Ilya caught a brief flash of a smile on Danya's face. If what it took for Danya to have normalcy was to bicker with him forever, Ilya supposed he could tolerate it.

3

September 16th, 1927

Adjusting to life as a human had been difficult for Danya. He would get defensive over food, was quick to anger, and his sleeping habits were a nightmare. He took care to remember himself, but Ilya's patience was threadbare. He needed space.

"I'm going into town today. Will you need anything?" Ilya asked.

Danya was on the couch, knees pulled to his chest, an aura of darkness surrounding him that sucked all the joy out of the room. He glared at the wallpaper next to the fireplace and eventually shook his head.

"I'll find something for dinner, but you're on your own for lunch."

"Got it."

Ilya knew he could be broody and miserable, but Danya took the cake today. He gathered his shopping basket and left through the church without another word. It was warm outside, Sun shining above the town. He hoped the mud would dry out, at least a little. There was a light breeze that blew the orange and brown leaves around him. He took a deep breath, feeling the crisp air fill his lungs. He supposed he should enjoy the clinging warmth of summer until the misery of alpine winter set in.

Ilya braced himself as he approached the town square, admiring the small clocktower that stood in the middle. It was one of the only pleasant sights in all of Velak.

The townsfolk were milling about, casting sidelong glances his way and whispering to themselves. They muttered about how shocked they were that he was alive, that he must have been lying and able to fight this whole time, how dare he show his face, how dare he let them die for so long. Ilya had no idea how to please these people, who were determined to think the worst of him. How could he convince them that he'd been truthful if they never believed the truth of him to begin with? There was futile hope in perhaps the mayor putting in a good word. Just once.

The town hall was at the head of the square, built tall from red brick with arched windows and a tile roof gone white with age. It was second only to the church in its grandiosity. It made sense to him why Mayor Ivan resented the church so much; the vision of his authority would always be smaller.

Ilya pressed open the front door, painted dark green. A bell rang above his head and he spotted Ivan's secretary perk up from her desk. Her eyes grew big as a doe's at the sight of him. Clearly, nobody had expected him to be alive.

"Ilya, I'm surprised to see you," she said. "Were you successful then?"

Ilya ground his teeth together. "Well, as you can see, I'm not dead, and there have been no more attacks since all of you cornered me. Does that answer your question?"

She balked at him and nodded, kind enough to be embarrassed for asking. "Yes, it does. I assume you'd like to speak with the mayor?"

"Yes. Now, please."

She rolled her eyes at him but walked into the back to find the mayor. Ilya sat by the entrance in a huff, staring at the door to Ivan's office. Standing up for himself was difficult, hands trembling despite his words. His courage had long been beaten out of him by both the town and his mother over these two long decades. It might as well have been centuries.

Despite that, he'd done as they'd asked. It would be nice if they didn't treat him like a pariah. If they made him fight again he wasn't sure how he'd handle it. Priests learned the will of the Sun, became a source of light and warmth for their communities, burning out their eyes to truly see Her. It was the Moon that granted the strength to protect from the evils of the night. That was where the hunters drew their power from, shrouded in shadow to see every bump in the night.

There was a time as a child when Ilya thought himself hunter material, but ultimately he found he wasn't cut out for it. He was too soft a heart and too weak of will, like his father had been. Instead, he followed in those footsteps, becoming a priest.

Not that Ilya could ever measure up to him. His father had been so skilled he could stitch limbs back together like new. Ilya could barely manage bone fractures, if that. He wouldn't be surprised if Danya's limbs ached from lingering injury due to his lack of talent.

Ilya pulled himself out of his mental flagellation when the door to Ivan's office swung open. It was about time.

Ilya got to his feet, crossing his arms, hoping to shield himself from the inevitable difficulties.

"Ivan."

Ivan was unphased by Ilya's demeanor, approaching casually. "Ilya! What a surprise. Genuinely. We haven't had any other attacks but you hadn't shown your face. We assumed you were being snacked on. Nobody wanted to search for your body."

"You know, if any of you came for ceremony for once in your miserable lives you would've found me."

Ivan barked a laugh and mimed wiping a tear from his eye. "No offense, Father, but unless you bring your predecessor back from the dead, your church will remain empty. However, if you didn't fuck up and lie to us," Ivan lowered his glasses to look at Ilya over the rim, "then I'm sure we can leave you to your misery once again."

Ilya threatened to chew through his teeth from how hard they ground together. "Yes, I'm sure. I'm also sure you wouldn't mind spreading the word so the townsfolk would stop spreading rumors about me?"

"You and I both know that won't happen. Think you'll have to suck it up."

His nails dug into his palms as his chest grew tight. He should have expected it, should be used to it by now, but he ached all the same. What did he have to do to get so much as bare *tolerance* from anybody in this place?

Ilya whirled around to avoid embarrassing himself, leaving the office without another word. He pulled his hood down low over his face so it was shielded from the view of passersby. He wound through the alleys behind the town hall, stones still damp with snowmelt in the shadows of the walls.

Days like this made him ask what the point of anything was, why he had to be here. He'd petitioned the church countless times, begging to be transferred *anywhere* else, but they wouldn't listen. He was his father's son, and thus he had to remain in Velak where his father had worked. How dare he snub his father's memory by even asking? If he left on his own, he'd be cast out of the church entirely, hunted down as an apostate despite any beliefs he still held. He'd have nothing left. No family, no friends, no church.

He was powerless, hopeless. What was he even good for?

A wave of grief washed over him. Ilya pressed a hand to the alley wall to keep from collapsing. His hand curled into a fist, his jaw tightened, and he slammed his eyes shut as his eyes stung with tears. He took in a breath, sharp, short, until finally a sob leaped forth. He pressed his forehead against the stones, pulling his hood closed.

Hot shame roiled in his stomach. This was such a childish display of emotions, unbecoming of a town's religious leader. He remembered his mother saying the same at his father's funeral, remembered the way the other adults of the town looked at him without an ounce of empathy. They'd even asked why he was crying, had accused him of being the reason his father was dead in the first place. What right did a murderer have to cry over his own father?

He didn't understand then and he didn't understand now.

Ilya's head spun, flooded with horrific memories. Every wrong that had ever been inflicted on him flashed, no matter how long ago or how slight. They all hated him for who he wasn't. He wasn't his father, he wasn't as skilled, wasn't as warm, wasn't as knowledgeable. All they saw was a lost child. He was a waste of space.

He couldn't be Father Sokolov, always just Ilya. Even risking his life to save everyone hadn't been enough. They had wanted him to die, hoping to get somebody new, somebody better. The people of Velak would rather be ravaged by a monster than have him exist.

Ilya removed a leather glove to wipe at his eyes. A feeble attempt at looking presentable was made until he gave up, replacing the glove as he shoved on through the alleys. That was enough of town for today.

The climb up the hill was terrible as ever, mud splashing onto his clothes as he walked. He wanted to get home and sequester himself away until the need for groceries arose at a later time.

Ilya froze in place as it hit him: he hadn't bought anything for dinner.

Palm collided with forehead in his aggravation, dragging it down and growling under his breath. He stared at the ground and did his level best to compose himself. Everything was being held together with a hair thin strand; if one more thing went poorly today he'd do something drastic.

Unfortunately, being that he was a priest, he was highly profi-cient in self flagellation. Finally Ilya had a patient, somebody to look after, to use all of his training on, and he couldn't even feed him. Not even this one thing.

Ilya's hands ached with his misery, a sensation that extended out to his arms, snaking through his chest to constrict his heart. Breaths came in shaky gasps, and while he tried to settle himself, he found it was a losing battle.

ONCE INSIDE THE church Ilya collapsed onto a pew in the back. He pressed his hands against his face and leaned so far forward he was bent in half. Whispered prayers left his lips, begging the Sun to release him from his pain, to give him anything to look forward to, anybody to be kind to him.

Letting go of everything was all that came to mind. Of the world, of life. Maybe he would once Danya was better. This could be his last good deed before he made one final, selfish decision.

It was a struggle to keep quiet inside the church. It was ten times larger than it had ever needed to be, with its high arched ceilings painted black and embedded with gems to mimic starlight. Every surface was luxurious stone and open air. It was all disgustingly grandiose with its alabaster walls and black marble floors, broken up by the symbol of the Sun in front of the altar made of polished gold. The acoustics were lovely for singing, but he had no choir nor talent of his own. It also meant his sobs were *extremely loud*.

Once he'd had a moment to get his emotions out, he slumped back in the pew, looking to his right to admire the stained glass windows. There was a skylight directly above the symbol of the Sun on the floor. When the noon light hit perfectly, it would cast the entire room in gold. It was bright enough you could see the rainbow glass glowing from *inside* the church.

There was beauty in this place, but Ilya couldn't help feeling it was one more reason to be despised. Most of the townsfolk lived in their modest wood, plaster, and thatch homes, and here he sat in a building of pure art. There was love for his deity, the celestial body that gave all the world life, but none for the rest of its denizens.

The door to the rectory opened and Ilya snapped his head so hard toward it his head spun. Danya walked past the two dozen pews to reach him, soft steps echoing through the church. His hand ran across each bench as he moved closer, brows furrowing when he looked at Ilya.

"Why are you hiding back here?"

Ilya's stomach turned as he struggled to find an excuse that would keep his pride intact. "Just praying for a bit," Ilya replied, clearing his throat. "It's lovely out here. Have you spent much time in the church yet?"

Danya sidled up next to Ilya's pew and leaned his weight against it. There was a quizzical look on his face; he clearly didn't believe Ilya. Ilya stared ahead at the altar, refusing to make eye contact. He'd stomached too much shame today.

"I haven't. You find anything for dinner?"

Ilya's eyes turned up to the ceiling. He bit his lip to keep it from quivering. Grief roiled in his chest, his palms ached all over again. Finally, he met Danya's gaze.

"No. I *fucking* forgot."

Danya raised his eyebrows. Ilya tried to not swear, but he was at his limit. It didn't help that Danya swore like a sailor and it was rubbing off on him.

Danya grabbed his shoulder. His touch was gentle, his hand radiating warmth. His thumb stroked the fabric of his vestments and Ilya did his best to ignore how hot his body grew from the gesture.

"There's plenty around I'm sure. It'll be fine, Ilya."

Ilya swallowed hard and looked down at his hands. "I'm supposed to be taking care of you while you recover. I should be able to make you a nice dinner."

"The fact that you didn't kill me in the woods is already more kindness than I deserve, Ilya," Danya whispered. "Now come on, stop crying in the corner."

A sigh rushed out of his lungs, but he did get up. The heat from Danya's hand lingered on his skin, spreading through his body. It brought a comfort to him that he couldn't quite grasp.

Perhaps Danya was the sign he'd been looking for all this time.

DESPITE HIS PANIC, Ilya managed to find all the ingredients he needed for a very average vegetable soup. It was better than nothing, and the fact that he could provide for his guest at all eased his mind. The bread in the pantry was a bit stale, but stale bread tended to be fine when paired with soup of completely average make. Everything was *fine*. He was *fine*.

He began to chop everything he'd need. Danya loomed behind

him as he worked and set his nerves on edge all over again. Ilya squinted at him over his shoulder.

"Can I help you?"

"Was about to ask you the same question."

Ilya turned and held up the knife in his hand. "If you come anywhere near me while I'm cooking I'm going to gut you and add you to the dish."

Danya backed up several steps, hands held up in surrender. He shook his head and went to lay on the couch, sighing loud enough to make sure Ilya heard him.

"Just wanted to be useful. I feel so... helpless. Like I'm some fucking child that got left on your doorstep. I'm just sitting around here doing nothing while you do all this shit to help me!"

Ilya shook his head. "Yes, well, your goal is to get better and remember your past life. If you want something actionable, we're going to need more firewood, and I hate chopping. I'm going to have to cross the mountains into Kursiya in a few days to get all our stock for the season. The larder is a tad sparse and I refuse to try and fish from the ice to have anything to eat."

Ilya finished his chopping and tossed everything into a giant cast iron pot. He filled it with water and brought it over to the fireplace. It was hung on the hook in the center and the fire was lit. What he wouldn't give to have one of those electric stoves that all the houses in the city had; he was so tired of firewood.

Danya sat up as he watched Ilya work. "Might be nice to go fishing actually. Get out of this fucking building if nothing else. No offense."

Ilya snorted. "None taken. I hate it here too. Lacks in personality."

"So why not redecorate?"

It was a simple question with an equally simple answer. "Guilt. I grew up in this place, at least for a while. It's a wonder I was able to get my mother out when the time came... But my father, Pavel Sokolov, was the last priest. He made this place what it was. I don't have the heart to change it."

Danya was silent for a long while after that. Ilya could *hear* him thinking, perhaps trying to recall memories of his own family. He went back to the kitchen to clean up in the meantime.

Finally, Danya called back, "Don't remember my parents. At least you've got yours I guess."

Ilya paused in wiping the counters, anger lancing through him. "Hardly."

Danya huffed. "You've been in a fucking mood today. What's your damage?"

Ilya ground his teeth and stormed back over to the couch. He leaned over the back of it, grabbing Danya by the front of his shirt to get directly in his face. "My father died when I was eight and my mother is an awful hag who, along with *this entire Sun forsaken town*, blames that death on me. They shamed me for crying at his *funeral* because they think I'm a murderer because I was a *child* who didn't have the power to heal his father's illness. They're probably annoyed that you didn't eat me. *That* is my damage, Danya. What's *yours*?"

Rage coursed through his veins, breath coming in heavy. Ilya was a pot boiled over, every last drop evaporated, nothing but candescent heat left.

His eyes finally refocused, the look of fear on Danya's face giving him pause. He let go of Danya's shirt, smoothing it out and going back to the kitchen. This wasn't him. This was his mother, this was Ivan, this was Velak as a whole. This rage? It wasn't him.

Shame compelled him to ignore the sounds of Danya moving behind him. His shoulders tensed, unsure of what might happen. Would Danya leave? Would he lash out? Ilya wouldn't blame him either way.

Warm arms wrapped around his body, firm in their grasp. Danya's face pressed against the back of his head, nosing into his curls. Danya's breath ghosted over his scalp and the backs of his ears. Ilya broke, went limp in Danya's hold. He heaved a sob, head hanging even lower. There was a thick silence that filled the room, broken by the crackling of the fireplace and Ilya's sniffling. He hated making noise when it was this quiet, especially ones as loud and undignified as this.

"I'm sorry," Ilya sobbed, "I shouldn't have done that."

Danya turned him around, embracing him once more, hooking his chin over Ilya's head. Ilya pressed his face into the crook of Danya's neck, breathed him in, took in his scent. An immediate calm washed over him, body sagging once more.

"You smell like cinnamon," Ilya croaked.

Danya snorted and squeezed him tighter. "Didn't realize."

Another long moment of silence passed between them, neither man willing to budge. Ilya fought his shame, choosing to enjoy this gesture while it lasted. He'd cried far too much today; it was undignified. He refused to let everybody keep getting to him like this. At least maybe now he'd have a friend to weather the storm with.

Eventually, Danya did let him go. "We should check on dinner."

Ilya used the collar of his shirt to rub at his eyes, cleared his throat, and nodded. "Yes. Let's."

Things were quiet between them as Ilya checked on the cast iron pot. He wasn't proud of his outburst, but Danya didn't seem to be interested in prying. Ilya was happy with that.

4

I t took Ilya a few days to find the will to go into town again. Subsisting off of middling vegetable soup from the icebox certainly became a motivating factor. In the meantime, they both had taken care to convert the attic into a more hospitable space for Danya to call home. He was going to be here a while yet, and Ilya wanted him to have privacy. The attic had become overstuffed with his father's old things, but it had a suitable enough bed and a spare desk. Danya was plenty grateful at least.

The morning Ilya left Danya had been acting peculiar. He seemed eager to have Ilya out of the house, made most curious by Danya's new private room. If he wanted the space he could simply climb the ladder and get away. He was nervous for what might await him on his return.

Thankfully the trip into town was mostly painless, though bringing home extra food to accommodate a second mouth made the walk home *infinitely* worse. He slid around in the damp earth, arms aching as he lugged his bags up the hill. He'd have to make Danya come with him from now on.

It was utter chaos in his kitchen when he finally shoved open the door to the rectory. There were tiny metal parts strewn about the table, wooden panels on his counter, and dust all over the floor. Panic rose in his chest, eyes roaming across all the mess until settling on Danya sat at the table doing Sun knew what. He didn't look ashamed, necessarily, more like he'd been caught with his pants down.

"Fuck sake, I thought you'd take longer."

Ilya set the bags on the floor and rushed to the table. "What *are* you doing?"

Danya turned back to whatever he was working on. "Well, I had a breakthrough while we were going through all that shit in your attic yesterday. I remembered... I think I used to work with machines? I was an inventor's assistant. It all came in a flood, and I spotted this broken phone in the corner upstairs. Phones were our speciality, so... I thought..."

Ilya took in all of Danya's babbling, tilted his head as his voice trailed off. "Are you... fixing it?"

Danya nodded. "Yes. You've done a lot for me and I've been fucking useless in return. As soon as it all came back, I wanted to try doing something. So far I've filled in the wood and sanded it, scrubbed all the rust off of the metal parts, and made a new dampening spring. Still got work to do, but it's getting there. Won't be as good as new since all the nickel plating came off the outer parts and I don't have shit to do *that*, but it'll be pretty fucking good anyway. You can count on that."

Ilya blinked in his surprise, taking everything in. It was a lot of technical talk that went over his head, but he got the gist of it. Danya had relevant memories come back to him, saw something broken, and wanted to fix it. He was touched that he was going to so much effort to fix this, to try and make up for existing in Ilya's space. An idea came to him at that moment.

"You know, there's a junk shop in town. The woman who runs it is... nice enough. She lost her husband recently, so a lot of machine repairs have gone by the wayside. Perhaps you could convince her to let you work for her. Might give you something productive to do, so you don't sit around here thinking about so much all the time."

Danya stared back at him, chewing his lip. He could see the hesitation on Danya's face, but Ilya couldn't say why. Danya finding his independence was important; Ilya didn't want to be, nor *could* he be, Danya's entire world. That sounded far too isolating and highly inappropriate.

Danya finally replied, "Maybe, I guess. But won't it be weird to have a new guy suddenly show up right after a fucking night creature has been attacking everybody? If they're as suspicious of you as you say, they'll probably think I'm some lunatic."

It was a fair point.

"I'll have to ponder on that for a bit… Though at this rate you could blame me and let me take the fall. They'd be glad to ignore anything strange about your circumstances in favor of finding a new reason to hate me."

Danya frowned. "Well I don't love that."

Ilya snorted and began putting all the groceries away, leaving Danya to the task of fixing his telephone. He'd need time to think of a good excuse for Danya suddenly being in Velak. He couldn't say he was sent by the Church. The people would refuse to believe the Church ignored them in their time of dire need but were perfectly happy to send a charity case their way (even if that was likely).

There was Kursiya, the next town over. Most people in Velak visited Kursiya when they needed a specialty item and didn't want to go all the way to the Capital for it. On foot, Kursiya could be reached in a day if you timed everything right, while the Capital was over a week away. Nobody in Velak was fortunate enough to afford cars yet, and certainly none of the roads were suitable for them anyway. Ilya could recall seeing only two during his training in the Capital.

Saying Danya was from the Capital would then likely be foolish and unconvincing. At the very least, if he didn't have a horse or wagon with him, it would be hard to believe. Saying he was from Kursiya and looking for work outside his home town, that he'd come to the church first to seek aid and guidance would be believable enough. Strange to not go to the town hall first, perhaps, but most people trusted the clergy when in need. Velak was a *special* case.

"I believe I have a solution to our problem," Ilya said. "Would you like to tell me if it suits you?"

Danya was in deep concentration, hunched over the wooden case for the phone, carefully placing a piece of coiled wire back into the contraption. Perhaps the dampening spring he'd mentioned. He had several screws he was holding between his lips, brow furrowed as he handled the delicate machinery. There was a light *snap*, and then Danya leaned back in his seat to look at Ilya.

"Shoot."

Ilya snorted at how much of a mess Danya had become. His face and hands were covered in dust and grime from the broken telephone, and he was practically eating the screws he held. Ilya had to admit that it was endearing.

He relayed his thoughts to Danya, explaining Kursiya and how he would claim he was seeking work. Ilya would take him to the junk shop to help corroborate the story, and that would hopefully be enough.

"Does that all make sense?"

Danya hummed and removed the screws from his mouth. "I think so, yeah. Still really fucking nervous about it, and the towns-folk are super weird, but I guess I'll be fine."

"It should be. At most they'll be at mental odds, wanting to believe an innocent stranger who's done nothing wrong, but who has gone to me for aid so must be suspicious. As long as you act like yourself I'm sure it'll be fine." Ilya rolled his eyes for good measure.

Danya rolled them right back, returning his focus to the phone box. "Yeah, sure, I really know how to do *that*. Now gimme a minute, this transmitter looks like dogshit."

THEY DREW attention as they came into town, but Ilya was positive it was more him than his strange roommate. Nothing new here. Danya was tense as they stepped into the town square; so tense he was sure Danya could be coiled up and made into his telephone's dampening spring all on his own. The junk shop was easy enough to find, being diagonal from the town hall. It helped that in front of it were half a dozen tables, organized into evenly spaced rows, but covered in so many spare parts, antiques, and random housewares that it was rendered nearly pointless. They had to squeeze through a narrow aisle between the tables, Ilya trying to not let his cloak snag on precariously placed candelabras, and Danya desperately sucking his stomach in for good measure.

They paused on the wooden porch and exchanged a look. Ilya cracked first, and Danya followed, both sharing a quiet laugh.

"I'm shocked you can even stand on the damn porch," Danya said.

Ilya smiled as he shook his head. "Berta enjoys standing out here, smoking her cigarettes and judging all who pass by. If the porch was full of junk she wouldn't be able to see all the targets of her scrutiny!"

"Incredible she can even see over those tables. I'm too big for that space."

Ilya refrained from making any comment, instead opening the door to the shop.

There was a light jingle from the bell over the door as they stepped inside. Ilya hadn't been here in ages, not since Berta's husband had died, but it was as he remembered: a nightmare. Nothing but messes and piles of useless shit that reached the ceiling, sitting on countless tables and shelves and crates. His skin itched and stomach turned. He crossed his arms in front of his chest and scratched at his arms, tensing his jaw when it brought no relief. It smelled of tobacco smoke accumulated over decades, earthy and acidic. There was an unmistakable metallic scent that mingled with the damp of mildew. It would shock him if there weren't at least a *baker's dozen* of spider nests amongst everything.

The clearest spot was the checkout counter at the front, an aged brass cash register set on top of glass display cases filled to the brim with even *more* shit. It was incredible there was room to *breathe* let alone *move*.

"This place is... something," Danya whispered. "Pretty sure the last shop I worked in was kind of a mess, but not... this."

"Junk shops are a special kind of monstrosity that fell out of the gaping, endless maw that is the Realm of Eternal Night. They are a sign the Sun does not love us as much as She claims, for how else would such a nightmare be allowed to exist?"

Ilya scratched at himself, dragging his nails across his cheek. Danya's eyes bored holes into the side of his head, but he couldn't possibly care less. This was his neurotic burden to bear and judgemental looks were hardly the salve that would make it stop.

Danya began to speak, "That's pretty dramatic—"

Danya was quickly cut off by shouting from the back of the store. Ilya winced as the sound of a thousand metallic objects crashing into the floor rang throughout the shop. Eventually, an old woman emerged from a back aisle, dusting off the front of her flower-print apron.

She was short and stout, much like the pile of teapots on the shelf next to her. Her snow white hair peeked out from under the bright pink and white paisley scarf she had wrapped around her head and shoulders. Her eyes were nearly bulging out of her skull from how big they were, made further like a bug's by the thick, round glasses that were threatening to slide off her nose.

She'd shrank since he last saw her, but indeed this was the same Berta he knew.

Berta adjusted her glasses, squinting at Ilya and Danya. She turned to Ilya first.

"Sokolov. I'm very surprised to see you. What brings you here?"

Curt, but not rude. Ilya would call it an improvement in treatment, but he was sure Danya being around helped.

"I've brought a man from Kursiya who's been trying to find work," he replied. "This is Danya. He used to work with an inventor until the shop closed. He reached out to me in the hopes I might have an answer. I thought since your husband isn't around anymore having a new set of hands might help you."

Berta glared at him briefly then looked at Danya. She stepped up to him, tilting her head back to get a better look at his face.

Danya stared down at her awkwardly, clasping his hands together. "Uh… I can show proof if you need it."

Berta examined him for a few moments more and then said, "I'd be thrilled to have paying customers again, and if it means bringing on some strange new boy then so be it. Come back to the workshop, show me what you can do."

She led them to the back, navigating the labyrinthian piles of knickknacks with ease. Once more, Ilya and Danya both tried their best to not cause a disaster as they followed. Ilya was relieved the workshop was more spacious than the front once they arrived. There was a long workbench along the right wall, a pegboard full of tools that extended to the ceiling. There were shelves full of bits and bobs and broken things that needed repair. There was a door that led to the back porch and the courtyard that contained the Sunset Tavern, as well as several other homes. To the left was a set of stairs, likely up to Berta's living quarters. There was hardly room in Velak, most couldn't afford to live in homes separate from their workplaces.

Ilya's mind began to wander as Berta interviewed Danya, who seemed to be taking it all in stride. His arms were crossed, but he held his ground.

Despite the markedly better state of the workshop, Ilya found he was too desperate to be away from all the junk and headed to the back porch. He let out a sigh of relief once the chill of the air hit his face, a cloud of vapor forming around his head. A wave of tobacco smoke hit him as the breeze passed, and he sent a glare at the bar across the way. Everybody seemed to smoke but him. Ilya couldn't find the point in it; not since his father died from it.

After a few more moments Danya and Berta joined Ilya. Berta placed a cigarette between her lips and lit it, offering the same for Danya, who took it with ease. Ilya glared at him, Danya rolling his eyes in return.

"I had no idea you smoked, Danya," Ilya said curtly.

Danya ground back, "Everybody else seems to, so why not? Better to be sociable, *isn't it*, Father? Fit into a new town?"

Berta broke their argument. "You know, I'm surprised, Sokolov. Normally I wouldn't trust anything from you, but this boy knows his stuff, and he knows to give you shit. It'll be nice to get work done again... Good job."

It seemed it truly would kill the citizens of Velak to say "thank you" to him, but he supposed this would have to be enough.

"Of course. Danya and I both need a bit more separation from each other for the moment, and helping you will do you both some good."

Berta snorted and blew out a cloud of rancid smoke. "I didn't know you cared about us."

Ilya bit the inside of his cheek to fight the acerbic comment creeping up the back of his throat. He turned his focus to Danya again, who mirrored Berta's motion. Ilya's eyes fell to Danya's hands, staring at how they were shaped holding his cigarette. Danya's hands were surprisingly delicate; it made sense for somebody who worked with small machine parts. His knuckles bulged from his deep brown skin, covered in a dusting of those darker freckles. Maybe it was odd to remark on how *pretty* Danya's hands were, but they were.

"Ilya has been a wonderful caretaker so far. I'm not sure why you seem so surprised babushka," Danya mumbled, bringing the cigarette to his lips again.

"Haven't been called that in years," Berta laughed, a low, gravelly sound punctuated by a wet cough. Ilya winced from the sound; just like his father.

"I'm going to leave the two of you here, you seem to be getting on fine. I'll start on dinner, it'll be done by the time you're back I'm sure."

"Sure thing, Sokolov," Berta replied, "Need to finalize things with this kid anyway."

Ilya caught Danya's eye long enough to spot the ghost of a frown on his face, but he ignored it and navigated back through the disaster of a shop until he could exit. He breathed a sigh of relief, glad to be free of the mess and the smoke. It would stick to his clothes for days until he laundered them, though if Danya had a new habit he was going to pick up, it was probably pointless.

Couldn't remember the majority of his life, but suddenly he

could remember to smoke when prompted. Ridiculous. He understood it was to try and fit in, but it set his teeth on edge. He hoped Danya would find better things to smoke than what Berta had; the clove cigarettes his father had used at least had a more pleasant odor.

Clove and cinnamon would certainly be a more pleasant combination.

5

October 15th, 1927

Danya had been working for Berta for a few weeks now. He wished he'd given in to Ilya's bitching and foregone picking up a smoking habit to fit in with his new boss, being that it was expensive and burned the shit out of his hands, but thus was life. Now he was smoking half a pack a day like the rest of them. Ilya made him do it outside, which was cruel and unusual now that winter was settling in. He didn't get cold, but it was isolating all the same. Ilya said he hated the smell, but there was a pang in his voice that Danya couldn't place. Ilya always seemed to have something that brought him pain, and now that Danya was spending more time in town, it was hard to say how much of it wasn't his own making.

It wasn't that he didn't believe Ilya when he said he was mistreated. Ilya was too direct with him for him to bother lying. He'd gotten angry enough to physically threaten him that one time, even if he'd cried and apologized later. As he got to know Berta and the other townsfolk that came through looking for help, it seemed exaggerated. These people were nice to him, welcomed him with open arms. He made a habit of grabbing a drink once he was out of work, and he liked chatting with everybody. They were normal people.

Ilya wasn't unpleasant company, but he was good at isolating himself and was incredibly neurotic. He was highly particular, the smallest thing out of place setting him on edge. Ilya complained when he smoked, complained even louder when he drank, even when it was a single beer. If he smelled anything stronger he'd crow about how he couldn't be anywhere near him. He figured religious types were bound to be picky and judgemental, but Ilya was ridiculous.

Danya was smoking and squinting into the sunrise when an unease made the hair on his neck stand up. He glanced over his shoulder and spotted Ilya staring at him, gaping like a fish at having been caught. Ilya stepped away from the window and Danya scoffed. More shitty, annoying judgment.

Things had been hard enough without Ilya having an opinion on every action he took. He couldn't remember jack from shit outside of being a mindless animal who wanted to *eat*. He wanted to be normal.

He dropped his cigarette on the dirt, snubbing it with the toe of his boot. He straightened himself out and then made his way down the Sun forsaken hill that Ilya lived on. He was positive that Ilya's glutes had to be ridiculous from how often he made the climb back up. Too bad he was hiding under all those layers of vestments. Strange how stuffy they were even with a giant hole in the chest.

THE 76 DIFFERENT clocks in the main shop (he'd counted) all chimed to signal the hour when he was finally freed from work. He put all his tools away and removed his safety glasses, heading to the front of the shop to check with Berta.

Berta was sitting at the front counter, smoking a rancid, cheap cigarette. He *had* taken Ilya up on the compromise of smoking better smelling things. At least he'd finally given him an inch. Danya needed his own place, but he'd worry about that later.

"Clocking out now. Need anything else?"

Berta hummed then nodded. "Come have a drink with me. It's the weekend now, everybody'll be at the tavern. In fact, make it a night out. You spend way too much time with that Sun forsaken priest, I can tell it makes you far less fun. Get to know the town better."

Danya could hear the complaints Ilya would level against him already and he rolled his eyes. "He's very stiff. Swear he has a stick lodged up his ass."

"Too right, Danylko," Berta chuckled. Danya raised his eyebrows at the nickname; perhaps Berta had grown fond of him after all. "He's always complaining about us and how we don't go to ceremony. Have you seen that hill? And he'll never be better than his father anyway, why bother?"

A chill wrapped around Danya's stomach at the comparison. He wasn't above gossiping — more and more he was discovering he was an asshole — but the comment struck him in a way he hadn't antici-pated. He decided it was better to be diplomatic, lighting a clove cigarette to seem casual.

"Yeah, that hill sucks. Why the fuck is the church all the way up there anyway?"

"To be closer to our Mother Sun," Berta replied. "All the churches are built at the highest points of every town, don't you know this, Danylko? Oh, but I'm sure the priest in Kursiya is shit, and Ilya is a shitty little child who's terrible at his job, it's no wonder you don't know. The previous Father Sokolov was truly a special man…"

Danya cleared his throat. "So, night on the town, you were saying?"

"Oh! Yes, yes, my dear boy, come, let's go to the tavern. Every-body spends time here once the work week is over."

Berta jumped from her stool and grabbed hold of Danya's free hand, leading him out the back door into the courtyard. It was bustling with townsfolk, dozens filing in for the evening, a few stragglers hanging outside to have private chats. It was loud as they stepped in, which surprised him. Velak was so quiet you could hear a pin drop. The tavern was deafening by comparison.

Berta ordered beer for the both of them and then found a place to sit. Danya set his cigarette on the ashtray in the center of the table so he could sip from his mug, glancing around at the other people nearby. The people of Velak trended old. Danya was out of place as the youngest person in the bar.

Several people came by to sit at their table, greeting Berta and exchanging hugs and cheek kisses. Danya gave them a nod, and most of the men seemed to approve of how stoic he was. Awkward was more like it, but he'd take what he could get.

It continued to be awkward as more and more people came to chat and left him out of it. He wasn't making much of an effort to speak, enjoying the beer refills and whiskey that Berta's friends would force upon him. The bar whirled around him as the night pressed on, the energy of the people reaching a fever pitch. The silence that permeated the town most days wasn't pleasant, but the quiet conversation he'd have with Ilya was sounding more and more appealing. At least Ilya knew he existed.

Danya was on his third cigarette of the night when another large group came to visit, all eyes on him. An older man with hair combed over his half bald head used his mug to point at him, beer sloshing out and splashing him in the face. He wiped it away with a thumb as the man shouted at him.

"You! You live with that stupid fucking priest! Ilya! Do you know you live with a fucking *murderer?*" he asked.

Danya recalled Ilya saying the town blamed him for his father's death, and now he was about to get another earful about it. All anybody seemed to say about Ilya was that he was shit compared to his father, and now an accusation of murder? If he was a murderer why was he even *here* then? Ilya wasn't his favorite person in the world, but this was exhausting. Didn't they have *anything* else to talk about?

"Do I?" Danya finally answered.

The man slurred back, "Yes! That fucking brat killed his own father! Did you not know?"

Berta cut in, shaking her head, "The last Father Sokolov was such a good man! The best healer in the country! He was so good to us all! That brat let him die, but I wouldn't call it murder. Neglect for certain!"

They were both waving their mugs around to punctuate their words, sending more beer across the room and onto him. Danya leaned out of the way to dodge most of it, frowning when his shoulder got wet. He didn't have many clothes and he wasn't sure where to get new ones. This would be a pain to launder and Ilya was going to chew him out for smelling like alcohol again.

"Why would he kill his own father?" Danya asked.

Another old man cut in, this one with frizzy white hair that puffed out in a halo all around his head. "Because he's fucking useless! Can't even heal his own father, how can we expect him to do shit for us!"

Pain formed behind his eyes as irritation and exhaustion set in. The lone clock in the tavern said it was well past two in the morning already, and hearing old people complain about the same shit over and over made every minute drag.

Danya took a long, deep drag off his cigarette and made a point of blowing the smoke in the old men's faces. "Is it true Ilya was eight years old when his father died? Wouldn't he just not have been skilled enough yet?"

Berta scoffed and blew her own rancid, acidic smoke back in his face. "That's the excuse he gives every time. He spent years in the Capital before his mother made him come home to try and fix it! Why even bother?"

It seemed all too convenient to blame a child for such a tragedy. Fire burned in his chest at the contempt of these townsfolk. He was at his limit with this shit.

"Can we fucking talk about something else? Sun's sake, you geezers are so annoying."

The men crowed at him about disrespect in unison and he pinched the bridge of his nose in his frustration. Berta eventually shooed them away, though the look she was giving him suggested she was disappointed.

"You were telling me earlier about how annoying you found him, Danylko," she said, refilling her mug while looking at him over the rim of her over-large glasses.

Danya scowled at her. "Just because he's annoying doesn't mean I want to keep fucking hearing you all bitch about your dead priest. He's gone! It's been what, two decades? Find something else to gossip about, *shit*."

Berta looked ready to reach across the table and smack him, but she stopped short as somebody stepped behind him. He turned around in his seat and looked up at a woman, younger than Berta but definitely older than he was. Her skin was sheet white, a feat considering Ilya had to be the palest soul in the whole town. Ratty platinum blonde hair was tied in an uneven bun. She had on a black and white dress covered in stains. A golden sun-shaped pendant around her neck was the final touch, the same symbol Ilya had on his chest. She swayed and grabbed the back of Danya's chair to hold herself up, glazed eyes staring down at him.

"You live with my son?" she asked.

Danya blinked and tried to process what she'd said. This was Ilya's mother? She was a complete mess.

"I do, yeah. What about it?"

"You should know some things. Come to my home," she slurred.

The hairs on the back of his neck stood up, every instinct he had was telling him this woman was nothing but trouble. He glanced back at Berta who was boring holes into Ilya's mother's skull from how much hate that radiated off of her. It surprised him, if he was being honest. They adored Ilya's father, but hated Ilya and his mother? None of this made sense. It was so fucking stupid.

He finally asked, "What things?"

"Just— Just come. Don't ask dumb questions, boy." She patted his cheek harder than he would've liked and stumbled towards the door.

On second thought, he wished she hadn't touched him at all.

Her touch lingered on his skin like grease. He rubbed at his cheek to try and get rid of the feeling, but it persisted. Great.

"Don't you follow that hag of a woman," Berta hissed. "She's a burden on us all, it's a miracle there's somebody worse than that child you live with."

Danya looked back at her, staring into her eyes to glean anything he could. She seemed so angry, even compared to how she talked about Ilya. If Ilya was the town whipping boy, it seemed like his mother was the town witch.

"Unfortunately, I'm curious," Danya admitted.

Berta scoffed and leaned back in her chair, angrily taking a drag off her cigarette. She blew the smoke out of her nose and refused to look at Danya anymore. "Obstinate boy. Go then, see what you learn. Watch your step in that wretched place."

Danya smudged out his cigarette in the ashtray, left a few coins on the table for a tip, and then followed Ilya's mother outside.

She hadn't gone far, stumbling and swaying her way through the courtyard before rounding the corner. He rushed to catch up with her, falling in step behind her.

"What do I call you?" he asked.

"Irina. Took you long enough to catch up."

She led him down the main road, turning right into a narrow passage. There seemed to be a clothing shop (thank the Sun, he needed better fitting things than Ilya's hand-me-downs), a ramshackle wooden home next to it. Irina stepped up to the door, forcing it open and leaving it open for Danya. He stepped onto the threshold, scowling as the overwhelming stench of rot and sour beer hit him in a wave.

If the junk shop was crowded, this place was on another level. Trash was piled high, nearly touching the ceiling. The floorboards were warped and stained, cobwebs stretched across every available corner, and what carpet he could spot under all the piles of trash was dingy and molded. He closed the door behind him, grimacing at how sticky the knob was.

There seemed to be a mostly clear path from the door to the kitchen, one veering into what he assumed was the living room, and one to what seemed to be the door to a bedroom. Irina was shuffling her way to the kitchen, and he did his best to follow without knocking down the towers of mess. At least if anything in Berta's shop collapsed on him, he'd probably die instantly. If this shit fell over, he'd suffocate on fumes while the roaches chewed on his still living body. He wouldn't be shocked if there were long lost pets that had been entombed in the piles.

In the gaps between the towers he could spot a number of framed photos. The images were faded, but they showed Irina, a man who he assumed to be the famed previous Father Sokolov, and a smaller figure that had been burned out of every photo. The glass over the burned figure had been smashed as well. Danya knew who it was. He wanted to smoke through an entire pack of cigarettes from the tension that formed in his neck thinking about it.

The kitchen was surprisingly clear, but there were beer bottles on every horizontal surface in view. Flies buzzed around in the room and Danya had to keep swatting them away.

Needless to say, he understood why Ilya was so neurotic about cleanliness now. He'd never give him guff about it again from how deeply he understood.

Irina pulled two bottles out of the icebox, cracking them both open and handing one to Danya. He took it and sipped at it gingerly, feeling his stomach roil. Part his body protesting the further consumption of poison and part disgust with the woman in front of him, if he had to guess. He'd probably vomit on his way back up that Sun forsaken fucking hill from the exertion.

"So. How long have you been living with my son?" Irina finally asked.

Danya had to do quick math to make sure he didn't out himself, raising an eyebrow as he said, "A couple months now? I'm guessing you're going to tell me that's a bad thing."

The laugh that came out of Irina was dark. Danya's discomfort was growing by the second, sipping his beer to give him anything else to focus on.

"He's an annoying waste of space, isn't he? I don't think I've ever regretted something the way I regret him."

Danya couldn't help himself. "That seems like a terrible thing to say about your own child."

She whirled on him and threw her bottle on the floor, shattering and sending frothing liquid across the sticky tiles. "That *thing* is no child of mine! You know you live with a murderer, don't you? He's nothing but a killer! He killed his own father! You should get away from that mistake as soon as you can. Better yet, go back where you came from. This place is *cursed*."

She broke down into hysterical sobs, collapsing into a chair and throwing herself against the table dramatically. She sent bottles flying off the table, rolling across the ground. Danya set his own on the floor; he figured it would hardly go noticed amongst all the other mess.

"What makes you say he's a murderer?" He kept his tone even as best he could, but it was a struggle.

"He let Pavel *die!* We sent that brat to the Capital to learn magic and he comes back and knows nothing! He did it on purpose! He always hated me, his Father loved him more, he let Pavel die to spite me! Then they made me *live* with him in this shithole! He didn't even have the decency to die! He would *keep getting up* after everything I did! *I HATE HIM!*"

The hysterical crying had devolved into screeching. She thrashed in her seat, sweeping her arm across the table and sending more bottles flying. Danya threw his hands up in time to block one that almost hit his face, grunting as one slammed his stomach. Now he was *definitely* going to puke.

Irina stumbled out of her chair, throwing herself onto the floor to wail and writhe on her back. She smashed her fists against the tiles and screamed as loud as she could. Everything about this woman was a sad, shameful wreck. That she was openly admitting all of this to Danya disgusted him. If he'd ever lost somebody close to him, he couldn't remember. He couldn't begin to know her grief, to know what had pushed her to get this way.

But he knew one thing: no matter what she'd experienced, this woman was rotten, and anybody who felt the same as her? Equally rotten. That they rightfully condemned her and her behavior while sharing the same feelings about their current priest? That they all did her work for her in making his life miserable? It was unconscionable.

Danya couldn't believe he'd ever been annoyed with Ilya at all. Ilya, who had broken his curse, healed him, clothed and fed him, gave him a home, helped him find work, a purpose in life, who did everything in his power to make him feel human again. Danya had given in to all their gossip, let himself be like them for even a moment. He couldn't forgive himself.

He turned to leave, stopped short by Irina grabbing onto his ankle.

"*Don't* you go back there! He's not to be trusted! He'll kill you too!"

Danya snarled and kicked her hand with his free foot, yanking his other out of her grasp. He hadn't known a fury like this since he'd been cursed, since all he knew was rage and hunger. He hated this woman for bringing it all to the surface again.

"You disgust me. I never want to see you again, you hateful witch."

Irina shrieked as he rushed for the door, slamming it shut behind him in time to hear her body smash against it. He held it closed as she pounded her fists against it, her voice going out from how loud she screamed. Time dragged on until she gave up. There was a thump against the ground as she whimpered to herself, cursing Ilya's birth yet again. He waited a few more moments then dashed away, groaning in relief as he finally came back into the main square.

He glanced at the clocktower in the center, squinting in the dim light. It looked to be four in the morning, and it would take at least another hour to get back home.

He supposed this would be his punishment for ever giving in to the town gossip.

DANYA DID in fact vomit halfway up the hill. The exertion of the climb and the bottle that hit him earlier was too much. His head was pounding, his ears were ringing from all of Irina's fucking noise. If somebody shoved an ice pick into his tear duct he wouldn't know the difference. If Ilya actually killed him when he got home he'd be *thrilled*.

UNFORTUNATELY, Ilya liked to wake up at the crack of dawn and very much noticed when Danya got home. He threw open the door to the rectory, marching outside and clenching his fists at his side.

"Do you have *any idea* how long I've been waiting for you to come home? I was worried sick! I didn't know if you fell into the ravine or if they'd found your secret and hurt you or— or anything! And for Sun's *sake*, you smell *terrible!* How much did you even drink? No, I can't be near you, get to the attic right this second and get away from me—"

Danya was so tired, and he was so very tired of the Sokolovs yelling at him. He did the first thing that came to mind and wrapped his arms around Ilya, bringing him into a tight embrace. He buried his face against Ilya's curls and breathed him in. Ilya had once remarked that he smelled like cinnamon. For his part, Ilya smelled like all the incense he burned. Sandalwood and frankincense, earthy, grounded. He hadn't realized how much comfort that smell had brought him, how much comfort it held now.

"What are you doing? Let *go* of me you— you..."

The fire went out of Ilya almost immediately. He slumped in Danya's arms, crying quietly into his chest. He supposed he knew where all the crying came from now.

"I was so scared they'd killed you. I was worried I'd failed you."

Danya squeezed him tighter, setting a hand on the back of Ilya's head so his face was in the crook of his neck. Ilya let out a sharp breath against his ear, skin growing hot under his touch.

Finally, Danya whispered, "I'm sorry. I'm an asshole. It won't happen anymore."

Ilya cleared his throat and replied, "I believe you."

Ilya made no move to break away, and Danya wasn't sure he was ready to let go either. Despite all the cruelty that had been lauded at him for years, Ilya hadn't become unkind, had been merciful to him, a single-minded monster whose sole satisfaction was killing and consumption. He was a soft soul who's wounds were never allowed to heal. Ilya cared for him so much, even when he didn't need to. Even when he didn't deserve it. He'd been such a fool.

Ilya meant more to him than he'd realized.

6

October 20th, 1927

The first frost hit Velak like a hammer. Ilya managed to stock up for the snow, crossing the mountains into Kursiya for a few days. He was nervous to leave Danya by his lonesome; when he got lonely he got bored, and that meant he'd come home to more chaotic mess as he did handiwork around the rectory. He appreciated it, truly, but the mess also made him want to die. Ever since Danya had come home at the crack of dawn, however, he'd been much better about trying to be neat. He wouldn't say why he'd become more considerate after Ilya had pried, but he wouldn't look a gift horse in the mouth.

Danya's memories seemed to come in flashes, fleeting things that fell through his grasp like sand. Ilya made him keep a journal so he could write it all down, hoping it might help him keep track. Not much had come back to him beyond the workshop he assisted in. He kept working for Berta, though their relationship had become notably strained. Danya once again refused to say why, and Ilya wasn't keen on prying into Berta's thoughts on the matter. Danya kept busy and stopped staying out so late. Ilya was satisfied with that.

As the weeks had been going by, he noticed Danya's strength growing by the day. He was on another level entirely. Ilya had him preparing firewood to store for the season and he made quick work of it, not breaking a sweat. He'd spent almost half an hour gazing out the window watching him, completely enraptured.

Simply because the feat of strength and endurance was incredible, and for nothing else whatsoever.

Ilya couldn't allow anything otherwise.

Not when Danya was his charge, his responsibility. The man had barely remembered his name let alone his previous life. Ilya would never dare to presume he could intrude on that. What if he had a wife? Children? Friends who missed him? No. Ilya wouldn't dare be so selfish to believe he could keep Danya away from that. His own feelings had no place in this matter.

Who knew if Danya wouldn't turn around and hurt him in his disgust anyway.

Ilya strode into the nave as he finally came home from his trip, bundled up tight as he tried to avoid the first flurries outside. The rectory had finally had proper heating installed a few years ago, but the main church building hadn't been so lucky thus far. There was a great fireplace in the chancel, but the single source couldn't do much for what amounted to a stone ice box. He had few visitors to begin with, but winter was always dead. He could wrangle a few people for the solstice, but that was rare. Nobody wanted to sit in a stone room that was colder than outside, and he couldn't blame anybody for it.

He rushed into the rectory and sighed in relief as the warmth washed over him. He spotted Danya at the kitchen table, junk strewn across the surface and a lit cigarette in his mouth. Ilya frowned as he tugged his gloves off, brows knitting in his confusion. Not only had Danya fixed his phone over a month ago, but he had a workshop if he needed to bring work home. He'd been better about his messes in general.

"Danya. What is this?"

Danya's head snapped up, expression owlish in his shock. It faded into a sheepish grimace as he glanced at everything on the table. He plucked his cigarette out of his lips and said, "If it helps it's all on this table."

Ilya's eyes flicked across the room to verify, finding nothing else out of place. Good, then. "It does, but that doesn't explain why it's down here."

Danya placed his cigarette in his ashtray and shrugged. "Well, I figured down here would be a better place for it when I finished. It's a radio I found in my room. Looked busted but not too bad, and I wanted to try fixing it for you…"

Heat swam up Ilya's neck with such immediacy he threatened to burst into flames. He swore it was because his body was adjusting to the temperature differences between here and the church. Nothing untoward whatsoever.

"Oh. I see… thank you, then. I was sad when it broke, and Berta's husband died before I could get it fixed."

Danya had gone back to focusing on the work, hunching over a series of parts he seemed to be struggling to puzzle back together. His posture was atrocious and he was squinting despite having a perfectly good magnifying glass next to him. "Still had the instruction manual and the schematics thankfully so it's not too bad… The oscillator coil looked like horseshit so that's probably what broke it in the first place, but some other parts have gone bad over time. Finishing some cleaning and then it should work again."

Ilya walked around the table behind Danya, placing an icy hand on the back of his neck. Danya yelped and sat up straight in his shock, glaring at him. "Maybe I should say fuck it."

Ilya scoffed and rolled his eyes. "Don't be like that, we're friends enough. Besides, you're going to destroy your back if you keep sitting like a sausage link."

Danya made a face at him and shook his head. He focused back on his pile of parts, replacing his cigarette once more. "Sausage link… Whatever."

Ilya let him be as he finished getting out of his travel clothes and putting all their supplies away. He left out a few things for dinner and then went to collapse onto the couch, groaning to himself. He was so utterly exhausted. Danya would have to live with stew for dinner, it was all he had the strength for.

"How are things with Berta? It seems like you two aren't as close anymore," he called out.

"She's pissed at me for saying shit she doesn't want to hear. Either she'll get over it because she knows I'm right, or enough time will pass that she gets bored of being mad. I don't know what to expect from people in this town anymore, everybody's full of toxic fucking gas."

Ilya didn't reply, dozing as he ruminated on everything. He was under the impression Danya was chewing at the bit to be away from him, to get to know other people, but things seemed to have changed. It was nice to have a friend on his side. He wasn't used to that.

A SUDDEN, loud noise shocked him awake, sitting up with a gasp as he clutched his chest. It was dark in the rectory, only the fire and the kitchen lamp for light. He peeked over the couch and spotted Danya standing at said table, radio put back together and blasting static. Danya snorted and smiled at him.

"Sorry. It works again though."

Danya looked so proud of himself, Ilya couldn't help the faint smile that spread across his lips. He came up next to Danya to examine the radio, turning the dials until he managed to find the old station he liked that played music.

"I never thought I'd get to hear this thing work again."

Ilya looked back at Danya, enraptured by how his golden eyes shone in the low light. He was utterly stricken by how handsome Danya was. Ilya wasn't going to deny the man his appearance.

As the song on the radio came to a close, Danya swept Ilya up in his arms. He placed a hand on Ilya's waist, using the other to swing him around as the next song began. Heat radiated through Ilya's body, ears burning so hot he was tempted to bury his head in the snow outside. He was too stunned to react in any way, gaping like a fish as Danya led them along.

"No smartass comments, Father Sokolov?"

Ilya swallowed audibly, searching for the ability to speak he was sure he had moments ago. "No– No. Not this time."

Perhaps it was a trick of the firelight, maybe his groggy, adrenaline-addled brain was making his imagination go wild. He swore Danya's hair was growing bright in color, fading from warm black to red. Pure scarlet, in fact. Like the inky fur of the drekavac melting away with rising sun on the day they first met.

No, he had to be delirious, there was no possible reason for this to be happening.

Ilya focused his attention on the warmth of Danya's touch as they danced. Danya had embraced him several times now and Ilya was familiar with how warm he was, but now it was a heat that permeated through the fabric of his clothes, past his skin, and deep into his bones. Not like a fever, nothing sickly. It was like the fire in the hearth, a comfort from the frost outside. It reminded him of the glow from their Mother Sun.

On top of that, he'd never done anything like this with a man. He'd never even dreamed it would be possible, that he'd die alone in Velak never having experienced anything close to romantic. In his heart of hearts, he knew if anybody saw them it would only bring more cruelty. Part of him believed he didn't deserve this, shouldn't have this.

He'd spent his life being told he was a waste of space, that he didn't matter. He repulsed everybody around him, rejecting him without ever knowing him. It was a life of isolation, and suddenly Danya was here in his space. Danya clearly cared for him. He wasn't stupid enough to ignore the implications of what they were doing.

There was the negling fear that once his memories came back, once the right trigger was found, Danya would leave him to go back to his life. He'd be alone again.

Part of him said he should enjoy it while he had it. Part of him said giving in for even a moment would make it hurt more later.

"Something wrong?" Danya asked.

Ilya's eyes focused on Danya's face again, swallowing hard as he tried to compose himself. "No. Not a very good dancer is all, concentrating so I don't break your toes."

Danya chuckled, light and soft in its tone. It sent an arrow through his chest and he was *furious* that he'd allowed an ounce of this school boy crush to enter his heart.

He was Danya's caretaker, helping him in his time of need, helping him when he was most vulnerable. It would be taking advantage to even entertain this further than he already had. He was allowing this dance because Danya initiated it.

Ilya pulled away from Danya the moment the song came to an end. Danya smiled at him, but there was a tightness at the corner of his eyes. A new wave of guilt washed over him. He didn't want to hurt Danya's feelings but he had to be responsible and keep his distance.

"Why don't we go into town in the morning?" Ilya asked, hoping the change in subject would distract Danya. "We need to get you some better clothes before the blizzards really settle in."

Danya turned the radio off as a new song began, refusing to meet Ilya's eye. "Sure. Sounds like the last chance to get away from you for a while anyway."

His chest ached and hands clenched from the contempt, but it was necessary. Danya didn't need to care about him, he needed to care about getting better, becoming independent again.

Despite all that, Ilya couldn't help the acid on his tongue. "Yes, well, I can't *wait* for the season to be over so you get out of *my* home."

Ilya stormed off to his room, managing to not slam the door. His eyes stung with tears, vision blurring as he sat on his bed. He was so *stupid*. He'd told himself he couldn't be with Danya, that they couldn't be closer than this, why was he acting this way?

It was for the best, though. He'd keep telling himself that. They could never be more than friends, if that's what they were at all. Months of doting on somebody like an annoying nurse hardly made for a friendship, didn't it?

It was for the best.

7

October 21st, 1927

Tense was a good way to describe the air between them. He wasn't sure if Danya would still want to go into town with him, if they would even speak beyond the bare minimum. He started on breakfast to try and preoccupy himself, turning on the radio to play quiet music as he worked.

It genuinely meant a lot to him that Danya fixed his telephone and his radio. He was used to the silence of his daily life, the emptiness of the church. Even when Danya left, at least he'd be less cut off from the world. Breaking up the monotony with music made the isolation more bearable. Perhaps he could find a news channel, hear what was going on in the Capital and the rest of the country.

Having company was better, though.

He was cracking eggs into the pan when the ladder for the attic dropped down. He resisted the urge to glance behind him as Danya shuffled off to the bathroom. He let out a beleaguered sigh and began scrambling the eggs.

A shout from the bathroom made him whip his head around

then rush to the door. Danya was staring in the mirror and pulling at his hair desperately.

It hadn't been a trick of the light after all: Danya's hair was *bright* red, that beautiful scarlet he thought he'd been imagining. Ilya came to Danya's side, grabbing hold of his arm with both hands to stop him from yanking every strand out of his scalp.

"Danylko– calm down, let me look, okay?"

Danya froze at the nickname; Ilya hadn't even thought about it. Danya's shoulders slumped and he looked on the verge of tears and confusion. Ilya put a hand on his cheek then took a lock of Danya's hair, examining it in the light. Where Danya's eyes had perhaps been deniable previously, there was no room now. It was very noticeable. Everybody in town would be talking, wondering what had happened. He'd get flack for it, but maybe that would be a good thing.

"What the fuck is happening to me?"

Ilya met his eyes, sharing in Danya's grief. "I don't know, I'm sorry. Do you remember anything?"

Danya pressed a hand to his forehead, face screwed up trying to recall *anything*. He growled and sighed, pressing his palms against the sink.

"I think I danced with my old boss? She... I don't even know if she was completely my boss. I don't *feel* different though."

A tug at his heart. Danya and his boss had to be involved with one another. Maybe they came from a more progressive part of the country. The Capital was definitely a little more loose, but polite society said men and women shouldn't be close unless they were courting. Ilya shoved everything down and tried to focus on the Danya in front of him, to do his duty as his caretaker.

Danya continued, "Nothing hurts, nothing feels weird, just... What the *fuck*."

"Aptly put."

"Who asked you?"

Ilya smacked Danya's arm and glared at him. "I'm agreeing with you, shithead."

Danya's eyes grew three sizes. Ilya didn't swear often, but in this moment it was warranted. Might as well meet Danya where he was at, what with the sailor's mouth he had. Thankfully it seemed to have the right effect, Danya having the decency to look ashamed.

"I'm sorry... For last night too. I seem to keep being shitty to you when you've done so much for me and I'm such a fucking asshole about it."

Ilya sighed, placing a hand on Danya's arm again. "It's not your fault. I was overreacting, getting in my own head... You don't deserve that."

Danya glanced at his touch, lingering long enough to make Ilya take his hand back. Perhaps too close, especially if he was remembering a past relationship now. He had to control himself. "Sorry... It's instinctual."

Danya took hold of Ilya's hand, placing it back on his arm and huffing. "You're my friend, you can touch me. I don't care."

That heat crawled up his cheeks once more and he turned around rapidly. His skin was translucent, he was sure all his blushing gave him away in seconds.

"Anyway– If somebody asks you can tell them I messed up trying to cure a migraine or something. They already think I'm bad at my job, they'll believe it."

Ilya made his way out of the bathroom, relieved to find their eggs were only *a little* burned. Danya followed behind him, huffing again.

"Do they need more reasons to give you shit though? I don't wanna keep contributing to that."

Ilya set their plates on the table and stuffed his face rather than answer the question. It didn't matter; the citizens of Velak hadn't let go of their hatred in 20 years, they wouldn't let go of it now. It wouldn't be anything he hadn't heard already, and if it meant people *gawked* at Danya instead of getting out their torches and pitchforks, it was for the best.

"*Ilyushka.* You can't ignore me when I'm concerned about *you* for once."

Ilya looked across the table at Danya. He looked exasperated, eyes pleading with him. Ilya couldn't remember the last time somebody had used that pet name for him. His mother had never used it, that was for certain. He hadn't been to visit his friend Oyuna in a while, but he couldn't even remember her using it. Probably his father had been the only one.

Nobody had held enough affection to use it for him in a very long time.

Ilya refused to cry this early in the day, over a diminutive of all things.

He really, *really* wanted to, though.

Ilya cleared his throat and replied, "I appreciate it, Danya. But I really think it's the easiest way to take the heat off of you. Might as well preserve the good will they have towards you. Mine's been gone for years."

Ilya finished his food, going to rinse his plate in the sink. Danya huffed behind him but stopped pressing the issue. He could be upset on his behalf, and it did mean a lot, but that didn't matter right now.

"Now, let me see if I can't find you a proper coat before we go out."

THE WALKSWAYS WERE full of snow, but thankfully the sky was clear enough that it was melting away. There was a foot of it to wade through, but at least it had stopped snowing. Ilya wrapped Danya as warm as he could manage, but Danya threw most of it off, declaring himself too hot.

Ilya had checked him for a fever but Danya shoved him away, saying he felt fine. He wasn't sure he believed it, what with Danya's skin being as hot as the radiator, but he couldn't make Danya do something he didn't want. If he got cold he'd have to cry about it.

In the light of day, against the stark white of the snow, Danya's hair stood out like a beacon. It was like pure fire, like what their Mother Sun was said to be made of. Ilya wished he hadn't let go of the lock he held earlier. The strands were like silk and he couldn't stop admiring the gorgeous color.

"You know, it suits you. It looks good with how dark your skin is," Ilya said.

Danya blinked and glanced at him. "Yeah? I dunno, it seems kinda weird."

"It reminds me of the sunrise. There's a reason I get up at dawn every day."

Danya scoffed. "It's not because you're neurotic and weird?"

Ilya rolled his eyes in kind. "No. At least that's only part of it… You're sure nothing else has come back to you?"

"A little, actually? I remember a big city with a bunch of tall, white buildings… I think I was protecting somebody? My boss maybe? I don't fucking know." Danya sighed, long and lethargic. It had to be exhausting, struggling to piece together who you were.

What had Danya been in his past life? An inventor's assistant? That didn't explain why he was so strong or why he was protecting his boss. Was he a mercenary? Was he a hunter from the church? That didn't explain his appearance, though.

"I wonder if your appearance changes when more comes back to you." Ilya figured he might as well posit that out loud. "Though I don't think anything changed when you remembered you were an inventor… Your eye color changed long before that."

Danya frowned at that. "My eye color changed?"

"It was darker when you were uncursed, but I noticed it got lighter when I brought you home. I thought maybe I was imagining it. The red is a little harder to ignore though."

Danya guffawed. "No fucking kidding."

THE MOMENT they stepped into the main square there were eyes on them. That wasn't a surprise to Ilya, but what did come as a surprise was all the younger girls who kept staring at Danya. That raised his hackles in a way he hadn't expected. He breathed deeply out of his nose to collect himself, a cloud of mist forming around his face like a dragon. He half wished he could turn into one and eat everybody so they'd have peace.

It was Berta who approached them as Ilya led Danya to the clothing shop, stepping off of her porch and avoiding the tables of junk expertly. She blew out smoke and squinted at the both of them, eyes turning to Ilya.

"Sokolov. What in Sun's name did you do to my employee?"

Ilya huffed a laugh and tried to act casual, "Oh, it was a silly mistake on my part—"

"I woke up like this," Danya interrupted. "I have no idea why the fuck it looks like somebody set my fucking head on fire."

Ilya stared at Danya, who refused to look at him. Berta looked between the both of them with narrowed eyes, finally settling on Danya. "You don't have to defend him, Danylko."

"He didn't *do* anything to me. You calling me a liar now, *babuskha?*"

Ilya wasn't sure what to do with himself, too stunned that Danya had thrown their plan out the window. He was torn between gratitude for the defense and frustration that suspicion would be lauded at Danya now and make *both* their lives harder. Stupid man!

Berta scoffed, holding out her lighter as a gesture of peace. Danya held out a clove cigarette, placing it between his lips when it was lit. They both took drags off what they were smoking and Ilya had to fight the urge to make a face. Danya's cigarettes were irritating if a little nostalgic, Berta's clearly came from the Realm of Eternal Night. He had no idea why she had to pick the worst shit.

"I don't know how much I believe you, but if you're going to insist," Berta finally replied. "Think I always knew you were an odd duck anyway. Didn't really care 'cause you know your stuff, think I still don't really care. Long as you keep my business open. And for the record, you're the closest thing I've ever had to a grandson. My ungrateful daughter would never give me any."

Danya's face softened, clearly touched by the sentiment. Ilya resisted the urge to reach out and touch him, turning his attention to a younger girl calling for him.

"Oh Ilya!"

It was hard for him to know everybody in town since they never wanted to meet with him, but he knew this girl. This was Polina.

Her dirty blonde hair was tied together in a long braid that went over her shoulder and down her chest, her big eyes blue and bright. Her and her gaggle of friends were menaces upon society and were the worst product of their parents' upbringing. It was pure misery every time he interacted with them, but hopefully the buffer of Berta and Danya both would keep Polina in check.

"Ilya!" she repeated. "Who's this mysterious man with you?"

Berta snorted and got back to smoking. Ilya could *feel* Danya's incredulous look on the back of his head.

"Yes, hello *Polina*. This is Danya. He looks different today, I know. We aren't sure what happened."

Polina crooned back, "I'm sure it was something you did, but it looks very handsome Mister Danya. I've never seen a color like it on anybody."

Ilya could hear the restrained noise of pain in the back of Danya's throat and he had to bite his lip to keep from laughing, focusing on Danya instead of Polina. Danya gave an awkward wave with his fingers and Ilya almost broke again at the blush on his face as Polina giggled. Berta rolled her eyes and walked away without another word, leaving them alone with this *very bold* teenager.

"Ilyushka didn't do anything to me," Danya said. "My hair is just like this now I guess."

Polina batted her eyes at him and the defensive irritation came back to Ilya in an instant.

"Ilyushka? That's a very familiar way to address our useless priest. Would you like to get more familiar with me, by chance?"

Danya squinted at her. "I'm okay."

Ilya rolled his eyes hard enough his head went along with the motion, immediately walking away from the two of them. "Danya we need to find you new clothes, quit flirting!"

"You can't keep him away from me forever, Ilya!" Polina called back.

Danya rushed to catch up with Ilya, plenty eager to get away from this girl. Ilya raised an eyebrow at him and Danya groaned.

"I don't remember shit but I know she's not my type."

Ilya hummed. "And what type of women *do* you like?"

"Not teenagers! I guess I could be with an older woman though."

"I won't have somebody's husband whom you've wronged coming to my church to chase you around with an axe."

"You'd laugh at me, don't lie."

Ilya could hear the smile in Danya's voice and he snorted. "*You* won't be laughing when he's cut off your cock and balls and made you a eunuch."

"*Ilyushka*. So *vulgar*. Besides, I'm sure you could fix me up, you're a healer."

Ilya's fingers prickled hearing the nickname again. It was so familiar, it made his heart ache with longing.

"I'm a healer, not a miracle worker. The regrowing of body parts is beyond even the best of us. For once it wouldn't be because I'm shit at my job. Anyway, don't fool with any of the women of Velak, they'll do you no good."

Danya scoffed. "Guess I'll have to fool around with the men then."

Ily's heart clenched. He clutched the front of his winter cloak to calm down as his ears burned again. He decided to not dignify Danya with a response, pulling him into the alleyway where Oyuna's clothing shop was. He had mixed feelings every time he visited; Oyuna was the only person in Velak (aside from Danya now, he supposed) who he could claim was a friend. But, her home was right next door to his mother, his old house. She'd been their neighbor growing up and was the only one to show him kindness when his mother turned and became evil to him. As much as he loved Oyuna, he had to be careful that his mother wouldn't accost him.

Thankfully it was before 6 in the evening, so she likely wouldn't be awake yet.

Ilya was surprised to find Danya hesitate when they came down the alley. He glanced back at him and spread his hands incredulously. "Danylko. It's down here. What's with you?"

"I just thought... uh... Irinia, your mother is right here, isn't she?"

Ilya frowned. "How do you know that?"

"I, uh. Visited a while ago. It was… illuminating? It helped me understand you more, let's say."

"Not in a bad way, I hope," Ilya whispered, swallowing hard as his anxiety peaked.

Danya waved him off. "Nah. You make more sense to me now. If I had to live there for an extended amount of time I'd be fucking miserable."

Ilya sighed. "Yes, well. It certainly was. Anyway, let me show you to Oyuna."

A bell above the door signaled their arrival. The shop was modest with its wooden floors and paneling on the walls. There were sparse shelves and racks with a variety of colorful pieces. Velak wasn't big, so keeping a large stock wasn't entirely necessary. Not unless Oyuna was feeling particularly bored, anyway.

The bell brought a very, very short older woman from the back. She had a red patterned scarf wrapped around her head which perfectly matched the rosy tint to her tan cheeks. She had thin, dark eyes and an infectious smile that made her eyes appear thinner. Her shirt was yet more red with an array of patterning around the collar and cuffs. Truly, Oyuna was a beacon of color. She matched Danya's new hair perfectly.

"Father Sokolov! It's been so long. Who's this flashy young man with you?"

Ilya couldn't help but break into a smile. Oyuna was the grandmother he'd always wanted. He couldn't find the nerve to visit her often, but it was wonderful every time he was able.

"*Babushka*, this is Danya. He's from Kursiya and works in Berta's shop. He wasn't so flashy yesterday, if you can believe. He's also lacking in winter wear. Do you have anything for him?"

Oyuna stepped up to Danya, barely taller than his waistline. She held her hands behind her back and examined him, swaying this way and that.

Danya blushed and croaked out, "Uh, hi."

"What a pretty hair color. You're a very large young man, but I might have a few things. You'll have to not be picky, you understand."

"I'll be happy with whatever you can find. As long as it gets me out of Ilya's spares," Danya laughed.

Oyuna cackled as she began making her way over to a rack in the back of the shop. "No, I suspect no handsome young man wants to bury themselves in stuffy priest's clothing by choice! Show off what you have while you have your youth! Isn't that right, Father Sokolov?"

"I like these, Oyuna, you know that," Ilya huffed. "They're... mostly modest. I don't need to show off anything."

Danya clucked his tongue and caught Ilya's attention, though it was quickly drawn back to Oyuna as she spoke again.

"Oh, but it might help you to find a wife one of these days if you did. If not to raise your own son, at least get you to stop being so *dour* all the time. A woman in your life would do you good!"

Danya barked a laugh that startled him. He covered his mouth to feign being polite when Ilya narrowed his eyes at him. Danya's eyes were practically sparkling with his mirth as he suppressed his giggling.

"Ilya has too much of a stick up his ass to attract most people, Oyuna."

Ilya's jaw dropped, unable to help how offended he looked. The nerve of this man!

Oyuna practically howled as she sifted through a crate. Ilya's face burned with shame; he was used to Oyuna and Danya's teasing, but teaming up together was too much.

"Well, it's only most people! The right person will come along for our silly boy," she finally said, "Then I'm sure she could pull it out for him!"

Ilya guffawed. "Don't be so crass, both of you. I'm a fucking priest."

The other two snorted in unison when he swore. Danya threw an arm around Ilya's shoulders, giving him an affectionate squeeze. He rested his head against Ilya's and smiled.

"I'm glad I've become a bad enough influence on you, Ilyushka."

Ilya's head was swimming from the contact, body enveloped in Danya's warmth. Their sides were pressed together, Danya's heat burning through to his skin. Those silken red threads brushed against his cheek and all Ilya wanted to do was wrap it around his fingers and keep it forever.

He leaned against Danya in return, allowing himself this indulgence. He could return the affection this time, in good nature, in the company of the woman he trusted more than his biological family. Danya looked down at him, cheeks flushed with his joy. Ilya met his honey-colored eyes and then stepped out of his grasp on instinct.

No. It was too close. It gave him too much hope. Danya was with his boss, he'd want to go back to her any day now. He couldn't do this to the both of them.

"Here!" Oyuna declared. "I've managed to find some things. Danya, my boy, come back here so you can try them on."

There was a pile of shirts, a couple knit sweaters, a few pants, and one good coat that Oyuna had gathered. They were all reds and dark browns, colors that would look brilliant on Danya.

Danya gratefully accepted the pile, heading into the room Oyuna had sectioned off so customers could try things on. She waited a moment after the door locked before turning her sights on Ilya again, stepping up to him and craning her neck to look at him.

"Now Father, you know I only meddle in your business a little bit, but I can tell when you're more emotionally constipated than normal. What's with this man, then?"

Ilya wasn't sure where to begin, what was safe to reveal about Danya. That should be up to Danya.

"Nothing, *babushka*. He's become a friend to me though. I... will be very sad when he leaves soon."

Oyuna hummed and nodded her head sagely. "You're a very lonely man, Father. You leave this poor old woman to be as lonely very often, you know! But what makes you so certain he'll leave?"

"He has his own family, and I think a wife, or at least a woman he cares for... I doubt he'll want to stay away for long. And who wants the company of a stuffy priest who's bad at his job anyway?" Ilya swallowed hard to keep from breaking, tension making his shoulders go taut.

Oyuna's eyes roamed over his face, trying to divine anything she could about Ilya's inner thoughts. She was good at reading him; it came with knowing him since childhood.

"May I speak plainly, father?"

Ilya huffed a laugh and replied, "You always do."

Her eyes crinkled at the corners as she smiled, the deep lines of her face settling into their favored position. She stepped closer to him and took one of his hands in both of hers. "I know how wicked this town has been to you, how terrible that witch next door is to you. But you deserve to be happy, my boy. You should tell the people you care about that you want them around. If you're holding back, let it go. We only have so much time until the Great Mother brings us home. Let your friend know you want him to stay."

There was a lump trapped in his throat, choking him as he threatened to burst again. She wouldn't understand everything about why he was so upset, how his affections for his charge were growing every day, but she was right. He didn't know if he had the heart to act on it, but she was right.

Oyuna yanked him down, leaning on her tiptoes to kiss his cheek, smacking the other several times affectionately. Ilya made a face and pretended to be grossed out. She chuckled, releasing him as the door to the changing room opened.

"Ah, so you didn't break your head in there!" Oyuna called.

Danya rolled his eyes and stepped out, twirling once so they could get a view of him. "Seems like you got my size right, so how's it look?"

The sweater was snug on Danya, hugging his lithe but sculpted form. Its deep red color made how sharp his hair was stand out even more, brought out the deep, warm tone of his freckles. It made him look soft.

Danya was so beautiful.

"It looks good on you, yes," Ilya whispered, "Oyuna knows best."

Oyuna chuckled and smacked Ilya's stomach affectionately, forcing a wheeze out of him. "Quite. Now Father, I know it's been a minute since I've come to pay my tithes, so please take these as a gift from me. I'm sure our new neighbor could use the kindness as well. I'll come around for the Longest Night, though, I promise."

Ilya clucked his tongue and suppressed a smile. "Well, I suppose clothing my charity case will have to do. If you do visit and it's just us then please come to the rectory. I'll make dinner."

Oyuna smiled and nodded. "I'd like that very much, Father Sokolov. Now Danylko, let me pack the rest of your things."

She packed everything in brown paper and twine, patting Danya's arm as she handed everything over. "Make sure you take care of the Father here. Sun knows he desperately needs a good friend."

Ilya blushed and avoided turning away despite himself. "I'm sure I'll manage, *babushka*. Come Danylko, I'm in the mood for a cider."

"Thank you *babushka*, I'll do my best with Ilyushka whether he likes it or not."

Ilya shook his head and marched outside. He stared up at the dark gray sky, blinking away snowflakes that fell on his eyelashes. He took a deep breath and embraced the cold, willing away the heat in his face. He glanced at his mother's house and quickly made his way out of the alley and onto the main path, eyeing the Sunset Tavern across the way.

"Ilya," Danya said, voice soft.

Ilya looked over his shoulder, stricken by how much *affection* was plastered on Danya's face. How could somebody so beautiful even deign to look at him that way? Even knowing how bad he was at his job, how lonely and particular and over-emotional he was? He could never measure up to whatever image Danya had in his mind. He wasn't good enough, and he never would be.

Ilya turned away without a word and made his way to the tavern. There was a long pause before the snow crunched behind him, though not enough to mask Danya's drawn-out sigh.

8

November 6th, 1927

Sundays were for the Sun, of course. It was the day for weekly ceremony, celebrating the Eclipse, the union of Mother Sun and Father Moon. He changed into the white vestments for this, made of similar finery to his regular ones, but with no hood and *much* larger sleeves. Arguably a larger window over the chest, all to let the light of the Sun into his heart. Awful.

Oyuna came for ceremony when she could, but she was old and the hill was brutal on her joints. The only person who showed up these days was Danya, and that was because he lived with Ilya. He couldn't skip and go unnoticed.

Ilya went through the motions the first time to show Danya, but now they ate the circular chocolate and vanilla eclipse cookies and chatted. No point in wasting the effort, especially since Danya wasn't deeply interested in scripture. He'd listen to Ilya talk and kept telling him he liked listening, but Ilya was too awkward. He couldn't do it. So, they'd talk about how their weeks had gone.

Ilya's were uneventful in a stark contrast to Danya's, which were hardly eventful to begin with. Mostly it would be Danya explaining the next gadget he was fixing, bemoaning the "fucking dumbass geezers" who treated their things with a learned helplessness that infuriated him. Ilya loved hearing Danya think out loud, pondering how to fix something he was unfamiliar with, or explaining something he knew well. He adored Danya's intelligence and all the chances he had to admire it, even second hand.

Danya was in the middle of explaining how to repair phone lines when the great oak doors at the front of the church were thrust open. Ilya was shocked; the church was cold as ice this time of year, even with the fire in the chancel lit. Who dared bother?

"Father Ilya," Polina called, "Are you holding ceremony today?"

Danya groaned and Ilya managed to stifle himself to a snort. He got to his feet, frowning deeply as he realized more of Polina's crew had joined her. There were light flurries coming down outside and he wished it was blizzarding so he wouldn't have to deal with this. He supposed teenage girls could work through anything if it meant a chance at flirting with their crushes, no matter how much that object of affection wanted it. Or not, in this case.

Despite the question being directed at Ilya, Polina had only eyes for Danya. Frankly, so did the rest of her group. Ilya caught Danya scowling out of the corner of his eye and something inside his chest flared. He was possessive of Danya, as childish as it was. Polina had no chance, Danya had made that clear, but that she could openly flirt with Danya with no repercussions frustrated him. Ilya knew if he did the same they'd have his head.

Ilya took a small, sick comfort in the fact that when Danya left, that even if he would be back to a lonely, miserable life, so would these annoying girls. It was a cruel thought to have, but Ilya would never have claimed to be a kind person anyway.

The girls walked to the front pews, sitting behind Danya and surrounding him. Ilya counted eight among Polina's group. They all began cooing at Danya and asking him inane questions.

"How's your hair that *amazing* color? It has to be magic."

"I have an uncle in Kursiya, do you know him? Maybe our families are friends!"

"Would you like to come to the tavern with us later for company? I'm sure Father Sokolov is *such* a bore."

Danya looked like he was sucking on a thousand lemons. If asked, Ilya imagined he'd prefer to be doing that over whatever in Sun's name *this* shit was.

"Ilya is my friend, I'm very fine with being in his company," Danya finally managed.

Polina chimed in, "First name basis with the Father? I didn't know he had enough of a heart to make friends!"

The girls all giggled and looked at Ilya. For his part, Ilya rolled his eyes and stepped up to the altar to prepare for ceremony.

Polina crooned again, "Who wants to be around a man like him anyway?"

"He's been nice to me, I don't know what your damage is," Danya gruffed.

The youngest girl replied, "Just wait until he gets bored, then he'll abandon you like he did with the rest of us."

"And he's not even that good of a healer! He probably can't even heal all the cuts your big, strong hands get while repairing all the town's junk, huh?"

"Sun's sake," Danya groaned.

Ilya pulled out the enormous tome that contained all the edicts of the sun and slammed it on the marble altar as hard as he could. It sounded like a bomb going off, echoing off the massive ceiling in the church. It was enough to finally silence everybody.

"Now! If we could all settle down and pretend we have real reasons to be here, I'll begin ceremony!"

Ilya flashed the group a tight smile, disdain barely concealed. He paused to make sure they were going to stay silent, hands held up in anticipation. When they remained such, he began working his magic.

He swayed from side to side, rings of light pulsing from the center of the altar in a steady motion. He stepped on a padel under the altar to make the skylight close. The disc of blackened metal crossed in front of it, leaving a thin circle of light around it that shone on the ground below.

"We sit in this holy darkness during the daylight, mimicking the lovers' union of our Mother Sun and Father Moon. We show gratitude for the life the Sun has to give, and for the quiet comfort of the Moon. Though this moment is as fleeting as the Eclipse itself, we cherish this moment before our Mother Sun shines upon us once more."

Ilya waited a beat, stealing a glance at Danya. Danya started back at him and smiled. Even with only the faint ring of light, Danya's eyes glowed. They were golden and gorgeous.

He checked the position of the light then lifted his foot off the pedal, the metallic disc in the ceiling beginning to retract.

"And now we celebrate the perfect light of the noon, when our Sun's power is strongest. We wish for the Great Mother to be intertwined with her lover soon, and pray for their reunion once more."

He was silent again as the light blared through the skylight, casting a beam directly onto the polished gold symbol of the sun in the floor. It was blinding as it filled the room with light. It was mere minutes of spectacle until the beam receded, leaving the room in regular daylight.

Ilya looked out at the small crowd, seeing Danya and the girls raise their heads from prayer. He reached under the altar for the box of Eclipse cookies, holding the first up.

"Please take your turns and come accept the symbol of the sun."

Danya wasted no time escaping his seat, holding his hand out for Ilya.

"May you delight in the fruit of our Mother's labors."

Danya's fingers brushed against Ilya's palm, lingering a moment before plucking the cookie and popping it into his mouth. He walked behind the altar to wait with Ilya as Polina and her friends all accepted their treats. If he shoved his own cookie into his mouth a little more frantically than he should have, who was to say?

"A beautiful ceremony as always, Ilyushka," Danya said.

The gaggle of girls all made faces at Ilya's nickname, and the reaction made him crave it more.

"Ugh, you're calling him *that?* Seems pretty familiar, Mister Danya," Polina said.

"I'm *very* familiar with him. Does that bother you?" Danya asked.

Ilya's face burned from the implication. He could tell the other girls were reading plenty into it, all eyes staring daggers into his soul.

Danya continued, "Even still, I'm not as familiar as I'd like to be. Father Sokolov is very stubborn and distant, but since you're a pious, righteous group who comes to church regularly I'm sure you know plenty about him already."

The girls exchanged looks, looking a combination of frustrated and chastised.

"It is a bit silly none of you will even show up for holidays," Ilya mused. "Even the least pious in the Capital will do that."

Another of the girls spoke up, "Maybe if he was better at his job we'd come."

Danya tilted his head. "What exactly did he do wrong?"

A tense silence followed the question. Ilya braced himself, gripping the edge of the stone altar for stability. Here he believed Danya was *at least* his friend! Inviting such criticisms! He could hardly believe this.

"I guess nothing," Polina sneered, "But it's super boring."

"Whatever, Polina," Ilya scoffed back. His patience had been ground down and he couldn't pretend to be civil anymore. *Whatever*.

The girls rolled their eyes at him and made their way to leave, the youngest of the bunch asking, "You'll come into town more often, won't you Mister Danya?"

Danya snorted. "No. I don't think I will."

Ilya managed not to laugh at how crestfallen all the girls were as they left the church. He heaved a drawn out sigh when the great oak doors shut, crumpling across the altar in a heap. He yelled into the tome, breathing in the musty old paper to calm himself. Nothing like old book smell to find peace.

A warm palm pressed against the center of his shoulders, massaging in circles. Ilya groaned as his body sagged, tension melting away like butter. He peeked from behind his arm when Danya's hand went still, catching his eye. It was hard to tell with Danya's darker complexion, but Ilya could swear he was blushing.

"Uh, anyway– don't let them get to you. It's really fucking weird they never even knew your father and act that way. Also fucking weird they expected me to go along with it."

Ilya pulled himself up from the altar and dusted off the front of his vestments with his hands. "Well, I am insufferable and easy to bully. I wouldn't have held it against you."

Danya leaned back against the altar, crossing his arms and frowning as he crowded into Ilya's space. "Why do you think I'd *ever* do that? I care about you, Ilyushka. You take care of me, you *saved* me. You're basically my whole world."

Ilya turned away from him. He couldn't stand hearing that, it made his chest ache. "I don't deserve that. I'm very selfish, actually. I've been keeping you from your real home, your previous work. You should probably leave soon."

"Would you *knock it off* with that? Sun's sake, Ilya, if I wanted to leave then I would. I still barely know who I am. I was cursed! People don't end up with curses because their lives were going swimmingly. And besides, I *like being around you*. Even if you never believe me."

"You're right, I don't."

Ilya sighed and began to step back towards the rectory. He didn't expect Danya to yank him back by his enormous sleeve and hug him. Danya seemed to enjoy hugging him, and it shocked him every time. Danya's face was pressed against his shoulder, sighing against his neck. He was too stunned to be flustered, lifting his hands as he tried to figure out a response.

"Stop, okay? I like you. I want to stay here. I don't give a shit about my past life. I'm living this one right now."

Ilya stared down at the flash of red hair cascading across his front. He reached for the end of a lock, curling it around a finger. Danya snorted and finally pulled back, making the hair slip out of his grasp.

"What is it with everybody and my hair?"

"It's a very pretty color," Ilya chuckled. "Only I know how soft it is, though."

Danya blinked, that owlish look returning. It happened every time Ilya surprised him. He could never tell if it was good or bad.

"Anyway, how does lunch sound?" Ilya didn't wait for a reply as he whirled around to head back to the rectory. He wanted out of these vestments and to stop hearing Danya lay his affections bare.

Danya sighed and followed him back.

9

November 23rd, 1927

They were deep into the snowy season now. Nary a day went by without snow. Icicles had formed inside the church, scattered across the vaulted ceiling. The marble floors were so frigid that it leached through Ilya's boots. Never one to be bothered by the temperature previously, even Danya complained of being cold. This was a misery that Velak hadn't known in a long time. Ilya was ever grateful for the electric heating in the rectory, but even that wasn't strong enough. He had Danya marching through the ice to get firewood *constantly*.

Today was yet another terrible storm. The windows rattled from the force of the gales outside and the power kept flickering. The radio hadn't been able to get signal in days, the telephone lines were down, and Ilya was sure the electricity would die at any moment. He had a generator outside, but it would awful to reach right now.

Ilya stoked the fire under the pot that hung in the fireplace as he waited for Danya to bring in more wood. He kept glancing out the windows, searching for that wisp of scarlet amongst all the white and gray. He jumped out of his skin when there was a knock on the door, sighing when he opened it to find Danya. Danya kicked the snow off of his boots and closed the door. Meanwhile, Ilya set to the task of brushing the snow off Danya's hair and shoulders.

"Even if you never *feel* cold, you need to keep warm. If your fingers go black and fall off I won't be able to fix it," Ilya tutted.

"You don't need to mother hen me so much," Danya huffed. He dropped the bundle of wood strapped to his shoulders, pressing his hands to the small of his back and groaning as his spine popped a thousand times. "Fuck—"

"Go lay down, we should be fine for a couple days with all this. I've got a stew going that should be done in a few hours."

Danya kicked off his boots and, for once, did exactly as Ilya told him, going to lay faceplant on the couch. Ilya went to check on the stew, gave it a stir, then loaded the wood into the fireplace rack. It would need time to dry out, but they'd be fine for a few hours.

The lights flickered as another gust slammed against the rectory and he glared at the ceiling. "I have no idea what humankind did without electric heat. Frankly I have no idea what *I* did."

Muffled by the couch cushions, Danya said, "I hear people huddled for warmth. Shared body heat and stuff."

Ilya scoffed. "We don't need to be in each other's personal space like that. We're grown men."

Danya pushed himself up from the couch to peek over at Ilya. "I'm being serious, isn't that what we're supposed to do? Stop being weird about it, you damned stuffy priest."

Ilya meant to glare at Danya but he was distracted by how the golden color in his eyes seemed to glow in the firelight. They were as bright as the Sun that he so *dearly* missed right now.

It seemed as soon as he wished for brighter days, the power went out. Ilya leaned back and let out the longest sigh he could manage. *Of-fucking-course*, as Danya would say.

"I suppose I'll have to go turn on the generator," Ilya grumbled to himself as he went to the coat rack, pulling on his warmest cloak and gloves.

"Ilyushka," Danya whined, "You're going to freeze to death way before I do, let me go back out."

"*Danulyachka,*" he hissed, "You're going to throw your back out if you don't *quit,* now get back on that couch or so help me–"

"Ooh, what's the big bad priest going to do to a naughty little boy like me?" Danya cooed. Despite himself, Danya's face was bright red. The overextended diminutive was definitely over the top, but it got Danya to stop in his tracks, and that's all that mattered to Ilya.

"Hit you in the head with a pot of boiling stew if it will make you *rest,*" Ilya hissed.

Danya scoffed but settled back on the couch as Ilya asked. Ilya finished dressing and came back over to Danya. He let his palm spread over the small of Danya's back, warm light emanating from his hand. He could ease Danya's pain, which would hopefully get him to settle long enough.

Danya melted against the cushions, finally going still. Ilya took that as his cue to go outside. He pulled up his hood, pinned it together so it wouldn't fly off, then tightened his cloak. Finally he opened the door to brave the ice.

Saying his vision was limited would be generous. The wind bit and lashed at his skin like a cornered animal, howling like a wolf. It threatened to toss him to the ground, as if he were nothing but gossamer. Ilya pinned his shoulder to the wall, following it as he searched for the generator. The snow was halfway up his shins, and he worried he wouldn't even *find* the stupid generator because of it.

He trudged on through the snowbanks, relieved when his boot slammed against something metallic. He brushed the snow away and lifted the cover for the switch panel. Despite being covered, it had iced over. He smashed against the ice with a fist to get it to fall away, but to no avail. There was no way he'd be able to get it working. On top of it all, if he spent any longer outside, his nose would freeze off his face. Damn it all.

Ilya trudged back in his defeat, shouting as a sudden gust threw him forward. He slammed into the hard, icy ground. Even with the wind howling as it was, he heard the crack of his face hitting stone. His teeth ached and a thick warmth immediately gushed down the back of his throat. He gagged and spit out way too much blood, red droplets stark against the pure white ground.

He much preferred Danya's red.

"Fucking– stupid generator–"

His hanky did well enough to stop his bleeding nose from making a mess of his vestments, but not enough for the same. Thankfully, going in the direction of the wind made it quicker to get back inside. He threw the door open, terrified it would get torn off its hinges as it slammed into the wall. Danya shot up from the couch and stared back at Ilya in disbelief.

"Ilya? What happened?"

"Just close the fucking door," he spat back. He rushed over to the kitchen sink, turning the tap. The pipes groaned and Ilya shut the tap off. Perfect. The pipes were frozen.

Ilya's shame and rage threatened to boil over in combination with his pain. He dressed down, careful to navigate around his hanky, stained red all over. He tossed his boots halfway across the room and threw his coat at the couch. Everything was *terrible*.

Danya stepped up to Ilya after closing the door, placing a gentle hand on his arm. "Ilya. Calm down, okay? What happened? Are you able to heal yourself?"

"No! I fucking can't, remember! No healing for the healers! Too selfish or some other– stupid– fucking bullshit– Why my *stupid* father died and the *stupid* fucking town blames me for *everything*, can't do *shit* for ourselves, nope, never!"

Ilya snarled as he went into the bathroom to find a spare wash-cloth. They'd be stained forever with no water to rinse with. Damn it all!

He whirled around against his will, arms pinned to his sides by Danya moving him. His head was spinning from immediate vertigo and he slammed his eyes shut to try and settle his headache.

"Ilyushka," Danya whispered, "Let me help you. Okay? You're swearing more than me."

Ilya fought the urge to swear at Danya, trying to calm himself instead. He hissed and grit his teeth as Danya patted his nose dry, holding a rag against his face until the bleeding stopped. Every brush of Danya's warm fingers against his cheeks released more tension from his shoulders. Finally, the fire in his soul went out, nothing but a smoldering coal of ache in his face remaining.

"You'd probably know better than me, but it doesn't look broken. For what it's worth."

Ilya sighed. "Tiny miracles from the Great Mother. Proof that she hasn't decided to abandon us yet."

Danya huffed a soft laugh, digging through more cabinets. "You have a first aid kit then, since you can't heal yourself?"

"Under the sink. Try to not hit your head on the counter."

"I can manage, Ilyushka."

Danya kneeled to rummage through the cabinet. It was so *pedestrian*, needing things like bandages when he had magic, but alas.

There was a loud *thump* followed by Danya swearing. Ilya rolled his eyes.

"What did I say?"

"Shut up!"

Ilya smiled until the pain in his face became unbearable. He whimpered and reached for the rag Danya had used to clean him up, soaking up more blood from his nose. He tilted his head forward to try and catch it all, gulping down air. There was copper in the back of his throat and wished so desperately that he could wash it down with water.

Danya came up from under the sink, leading Ilya out to the living room so they could use the firelight to see. He pulled out ointment, gauze, and probably too many bandages, doing a hack job of wrapping Ilya's face. It was extremely amateur, but he was calmer now that it was taken care of. He was too flustered to do it himself.

It was odd to be doted on like this, after all this time. All his past months had been dedicated to taking care of Danya. Danya seemed happy being able to help in this way.

"Not just a big meathead you can use for all your firewood now, huh?" Danya teased.

Ilya frowned, hissing in pain before straightening his face. "I never said that. You're good for other things."

"Oh yeah? Tell me."

"Well, you're very good at going through my things to find broken stuff to fix. Carrying all the heavy groceries is also helpful. Oh, and there's being a pain in my ass…"

The line of Danya's smile made his heart flutter. Ilya pushed past the pain as he smiled back.

A chill ran through him and he hugged his body. The cold was settling in. He'd have to *sit* in the fire to be warm enough. He stepped up to the fireplace, holding his hands up and wiggling his fingers. They were a bit numb, admittedly.

"Hey, you remember what I mentioned earlier?" Danya asked.

Ilya squinted over his shoulder. "What about it?"

"Can you not be weird and avoidant for like, five minutes so we can try this?"

"What do you mean *weird*–"

The answer came in the form of Danya dragging him back to the couch. He laid back and pulled Ilya on top of his body, yanking a quilt down from the back of the couch to cover them. Ilya was suddenly *hot* all over. This was too intimate, he couldn't handle it. He started to push himself off, but Danya held tight onto him.

"Hey, no you fucking don't. I told you to stop being weird and avoidant. You're gonna freeze to death."

Ilya whined, "This is too much, Danylko, let me go–"

"I'm hot as the Sun and it's gonna be cold as balls with the heating out. Let me do this for you, okay?"

Ilya sighed and settled across Danya's chest again. He crammed his face against his neck and grumbled out, "Whose balls are you touching that are as cold as a blizzard?"

Danya snorted. "Would you shut up and relax? I'll let you go when dinner's ready, all right? We can talk balls later."

"I think I have meatballs in the icebox actually–"

"*Ilyushka*, darling, I'm going to smother you if you don't stop talking and sleep."

The one-two punch of nicknames was enough to silence him. His heart was palpitating from everything happening as it was. This closeness was overwhelming, but it was very warm. That scent of cinnamon, clove, and tobacco lingered on Danya's skin. It washed over him as the gentle heat from the man under him permeated into his skin. His teeth and nose ached, but the pain had reduced to a dull throb he could ignore as he dozed.

He focused on Danya's broad hands spread across the small of his back. He was so small compared to Danya and it made his heart pound harder. He never believed he'd know intimacy like this.

Even if Danya was only a friend. That was all this was.

Ilya refused to admit to anything serious; that perhaps, just maybe, something was starting to bloom inside of him.

TRUE TO HIS WORD, Danya woke him a few hours later when the stew was ready. Broad hands stroked his hair, fingers digging into his curls and making him shiver. Danya spoke in a low, gravelly tone, "Ilya… we should eat."

Ilya whined in reply. His face hurt even more than earlier now that the adrenaline had worn off. Everything was awful. He managed to peel himself off of Danya with a groan, trying to not think about how close they'd been. He approached the fireplace, grabbed a mitt to pull the pot out of the fire, and made his way to the kitchen carefully. He dished them up and then sat on the couch with Danya, making a point to sit on the opposite end from him. He couldn't keep indulging his feelings like this, living in the fantasy they could ever be together.

"Why are you always avoiding me?"

Ilya stared back at Danya. It was hard to avoid Danya when they'd been living together for months. He supposed maybe they didn't know each other as well as Danya hoped, but Ilya thought they were very close. As close as one could be when one of you had half a memory and the other had nothing of note happening to them at all times.

"I don't try to. I just think it's a bad idea that we're too close."

"But *why?*" The pain in Danya's voice tugged on him. He didn't expect that. "Ilya, you're one of, like, three people I have right now. Do you understand? It hurts."

Danya's voice cracked as he pleaded with Ilya. It crushed Ilya's very soul to hear. He fought the urge to hold Danya's face and wipe his tears away.

"I'm sorry, Danylko. I don't mean to hurt you. I keep thinking about how close you and your boss must have been. Why would you need me when she's probably waiting for you to come home? I can't have you getting too close or it'll hurt too much when you leave."

Ilya finally looked at Danya, shocked by his expression. Ilya might as well have hit him in the face for all the damage his words had done.

"So you think I'm going to abandon you? *Still?* You are so *frustrating!*"

Him? Frsutrating? After the stunt Danya had pulled? No. Ilya would have to be foolish to think he was anything but a temporary fancy. A place to call home until everything came back. He'd mean nothing in time, like everybody else in his life.

"And what if you have a family, Danya? What if you have a whole life you're ignoring to stay here with me? Are you going to abandon everything for a priest from a shihole town in the middle of mountainous nowhere? I don't believe you'd do something so selfish and cruel."

Danya opened his mouth to speak, seemed to think the better of it, and shoveled stew into his face instead. Ilya did the same, glaring at the blizzard outside the window. The snow piles were up to the windows, trapping them. Wonderful time to have an argument with one's roommate.

Danya set his bowl on the coffee table and continued to glare at the fire. Ilya finished his food and made to grab for Danya's bowl, but a hand wrapped around his wrist stopped him.

"She's dead, Ilya."

He blanched at that. "What?"

"She's dead. That's why I was cursed. So they could kill her. I… I keep seeing blurry faces, but they look like black-eyed monsters. I don't remember why it happened. I know they did it."

Ilya set his bowl on the table again, sitting next to Danya. "That sounds like the Hunters from the church. I'm sorry."

"Do you understand why I haven't left, now?"

Ilya laced their fingers together, setting another hand on top of Danya's. "I'm sorry. I… I keep assuming the worst. I'm so used to it… Forgive me."

Danya sighed and squeezed Ilya's hand. "It's okay. Just… know I'm happy here, with you. I like my life here so far."

For once, Ilya initiated their embrace. Danya buried his face against Ilya's shoulder, choking on a sob. Mourning a life you could barely recall had to be difficult. He did want Danya to stay, and selfishly, he was glad he wouldn't leave. He hated the pain behind it, hated that he was even a *little* happy about it. But, he was only human.

"Ilyushka," Danya croaked, "It's still gonna be cold. Will you let me keep you warm?"

Ilya sighed, weighing the options. Either he could send Danya, who had confessed something deeply personal, to freeze in the attic while he froze in his room. Or, he could be warm, and be there for his friend. If he could bring comfort to his charge, care for him as he was supposed to, then he would.

Not the least bit because he enjoyed sharing warmth with someone.

It was a bonus, though.

"All right, I give in. Come to bed then."

Danya lifted his head immediately, eyes wide in his surprise. The look of joy that crossed his face made the decision worth it. Ilya's heart pounded and he was blushing up to his ears again, suddenly hotter than the fire. Danya was easy to look at anyway, but that happiness? Made him breathtaking. Ilya never wanted to stop drinking in that bliss. He wanted to see it every day if he could help it. He'd cherish it for the rest of his life.

Whatever was happening between them, he knew that being close to Danya was important to him. Danya's happiness was important to him. Even if this was a fleeting moment, a blip in both their lives, he wanted to enjoy it.

They didn't speak further, quietly making their way back to Ilya's bedroom. The walls were black and the sheets were gold. It was almost entirely void of knickknacks or personality aside from the bookshelves across the room from his bed. A portrait of his father rested on the desk that was nestled under the window and there was a nightstand with a tiny lamp. He'd never had the heart to decorate, to make it more of his own. The room was a bit depressing in that way.

Danya said nothing as Ilya crawled under the covers. He shivered from how cool the fabric had become, lifting the blankets so Danya could slip in next to him. Ilya laid flat on his back, staring at the ceiling as Danya tossed an arm across his chest. The bed was definitely on the side of too small for two grown men, but if they were going to snuggle up then he supposed it was enough. The whole point of this was to get close and share body heat anyway. It was fine.

Ilya's face throbbed, Danya's warmth soothing him. He drifted off quickly, eyes fluttering shut. Despite his whining, he was comfortable. At peace.

As he drifted, he swore he saw flecks of glowing gold scatter across Danya's cheeks.

10

November 24th, 1927

I lya woke up surrounded by warmth despite the cold against his aching face. It was so cold it hurt to breathe through his nose, nostrils burning from the chill. He groaned and angled his face against the warmth elsewhere. He took a deep breath, wrapped in the scent of spice and smoke. He buried his face deeper into it, letting out a contented sigh.

His eyes shot open as everything came back to him. He pulled away from Danya in a panic, pausing to stare at the glittering flecks on Danya' cheeks. His breath gathered in a fog around his face as he drank it in, the icy air bringing clarity back to him.

Danya groaned and rubbed his eyes, blinking and looking at Ilya with knitted brows. "Ilyushka...?"

Ilya was too stunned to reply, lips parted in his shock. The gray sky left the room in darkness. Danya's golden freckles looked like fireflies on a summer's evening, shifting as he sat up. Ilya was entranced.

"What *are* you?"

Danya paused in rubbing his eyes, pulling his hands down to frown at Ilya. "What's that supposed to mean?"

Ilya pressed a hand to Danya's cheek, forcing their eyes to meet.

Even his eyes were glowing now. It looked like the glint of a skulking animal in the night, like the wolf Danya had been not so long ago. He rubbed a thumb across Danya's cheeks, watching the glow disappear under his touch. The light from Danya's eyes cast on Ilya's pale skin. This was real.

Danya was beautiful.

"Go look in the mirror, Danya. It's unbelievable."

Ilya threw the covers off and nudged his begrudging bedmate with his hand until they were in the bathroom. Danya whined about not wanting to leave bed yet, but the immediate silence said everything.

Danya pulled at the skin under his eyes, stared at the tops of his hands, smacked his palms against his cheeks. His freckles and eyes were the only things visible in the darkened bathroom mirror.

"What *am* I?"

"I don't know," Ilya whispered, "But I think you're more important than I ever knew."

Danya was quiet as he continued to examine himself. It gave Ilya the time to notice smaller things about him, all crystalizing together. Where Ilya's breath was a small cloud, Danya's came out in great heaps, like a volcano spewing smoke. There was his resistance to the cold outside, the fiery red hair, the immense strength despite his frame suggesting less. There was something magical about Danya.

How could somebody so special become a monster against his will? People didn't bestow curses for no reason. Either Danya's past life was something to fear, or he had enemies of immense power. He'd mentioned seeing the Hunters, but they were supposed to kill monsters.

What manner of monster could Danya possibly be?

"Do you remember anything new?" Ilya asked.

Danya pressed his hands against the sink and closed his eyes, face screwing up as he tried to think. "My boss... Her name was

Tatyana. I was supposed to be protecting her? I... Fuck, I don't remember anything else. I don't remember!"

Danya growled and slammed his hand against the sink. Ilya jumped, staring at the crack that formed in the porcelain. Ilya was torn between fury at having his sink damaged and arousal from the sheer strength Danya possessed. It was both, if he was being honest with himself.

"I'll fix that when the weather clears up, get the supplies in town," Danya groaned. "Fuck, sorry..."

Ilya touched Danya's arm in an attempt to soothe him. "Everything is coming back to you, slowly but surely. You're getting there. It'll be all right."

Danya sagged and gave him the most forlorn look imaginable. Ilya could see how he was struggling. He wanted to make this poor man happy, but he couldn't get too close. Danya was something special, a magical being with so much potential hidden behind a wall of memories. How could he dare presume he could measure up to whatever Danya was?

Ilya would always find a justification for why they couldn't be closer. Part of him knew it was denying himself happiness because happiness scared him. The fear of something new and unknown, something he'd dreamed of having. He'd convinced himself long ago that he'd die alone, that perhaps it wouldn't even be of old age. The idea that everything he'd come to terms with wouldn't have to be true was hard to parse. He refused to believe it.

Ilya didn't know how to be happy. Constantly having his happiness presented to him was terrifying. Danya was everything he could've ever dreamed of, but he'd still give in and push him away.

He decided a change in subject would be best for the both of them.

"Well, I know it's not exactly fun... But now the snow has stopped, maybe you can help me unbury the generator. It'll give us other things to think about. Additionally, my dick is going to retreat back inside of my body if I'm in this cold a single second longer."

Danya guffawed at how crass Ilya was, but he smiled anyway.

Ilya warmed a little seeing that smile. Danya was like a beam of sunlight, that little thing to make his life brighter.

Even if he knew it wasn't meant to be.

To say he was in pain would be an understatement. Shoveling snow was terrible anyway, but having to smash ice off the generator so it was usable made it worse. Ilya groaned as he kicked his boots off and spread himself out on the couch. It was freezing in the rectory, but he could hear the creaking of the coils for the heating. What sweet music.

Danya shoved Ilya's feet out of the way so he could flop down on the couch as well. Ilya groaned again and moved his feet into Danya's lap in protest. Danya huffed a laugh and took his boots off as well.

They caught their breath and relaxed as the room slowly began to warm. The windows fogged and the heavy condensation dripped down the panes, forming puddles that needed to be mopped. Ilya was deeply unmotivated to do any more physical labor.

"I'll deal with it later," Ilya gruffed.

Danya snorted and let out a deep sigh. Ilya had just shut his eyes when Danya's hands wrapped around his foot, jerking it away on instinct. He blinked up at Danya who grabbed his foot again.

"I know you're not about to complain about a foot massage you stuffy weirdo," Danya huffed. "Lay down, Ilyushka."

Ilya was too tired to protest, flopping back on the cushions. His body hurt, his face throbbed; he was ten seconds away from having a toddler tantrum at the age of 30. Maybe a foot massage would be good.

Danya's thumbs worked into the soles of his feet and Ilya couldn't help the groan that escaped him. Danya's hands were strong and warm, everything he needed. He closed his eyes again and dozed lightly as Danya kept working, eventually switching to the other. Ilya couldn't remember the last time he was this relaxed. Occasionally in the summers, when the breeze passed through the rectory just right while he sat with a new book, he was equally content. Rarely, though.

Ilya whispered, "Do you remember what she was like? The inventor woman you were with?"

Danya paused. He was silent for a long, long moment, then began working his thumbs into Ilya's ankles.

"Kind of. She was… really smart. I was so naive when I found her, I knew nothing about the world… She showed me how incredible it can be. She liked communications, her telephone was the most advanced in the city… I think she designed them. She wanted the whole world to be able to talk, so ideas, culture, could spread. To let people who are isolated find connection, find their power… She was incredible."

"It sounds like it. I'm sorry."

Danya sighed and settled his hands on Ilya's shins. "Thanks. It's weird, missing somebody that I barely know. I know I loved her, that I was protecting her. I know she was brilliant and would've changed the world. But that's it. Concepts, ideas of a person. Not a fully realized being."

"I feel that way about my father sometimes." Ilya paused, opening his eyes again. "It's been so long, and I was so young when he died. I can barely remember him, only that he was good to me and I loved him. Most of what I know of him now is how his memory has been tainted by everybody around me… I hope you never have to suffer through that, Danylko. I hope her memory stays with you as long as possible, and that it remains good."

Danya squeezed his leg, staring down at him. Ilya tilted his head forward to meet his gaze.

"If the weather stays clear enough, wanna go into town tomorrow? I have some parts I need to grab for a job. And… I want to try something for you."

Ilya raised an eyebrow. "What is this something, exactly?"

"Well, you make me dinner all the damn time like you're my fucking househusband and I'm useless. I wanna do something for you for once."

Ilya stared up at the ceiling as a blush crawled up his face. It was two sentences and they sent him into orbit. *Househusband. Dinner.* Quoth Danya, 'What the fuck.'

"I see. That's kind of you... I'd appreciate it, Danylko. Whatever you want to do."

Danya huffed, "The point is feeding you, dummy. Tell me what you want."

Ilya could barely remember food he *enjoyed*. Most days he ate to sustain himself. Part of that priest training, never be overindulgent. Food was always an indulgence. If it was a gift, if it would ease the mind of his grieving charge, then surely it would be worse to not oblige, right?

"I... liked stroganoff a lot, as a kid," Ilya finally said.

Danya snorted. "Stroganoff? That's a little too much information, Ilyushka."

Ilya sat up and smacked Danya's shoulder. "I'm being serious, *Danulyachka*."

Danya barked a laugh at the hit, patting Ilya's knees. "I know, I'm sorry. I think I can manage that. I'll try very hard not to poison you, I swear."

"I feel very reassured for my safety and wellbeing." Ilya smirked and then laid back on the couch, trying to not think about their closeness. Danya leaned back and closed his eyes, rubbing his thumbs into Ilya's shins as they went quiet and enjoyed the return of the heat.

Danya cared about him so much and he didn't understand it. When everybody had spent so long telling him he was worthless, unlovable, evil... Having somebody who seemed to enjoy his presence was hard to process. He couldn't believe it, no matter how much he was presented with reality.

It was nice, just enjoying each other like this. Ilya was resistant to physical contact of any kind, but Danya had been slowly chipping away at him. While he'd protested vocally, his body seemed to be challenging him every step of the way. Subconsciously, he wanted this. Any time Danya touched him, held him, he didn't want it to stop. He wanted more, in fact.

He hated to even *think* he might be falling for Danya. Perhaps he'd been falling for Danya this whole time, but he couldn't. It was wrong, he was taking care of Danya.

Part of him said he didn't deserve Danya.

Danya was clearly something special; even outside of how handsome, intelligent, charismatic, and vexing he was. The red hair, the golden eyes and freckles, the unnatural warmth, the extraordinary strength. He had no idea what Danya could be, but he clearly wasn't human. He wasn't a night creature, that much Ilya was certain of. He had to be a being of light, something borne of the Great Mother herself.

Why would a creature of the Sun ever settle for a pale, gangly, stuffy priest? Ilya was more walking dead than suitable partner. He had far too many issues to foist upon somebody he cared about. Danya didn't need to deal with him more than he already was.

A hand migrating up his shin and settling on his thigh was enough to break him out of his spiral. He lifted his head to stare at Danya, brows knit together. Danya stared back and it made Ilya's heart pound. Danya gave him a squeeze then lifted Ilya's legs off of his body, sighing as he got to his feet.

"I'll mop everything if you make lunch? I'm starving."

Ilya swallowed hard and nodded. He got up and rummaged around the pantry and icebox, settling on breakfast foods. They'd been too distracted to actually eat, so this would have to make up for it. He turned the tap and sighed in relief as the pipes groaned and water trickled from the faucet. He left the water running to make sure they wouldn't freeze again; he wouldn't be forgetting that.

He set their plates down once he was finished, groaning as he dropped into his seat. He was sore all over and it was miserable. "Fuck *me*."

The mop clattered to the floor and Ilya jolted, turning his attention to Danya. Danya looked like a deer, wide eyed and terrified. Ilya furrowed his brow and held his hands out palm up, completely incredulous.

"What, Danya?"

Danya cleared his throat and picked up the mop, shaking his head. "Nothing. Hand slipped from all the damp."

Ilya squinted but dug into his food, scarfing his sausage with a furor. He'd ignore how strange Danya was being. A lot was changing within him, he'd give him a break.

Danya ate with him after a few moments, frowning slightly. "Do you need to shovel the snow in front of the church too, or does somebody else get to do that?"

Ilya smacked a hand to his forehead. He should've known he'd forgotten something.

11

I took them forever to shovel the church enough to navigate around it, but it happened. It made the trip into town all the more rewarding, at least. Ilya was thrilled to be out of the house. Danya's closeness was getting to him.

They were careful as they made their way down the slippery hill. Ilya's face was now a *wonderful* shade of yellow-green and he didn't want to refresh his injuries. At least if Danya ate shit he could fix it right away.

Unfortunately, Danya had the terrible habit of grabbing on to him when he slipped. Danya yanked on Ilya's hand, nearly pulling his arm out of its socket as he righted himself. Ilya steadied his feet and glared back at Danya.

"I see things haven't changed."

Danya squeezed his hand and flashed an innocent smile. "Sorry."

Their hands remained linked as they continued, Danya's grip like a vice. Ilya decided he'd allow it for the trip down; the ice was making it difficult anyway. Perhaps he'd get to give Danya a taste of his own medicine.

As the ground leveled and they approached the square Ilya let go of Danya's hand, only to find it reattaching.

"Ilyushka, my hand is cold, let me keep holding yours."

It was the lamest, most ridiculous excuse Ilya had ever heard in his life, tantamount to a child on the playground. Danya constantly complained that he wasn't cold, throwing off all the layers that he'd been gifted in favor of single sweaters. What a liar!

And despite all his grouching, Ilya stopped trying to let go.

"You should wear the gloves you have," Ilya grumbled.

"Maybe," Danya chirped back.

Their hands swayed as they walked, Danya's thumb brushing over his knuckles. Ilya never imagined he'd get to do something like this with another man; even if it was because his roommate was being ridiculous. Finding people who *tolerated* him, let alone men who could perhaps love him, was impossible.

He wasn't stupid. Danya had been flirting with him for a while, but he was also mourning the loss of a woman he hardly remembered; their interactions of late were because of that, surely. Ilya would enjoy this while he had it, until Danya woke and realized he didn't need to be doing this with him to fill a hole in his heart.

THEY WERE GETTING stares the second they arrived in town. Nausea bubbled in his stomach and he wrenched his hand out of Danya's grasp. For a moment he'd been living in a world where holding hands with Danya in public was something he could do without repercussion. Danya reached out again and Ilya avoided it by shoving his hands into the sleeves of his vestments. He refused to make eye contact, marching ahead to Berta's shop. The space between them grew wider, physically and emotionally. He knew Danya must be hurt, but Ilya didn't have the heart for more scrutiny.

A younger woman approached them, a look of confusion on her face as she scrutinized Danya next to him. "You're Danya, yeah? I heard about the hair but now you're *glowing?* What's your deal?"

Ilya finally looked at Danya, seeing how taken aback he was. "Uh. I don't know? I woke up like this."

The woman turned to Ilya and glared at him. "What did you do to this man?"

"Nothing," Ilya huffed back. "Don't you know it's rude to ask somebody why they're glowing? He's blessed by our Mother Sun, obviously, why else would he look like this?"

"So you've been hiding him from us then?"

Danya stepped between them, placing a hand on Ilya's chest. "I was literally about to go into Berta's, where I work, and anybody who comes in has been able to see me for like, three months. Get over it."

The woman scoffed and walked away. "Don't know how somebody so rude could be blessed by the Sun."

They watched her go and Ilya sighed. He glanced at Danya's hand on his chest, relishing in the warmth that reached his heart. Danya finally pulled back and Ilya was torn between relief and want. He supposed this was his own doing.

"Shall we visit Berta then?" Ilya asked.

Danya looked at him and nodded. He seemed distant. Ilya understood, he'd forced this, but he was sad all the same. They were still getting stares, Ilya's stomach roiling with shame. Of course Danya's glowing was the reason for the staring. What else would it be? Why would they care about the two of them holding hands when Danya stood out so much? He was being foolish.

Ilya reached for Danya's hand, lacing their fingers together and holding on tight. Danya looked at him, golden glowing eyes wide in his shock. The look of surprise melted into a warm grin. He looked positively radiant like this, expression full of joy. Ilya wanted nothing more than to look at that smile.

Ilya was grateful that Danya said nothing about his strange, wishy-washy behavior. They could discuss it later if they needed. All it amounted to was Ilya was too inside of his head, too used to the town focusing on him to realize somebody else stood out more right now. He was sure Danya understood.

They stepped into the shop, Danya letting go of Ilya's hand as he made his way back into the workshop. Berta popped out from behind a shelf, watching Danya go into the back then approaching Ilya.

"Father Sokolov. It's been a while since I've seen you in my shop. I thought you hated it," she chuckled.

"Oh, make no mistake, I still wish to leave immediately, but Danya needed something for a project. I'll stay here by the door and hope my breathing doesn't knock the shelves over."

Berta let out a hearty laugh, shaking her head as she approached the front counter. Ilya enjoyed their more cordial rapport. "I suppose I understand why you're so stuffy, coming from that hell-hole. I don't know how you deal with my boy when you're like that though."

"I'm your boy now, *babushka?*"

Berta turned to look at Danya, gasping and placing a hand on her chest. "Danylko! You're glowing!"

Danya snorted, shoving a fistful of screws into his pockets. "Yeah? What about it? Ilyushka says I'm blessed by the Sun or something. I woke up like this."

Berta whirled back around to look at Ilya. "Is this true? He's been blessed?"

Ilya shrugged. "That's my only guess. It would explain the hair too… It looks like the sunrise, doesn't it?"

Berta was gobsmacked, looking between the two of them in disbelief. Ilya glanced back towards Danya, seeing how he was staring at him. Danya was so intense! He didn't understand!

"Well, whatever blessing you have, I hope you don't squander it *vnuk*. You understand me? You can be a real shithead sometimes, you know that?" She came up to Danya and hugged him tight, patting his back firmly. Danya hesitated then returned the gesture. It was brief and the most awkward thing Ilya had ever seen, but it was sweet and sincere all the same.

They parted and Berta reached to pat Danya's stomach. "I do have a project I need to discuss with you before you run off. Come back with me for a moment?"

Danya glanced at Ilya to check on him. Ilya shrugged in response. "I'll wait outside. Take your time, Danylko."

Ilya stepped back out onto the front porch of the shop as the other two went back into the workshop again. He breathed in the cold, crisp air, feeling how it burned his nostrils. Better than rust and dust, at least. He folded his hands in front of himself, watching everybody flit about the square in their daily routines. People glared when they noticed him and Ilya sagged in defeat. Perhaps the rumor that he'd been hiding Danya from everybody had already spread.

Ilya had been ground to a fine powder by Velak. Perhaps he was too sensitive, too quick to react. Maybe he was imagining things, reading neutral expressions as hostile. He'd found it hard to thrive in this town. He wasn't even sure he considered himself *alive* until Danya came into his life.

The only thing in his life brighter than Danya was the Sun Herself. He was like sunbeams after a rainstorm, determined to break through all the gloom and reach him. Ilya knew he was being stubborn and ridiculous with their relationship. Danya was patient, but he could hold out forever. Ilya knew it was self-sabotage to hope he could deny Danya for long enough he'd move on, but he wasn't worthy. If Danya had been blessed by the Sun, he'd never be worthy.

And yet.

Ilya thought of Danya's hand, how happy he'd looked when his affections had finally been returned. He imagined how it might feel, skin on skin. Danya was so warm he wouldn't even need to wear a glove to deal with the cold. He closed his eyes and kept trying to picture it all. After working with machines all these months his hands would probably be a little more rough, callouses across his palms from all his tools. His hands were slightly bigger than Ilya's, they could overtake him with ease.

He slipped a glove off and let his arm hang by his side, wiggling his fingers as they adjusted to the chilly air. Warmth encompassed his hand and Ilya sighed, soft and content as he relished in the feeling. He wanted every last ounce of it, the Sun held in his palm. A rough thumb moved across the interior of his wrist and Ilya snapped his head over to meet Danya's eyes. Danya's grip tightened, not enough to hurt, but enough to make the message clear: please don't let go again.

"What was the project?" Ilya asked. Fog gathered around both their faces as they breathed, but it wasn't enough to mask the look of determination on Danya's face.

"Talking about stairs for that stupid, shitty hill. About time," Danya whispered.

Ilya was stricken by how quiet he was. They'd had their quiet moments, but this was different, intimate in a way they hadn't shared previously. Ilya's heart was pounding so hard he worried Danya could hear it.

"I'm sorry you hate it here so much... I know you'll want to leave soon anyway. It'll be a nice parting gift," Ilya whispered back.

Danya squeezed Ilya's hand again, thumb pressed against the pulse point below the heel of his palm. "I don't like it here, no. But you're here, so I'm staying. I like being around you, Ilyushka. You've done everything for me. I'm returning to myself because of you. You care so much, and I don't want to lose that. Not ever."

Ilya wasn't sure how to handle the sudden outpouring of gratitude and affection. He couldn't remember the last time somebody had thanked him for anything. Ivan hadn't even thanked him for saving the town. The people didn't even *know*. He'd certainly never been thanked for anything else he'd done. He was *expected* to fix everything, to heal everyone who came to him, but they never seemed to appreciate it.

Ilya blinked and a flood of hot tears rolled down his cheeks. His lips parted as he took a deep breath, a flood of emotions washing over him.

Danya used his free hand to wipe Ilya's tears away, deep frown on his face. He whispered, "Why are you crying, Ilyushka?"

"Because you're nice to me," Ilya croaked, lip quivering as he tried to find his words, "And I don't know how to deal with that."

Danya pulled him in tight against his body and Ilya hid himself away in the crook of Danya's neck. That spiced scent mixed with metal and tobacco brought more comfort than he could describe. It had bothered him at first; this rude, flirtatious, short-tempered man continually invading his space and making him constantly worried for his wellbeing. Now Ilya couldn't imagine his life without the traces of it Danya had left on his home. Danya was devoted to protecting Ilya. For all that Ilya had done to save Danya from himself, Danya had been returning the effort.

"Whether you believe it or not, I think you're a good man, Ilya," Danya murmured, lips pressed against Ilya's curls, "I wish you'd stop listening to their lies."

Ilya never wanted Danya to let go. He could live in this spot forever.

His heart shattered when Danya pulled back. He cupped Ilya's face with his free hand again, swiping a thumb across his cheek. "Let's go get those dinner ingredients and then I'll treat you right, okay?"

Ilya supposed Danya treating him was good enough reason to pull apart. Ilya used a sleeve to rub at his eyes and wipe his nose, sniffling and clearing his throat. "Yes. That would be lovely, Danylko."

"Let's go then."

Just this once (as he'd told himself so many times before), Ilya would relent and let Danya keep holding his hand. He let his defenses down, and allowed Danya in.

12

Danya was thrilled. Ilya was a tough nut to crack; he had so many walls that he put up, but Danya had been working to tear them down, bit by bit. Now they were holding hands. Ilya had *initiated* holding hands earlier, and now he'd stopped fighting the gesture. He was so close to getting what he wanted, what he *knew* Ilya wanted. It has been one step forward and two steps back with their relationship thus far, but something told him the fall back wouldn't come this time.

Or maybe he hoped it wouldn't come this time.

Danya wouldn't call himself a patient man. He had a short fuse on top of his impatience, which meant he was an ornery asshole most of the time. Berta frequently hit him with rolled up newspapers for running his mouth when he shouldn't.

Ilya's softness brought him back to Earth. It was that gentle spirit that had him holding back now and for all these months. He'd loved Ilya since that horrific confrontation with Irina, but he'd known then that Ilya didn't see him the same way. Not yet. Danya knew if he was going to be with Ilya, he needed Ilya to come to him. He had to be as patient as he could.

But he was nearing his limit. Not that he was going to give up on

Ilya; he was too in love with this fucking ridiculous, stuffy, obstinately depressive priest. He was in too deep and couldn't let go, not when it was so obvious that Ilya felt the same. It killed him that Ilya kept denying himself, kept denying what they had. Danya could fucking *scream* about his feelings from the church steeple. This adorable, sweet, damaged man who deserved the whole world served at his feet. Danya was reaching the point where he couldn't be silent, couldn't let Ilya keep finding excuses. He couldn't keep his feelings to himself much longer.

He refused to let go of Ilya's hand as they walked home. This was his prize, something he'd wanted more than anything. Any time Ilya touched him was magic. Ilya thought he was a terrible healer, but Danya was positive that it was his care that had brought his memories back. Painful, terrible memories of a woman he'd once loved dying before his eyes, but that helped him remember who he was. He would never have become himself again if not for Ilya.

The walk up the hill was still perilous and the need to hold on to each other became very necessary, but Danya was relieved when Ilya held on as the ground leveled out. His heart was pounding as they entered the rectory. Ilya helped him unpack all his ingredients and pulled out a recipe card from a book hidden away in a cabinet, pat his shoulder, and went to lounge on the couch.

Why the *fuck* did he offer to do this? He was so fucking stupid. Ilya was an incredible cook and Danya didn't know jack from shit. He'd end up poisoning the love of his life and then they'd never be together. Why would Ilya want to be with a stupid, glowing man who was so shit? Stupid!

Danya pressed on, determined to put in the effort anyway. He owed Ilya so much. It would be impossible to ever make up for it. Sweet man that Ilya was would say Danya owed him nothing, but that wasn't good enough. He wouldn't stop until Ilya felt as good about himself as he deserved.

He'd start with the stroganoff and see where things went.

He started by cutting all the veggies, hissing and rubbing at his eyes with a dish rag in a futile attempt to stop the onion fumes from burning him. Ilya peeked at him from the couch and raised an eyebrow.

"Do you need help, Danylko?"

"Fuck you, I can do this," he hissed, voice cracking on the last word.

Danya hated swearing at him, but Ilya's laughter eased the worry. Perhaps this priest had a more sadistic side to him. If his mild and temporary suffering got Ilya to laugh, he'd accept it. He'd make an absolute fool of himself any number of times if it made Ilya happy.

His stress didn't ease even remotely as he got everything frying. His hands twitched and all he wanted was a cigarette, but Ilya *hated* them. The one time he'd tried smoking in the attic Ilya had caught him in seconds. He pulled one out of the pack anyway, placing it between his lips and letting it be. It soothed him, helped ease the urge.

Ilya wandered from the couch to sit at the table and watch him and Danya wanted to throw himself into the fire. Now he understood why Ilya threatened his life when he came into the kitchen. It was so stressful!

"You can smoke if you want," Ilya said.

Danya's head snapped to look at Ilya over his shoulder, brows knitting together. "You serious? Thought you hated it."

"Yes, but I can tell you're stressed and it's making *me* nervous. Do whatever you need, Danylko."

Danya paused and threw open a window. He'd impose as little as possible. This dinner was for Ilya's benefit, and he'd do his damndest to make him happy. He needed Ilya to learn how much he cared.

He lit his cigarette and took a long drag off of it, blowing the smoke out the window then stepping back in front of the stove.

"You look handsome when you smoke," Ilya said. "Is that bad to say? Being a healer and all…"

Danya paused and looked back at Ilya. There was so much he wanted to say, had to resist every urge to shout. He didn't think Ilya was being intentional in toying with his emotions, but it tore him to pieces every time it happened. Hearing Ilya call him handsome made his heart pound and he wanted so, so much more. He wished Ilya would make up his mind.

"Do I?"

"Danylko, the mushrooms are going to burn."

He swore and paid attention to the stove again, dumping the rest of the ingredients in to keep it all from becoming a mess. He was trying so hard.

He loved Ilya. He wanted to be with him more than anything. He'd get a taste of what things could be like every so often, like earlier, like when they shared a bed to keep warm, like now. They could be so good together, but Ilya kept resisting. Danya had to remind himself that nobody had been kind to Ilya in a long time, that it would *take* a long time.

But would it be so terrible if he confessed? Would it be awful to tell him?

He didn't know what to do.

"So I'm handsome?" Danya finally asked.

"When you smoke, yes," Ilya teased back.

"Is that why you always watch me do it?"

Ilya didn't respond and Danya sighed through his nose quietly. Being in love with Ilya was an exercise in fortitude.

He added the pasta to the mixture and then went over to the couch, hanging over the back of it to look at Ilya.

"You didn't answer my question, Ilyushka."

"You need an answer?" Ilya fired back.

Damn this man. "*Need* an answer? No. Like? Very much. Stop acting cute."

Ilya laughed. "Now I know you wouldn't want that, Danylko."

"No. But come on." He cupped Ilya's cheek, swiping his thumb across the mound of it. Ilya's face was thin and bony, but his cheeks were full. He wanted to cover them in kisses and *make* Ilya know how loved he was, but he'd take this. Ilya didn't seem to resist when he touched his face anymore. It had taken so much work, but he was grateful. Nobody else had ever been this close to Ilya. Danya knew how special this was.

Ilya's lips parted and his eyes went big. Danya let himself give in to a marginal temptation, tracing his thumb across Ilya's lower lip. It was soft and plump and all he wanted to do was place it between his teeth and nip it. Kissing Ilya would be nothing short of incredible.

"I... I do like looking at you, yes," Ilya stuttered. "Even when you aren't smoking... Your hands look nice when you hold them, though."

Danya smirked and went back to the stove, satisfied with the exchange. Somehow, their dinner wasn't completely ruined either. He got it plated and sat across from Ilya, watching him intently as he took the first bite.

"Good?" Danya asked.

A warm smile spread across Ilya's face and Danya couldn't help a smile of his own. Ilya almost never smiled, but he looked so fucking cute when he did. Every time he did it was because of something Danya had done. He'd keep doing whatever it took to make Ilya happy.

"Better than I remember," Ilya replied. "It's wonderful, Danylko. Thank you for this... You make me feel very special."

"You are special." He blurted the words without hesitation. Danya was glad he managed to hold his composure, deciding to only scream *inside*. Ilya's cheeks were bright red; they alway gave him away. It's how he knew Ilya reciprocated his feelings in the first place. He cleared his throat and changed the subject quickly. "Uh– would you come into the church with me when we're done? I wanted to do one more thing."

Ilya spoke between bites of food, "It's not Sunday, so I have no idea what you could possibly need from me in there. What are you up to now?"

"Can you just go with it for me?" Danya pleaded.

That flush came back to Ilya's cheeks but he nodded. "Yes, I suppose I could."

Danya grinned back at him. "Perfect. Meet you there."

He scarfed the rest of his dinner, tossed the plate in the sink, and then grabbed the radio from the living room to lug it into the church. Ilya was stunned as he watched. Danya knew he looked absurd, but it didn't matter. He had a plan and he was going to execute it.

HE WAS SEARCHING for an outlet when Ilya came into the church, arms crossed and playful smirk on his face.

"It's under the altar, Danylko," he called.

Danya sighed and set the radio on top of the altar, plugging it in and searching for a music channel. The sound bounced off of the stone walls and filled the vastly empty room with soft jazz. A lilting female voice managed to ring through the crackling static, sounding utterly heavenly in the space.

Danya looked up when Ilya huffed a laugh. Those pale cheeks had a tinge of pink to them, slight smile spread on Ilya's face. Danya bit the inside of his cheek to hold back all the gushing praise building in the back of his throat. He didn't want to ruin the moment and Ilya was far too deep in the throes of impostor syndrome to ever listen to it.

"Dance with me?" he finally asked.

Ilya rose to the altar, holding his arms out so Danya could lead. "I told you I'm a terrible dancer. I'm sure you've remembered more by now."

He snorted. "I wouldn't be so sure, Ilyushka."

Danya set a hand on Ilya's waist, guiding Ilya to set his hands on Danya's shoulders. They swayed back and forth, hardly moving at all. They were so close like this. Danya could look deep into Ilya's ghostly white eyes, count all the curly strands of dark brown hair that hung across his forehead. He wanted to coil it around his fingers, know how soft and fluffy it was. He resisted every urge to lean down and kiss this man.

Ilya was staring up at him with equal scrutiny. Danya could see how his eyes roamed over his face, counting his freckles. Did Ilya feel the same? Did he want the same closeness?

The woman on the radio crooned out words of love, of a

darling man she couldn't bear to be apart from, who was the sunshine in her life. Danya wanted to be that for Ilya.

He let his hands slide down to Ilya's hips, hooking his thumbs in the belt loops near the front. Ilya gasped quietly, eyes going wide for a moment. Danya made sure to keep his gaze fixed on Ilya, giving away nothing. This was another small moment, another wall gently nudged back. Ilya seemed to settle and Danya couldn't help but smile at him.

"I like this," Danya whispered. "We should do it more often."

"It reminds me of the holiday parties we used to have, when my father was alive... It mostly involved people playing instruments though. I think I prefer the radio."

"Did you ever sing for them?"

Ilya ducked his head, shy smile on his face. There was that gorgeous thing that he craved so badly.

"Sometimes. I was a bit young, so not very good... I'm probably no good now, what with no practice.."

"You should do it anyway. I want to hear you sing."

Ilya said nothing else, letting his words hang in the air. There was a palpable sense of comfort between them. Ilya was, for once in his life, completely relaxed. Danya was equally at peace. He was so attuned to Ilya's emotions sometimes he was sure it had to be part of his magic.

Because he had to be magical, right? You didn't get blessings from the Sun Herself for no reason. He was so protective of Ilya, all he wanted was Ilya's happiness. Seeing him so comfortable made his heart swell.

The song came to an end, the symphony in the background quietly fading out. Danya swallowed, hoped Ilya wouldn't let go, hoped that maybe this would be the one time he'd hold on.

"It's getting late, Danylko. We should head to bed."

Danya sighed through his nose, forcing a smile. "Probably. Hey, when's the next holiday?"

Ilya paused a spell to think, then continued down the steps from the altar. "The spring solstice. We're a ways off yet."

Quickly, Danya said, "We should do something for that. Even if it's just us."

Ilya wasn't looking at him. His heart clenched and his stomach dropped. Always, always, one step forward, two steps back.

"I'm sure we could, Danya. Are you coming?"

No, he needed a bit of a cry if he was being honest with himself.

"I think I want to listen to the radio for a bit longer. Good night, Ilyushka."

Ilya lifted a hand to wave in reply then headed back into the rectory.

Danya sighed and crumpled to the floor, leaning against the altar. He held his knees against his chest and closed his eyes. He listened to the soft jazz still playing, trying to remember how Ilya's hand felt in his palm. It was soft, the fingers long and elegant. Ilya would look gorgeous playing the piano. Perhaps in another life he would be in a band that was being broadcast to them now. He could've been heard the world over.

He dragged a hand over his face as he tried to picture how Ilya would look underneath him. How flushed he would look, how he would sing when brought to the edge. He wanted to touch all of Ilya's skin, to ravage him until he stopped thinking about anything but pleasure. Ilya thought way too hard, way too much. All Danya wanted to do was distract him from his pain, help him see that he could have more. *Deserved* more.

He fell asleep as the last song faded into static, remembering the softness of Ilya's lip under his thumb.

13

November 25th, 1927

All Ilya dreamed about was Danya touching him. Feeling his admiration, those warm, brown-skinned hands running across his body, feeling every inch. Ilya wanted to do the same, to kiss every sparkling freckle on Danya's face, to wrap his hands in that gorgeous red hair, taste the sweat on his skin. He wanted to meld together with this man, to give him his very soul.

Ilya was in love with Danya.

He could admit that now. It began to sink in ages ago, but it dawned on him when Danya made him dinner, and it hit him like a freight train when Danya touched his lip like that. It was past casual intimacy, well beyond anything he could dismiss as friendly affection. He'd seen the heat in Danya's gaze and he pictured it now so clearly. He felt *human*. He felt alive in a way he hadn't been in years. He thought he'd died all those years ago, right alongside his father. He'd never been the same since, had never been allowed to know anything but his unending grief and melancholy.

Danya shattered every expectation he had for himself. Even as a beast, Danya had compelled Ilya to merciful action. Ilya had invoked the love of the Sun to heal a creature that nobody would argue deserved to live, a creature of pure consumption and violence that left the town scarred and traumatized. Ilya had given Danya a piece of his love, the love he was meant to carry for all things as part of his duty. That was all it took.

Danya had returned that piece tenfold. Danya was *determined* to love him. He'd been patient so far, had endured all the barriers Ilya threw up, all while tearing them down again. He never pushed too far, only enough for Ilya to let his guard down and *be*. Ilya had never been this close with someone.

His mind wandered from fluttering affections to something more carnal. He wanted to know what it would be like with Danya, to have that powerful, Sun-blessed body over him, consuming him completely. Danya's lips would be so warm, enough to melt the lingering winter chill that clung to Ilya's skin. What would his mouth taste like? What places would it touch on his body?

Ilya gasped awake and slapped a hand on his chest, staring at the ceiling as he caught his breath. He was *throbbing* from his dreams of Danya. He was being a ridiculous teenage boy, imagining himself with any handsome man his mind conjured for his fantasies.

This wasn't any man though. He had nobody but Danya on his mind.

Ilya bit his lip hard to keep quiet. Danya's room was above his; it wouldn't surprise him if the gasping had already woken him. His hand moved rapidly, wrist aching as his desperation grew. He needed to get this out of his system if he was going to even *attempt* to face Danya today.

He fantasized Danya above him, kissing him, lips moving over every inch of his skin. Danya's powerful body pinning him down with all his strength, like Ilya was nothing more than a twig he could snap. He'd seen Danya's nude form on that first morning and tried to recall any details he could, but it was all too fuzzy now. He'd been so focused on not being rude and now Ilya wished he'd given in to Danya's early teasing.

He imagined the heat of his palm was Danya's and that was enough to push him over the edge. He let a sharp breath out through his nose as he finished and slumped back into the pillows. His body cooled as his passions calmed, heartbeat slowing to normal speeds as the fog of lust lifted.

Ilya was determined to be *normal* around Danya today. He couldn't give away a single thing. It had to seem as if nothing had changed.

He found a spare rag to clean himself, then peeked out of his door into the rectory. The curtains were drawn and there was no sign of Danya. A relief. He grabbed his vestments and then bolted to the bathroom, blasting himself with the hot water.

He scratched at his skin as he tried to get clean, overcome with guilt in using Danya for his fantasies. A pit formed in his stomach as the violation of what he'd done overcame him. How was it right of him to constantly run from Danya's affections but use them to pleasure himself? It was shameful.

He got himself together once he finished bathing. It would all be *fine*.

It was strange that Danya hadn't come down by now. Ilya knew he was the early riser between them, but Danya wasn't the type to be *this* late. He went to drop the ladder for the attic, lifting the door to peek inside. There was no sign of Danya in the room which had him panicking immediately. He rushed out into the church and sighed when he spotted Danya slumped against the altar. The radio was still playing soft jazz. He shook his head fondly.

Last night had been… intense. Danya had been so close, touching his lip, dancing with him. Ilya had run away again, and he was sure Danya's sorry state out here was because of him.

Ilya kneeled and took a gentle hold of Danya's chin, dragging his own thumb over Danya's lower lip. It was soft and almost hot to the touch. Ilya shivered and lifted his hand to run through Danya's hair, letting the silky red strands fall between his lanky, ghostly fingers. Danya grumbled awake then, slowly opening his eyes and blinking. His brows were knit together and he looked so sleepy. Ilya had to stop from cooing from how adorable he looked. A sleepy Danya was a sight that could thaw even the coldest of hearts.

"Ilya… Where…?"

"In the church. I'm guessing you never made it to bed," Ilya laughed.

"Mm. No. Don't think so." Danya smiled at him, a tiny, silly looking thing that had Ilya utterly charmed. The idea of having a stomach full of butterflies was absurd, but in this moment Ilya knew exactly what it meant.

He loved this man and his adorable face and his gorgeous skin and immense strength and his big heart. Everything. Every little thing.

"Well, you should probably at least get to the couch if you're going to keep sleeping," Ilya finally said. "Let's get up."

Danya took hold of Ilya's hand to help himself up, grimacing as he straightened out. "My back is fucking killing me—"

Ilya snorted. "Sleeping like a gargoyle will do that. Here, turn around and I'll see if I can't numb the pain a bit."

"Oh please—"

Danya faced his back to Ilya and Ilya froze in place. There were two decently sized lumps on Danya's upper back which couldn't have come from leaning against the stones. He pressed his hands against them and Danya hissed in pain.

"Ilyushka, what the fuck— I thought you were gonna fix it—"

"Take off your shirt right now."

Danya snapped his head to look back at Ilya, brows furrowed. "Excuse me?"

Ilya smacked Danya on the shoulder and huffed back, "You have two giant lumps on your back, get your shirt off so I can make sure you're not dying!"

Danya did as he was told. "What is it?"

Lumps was an ungenerous way of describing what these were. They were small, but covered in fluffy, cream colored feathers that glittered gold in the morning sunlight. It was a small pair of wings.

Ilya was too stunned to speak. He reached out to touch Danya's wings without thought, gently tugging one out to its full length. It was so soft, softer than even the finest silks from the East, and as warm as any other part of Danya.

Finally, he found his words.

"You're an angel."

"Thanks, but what the fuck is wrong with me, Ilyushka?" Danya sounded so stressed and frustrated, but he was being honest!

"I'm being serious you ass, come look at yourself–" Ilya grabbed Danya's wrist and dragged him back inside to the bathroom. He flipped on the light and turned Danya around, who gasped promptly.

"What the fuck are these– Ilya, what the hell am I?"

"I told you! You're an angel, Danya– It all makes sense now, everything about you, your strength, your appearance... You're not just blessed by the Sun, she's your *mother*."

Danya reached back to run his fingers over his wings, flexing and stretching out under his touch. Ilya was entranced as he watched, holding his breath for what might come next.

"Couldn't have been much of an angel if *these* are my wings, right?" Danya turned to Ilya and huffed a laugh, shaking his head in disbelief.

"You've been slowly gaining your real appearance back, so I doubt these are at their full potential. Even if they are adorable." Ilya reached out and ran his fingers across the feathers, rubbing the skin at the base of them. Danya groaned at the touch and Ilya drew his hand back like it had been burned. Heat flooded his body from the sound, fingertips prickling. He swallowed hard to try and compose himself, thankful that Danya seemed unable to meet his eyes right now.

"That spot's, uh," Danya stammered, "Sensitive, I guess."

"Yes. Quite." Ilya promptly turned away from Danya. "I'm going to make breakfast now, good bye."

Ilya distracted himself by cracking eggs and staring out the window at the vast pine forest that stretched beyond the borders of Velak. His eyes roved over the rising sun, fading from its brilliant reds and oranges to the soft blue of the regular day. It was no wonder Danya looked how he did, he was the rising sun embodied, that hope that came with every dawn. Shame roiled in his gut once again, the muscles in his neck and shoulders tensing as everything settled into place.

If he was unworthy of Danya before, it was tenfold now. Danya was an *angel*, a supreme being of the Sun, Her ultimate messenger, Her ultimate purveyor of justice. Based on the memories that had resurfaced, Danya was an angel of protection, a guardian for the woman he'd loved. He'd been brought down to do a job and somebody had kept him from it, had killed his charge. What was an angel without a charge?

Danya would leave, as Ilya knew he would, but it wouldn't be for just anyone. How could he deny a being of pure light returning to his Mother, the great Mother of all life? How could he ever claim to be on her level? He simply wasn't, nor would he ever be.

Ilya was pulled out of his thoughts by Danya wrapping his arms around his waist, hooking his chin over Ilya's shoulder. He hadn't put his shirt back on and Ilya was *very* aware of Danya's skin. Their cheeks brushed together and he sucked in a breath as he tried to fry their eggs without breaking the yolks. Normally he'd be threatening Danya's life for distracting him like this, but the tension between them was so thick he couldn't think to do it.

Ilya managed to get their food plated despite Danya clinging to him, turning around in his arms to hand his breakfast over.

Danya was so close to his face like this. He was leaning in, noses nearly brushing together. Danya's heat warmed him from even this distance, the tickle of his breath as it made his curls move. Ilya was locked in a trance, throat dry. He was beginning to throb again, heat working its way down from his gut to his groin. He *definitely* couldn't have Danya know that. His vestments couldn't hide everything.

He couldn't go to his room, that would be too obvious; he refused to go outside for it either. He had *some* dignity left. That left the church, which he didn't love, but it was for the best.

Ilya broke out of Danya's arms and stepped towards the door to the church. "You know, I haven't taken confessional in a while, I'm going to do that– have my eggs if you want."

If Danya said anything, he didn't catch it for how quickly he left. Ilya was on a mission of relief now and he refused to hold out any longer.

ILYA HAD NEVER BEEN HAPPIER in his life that the priest's side of the confessional had a *lock*. He slotted the hook into the ring and leaned back against the wood, breathing in deep. It hadn't warmed up even a single degree since Ilya had dragged Danya back inside, and while it dulled the passion, it wasn't nearly enough.

Ilya made a circular motion in front of his chest, crossing his fingers over six times to make the symbol of the Sun and whispered, "Forgive me, oh great Mother, for how I am about to desecrate this sacred fixture for my own pleasure. Alas, I am but a mortal man, and I have a vice."

He continued to stare at the wooden ceiling, hoping to divine a reply, permission for what he was about to do, but he knew it wouldn't come. He sighed in his longing and continued, "If it means anything, he's one of yours. Perhaps if you hadn't made him so lovely, it wouldn't have come to this."

Another beat of silence to let it all sink in, to find the heart to go through with this. He lifted the front of the robes, palming himself through his leather pants. They clung tight to his skin and made him sweat more than he cared for. The way he was bulging was made all the more lewd by the material. He looked ridiculous.

One last silent prayer hoping that Danya wasn't at all suspicious, and then he unzipped his fly. He pulled himself out and held on tight, sighing in relief. He would need to keep his sounds in check, but it would be fine. Everything would be fine.

Ilya began moving his hand, eyes fluttering shut as he let his mind drift. He pictured it was Danya's hand holding him, those broad, beautiful hands encasing his cock. He wanted those strong arms wrapped around his body to keep him in place, at this angel's mercy. He'd let Danya do anything to him. He wanted to be stripped bare and made raw for Danya to touch all over, to bite, bruise, grab, scratch every surface of his body, to be completely claimed.

He belonged only to Danya.

Ilya rubbed his thumb hard against the head, whimpering out, "Danya–"

All his life he'd wanted a man to swoop in and take control, to allow him to stop thinking for a moment. He wanted to be blank, to be lost in his pleasure. He wanted somebody else to take the lead, to put his soul at ease.

Heat began to build in his gut, going tight as he grew closer. Ilya bit his lip to stifle himself, but another soft whine escaped him, "Danya…"

The other door to the confessional slammed shut and Ilya sat bolt upright. His heart beat faster than even when he was confronting the drekavac, his body prickled and soaked through with sweat. He wanted to vomit and die. He was going to run straight into the graveyard and claw through the frozen dirt and *bury himself.* If the roof caved in and conveniently crushed him under its weight, he would be *delighted.*

Ilya's ears were ringing, blood rushing in time with his pounding heart and making his head ache. He was so ashamed. Why was this happening to him?

"Father," Danya said, "I was wondering if I could talk to you about something that's been bothering me."

Fuck.

Danya heard him. There was no doubt in his mind. This was his punishment for defiling this booth, for having these thoughts, for wanting one of the Sun's perfect creatures. He deserved every horrible word Danya was about to spit at him.

He tucked himself away in his shame and glanced through the delicately carved grating separating them. He couldn't make out all of Danya's figure, but he seemed to be staring directly ahead. Small comforts, he supposed.

"Y-Yes, what is it my child," Ilya wheezed.

"There's somebody I'm very fond of, but he hates himself. He's so cruel to himself and it kills me." There was so much pain in Danya's voice as he spoke. More guilt thrashed around inside of Ilya; his palms ached from the intensity of it. Danya continued, "He's been beaten down his whole life, so I understand *why*

123

he's like this, but he won't let anybody be kind to him. He won't let *me* be kind to him. He looks confused every time it happens, doesn't understand why I ever would be... Why doesn't he understand?"

Ilya swallowed and tried to gather his thoughts. This was it then. "Perhaps kindness scares him. Perhaps it's been used against him so many times so that people can hurt him more."

"I would never!" Danya's fist slammed against the bench, utterly incensed. "I could never... He's done so much for me. He's been convinced that he's terrible and useless, that he's bad at his job, but it's not true! He's healed me without a drop of magic, he's incredibly kind when people want to accuse him of being evil and cruel! All they want to do is be terrible to him."

"Perhaps he is evil and cruel and you don't know it yet. Perhaps he doesn't deserve their kindness."

Danya shouted, "He doesn't need it anyway! They should be on their hands and knees begging for his forgiveness for how they've abandoned him all his life! He feels ashamed to exist, that he doesn't deserve to be loved, but it's not true! He wants to make the world better than he left it, and I see it every day in how he treats me. He just wants to be loved."

Hot tears pooled in Ilya's eyes, threatening to spill over at any moment. Being confronted with everything Danya felt about him, even the frustration, was too much. He could hardly believe it was about him, a part of himself still believed it had to be about anybody else. It could *never* be him.

"He won't let me love him, Father," Danya croaked. "I want to love him. I know he wants it too. He *must* want it too, but every time I get close he pushes me away. He shuts himself off every time we're even a little closer. I don't understand anymore."

Ilya's heart shattered into a thousand pieces. He couldn't bear the thought that he was the one hurting Danya like this. Tears rolled down his cheeks, gathering under his chin before dripping onto his vestments. He took a breath and swallowed, trying to hide how his voice wavered.

"Perhaps he doesn't feel worthy of you."

"How? I'm not worthy of *him*. His... Him loving me has restored me. He's made me whole again."

Ilya's brows knit together in his confusion. "What do you mean restored you?"

"His love for me, whether he'll admit to it or not, has helped me be myself again. I was a monster, he had every right to kill me and free the world from my evil, but he didn't. There was so much love in his heart that his first instinct was to heal me, make me a man again... And now he's made me an angel again. I would've never returned to myself if not for him.

"I want to give him everything he deserves, all that I am. He's my whole world, Father, and I love him more than I can stand sometimes. I want my wings to come back and I want to fly him away from this wretched town full of wretched people and take him somewhere he can be himself. I want to make him happy."

The silence stretched on between them. Ilya's heart palpitated out of time as he tried to process everything. He knew Danya had feelings for him, but he hadn't comprehended how deep they went.

"What if he doesn't feel the same?" Ilya asked.

"Well, Father, I've heard some things that suggest he does."

"I think you were imagining things."

"No, I don't think so, Father."

"Perhaps you should—"

Danya's fist slammed against the divider between them, cracking the wood from the force. Danya didn't know his own strength sometimes, and it was a combination of terrifying and arousing. Danya would never hurt him, but his fiery temper, as hot as the surface of the Sun, got the better of him sometimes. Ilya wasn't surprised that he'd frustrated Danya so badly that he reacted like this.

"*Ilyushka, please.*"

"Danya I have no idea what you're getting at—"

The door to the confessional slammed against the wall, followed by stomping footsteps that stopped at Ilya's side of the booth. The door was ripped open, lock tearing out of the wood in the process. Ilya's eyes bugged out of his skull, staring at Danya with his lips parted in shock. Danya dropped to his knees, prostrating before him. Ilya had never seen him look so small. Those golden wells for eyes looked up at him, watery with pain.

"Ilya, I'm begging you. *I love you.* I want to make you happy. Please stop punishing yourself because some heartless people have said you're not worthy of affection."

More tears rolled down both their cheeks. Ilya's vision was blurry from how his eyes watered. He was so ashamed of his behavior, reducing somebody as wonderful as Danya to this. "This isn't something you can magically heal, Solnishko. It won't go away today, tomorrow, or maybe even years from now. As much light as you think I hold in me, I am but a mortal man, and therefore also hold great darkness."

Danya perked up at the new pet name. It meant "sunshine" in the old language, which is exactly what Danya was. Pure sunshine.

"Well, turns out I'm a being of light or some shit, so I'll have to burn it out of you, won't I?"

Danya's hands moved to Ilya's knees, squeezing them gently. Danya rested his chin on top of them and Ilya throbbed to life again. Danya was so close to Ilya's embarrassment, but he had to know that already.

Ilya let out a watery laugh, using a wide sleeve to dab at his eyes. He cleared his throat and said, "You're as insufferable as the day I found you."

"You don't have to say it back. Ever, if that's easier for you, but please. Let me show you how I feel." Danya's voice was so *soft*, barely above a whisper. Another secret confession, only for him and the Sun to hear.

Danya wasn't going to let Ilya give up again. Even if he did, Danya would stay, still in pain. Ilya couldn't make this man be in pain because of him.

Not when he felt the same.

Just this once, he'd let Danya love him. Just this once, like the other times he'd said so.

"Okay. Show me then."

Danya leaned up, dug his fingers into Ilya's curls, and pulled him into a kiss.

14

Ilya's head spun as Danya kissed him, and he cried in his relief.
His heart pounded in his ears and he was leaning into Danya,
kissing him back, taking everything he was being given. He wasn't
sure it would ever be enough.

He was kissing a man. Never in his life did he picture that as a
possibility. With his luck he wasn't sure he could find *anybody* to love
him at all, but here was Danya. He was floating on air as the air in
his lungs was being drawn out in their mutual desperation. *He was
kissing a man.*

Danya was more than that, though. He was an angel in every
sense of the word. He was light and love and warmth and everything the Sun represented. He was dawn when he'd been trapped in
endless night, he was a fire in the cold of winter, he was an oasis in
the desert. Danya was everything.

Ilya loved him.

As much as Ilya had saved Danya, Danya had saved him. He'd
been lost in his melancholy, debating every day if life was even
worth living, asking himself if being killed by a horrific monster
would be such a terrible fate. That monster meant the world to
him now.

A shaking hand coiled into Danya's soft red locks, wrapping the strands around his fingers just as he'd imagined. Danya grabbed for Ilya's other hand, pushing him back against the confessional's divider, overtaking him, forcing as much of his love into Ilya as he could. Their tongues slid together as their passions intensified. Ilya relished in the sweet taste of his angel. He was more than happy to let himself succumb to Danya's every desire.

Danya pulled back, both of them gasping for air. Ilya couldn't help but frown in his confusion.

"Why did you stop?"

Danya pushed Ilya's thighs apart and placed a finger to his lips to hush him. Ilya pulsed to life all over again, nipping at the tip of Danya's finger. Danya huffed a laugh and nestled between Ilya's legs, face mere inches away from his stomach. Danya's eyes were completely blown out and full of hunger.

Danya kissed up Ilya's stomach and crooned, "Ilyushka, can I do something for you?" Danya's voice was low and full of gravel, vibrating throughout Ilya's body. He twitched in his pants as a shiver jolted up his spine, sending him back against the divider. This man was too much.

Ilya gasped out, "You said you would."

Danya chuckled as he lifted Ilya's vestments out of the way, reaching a hand into his still-unzipped pants. A whimper escaped him as Danya grabbed his hardness, pulling it out into the chilly air. Ilya couldn't remember being so turned on and terrified in his life. Despite being almost entirely clothed, he had never been more exposed and raw.

"Glad you couldn't finish the job before I caught you."

Danya's lips brushed against his hot skin, kissing up and down Ilya's cock, laving his tongue across the head. It was all too sweet, more affectionate than Ilya would've ever believed was possible. Danya's tongue was so *soft*. He was a mess of pathetic, mewling sounds. Danya had only just begun, but he wouldn't last long. Not when he had everything he wanted.

"Solnishko—"

Danya groaned low in his throat, glancing up at Ilya through his lashes for the briefest of moments before swallowing Ilya down entirely. By some miracle he kept still, grabbing a handful of Danya's hair to distract himself. Danya hollowed his cheeks to create more friction, bobbing his head over and over. Ilya slumped against the divider, eyes rolling back with him. He'd already been so close when Danya caught him, but he was desperate to hold on. He wanted to preserve this first moment for as long as possible, but his desperation wouldn't hold out. Ilya gripped tighter on Danya's hair and got a lewd noise of approval from his angel out of it.

"Close, Danya–"

Danya pulled off of him with a slick *pop*. His warm, rough hand returned to engulf his length again, grinning at Ilya, eyes sparkling with mischief. "How do you want it?"

"I surely have no idea what you mean by that."

Danya's grin doubled in size. Ilya wasn't sure how to take that.

"Then I'll have to surprise you."

Ilya opened his mouth to speak but found a whine leaking out when Danya brought him into his mouth again. Danya worked his way down until his nose was pressed against Ilya's belly, eyes flicking up to meet Ilya's. He was overwhelmed at being consumed, being completely down his lover's throat. It was *ludicrous*.

Danya kept taking him in deep, each pass making more and more heat build up in his gut, working its way down his body. He was enveloped in a fog of pleasure, working its way up his spine until his body shuddered with its climax. He gasped and bit his lip as he watched Danya. He pulled off, coughing and wiping at his mouth, flashing a smile. Danya tucked him away and replaced his vestments, patting his thigh. Ilya could cry from how polite Danya was.

"You look like the cat that got the cream," Ilya panted.

Danya snorted, resting his cheek on Ilya's thigh. "I mean, I did. And I'm very pleased about it."

"That can't have tasted good though."

"Mm, I don't care that much. It's you, after all."

Ilya pet Danya's head, stroking his thumb across his forehead to move the hair out of the way. He was at peace, finally touching

Danya freely. "You'll forgive me if I'm more hesitant. I want to please you too, Solnishko."

Danya shivered at the nickname, burying his face against Ilya's leg and breathing deep. "As much as I'd love to finally see what your pretty mouth can do, there's something else I'd like to do. We both can enjoy it, just... it might be uncomfortable at first, if you've never done it."

"I trust you." The words spilled out of Ilya's mouth without an ounce of hesitation. "I want everything you want to give me."

Danya lifted his head slowly. Ilya could see the gears turning in his head, that same look as when Berta gave him an interesting project to solve. What calculations was he running through this time?

Ilya shouted as Danya pulled him out of the confessional and into his arm, carrying him up the steps to the altar. He laid Ilya out flat, legs dangling off the edge. Ilya shivered from the chill trapped in the stone, goosebumps blooming across his skin.

"First the confessional, now this?"

"Hey, you started it with the confessional. Besides, I'm an angel. I make the rules or whatever."

Ilya rolled his eyes. "I'm sure that's how it works."

Danya kissed Ilya hard to get him to shut up. Ilya held Danya's face as was happy to be silent, kissing back with equal fervor. They kissed for ages, until the chill melted away into something comfortable.

Danya pulled back a fraction, lips still brushing across Ilya's as he spoke, "Let me worship you on this altar, Ilyushka."

"Please—"

Danya shucked Ilya's vestments, peeling back layers of black fabric to reveal pale skin underneath. Ilya shivered, nipples going taut from the air across his body. Danya brushed his thumbs over the nubs, making Ilya groan. Danya groped his chest, warmth permeating into his body as they traveled down, almost wrapping around Ilya's waist. He felt so small like this.

"I knew you were ridiculous under all that shit," Danya rasped. "I don't get it."

Mercy

Ilya giggled, tension melting away. Was his appearance really so baffling? He supposed it was nice to be desired for once. Danya looked at him so fondly, more warmth filling his heart. He was *loved*. Danya loved him.

Danya's hands slid down Ilya's body once more, rubbing his palm against Ilya's bulge. Ilya whimpered and arched his spine in reflex, pulling a laugh out of Danya. He yanked Ilya's boots off then slowly peeled his leather pants down, reaching under his body to grab his ass. Danya sighed in pure relief and Ilya couldn't help but laugh again.

"I'm sorry I didn't realize how desperate you were for me."

"Very much. What the hell is this thing anyway?" Danya was so incredulous! Ilya snickered nonstop from how silly his angel was being. "I'm serious! How could you hide this from me for so long?"

"It wasn't on purpose! But please enjoy yourself."

Danya needed no further permission, tossing Ilya's pants to the floor. He lifted Ilya's hips, digging his fingers into the pillowy flesh. His rear end wasn't something Ilya thought about much, let alone one that somebody would be losing their mind over. Fitting into his clothes was frustrating sometimes, certainly, being too large or too small depending on the area he accommodated. If Danya was thrilled he wasn't unhappy, though.

"Spanking you would be such a joy." There was so much longing in his voice! He was two folds tickled by how strange Danya behavior was and overjoyed at how intense the attraction was.

"Why don't you?"

Danya clucked his tongue. "Baby steps. We'll work up to every-thing we can do together."

Ilya rolled his eyes even as he struggled not to grin. "How is that you barely remember who you are but you can recall every aspect of *fucking?*"

"I have very clear priorities in life, Ilyushka, it's simple."

Ilya's eyes were going to pop out of his skull if he rolled them any harder. He was in love with the most ridiculous angel in the world; for such a holy being, he was terribly crude. He was charming in his own way.

Danya grabbed Ilya's knees and forced them apart, pulling a gasp out of Ilya. He was so exposed, curling his hands against his chest. Danya's lids lowered, fond smile spreading across his lips. Ilya sunk back into the pile of clothes under him, shivering from the stone and the look on Danya's face.

His teeth chattered as he whined, "I'm freezing, Danylko."

"Let me fix that, then."

Danya pressed two fingers to Ilya's lips, instinctually parting for him. Ilya sucked on them, laving his tongue across the digits. He whimpered as their eyes met, warmth spreading across his skin once more. Danya looked ready to eat him alive, filling Ilya with power. He had an angel ready to bend to his whims and it was incredible.

Danya pulled his fingers back, trail of saliva connecting them to Ilya's lips. His hand dipped to circle over Ilya's hole, pressing the first knuckle of each digit inside. Ilya breathed in sharp, goosebumps rising across his skin. It was strange but not uncomfortable. He'd never had the heart to do this to himself, had only imagined what it might be like. He wasn't exactly overwhelmed yet.

"Probably be strange at first, but I'll make it good for you, Ilyushka. I promise."

"I still trust you, Danylko. Go."

Ilya's breathing quickened as his anticipation built, shoulders tensed as the intrusion in his body grew deeper. He stared at the vaulted ceiling, eyes trailing over the intricate carvings to redirect his anxieties. Danya's fingers were hot, moving slowly to stretch him open. The heat soothed him, but he was gripping onto his vestments for dear life anyway.

A moan ripped out of the back of his throat when Danya's fingers rubbed rough over a spot inside him. It was like a bolt of electricity, forcing his spine to curve, sending sparks down to his fingertips, prickling with pleasure. Danya seemed encouraged by the reaction, rubbing his fingers in and out, pressing that spot over and over.

"You like that, huh? You made such a pretty noise for me…"

He nodded dumbly, eyes rolling forward to look at Danya. There was nothing but joy on that face, completely enraptured with pleasing Ilya. Danya kept rubbing his fingers over that bundle of nerves, making him writhe in ecstasy.

"Stop– I don't want to finish yet– Please."

He was too aware of the emptiness once Danya's fingers were gone. He gulped down air, throwing a wrist over his eyes in a feeble attempt to collect himself, overstimulated and on edge. His heart skipped a beat as Danya's belt jingled. He lifted his arm, trying to catch a glimpse of him, desperate to fill in the blank from earlier.

"You can look as much as you want, Ilyushka."

Ilya propped himself up on his elbows to watch, licking his lips as Danya dropped his pants. He was slow and methodical, teasing Ilya with every passing moment. He drank in the appearance of the base, clearly much thicker than his own. His own cock twitched in excitement. He only hoped Danya would fit.

Danya finally let everything hang out, heavy between his legs. Ilya closed his mouth, realizing his jaw had been hanging open in awe. His mouth watered at the sight, desperate to have Danya inside of him. He couldn't form the words to fully describe how terribly he needed this.

Ilya finally managed, "It's big." He smacked a hand against his face, groaning in shame. He sounded like such an idiot, he had no idea being with somebody this way would make him so *brainless.*

Danya barked a laugh, grabbing hold of Ilya's waist to pull him in closer. Ilya's ass pressed against Danya's hips, the heat of Danya's cock nestled between the cheeks. A shuddering breath escaped him as Danya laid his length across Ilya's stomach, heat permeating into his skin. Ilya reached out with a timid hand, wrapping his fingers around the upper end. Danya groaned deep in his chest, Ilya swelling with pride. In time he'd be able to give to Danya as much as he took.

"I've imagined this so many times," Danya rasped. "Fuck, it doesn't even compare to the real thing. Can I–?"

The question hung in the air as Danya thrusted into Ilya's hand, barely staving off his need. Danya licked his teeth, more than ready to ravage him. Ilya wanted to be nothing but a puddle on this altar and he knew Danya would be happy to give that to him.

"Come on and *fuck me* then, you Sun forsaken angel."

Danya needed no further prompting. He took hold of himself and pressed the head to Ilya's ass, forcing him open once more. Ilya's eyes bugged out of his skull, processing just how enormous Danya was. The near overwhelming heat from Danya's body spread inside of him as he pushed against the first ring of muscle. Ilya hissed through his teeth when it finally gave way.

Once the initial discomfort went away, Danya's movements were smooth and easy. He was full, processing the sting as he opened up. His head spun from all the new sensations, heat filling his core as Danya bottomed out. He swallowed and stared at the ceiling again, desperate to relax and process it all.

Danya pressed his knees towards his head before pulling back, just a fraction. Ilya sucked in air between his teeth, jaw hanging open with a moan when Danya pressed back inside. Everything was slow, methodical, and careful. He could cry from how considerate his angel was.

"You feel good?"

Ilya nodded, growling back, "I told you to *fuck me*, Danya."

Danya snorted in reply. "You're such a brat, you know that?"

His next smart comment died in his throat when Danya started slamming into him. Whatever spot Danya had found in him earlier was being hit over and over, sending more sparks through his nerves. Danya hit it every time he moved, his pace unrelenting. A burn worked up Ilya's spine, arching and writhing under Danya's body. Danya throbbed inside of him, dragging in and out. The smack of Danya's hips against his ass echoed throughout the church; it was lewd and preposterous and it filled Ilya with immense joy.

"You have the perfect cushions– It feels incredible."

Ilya slumped back, letting his head hang off the edge of the altar. He gazed out at the rainbow of stained glass above the giant oak doors at the front of the church, glowing from the afternoon light. His eyes lost focus as he took in all the brilliant colors, letting himself become nothing but a pile of sensations. The scent of spice and cigarettes mixed with sweat and musk filled his head, further dizzying. He was in a fog of bliss, ravaged by a celestial being.

Clarity returned when Danya bit his throat, dragging his tongue across the skin to soothe it. A whimper spilled out as Danya sucked hard on his skin, all over his collarbones, his chest, just under his jawline. They'd all bloom into bright red-purple bruises in no time, and Ilya wasn't sure he was upset about it a single bit.

"Mine," Danya growled. "All fucking mine."

His fingertips prickled as goosebumps crawled across his skin once more. This was all he'd wanted: to be consumed, to let Danya take complete control, to think only of his pleasure. Heat began working its way down to his groin, coiling in his gut the closer he got to his finish. Danya was ruining him and he loved it.

"Close again," Ilya whined. "Do what you want."

Danya chuckled, pounding into him with relentless fervor. He cried out, writhing against the icy stone as a burn worked up his spine. His eyes rolled back, filled with the vision of glowing rainbow glass again. He was in a daze of lust, focused only on feeling. He never could've dreamed his first time would be this incredible. Sweat poured down his body, curls sticking to his forehead and cheeks. Heat pulsed in his core with each of Danya's movements. He could never be cold again; not with Danya.

Ilya gasped, "I love you—" Danya groaned, pressing his face against Ilya's chest and licking a stripe up his sternum. Without hesitation Ilya's fingers tangled in that sunrise of hair, nails scraping his scalp. Danya didn't let up for a single moment, lifting his head to kiss Ilya with equal ferocity, teeth clacking until it became nothing but lips and tongue moving together. More colored light crossed his vision, shades of purple and gold and blue fading into that perfect scarlet. He was in another world entirely.

"I'm—"

Ilya keened, body tensing and muscles flexing as he spilled across his stomach. His ears pounded with the rush of blood through his veins, punctuated by the beating of great bird wings, like the eagles that passed through the woods. Loose feathers the color of wheat floated across his vision, soft and ethereal. His lips parted first in shock, again when Danya slammed into him one final time.

"Fuck, Ilya, I love you too—"

Ilya sucked in a breath as Danya finished, shivering from the feeling. He settled against the cold stone, eyes rolling up to gaze at the vaulted ceilings. He gulped down air, skin clinging to his ribs as he breathed, collecting his brain off the proverbial floor as his sweat cooled. Danya's fingers were still digging into his waist, hard enough that Ilya was sure he'd bruise. He ached all over in the best of ways, the kind of mild pain that he wanted more of. Or, he would, if he wasn't *exhausted*.

Danya panted above him, brushing his curls out of his eyes. Ilya's gaze turned lazily upon his angel, his lover, the only man he ever wanted to be with. He was stunned by the vision in front of him, not unlike the incredible murals and painted ceilings in the Capital.

Great fiery colored wings had emerged from Danya's back, ripping through his shirt without a care, freed at last. They glittered in the afternoon light, fading from white hot to a dark vermillion. They were like flames bursting free, like the surface of the Sun Herself. Danya was fully realized, returned to his true form once more.

He was utterly enraptured as they gazed at one another. A sudden realization had Ilya breaking into a giggle.

"Ilyushka, what's so funny?" The smile on Danya's face was so fond, so in love. Ilya had to stop from melting so he could answer.

Ilya laughed, "I can't believe you got your wings back because I'm that good of a lay."

Danya snorted as he shook his head, stroking Ilya's cheek. He looked upon Ilya with utter admiration. His wings spread as wide as they could go, twice the size of the aisle that ran through the center of the church. Ilya took in their beauty before being enveloped by them, hidden away in a warm, feathery cage. The last light of the sunset made Danya's feathers glow the same warm, golden shade as his eyes and freckles. It was so intimate, being locked away with nothing but Danya and his feathers.

Danya whispered, only *just* loud enough that Ilya could hear. "I like to think it was all because you chose to love me. You've saved me twice now, Ilyushka, healed me and made me whole. I don't think it'll ever be possible for you to know the true depths of what I feel for you, to understand what you've done for me. Not in a thousand of your lifetimes could I repay you."

Moisture pricked at the corner of Ilya's eyes, the familiar burn blooming across the surface. Danya spoke to him with such feeling, more serious and sincere than he'd ever witnessed. He never imagined he'd know love like this, but here he was with a blessing from the Sun; one of Her sons, no less. Ilya wasn't sure why it was now, of all times, that he'd been given this gift, but he would treasure Danya for all of eternity. He would love him in this life and in the Realm of Eternal Day until existence itself burned out of the universe.

A familiar warm, calloused thumb scrubbed across his cheek, drying his tears. "You cry so often, Lyubimi. How can I fix it?"

Ilya placed his hands on top of Danya's, lifting it to kiss the center of his palm, melting from the new pet name. *Beloved.* "This is the good crying, Solnishko. Don't worry. Any time I have shed tears because of you, it's been because you've made me happier than I can handle."

Ilya kissed from the center of Danya's palm to the heel, pausing over the pulse point. His eyes flicked up, gazing at Danya through his lashes, trying to appear as demure as he could muster. Danya sucked in air through his teeth, dragging his thumb over Ilya's lips.

"If you keep doing that I'm not going to let you leave this altar."

Ilya crooned back, "Would that be so bad?"

"You wouldn't want to move to your bed?"

The burning at the base of his spine throbbed, the icy stone leaching into his papery skin. "My back is killing me, yes… Perhaps we should."

Danya finished kicking out of his pants then scooped Ilya into his arms. "That won't let up for a while, I'm afraid. You'll get used to it."

Ilya rested his chin against Danya's chest, gazing at him longingly. "I see. Then you'd better get me to bed."

Danya laughed. "You don't have to tell me twice."

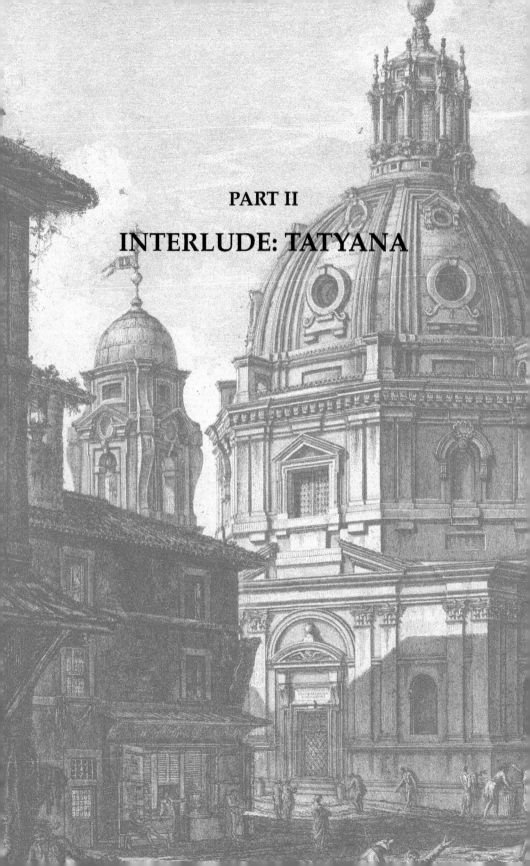

PART II

INTERLUDE: TATYANA

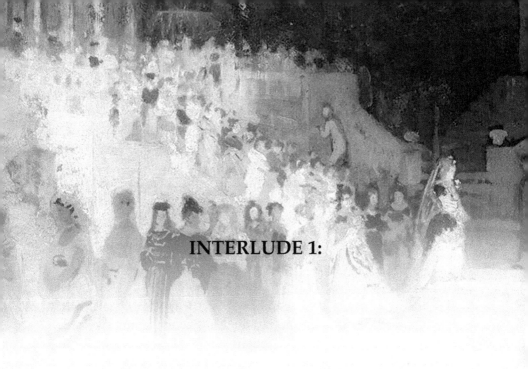

INTERLUDE 1:

Unknown time, unknown place.

There was fire. A great sphere of it, burning gold, larger than all his vision. Perhaps there should've been fear in his heart, but this ball of flame was gentle with him. She cradled him in wisps of glowing light, fractaled nebulae that were shaped into his being. His head erupted in flames, licking out from his scalp until they cooled red. More wisps traced along his back, stringing stars together to form feathers. Hundreds and hundreds, until they took the shape of great wings larger than his own body, glittering like galaxies.

She didn't speak to him, but somehow he knew Her will. He was an angel, one of Her beloved sons. She made him from Her own flames, from the celestial bodies She commanded. She had a task for him; a special one. He had to look after somebody important, somebody who would make the lives of others better with her mere existence. There were creations of Hers that had lost their way, that had given in to the will of the Eternal Night. While his siblings were tasked with changing their hearts, he would protect this one special person.

She named him Danil. But it was too formal, She said, She would only ever call him that when She was angry. She would never be angry, She assured him. He would instead be called Danya, a sign of Her affections. He would never be alone, so long as She shone in the sky. She couldn't always speak to him, but he need only call to Her, and She would aid him. He would be strong, though, strong enough to accomplish whatever he needed.

She had complete faith in Her Danya, Her youngest son. She had made him special. Once he was ready, he would begin his work.

His siblings whispered amongst themselves sometimes. "Yaya is Her favorite, surely. She put so much work into him." "Don't be silly, She loves us all. He's only new." "But why does he get such a crucial task? Who knows if he can do it!" "She made him special for it. Of course he can. Do you doubt Her?" "I would never doubt Mother." "Then leave it alone."

He did love them, but their conversations hurt.

Eventually the time came: he would be sent to Earth. He knew enough, had trained hard to defend his charge. Her name was Tatyana, a human woman. She was a brilliant scientist, Mother had said, unlocking all the secrets of the world that She had left, using it to create new things. She would be vital to the world, and Danya was to keep her safe.

His Mother cradled him in one last warm, golden embrace, tendril of light tracing all of his glowing freckles. She loved him dearly, and trusted him with this task. He promised Her to do his duty, that She had placed her faith in him correctly. Her light kissed him, and then the cosmos vanished.

May 16th, 1923

He was dropped in front of a great structure, white walls and black roof punctuated by gold fixtures. He looked around at everything, finding most of the buildings in a similar color. Far in the distance was a great domed building that towered above all the rest, golden roof reflecting the light of his Mother. It was a glowing beacon in this… city? He was sure that's what it was called. It was densely packed, but this area seemed quiet.

The building he'd been left in front of was covered in green moss. The front garden was a rainbow of flowers, bees gently buzzing from bloom to bloom. A pond sat in the middle, full of brilliantly colored fish that slowly moved through the gentle current. All this nature was familiar to him; he'd seen things like this in his Mother's realm, but there were puzzling things as well. A great metallic dish was attached to the roof, a tower of crossed metal beams reaching even higher into the sky. Lights blinked in a kaleidoscope of colors, reminding him of the brilliant windows that had lined his home.

It was a fascinating spectacle, and it seemed odd to be left on Tatyana's front… porch? Yes. That's what it was called.

He wasn't sure how to introduce himself. Did he simply open the door? Did he knock?

There was a button beside the doorknob, a bright white color in a golden frame. He hesitated a moment before pressing it. A chime of bells rang out, loud and brilliant. He jumped from the sudden noise, feathers puffing out in his confusion. He had no idea it would make such racket!

Steps came from the other side of the door, swinging open. All the air in Danya's lungs rushed out of him, taking in the sight of the most beautiful mortal creature he'd ever seen.

Her hair was black as an onyx gem, flowing down her shoulders like a waterfall of night sky. Her skin was warm like his, though it was barren of his golden flecks. Their gazes met and he became lost in the color, a rich color like amber. Her eyes were thin and unlidded, different from his own. He'd never seen anything like her. He'd met some of the angels of the Moon, but none of them compared to this Tatyana.

They were equally stunned by the other. Heat spread across Danya's neck, lips parted dumbly until he found his words. "I'm– I'm Danya. Mother asked me to look after you. Is that okay?"

Tatyana blinked at him in surprise then burst out in a brilliant laugh. It filled him with warmth the way his Mother's touch did.

"Oh, I had no idea angels would be so shy and silly! You're so cute. Of course you can look after me. Why don't you come in?"

Tatyana's home was even more brilliant on the inside. There were dozens of strange machines blinking and whirring with their function. There was hardly a surface that wasn't covered with documents, meters, and boards covered in yet more paper. Dark wooden shelves lined the walls of the main sitting room, all covered in hundreds upon hundreds of books. It was the most incredible library he'd seen, and that was saying a lot, considering his home. He looked around in awe, breath pulled directly from his lungs.

"I imagine it's a lot to take in," Tatyana said, breaking his focus. "I like to make things, especially if they can make everyone's lives a little better. Do you know what a radio is?"

Danya shook his head, watching her carefully as she approached a wooden box with a rounded top. She flipped a tiny metal switch on its side, and the box erupted in a horrific crunching noise. It sounded like the hissing of a snake and it made his feathers stand on edge.

"Oh, you puff up like a bird when you're nervous! Aren't you such a sweet thing? Don't worry, it doesn't hurt, I promise. I made this. It allows people to communicate from across the country! Perhaps one day the world, but for now, I'm glad for this. Some will let people talk to one another, though this one doesn't. This one does let you hear the brilliance of others, however."

Danya watched nervously as she twisted several dials, different voices cycling through until it settled on a gentle voice. She sang a sad tune about a lost love. Danya was utterly enraptured. He stepped closer to the box, kneeling to look closer. He traced a finger along the edge of the wood, taking it all in.

"This is amazing... you made this?"

Tatyana was beaming. "I did. I suppose they don't have radios in the Realm of Eternal Light?"

"No, not even close. This is so incredible... I see why Mother wanted you protected. She told me you're special."

Tatyana tilted her head curiously, eyes glittering with curious mirth. "Did She? Well, it's certainly an honor to have a child of the Sun watching over me. My own guardian angel... Who knew!"

Danya shifted on his feet, worrying his hands inside his shining silver gauntlets. Now what? What did he do?

"She was... unclear on how best to handle my task. She only trusted that I would know how to do it."

Tatyana laughed, stepping close to pinch both of his cheeks, shaking them gently. His face warmed, unused to having such beauty so close to him. She rivaled his Mother in brilliance. Even when his siblings would speak about him, he'd never been so weak in the knees.

"You're so naive and adorable. I'll have to teach you... many things. Why don't I show you the rest of my workshop?"

Tatyana had overwhelmed him with everything she had to show. She showed him a radio, both the kind that played music and the kind that allowed for communications. She had been the one to invent it, iterating on it so many times that now almost every home in the Capital had one. Music, news, and sports games could be listened to and enjoyed by all. Information about night creatures and attacks were spread by the church, allowing people a chance to flee and find refuge until the church's skill hunters could step in.

She showed him telephones, which allowed for even more distance. That people cities over could speak to one another was astounding. She spoke of opening up the world, making telephones and radios that could allow people continents over to talk. Free trade of information for the betterment of humanity was her goal, and she worked persistently to keep it in the hands of common folk.

Danya understood why his Mother had valued her so much. She was fiercely intelligent, constantly pushing him to learn as much as she knew herself. Beyond her brilliant inventions, she valued humanity. She spoke of the possibilities if people in small, rural cities could call for aid from far off, of friends and family connecting from worlds apart. News of disaster and misdeed could be heard faster, so the church might aid sooner. She had so many plans.

Beyond what she taught him about her work and her dreams for the future, she taught him the simple pleasures of human life. When Tatyana learned that he could read, she forced dozens of books into his hands. Grand tales of royalty and warriors in battle, documents on the cultures and night creatures around the world, books of all the sects of magic. He read scripture from the church, delighting Tatyana with all the corrections he made.

He read stories of love as well.

Danya was most fascinated by these. He loved his Mother. He cared for his siblings too, though not the same way. The love in these stories was so much more. It was akin to what his Mother and Father shared, an eternal bond of deep devotion that couldn't be severed by time or space.

He knew some of his siblings shared deep bonds with angels of the Moon. Some of them with each other; a not-unusual thing that didn't seem to happen with humans. Angels were all related and not at the same time, solitary beings made from the dust of the universe by their respective parent. He'd tried to explain this to Tatyana on a few occasions, and she *mostly* understood.

Still, he'd seen relationships like this. He'd known they existed in theory, but this was different. The grand gestures and declarations, the powerful emotions. They moved him, made his chest go tight with a displaced longing.

Danya began to look at Tatyana differently. He kept these thoughts to himself, simply enjoying everything about life on Earth. He couldn't ponder on these feelings too deeply, couldn't be distracted from his duty. The moment he faltered, her enemies, however unknown and impossible to him, could strike. He would be diligent.

Despite his wishes, Tatyana was brazen in showing him off. She brought him to parties with colorful dress and booming music, to museums full of treasures from the world over, to galleries full of art from the most brilliant minds, to public fairs where common people played games and shared snacks, to sporting events with incredible feats of human strength. The people came to know him, feeling blessed in his presence. Eyes were always on the two of them.

Tatyana pointedly avoided ceremony at the cathedral. Danya never asked, and Tatyana never bothered to explain. He felt his Mother's presence in all things; he didn't need a building if he wanted to speak with her.

None of that mattered. He loved everything she taught him about the world and the people around him, even just in her home city. Everybody loved her in return.

Over a year went by, a rush of color and feelings all new and unknown. By the end of the first year, Danya was sure he loved Tatyana too, the way they did in the stories.

The guilt overcame him. She was his charge, his responsibility. Was it right for him to want her? Would she feel crowded by him being so near if she didn't share his sentiments? Danya would never forgive himself if he made Tatyana uncomfortable for even a single moment. Frankly, he had no idea if his mother would make him leave earth for falling in love with his charge. Would she find him irresponsible, incompetent?

He spent weeks in quiet self flagellation until Tatyana brought him to an opera for the first time. She had a private box and had received a special invitation from the owner of the theater. For his greatest production, he needed the most culturally relevant woman in all the city, and he needed her guardian angel alongside her. Danya was happy to have Tatyana parade him around, to introduce him to all the most important people in the city. He met business people, other inventors, artists of all kinds, the whole breadth of humanity. It was overwhelming until they made it to their seats.

Their little private balcony was quiet and dark aside from the light and sound of the stage. It gave Danya plenty of time to stare at Tatyana, to admire her gorgeous features. She normally kept her hair tied up and out of the way, but tonight it was all flowing down past her shoulders. Even in the dim light of the box it glistened. He wanted to run his fingers through it, to know how soft it was. He wanted to wrap it around his knuckles and press it to his lips.

He marveled at how she could be one of siblings for how stunning she was. His Mother could only dream of making someone so perfect. Was it blasphemy for him to think so? He hoped She'd forgive him for these terrible thoughts. He couldn't help it.

He tried his best to enjoy the music, which was beautiful, but his gaze kept drifting back to his charge. On what was perhaps his hundredth time looking over at Tatyana, she glanced back. Their eyes met and she snorted in laughter.

"What's that look for, Danylko? You look like you've swallowed a toad."

No more fear. "I love you, Tanechka."

Tatyana blinked at him, lips parted in shock. His gut wrenched and twisted into knots. He looked away from her, head hung low in shame.

"I shouldn't have said that. I'm sorry."

The force she employed in grabbing his shirt collar was shocking enough, but the crash of their lips left him stunned. It wasn't a gentle kiss by any means; it was all heat and teeth and he swore his lip was going to split from how Tatyana was biting. Even still he gave in, eyes fluttering shut as he'd read in his novels. He was unsure of how to reciprocate, simply letting her take the lead.

It was as though she meant to kiss the breath out of his lungs, suffocating him. Her tongue slipped into his mouth and tasted of the sweet champagne she'd been drinking in the lobby earlier. Danya wanted to take all of it in, every taste her mouth had to offer, wanted to run his tongue across every surface until it was mapped in his mind. He could live a thousand years and never forget this moment, this first kiss.

He'd read of them being gentle, soft things in his stories, but that wasn't Tatyana. This was bold and feverish, just as she was. He shouldn't have expected anything else.

She broke the kiss briefly, her laughter quiet and breathless. "Have you ever experienced pleasure before, Danylko?"

He blinked at her, trying to regain his focus. "I... It's a pleasure to be near you."

"You're adorable." Tatyana giggled and pressed her hands to his chest. She groped each of his pectorals, fingers dragging down his stomach. She stopped just above his pant line, tilting her head with a smirk. "How shy do you feel, Danya?"

Tatyana smirked from how hard he swallowed, blinking rapidly. "I, uh... Not very, when I'm with you. Why do you ask?"

"I'd like to do something for you, and there's just a small chance we'll be noticed. That's all..." Her hand dropped to his groin, cupping him through his trousers. Danya inhaled sharp through his nose, back going board straight. He wasn't entirely aware of what she was going to do to him, but his skin blazed wherever she touched. He wanted every bit of heat. He'd never deny her a thing.

"If– If you want, I won't say no." His voice cracked on his last word. Danya scrunched his nose in embarrassment, deciding Tatyana's giggle of delight as well worth the temporary shame.

She was swift in undoing his belt and button, reaching a delicate, manicured hand inside. Tatyana's fingers wrapped tight around Danya's cock, eliciting another sharp intake of breath from him. He pulsed in her hand, goosebumps rippling across his skin as she pulled him into the open air.

"You're a big man I see– Bless your mother for Her generosity."

Danya didn't want to think about his Mother right now, actually. Tatyana was quick to erase Her from his mind when she kissed him once more. It was just as forceful and frantic as the first. The added sensation of her hand stroking up and down his length put him in an even bigger fog. He did his best to keep quiet, softly whining into Tatyana's mouth as she worked him.

"I love being with men that are new to this sort of thing... You make such cute noises. I bet you already want to finish, don't you? Oh, do you even know what that means, you sweet angel?"

Tatyana was being very condescending. Worse still was that he enjoyed it. No, he had no idea what any of this meant, only that

Tatyana wanted to give him this and it was incredible. Heat was building in his gut and working its way down his body, breath coming in fast. He thought he could only ever dream of Tatyana kissing him, let alone whatever it was she was doing now.

"It just feels good, Tanya. You're amazing–"

Tatyana kissed him harder, gripped him tighter, and moved her hand faster. Danya's brows knit together, soft whimpers escaping between Tatyana's kisses. He gasped as heat burst forth from him, sparks of pleasure working through him and making his fingertips tingle. He spilled out onto Tatyana's hand, groaning as it dripped onto his trousers. She chuckled and pulled out a handkerchief to clean them both, eyes glinting when he caught her gaze.

Danya slumped back in his seat, head rolling back to look up at the ceiling as a brief respite. If he kept looking at Tatyana he feared he'd make a mess again.

"It's also cute how easy it was to get you to cum. I'll teach you so much when we get home."

Danya's ears burned in hot embarrassment. She was too much! Unfortunately he was curious about what else she'd do to him. He wanted all of it, every touch and kiss.

He said it again, between breathless pants, "I love you, Tanechka."

Tatyana took gentle hold of his chin, forcing their eyes to meet again. Her expression was softer, more sincere than the mischief it had born just moments ago. "I love you too, Danylko. You sweet, special angel."

"Sorry to distract from the performance… I had to tell you. I… I wasn't sure if you'd hate me for it, if you'd want me to go away because I'd made you uncomfortable."

Tatyana pursed her lips, pecking his cheek forcefully. "*Stupid*, sweet angel. I wasn't sure if you could even reciprocate… I didn't want to make you break some sacred oath by jumping your bones. Know that I adore you, Danylko, and I'd love to have your heart as long as you'll have mine."

Danya was breathless once more, lips parted in his shock. It was hard to get Tatyana to be so serious. She meant every word.

"Forever, Tanechka," Danya rasped, "Until my mother burns out at the end of time."

Her facade cracked, lip quivering and eyes going glassy with tears. She kissed him, tenderly, softly. "Lyubimi… My beloved Danya. Let's go home. Let me show you all of my love."

Danya could only nod. "Yes. Let's go."

INTERLUDE 2:

February 8th, 1925

Tatyana came home in a fury. While she tended to be in her own workshop most days, every so often she would go into the city and leave him to his devices. More and more lately, she returned irritable and avoidant. Today seemed to be the pinnacle of her frustrations. Danya had never heard her slam the door so hard. She couldn't look him in the eye as she stormed into the basement. Danya followed quietly, worrying his lip. She tore through file cabinets, pulling out folders and documents that she threw to the ground.

Tatyana was usually calm and collected. He'd never seen her like this.

"Tanya? What's going on?"

Tatyana flinched at the sound of his voice. It brought her to a halt, frozen as she white-knuckled a folder in her hands.

"Danya. The church will be arriving soon. I have to burn my research for them."

Danya blinked owlishly, head tilted in surprise. "You've been doing research for the church? Why would you have to burn it?"

That prompted her into action again. She tore through more

cabinets, stepping over to the potbelly stove in the corner of the workshop. They'd had several winters together spent in front of this stove, tinkering and drinking coffee while avoiding the chill outside. It roared to life as Tatyana lit the fire, throwing piles of papers into the blaze. They crackled and snapped, a mound of ash forming in the bottom of the cavity as more burned.

"Tatyana. Please tell me what's going on?"

"I can't, Danya!" She whirled on him with fury in her eyes. Her hair, normally delicately coiffed, was coming undone. Stray strands were coming loose from pins, sticking to the sweat shining across her skin. Her black eyes held only the heat of anger. "The less you know, the better. Just stay out of my way right now. Go watch the door or something if you want to be useful!"

His wings sagged, feathers dragging across the dusty concrete. She would sometimes talk down to him to fluster him, in a playful manner. But this was supposed to hurt.

"Tanechka… Why are you talking to me like this?"

She threw another bundle of papers into the fire, breathing hard. "Just *go*, Danil. I can't look at you."

His chest and shoulders tensed, pain moving up the back of his neck. His throat grew tight, like it was closing off. Had he done something? Had he caused this? He was so confused.

Danya finally made his way upstairs, standing by the front door as she had asked. Once he was out of view he coughed out a sob, rubbing at his eyes. The house smelled of smoke, filled with the sounds of stomping, rummaging, and muttered swears from the basement. It was nightfall by the time Tatyana came upstairs. Her demeanor seemed more settled then. She pulled the chains for several of the lamps, busying herself so she wouldn't look at him.

"Tatyana. Please tell me what's going on."

Pain. He was in so much pain.

"I can't, Danya. For your safety… and because I'm ashamed of the truth."

Danya stepped towards her, gently grabbing her arm. "Please, Tanechka, I love you. Nothing will ever change that. I just want to understand."

The front door flew off its hinges, slamming into his back and knocking him onto the floor. He narrowly missed hitting Tatyana, jaw slamming against the wood floors. His vision spun in circles for a moment. Danya fought to get to his feet, pushing himself up as a dozen strange men flooded into the foyer. Their uniforms were all dark leather and black fabric, wide brimmed hats shading their faces. All their eyes were glassy black, as if they were creatures of the night.

"Stop! What are you doing?"

Tatyana screamed again, two men dragging her to the front door. She dug her heels in, tried to be dead weight in their arms, but she was no match. Tatyana was a brilliant scientist and a socialite, but she had never been a fighter. That was Danya's job.

He managed to get back to his feet, holding on to the couch for support. "Stop! Let her go! I am an agent of the Sun, our Great Mother, and that woman is my charge!"

Danya met the eyes of another of the men. He seemed calm, flashing Danya a serene smile. "You don't know what she's been doing, do you?"

"No!" Tatyana screamed when they pulled her outside, and that was his final straw.

Danya flicked his wrist, bright silver sword materializing in his hand, plate armor clinking into place in a flash of brilliant light. The men around him covered their eyes and hissed in pain. Danya held his sword point out to all of them, extending his great wings. If he managed to intimidate them, perhaps he wouldn't have to resort to violence.

"I will ask only one more time! Let her go and I'll spare you."

The man who spoke earlier approached him. Danya kept his sword extended, tip pressed to the center of the man's chest. The man tilted his head, perhaps assessing how much of a threat Danya was.

"All of your siblings are the same. It's no wonder we human beings have had to take carrying out your Mother's orders into our own hands. She can only make naive fools."

It was just enough to make Danya hesitate. "My siblings—?"

Chains wrapped around his neck from behind. He grabbed at them in a desperate attempt to pull them off, burning to the touch. Smoke rose from the contact points and made him cry out in pain. Danya threw his head back in an attempt to free himself, wings flapping rapidly to beat the crowd of men away. They slung more chains across the length of his wings, pinning him to the ground. He struggled against his bonds, liquid gold blood leaking down his feathers and onto the slick wooden floors.

Danya snapped his head toward the door, the clattering of wood echoing through the foyer. He glared back at the man who spoke to him earlier.

"What do you think you're doing?"

That sickly, serene smile spread across the man's face again. "Your Tatyana has committed crimes against the church, and dare I say, all of humanity. A great many sins that she is going to have to pay for now."

Danya surged forward before the chains dug too deep into his skin, smoke clouding his vision, burnt sugar smell filling his nostrils. *"What are you doing?"*

The man clucked his tongue, folded his hands behind his back, and began to walk to the front door. "What we have always done with witches and sinners, dear angel. Danya, she said your name was?"

Again Danya fought against his bonds. The men pinning his wings seemed to be struggling; no mortal man's strength could compare to that of an angel. This man, their leader, was smug and enjoyed his suffering. He could work with this.

"Why did she tell you my name?"

The man turned his head back to him, mirthful glint in his eye. "She was going to give you to us for our project together, you see. Then it seems she fell in love and got cold feet. So much for science."

More rage coursed through his veins, a heat so powerful it threatened to burst from under his skin. Lies upon lies to justify hurting a woman whose power they feared. That's all this was.

But he had what he needed; their attention.

"I won't let you have her!" He focused all of his anger out of his body, white light flashing from atop his head. All the men in the room shouted and cried out with pain, clutching their eyes as they burned and bled. The Sun's purest light could burn out anybody, but these monsters who had made pacts with the night would know Her wrath the most.

The men holding him dropped his bonds in their agony. Danya surged forward, flapping his wings to launch himself through the door. He rolled onto the moonlit lawn, greeted by the sight of Tatyana tied to a post in the middle of a wood pile. Some of the other church men noticed him, many pulling more of those cast iron chains out of their coats. Danya tried to launch himself into the air, but found his wings too damaged to carry his weight. He settled for launching himself at the men surrounding Tatyana's pyre.

Silver sword crashed against iron chain and wooden crossbow. Sparks flew off the metal as Danya leapt back. His rage bubbled to the surface again, blade lighting aflame in scarlet. More and more men surrounded him to keep him away from the pyre. He caught a glimpse of Tatyana, defeat flashing across her expression. He wouldn't let this happen. He couldn't. This was his duty, this was why his Mother created him. If he failed this, what good would he be?

"Danya, I'm sorry!" she cried out. Danya told himself that Tatyana had nothing to apologize for. It was all lies. He would save her, she would explain herself more clearly, and they would live in peace.

He stole a single, longing glance, flashed her a reassuring smile. It was fine. It would all be fine.

Pain in his left shoulder blade. How did it pierce his armor? More Sun forsaken cast iron. Why did church men know how to harm an angel this way? Why did they dare?

Every nerve screamed in agony, ice clutching his veins in a vise. He whirled around; the church men's leader held a raised crossbow. Danya looked down at his hands, just enough silvery light to expose the ink that pumped through his veins. It was as though his organs had withered to dust. Endless emptiness. His teeth gnashed together, three sizes too big for his mouth. What had they done?

A woosh of air and crackling wood drew his attention to the pyre. Somebody he cared about was being burned. He tried to look at the flames, vision swirling from its intensity. He whimpered and threw his hands in front of his eyes, long black nails shielding him.

"Run Danya! Please! I'm sorry, please run!"

She wanted him to run. Who? He wasn't sure, except that perhaps he loved her. She was special. He loved her and she wanted him to run. He wanted to save her, but it was too late. He remembered enough for that. He'd failed.

"I love you!" she said again. "Forgive me! Please, get away!"

Clattering chains activated him, made him bolt in fear deeper into the city. He crashed into an alley, scrabbling on all fours as he rounded a corner. Boot steps behind him forced him to keep sprinting. His paw pads splashed into cold puddles of snowmelt still clinging to the spots of shade from the day. He crashed into garbage bins and other discarded waste that scratched him, drawing ink from below his piled black fur. He needed to get away from these men, and he needed to stay out of the light.

An iron fence blocked his path as he rounded another corner, but he made the leap anyway. His belly was grazed by the pointed tips of the grate, but he made it. The noise behind him quieted as he ran still, panting for air. He came to a halt when the twist of alleyways ended, just outside of the range of the dim lamplight on the street. His eyes, dozens, hundreds of them, all whirled around in a frenzy. Where would he go? Where could he hide?

One eye honed in on a bridge in a park across the street. There was a shadowed alcove, maybe a way out. He could hide from the light there.

The lamp light made his eyes burn and vision twist. He crashed down the hill to his target, tumbling into a darkened tunnel. He paused to pant for air again, exhaustion beginning to grip at him. Still he pushed on, padding deeper into the darkness. He could see clearly here, felt safe in the dark. He was left only with the sound of trickling water and rats.

Rats. He was starving.

He crunched on whatever vermin that wasn't quick enough to escape the snapping of his bony jaws. He wandered aimlessly, feasting and gorging. It wasn't enough. *He was so hungry.*

He didn't know how long he was in the tunnels. Sometimes he would find the unlucky cat or dog for a bigger meal, but all failed to satisfy. Even the biggest prey of them all couldn't satiate.

The men who he ran into were much more feeble than the ones who had been chasing him so long ago. They were easy. Confused, terrified. As they should be! He took joy in punishing each one, taking out his rage, his fear. He would rip flesh from bone, crush skull and brain matter then lap at the gray goo. Still his body remained hollow, his heart a burning coal in his chest that refused to go out. It would never be enough.

The scent of fresh air drew him out of the tunnels. He stared at the moonless sky as he waded through the murky shallows and into the deep river water. It was cold, washing away blood and other unknowable substances from his fur. He waded upstream until his pelt was heavy with water. He crawled up the bank, shaking himself out. It was quiet here, only the rushing river to break the silence. He padded along the bank, content that he had found true safety at last.

Now it was back to the hunt.

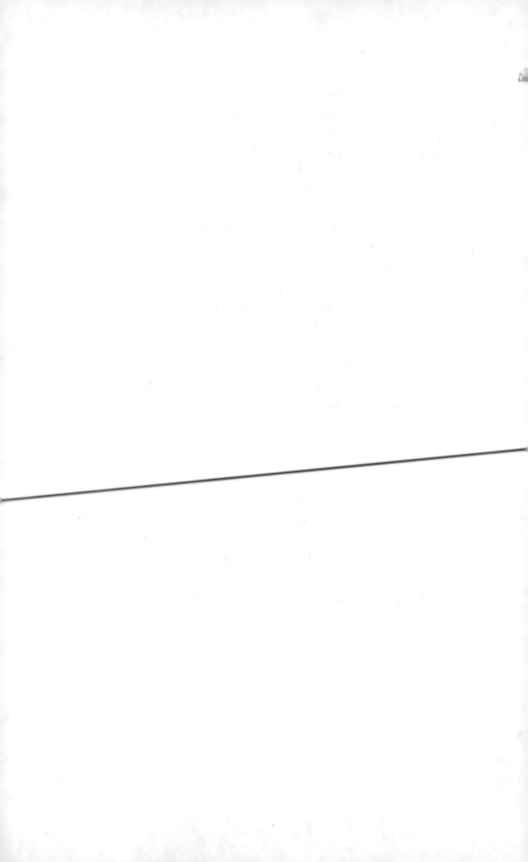

PART III

DAY

15

December 29th, 1927

Adjusting to life with an angel was easier than expected. Ilya had to get out his sewing kit to adjust all of Danya's clothes, but that had been short enough work. In the meantime, Danya being shirtless was hardly a bother.

He'd also informed Berta that Danya was ill and would miss work for a few weeks. They needed time to strategize revealing Danya to the world and the reactions thereafter. It would draw the attention of absolutely everybody. How would they deal with people one town over, let alone if the church got word?

They coped by enjoying their time together. Ilya couldn't remember the last time he was this happy. They were always touching, which Ilya welcomed. When you lived alone for years upon years with nary a soul to talk with, let alone have physical contact, it wore on you. Every touch from Danya was healing; from the gentle, roaming caresses, to the desperate, feverish ones that set his blood alight. Every moment of physicality brought him back to life again, like he *existed*. He wasn't just some ghost haunting the halls of the cathedral, he was real, present in his life again.

While he valued the primal parts of their physicality, the quiet moments meant just as much, if not more: nights curled up in front of the fire with his head on Danya's chest, listening to the beat of his heart; laying in bed in the early hours to count out every sparkling freckle on his face; walks in the woods behind the church, admiring the fresh snowfall before being pinned to a tree with a hot, passionate mouth. This was bliss.

As the weeks turned into a full month, rumors in town began to fly. Ilya had expected them; Danya was appalled. It was nice having somebody in his corner, who assured him that the way he was treated was unfair. Even still, he knew Velak's brand of crazy plenty well. When most of them considered his mere existence a personal slight, anything off was up for the highest scrutiny.

Now they whispered accusations of murder, that he'd grown jealous of how the town loved Danya and buried him in the church graveyard where nobody would be the wiser.

The people of Velak had leveled many horrific accusations towards him in the past. They could say whatever they wanted about how terrible a person and priest he was. He was used to these, all of their comments mind-numbingly absurd in their untruth, and certainly nothing he hadn't heard before.

But *these* lies? They were destroying him.

To be accused of hurting the love of his life? The man who saved him from the brink? He couldn't take it. They already called him a murderer for being unable to heal his father. Were they going to do this again?

Even Oyuna was cagey around him. That hurt him more than any of the other townsfolk. By contrast, Berta only seemed worried that Danya might need a hospital in the Capital. Her concern surprised him.

Still, Oyuna's doubts broke him into a thousand pieces, and it's what he brought to Danya when he'd hit his limit.

"Solnishko, I can't take it anymore. I can't keep hearing people call me a murderer again. I know once we open this box we can't put the demons back, but it must be time. I can't keep you here forever."

They were in bed, Danya's wings blocking out the harsh after-noon sun peeking through the curtains. Danya's arms wrapped around him in a protective shell, digging his fingers into Ilya's body reflexively.

"I trust Berta," Danya sighed. "I think we can show her. Do you think you could convince her to come here?"

"She adores you, and she's the only one who hasn't accused me. She'd come in a heartbeat. Maybe I can convince the Mayor to come too..."

Danya's feathers puffed out in his irritation. Ilya had to try very hard not to giggle; his angel wore his emotions on his wings.

"I fucking hate that man. *So much.* But if you think it'll help, fine. Hate this stupid town. Can't we just leave? Fuck off into the night never to be seen again? Or ask for a transfer? I don't understand why the church keeps you here when your congregation hates you."

Ilya took a hold of Danya's chin to pull him down for a kiss. Danya's wings relaxed back into their natural position, cowed by Ilya's affection.

"I've asked for a transfer so many times, but they won't budge. Not unless the town votes me out, and they won't. If I flee, then the church will assume I've abandoned my post. They'll send Hunters after me... they're not kind to deserters, Danylko."

"Seems like it would make everybody a lot happier. Stupid."

Ilya laughed, light and breezy. It was nice having somebody on his side, protecting him from the town. Danya must've been a guardian for Tatyana with how fierce he was in his loyalty.

"Well, I'll go into town and see if I can't convince them. I'm sure it will only be very frustrating."

Danya tilted Ilya's head back, kissing along his throat and sigh-ing. "At least let me ravish you before you go."

Ilya pulled Danya on top of him and smirked. "I certainly won't say no to that."

ILYA LIMPED his way into town, heart fluttering despite the undercurrent of anxiety. Danya certainly knew how to make a mortal man feel good. His nerves caught up as eyes trained on him, watching his every move. It was unbelievable that anybody in this awful place believed he murdered the one person who *liked* him.

Then again, some of them thought he murdered his father at seven years old, rather than his rapid illness. What did he know?

Ilya wove through the aisles of junk in front of Berta's porch, pressing open the heavy wooden door into the shop proper. Without Danya around, the junk shop had become *more* of a mess. It was a dark miracle from the Realm of Eternal Night.

He followed his nose to the back of the shop, finding Berta smoking in front of Danya's workbench. She glanced at him warily, blowing acrid gray clouds out of her nose. "Father. Is there any news on my boy?"

"Yes, in fact. He's still not sure about coming into town, but he wanted you to come by and see him for a visit. He got the feeling everybody in town was beginning to worry about him, but surely you can assuage their fears, yes?"

They stared one another down. Berta's gaze was intense, but Ilya's newfound confidence meant he could hold his own.

Ilya continued, "You can invite our dear mayor along as well, if it eases your fears. I'm sure he can help you spread the news that Danya is in fact alive."

Berta nodded, flicking her cigarette onto the cement floor without a care. "I'll fetch Ivan and meet you in the square, Father. Good day."

Berta sped out to the town hall. Ilya followed behind her, standing in front of the clocktower at the center of the square. He tugged his hood further forward, trying to block out everybody who was looking at him. Days like this were ones where the power of invisibility would be lovely. Unfortunately only the most dedicated of Moon priests could claim to do so, and alas, he was a devotee of the Sun; he could help anybody but himself.

He took a deep breath, crisp air filling his lungs. Hopefully soon he could have the town off his back. Just for a little while, he'd like to not have to care what people thought of him.

BERTA AND IVAN complained and kvetched the moment they started the climb up the hill. Ilya barely held back from rolling his eyes.

Ilya told them, "I'm sure Danya could be persuaded to install some steps here, but he'd get the work done faster if the town pitched in as well."

"Oh you know very well that won't happen, Ilya," Ivan replied, wheezing between words. "Not for you."

Ilya turned his head when he heard a smack, finding Berta glaring at Ivan. "We can't make that poor boy do all the work! Besides, we'll need them when they bring in the next priest! Start finding some people to help him!"

Ilya's eyebrows went up in surprise. He wasn't being defended exactly, but not many people bothered to confront Ivan when he was being cruel. It was more for Danya's benefit, but it was nice to have their *dear mayor* taken down a peg.

"If only so he can finally get back to working for you, is that right Berta?" Ilya asked.

"Damn right."

Ivan and Berta continued to bicker and complain as they walked. Ilya did his level best to tune them out and turn them into white noise, admiring all the conifers that lined the path. If Ilya pointedly walked far ahead to avoid the both of them, who was to say? Perhaps they were just old and slow.

They made it to the rectory soon enough, Ilya pushing open the door and calling for Danya, "Danylko! Berta and Ivan are here to see you!"

Ilya kicked off his boots and hung up his cloak then went to start the kettle for tea. He leaned back against the counter while he waited, arms crossed. Berta and Ivan took seats at the table, looking around awkwardly. He had no idea why Danya was taking his sweet time.

"Danylko, would you come out already?"

Perhaps he shouldn't be letting such pet names slip, but it was a force of habit now. He had to remain cautious, not knowing how Berta and Ivan felt about relationships like this. He was positive that Ivan would sell him out the second he got more than a whiff, if he was being honest. The punishment for romantic deviance was even more severe than abandoning his post.

Thus was the world they lived in.

Danya poked his head out of Ilya's bedroom, eyes moving between Ivan and Berta. "As you can see, I'm not dead! I'm very much alive, and Ilya is not a murderer!"

Berta rushed over to Danya without a second thought. She put her hands on Danya's cheeks, squishing them together. "My boy, I was worried you were at death's door! Father Sokolov said you've been ill for weeks, but you look glowing as ever! Have you been trying to get out of work?"

Danya snorted and shook his head. "No, I promise I have a legitimate reason for hiding. I made Ilya tell you all I was sick because I wasn't sure how to break the news. But," Danya narrowed his eyes at Ivan, a cat-like, facetious smile on his face, "I clearly underestimated how far you'd all go to make him the villain in all things. So here we are."

Ivan had been suitably cowed at seeing Danya, his smug aura fading. The mayor's lack of confidence *shouldn't* hurt Ilya anymore, but it did. A familiar ache flared in his palms, crawling its way up his wrists. He turned to finish with their tea, four cups with delicate saucers placed on the table. Ilya was surprised he had enough cups to serve them all, frankly.

"But Danylko, what are you hiding for?" Berta asked. "What a strange thing to say."

Ivan pointed at Danya with a thick finger, eyes narrowed. "And you're glowing, like all the rumors said. What's your deal, *zhopa*?"

The look on Danya's face clearly stated, 'I wish I could snap your neck and throw your body into the gorge'. Ilya wasn't in the business of stopping Danya from doing it. If anybody in town drew

Danya's ire more than Ilya's mother, it was Ivan. Ilya's heart swelled with joy to see somebody so willing to defend him.

Danya guided Berta away from the door so he could throw it open. The handle slammed against the wall and Ilya sucked air through his teeth; how many times had his mother done the same? He knew it was to intimidate Ivan, but it triggered something inside him all the same.

Danya stormed over to Ivan, grand wings spread wide, fluffed in irritation. He made a show of opening them as far as they'd go, glittering in the afternoon light. Berta gasped and collapsed against the wall, hand to her chest in her shock. Ivan shrank back, eyes wide in fear.

"My deal is that you're an insufferable, pitiable old man who's only source of entertainment has been making the life of my savior as miserable as he can manage for far too long. I'm sure my Mother will be *so* pleased to know what you've done."

Berta dropped to the ground, pulling their attention away. She was on her hands and knees, head bent forward to prostrate before Danya.

"Holy being of our great Mother Sun, I should have known of your divinity, please forgive my transgressions–"

Danya grimaced. He'd hated any of the praise Ilya tried to laud him with for being an angel, and this was many steps above general affections and admiration. He grabbed the back of Berta's dress and hauled her up, smoothing it out once she was upright.

"*Babushka*, you know I don't give a shit about that... Nothing's changed between us."

Ilya glanced back at Ivan. He was slack jawed, pale, and silent. The genuine look of terror was new for Ivan. Ilya liked it.

Berta kept muttering apologies under her breath, falling against Danya. Danya supported her frail body, feathers puffed up from his anxiety. Ilya snickered. This was only a taste of the praise he was going to get once word got out.

"This isn't some– some Sun forsaken, priestly trick?" Ivan spluttered, storming towards Ilya and shoving him back against the counter. "Trying to legitimize yourself, Sokolov? Making us think your charity case is a holy being? What spells have you learned while we were all dying from that fucking monster in the woods?"

Danya was wedged between Ilya and Ivan in the blink of an eye, the sound of wings flapping coming only after he appeared. He shoved Ivan back into the kitchen table, teacups rattling from the force. Ivan had always been able to overpower Ilya, both with his words and physicality; it was strange for him to appear so weak. Ilya was torn between fear and gratitude; fear for the memories that bubbled to the surface, and gratitude that Ivan was getting a taste of his own medicine.

"Does that feel real enough to you, *kozyol*," Danya spat "Have you had enough of tormenting him for no reason yet?"

Ilya touched the center of Danya's back, forcing the angel to pause. Danya glanced back at Ilya, wings sagging.

"It's okay, Danylko. I wanted people to know you're alive, and we've done that. This needn't go any further so long as people know you're safe. All right?" He glanced at Ivan, part confirmation, part warning. Letting Danya hit Ivan probably wasn't *right*, but it would be satisfying in the moment. Then again, justice didn't mean you couldn't defend yourself, and what as an angel if not the purest incarnation of justice there could be?

"I'm sure the town will be thrilled you've been keeping a son of the Great Mother hidden from us," Ivan spat back. "You manage to disappoint in new ways, Sokolov."

Ivan had the sense to run off into the church before either Ilya or Danya could process what he'd said. Ilya heaved a sigh and slumped against the counter, eyes turned to the ceiling. Could he beg to be transferred for the 68th time? Would it matter? It would be difficult to make his life more miserable than it had been all these decades, but an angry mob who *actually* acted on their darkest desires would do it.

"I don't understand him anymore," Berta said, her voice soft. Ilya met her hazy gray eyes, tried to search her face for her intentions. "Maybe if you'd asked when the drekavac was attacking, I would have said you were hiding Danya, that it was on purpose. But you got rid of it. I was bitter that it took so long, that the church ignored us, but you did it. And all these months, this boy has been in town, slowly changing in front of us... What was there to hide if you were paying attention?

"We all loved your father, Ilya. He was a man of the people, kind to a fault, generous to a fault. Then there was you, the only other magic in town, eyes burned out and blessed by the Sun Herself, unable to right this terrible wrong. We all blamed you... including your mother. That *witch* of a woman... I feel ill, thinking the same as her.

"Lately I've felt... I've been blinded by my grief. I lost my priest, my confidant, my friend... but Ilya, he was your parent. I never once stopped to think, in all these years, about how this must have affected you. And now I look upon Ivan's blind hatred, how he'll look for any excuse, even when it makes no Sun forsaken *sense.* When we have a child of the Sun in front of us, telling him he's wrong, assuming he knows better than an *angel!*

"It's too little too late, I'm sure, but all the same, young Ilya, I'm sorry. I'm sorry for what I've done, and for what you've endured. And I'm sorry it will get worse still, no thanks to that pathetic excuse for a man."

The silence hung thick in the air, clogged Ilya's throat and rendered him unable to speak. He never expected this would ever happen, that somebody would *change their mind.* All he'd wanted since that terrible day 23 years ago was for everybody to come to their senses, to apologize. He'd accepted his fate a long time ago, accepted that it would never happen, that holding out hope was a fool's errand.

But here Berta was, mind changed.

He was sure that Danya had everything to do with it. He didn't know what they talked about at work, but he was sure Danya spoke fondly of him, helped humanize him. Even just being *around* seemed to help soften Berta's shell.

He loved Danya so much. His protector angel, his champion.

The racing emotions brought tears to his eyes, rolling down his cheeks in fat streams. A warm, brown, gold dusted hand came to rest on his cheek. Danya's thumb brushed away the wetness and Ilya leaned into his touch. His eyes flicked up to look at Danya, a brief glance and silent thanks, then returned his attention to Berta. *Shit.* He'd been senseless to be seen like this.

"Thank you," Ilya croaked. "Why don't we see about tea now?"

Danya sat close, closer than he was comfortable with in this company. Berta had only just changed her mind about him, he didn't want to lose that so instantly. Ilya was positive at least part of the reason the townsfolk hadn't let go of their hate was because they knew about his proclivities. He'd never confirm it to them, lest he be hanged for it, but in the backs of their minds, they all knew. That Danya was being so risky had him on edge all over again. Loving a warrior of the Sun wouldn't save him if the time came.

"I'm sure Ivan is going to tell everybody now," Ilya sighed. "I'm worried for how people will react... I'm sure we'll be busy for ceremony tomorrow. I expect the whole town will show up for once."

Berta clucked her tongue and lit one of her awful, acrid cigarettes. "Oh, not just the town, boy, everybody from Kursiya to the Capital will be on us. Wouldn't shock me if a whole Cardinal made his way down here."

Bile crawled up the back of Ilya's throat at the mere idea. He'd rather walk straight down the hill, through town, find the cliff's edge, and drop into the river gorge than deal with a Cardinal. As much as he complained about the people of Velak, the men in power at the Capital cathedral made them look like *saints*.

"I haven't had to deal with a Cardinal since my lessons. They're dreadful."

Danya reached for his hand, squeezing it to reassure him. Ilya wanted to pull away, but Danya's grip was firm.

Berta barked a laugh, a cloud of smoke and ash wafting in front of her face. "I have no doubt. Even bigger geezers than me locked up all day reading their illuminated manuscripts and pretending they're better than the rest of us. I'm surprised you and your father weren't more insufferable."

"I'm still surprised to hear somebody admit that I'm not that bad."

Danya leaned into him, hooking his chin over Ilya's shoulder.

One of his wings curled around him, blocking off part of his face, trying to shield him from the world. Ilya wanted to be comforted by the gesture, and if they were alone he surely would have been, but every moment of closeness while another person was around was a risk. His teeth itched and his throat tensed.

"I'll admit I'm not so set in my ways that I can't learn. Danya's taught me newfangled things about junk in the shop and made me change my mind. Why limit it to gadgets? But enough of that." Berta paused to tap off her cigarette, ashes scattering across the floor. Ilya fought the urge to immediately clean it. "Danya, my boy, we should see about some stairs for the hill. I think the coming visitors will appreciate it."

"What if I don't fucking want visitors?" Danya grumbled. "I liked having the priest all to myself."

More like Danya enjoyed making Ilya desecrate his altar every week. *"I asked my mom and she said it's fine"* is what he'd said. What a bold, terrible lie.

"Well you'll have to just get over it, won't you, kid?" Berta shot back. "Now come on outside. We've had to deal with this mud for too many years."

Danya's mouth flattened into a grimace. "You've got me there. Fucking hate this stupid mud mountain."

Ilya laughed. "At least now you can fly above it. Now go on with your project. I'm sure there's plenty of trees around you can fell for your lumber while you're at it."

"You can just *say* you want me to collect more firewood, you know—"

It took Berta dragging him out by the ear to get Danya to finally leave, begrudgingly at best. Ilya went limp in his chair once they were out of sight, groaning in his contempt for the world.

ILYA HAD BEEN AVOIDING town for a while thanks to all the rumors, and thus the cursed vegetable soup returned. He wasn't sure if

Berta was staying for dinner, so something bulk was for the best anyhow.

Light-footed steps came in behind him, arms wrapping around his waist. Ilya tensed on reflex, checking to see if Berta had followed Danya back. Danya pulled away from him, brows knit.

"Ilyushka, what's the matter with you? You've been distant all afternoon."

Ilya heaved a sigh and looked up at Danya. "We can't... we can't be close like that in front of other people. Not unless we trust them completely. Do you understand?" Ilya clasped his hands around Danya's, kissing his knuckles in an attempt to reassure his poor angel.

Danya was positively incredulous. "No, I don't understand. What's the matter with us being close?"

"We're both men, Solnishko. It's a crime in this country. The church has said so... I could be hanged for it."

Danya bristled, hands clenching. "You're a priest. I'm an *angel*. What gives them the right? What in the fucking world makes them think they can decide that?"

"Men are of the Moon, women are of the Sun. To create the great Eclipse, there must be one of each. So they say. Nevermind that we aren't celestial bodies."

"I'm literally from the Sun!" Danya's exasperation was growing. Ilya had let go of his own a long time ago; he didn't have the strength to fight this battle, not when being alive in this place was battle enough. "Ilyushka, how could loving you be wrong? How could they claim to know better than Her?"

"I don't know, Solnishko. I wish I understood their heads. Perhaps one day you can make good on your threats and tattle to your mother. Maybe something will be done then. They're going to have my hide for not calling about you anyway... Better to not give them another reason to be angry."

Danya looked ready to cry. Ilya spotted the muscles of his neck tensing, trying to hold back. Ilya kissed him, a soft brush of lips. Danya broke free of Ilya's grasp and embraced him, as tight as he could without hurting.

"I just want to love you– I will *never* do something that could get you hurt. Even if it's *fucking stupid*." Danya sniffled in his ear, sucking in a shaky breath. "I made a vow to love you and protect you. If… If being private is what I have to do, then fine. *Fine*. But I'm ready to take you anywhere else the second things get bad."

Ilya pressed his face against the soft, silken threads of Danya's hair. "I'm worried Berta suspects about us… And I… I want to tell Oyuna. She cares about me, and I just… I want her to know. Would you be okay with that?"

Danya pulled back, brushing Ilya's dark curls out of his eyes. "Whatever you want, Lyubimi. But… I trust Berta. For what it's worth. She's not a bad woman, I promise. Okay?"

Ilya gave him an apologetic look. "I know. Forgive me, her kindness towards me is new. I… It's difficult to trust. You understand?"

"Yeah. I do." Danya kissed his forehead, trailing his lips down to Ilya's jaw. "Hey, wanna think about anything else right now? Wash off all this negativity? Now that we're alone and all…"

Ilya laughed, face pressed into Danya's shoulder. "Insatiable creature. Are you sure you're an angel and not the drekavac still?"

"Don't act like you don't initiate just as much as I do, you silly priest! Now do you want to fool around in the bath or not?"

Ilya stepped out of Danya's arms to start moving to the bathroom, a smirk on his face. "Come on then, silly angel."

16

Danya shoved him against the wall across from the tub as their lips crashed together, wings encasing him in a feathery cage. Ilya gasped against Danya's mouth, hot as the sun and overtaking him. Broad, tawny hands dragged down his chest, thumbs catching on the window over his chest. They reached back to undo the zipper of his vestments, nails scratching against his skin.

"I don't know how I'm supposed to start the tub if you're going to ravish me already, Danylko–"

Danya pressed his lips to the center of Ilya's throat and chuckled. "Can you blame me?"

He pulled back all the same and Ilya took the chance to get the bath filled. The pipes creaked as the heat came on, rattling from the effort. Ilya turned the taps to the appropriate settings and resumed undressing, shrugging out of the top of his vestments. A warm hand pressed against the center of his back, finger trailing down his spine and making him shiver. He giggled and turned to gently smack Danya's hand away. Danya grinned back at him.

"That tickles, you fiend. And don't make me do all the work, start stripping."

"Oh, we're being bossy now, is that it?" There was a twinkle in

Danya's eye as he lifted his cardigan above his head, tossing it aside in a crumpled pile. Ilya took the time to admire his body, eyes trailing over all the lithe muscle. He'd joked when they first met about Danya being big, but he really wasn't. Danya was a few inches taller and slightly more built at best. It made sense; you had to be light to fly.

"Should just get you that camera so you can stare all you want after all," Danya laughed.

Ilya rolled his eyes. "Like you could sit still long enough. And do you know how expensive those things are? They were 30 crowns last I knew!"

"On the low end maybe. But don't worry about it… Berta pays me fine." Danya remained chipper as he dropped out of the last of his clothes, pinning Ilya to the wall again once he'd done the same. He ground their hips together, friction making Ilya throb to life. Their tongues slid together as they kissed, Danya kissing his throat and sucking hard on the skin between his neck and collarbones. Teeth scraped against his skin, hot tongue laving over the mark to soothe the sting. Ilya wheezed, knees buckling beneath him as a jolt of pleasure ran through him.

It took every ounce of his willpower, but Ilya managed to pry himself away to turn off the water once the tub was full. Steam rose from the surface, fogging the glass of the mirror. Danya panted behind him as Ilya dipped the tips of his fingers into the water, hissing at the temperature.

"Too hot for me," Ilya sighed. Danya loomed behind him. Ilya glanced at him out of his peripherals, calculating for a brief moment.

Danya grunted as *he* was shoved back this time, expression turning owlish when Ilya dropped to his knees.

"Ilyushka?"

"I want to try something for you– do you mind?"

Danya shook his head vigorously. "Absolutely fucking not. I'd be a complete moron to mind at all."

A hand brushed back through Ilya's curls, settling on his cheek. Danya's thumb pressed against Ilya's bottom lip, forcing his mouth open by a fraction. Ilya's tongue brushed against it, holding Danya's gaze. His pale fingers wrapped around the base of his angel's cock, tight and firm. It radiated heat through the palm of his hand, working its way up his wrist and to his chest. Danya licked his lips, forcing his thumb into Ilya's mouth. Ilya wrapped his lips around it and swirled his tongue, stroking Danya in time with the movement.

Ilya broke free of Danya's hand, tongue flicking across the head of his cock, lapping up the salty bead at the tip. A shuddering breath escaped Danya above him. Ilya's pride swelled. His skills weren't at Danya's level, but he was determined nonetheless.

He licked the underside, rubbed the pad of his thumb hard against the head, could feel the rapid pulse of Danya's heartbeat as he throbbed in Ilya's palm. Danya's hand coiled into his hair, pulling tight. It didn't hurt, not exactly, but it was a pleasant tug that made his heart pound. He panted against Danya's skin and went back to stroking him, pressing the head against his tongue.

"Fuck, Ilyushka— you're gonna be the death of me."

Ilya chuckled, eyes sparkling in the low light of the bathroom before he wrapped his lips around him fully. They both shivered, Ilya breathing deep through his nose as he brought Danya into his mouth, swirling his tongue to create more sensation. Danya held tighter to his hair, gasping and slumping back against the bathroom wall.

Determination and far too much energy spurred him on. Ilya bobbed his head on Danya's length, slowly trying to take more of him in. He shuddered when Danya's cock hit the back of his throat, fighting against his gag reflex as tears pricked his eyes.

"Fuck *me*, you don't have to go all the way Lyubimi," Danya gasped. "This is enough for me."

Ilya pulled off of Danya, casting a glare his way. "Do you doubt my capabilities?"

"I'm a lot is all—"

Danya was silenced when Ilya changed the angle of his head, sinking down on Danya until his nose was pressed into the base of his stomach. Danya's musk was strong here and Ilya tried to breathe it in, groaning. Danya swore under his breath, hand slamming against the wall to steady himself. Ilya pressed the heels of his palms into the dip above Danya's hips, forcing them back against the wall. He could do this, but he needed Danya to be still.

Ilya relaxed his throat, letting his shoulders sag as he fought his body. He pulled back, breathing deep through his nose for a beat then sinking down again and again. It was slow and methodical at first, getting used to the sensation of having his throat filled. Danya kept a hold on his hair, grip relaxing and going tight again as he worked. Danya's other hand migrated to his throat, fingers brushing up against the bulge in Ilya's throat.

"When I tell you how much control I'm exerting to not just fuck your pretty priestly mouth," Danya growled. "One day–"

Ilya moaned deep in his chest from the thought, salivating in his want. He'd choke and die if they tried it now, which was a decidedly unsexy thing to do. Still, Danya exerting complete control over him, using his celestial strength to dominate his lowly human form, set his blood alight. He'd love nothing more than to not have to think, to be nothing but a pile of sensations as Danya had his way. Danya loved doing things to him and Ilya loved taking whatever he was given.

Danya caressed Ilya's throat as he kept working, hollowing his cheeks and breathing hard through his nose. It wasn't a firm grip, but Ilya wasn't sure he'd mind if it was.

"I'm getting close, Lyubimi. Can I finish on your pretty face? Fuck you'd look so gorgeous– Know it's a mess though and you hate it but we're gonna have a bath anyway–"

It was true, Ilya hated being filthy more than most things. This wasn't the same, though. This was Danya, this was an angel's pleasure at his mortal hands and he'd wear it with pride. Intentional filth when all he wanted was to be a writhing pile of bliss added to the fantasy.

Ilya pulled off of Danya with a slick 'pop', trail of saliva connecting his lips to Danya's cock. Danya's thumb shoved its way into his mouth again, rubbing against his tongue. Ilya heaved a breathless laugh as a grin spread across his face, eyes a glimmering haze as he crooned, "Do what you want to me, Solnishko."

There wasn't a hint of hesitation. Danya's thumb pried Ilya's jaw open, using his other hand to take hold of himself. He smacked the head against Ilya's mouth, rapidly jerking himself until the first rope splashed across, heat and salt coating his tongue. Danya let go of Ilya's face and shot out more hot slick, scattering on his cheeks and above his eyes. Ilya had to close one to keep from going blind, but he didn't mind. He was utterly debauched and proud that he'd brought Danya off this way. His chest heaved as he gulped down air, eye flicking up to check on Danya.

There was an overwhelming amount of affection on Danya's face considering what he'd just done. It took Ilya by surprise, even more so when Danya cupped his cheek. His thumb swiped away the mess on Ilya's eye, and he was grateful to be able to use both.

"Fuck it, I'm getting a camera for *me*, Ilyushka. I wish I could look at this forever."

Ilya snickered and pushed to his feet, flicking Danya in the center of his chest. "You're very crass. The people will be shocked by how much of a sailor-mouthed, temperamental pervert you are. It's no wonder it took so long for me to realize you're an angel."

Danya snorted, a tightness to his eyes. "I am kind of a shit angel, aren't I?"

Ilya shook his head, placing a quick kiss on Danya's cheek. "Only that your personality isn't anything like we're taught angels are meant to be, but it's part of your charm... I do think you're everything you're *supposed* to be. You're loyal, protective, intelligent... A beacon of hope in the darkness. My perfect angel."

Danya cleared his throat, rubbing at his eyes with the back of his fist. "Yeah, well. You wanna get cleaned up now? And maybe think of how I can return this incredible favor you just did for me."

"Start scrubbing and I'll let you know what I've thought of."

Danya had to force Ilya to not stress when the water splashed over the sides, reminding him of the drain in the floor. Ilya wished he wasn't so neurotic, but he was glad to have Danya now to help keep it in check. He distracted Ilya first by cleaning his face with a cloth, then by scrubbing out his hair for him.

The intimacy of the gesture gave him pause. Ilya had tried to fight it, but Danya told him to stop being weird and let it happen, so he did. His nails scraped against Ilya's scalp as he massaged the soap into his hair, the only noise in the endless quiet around them. Ilya closed his eyes as Danya scooped water with his hands to rinse him off, cupping Ilya's face and lifting it once he was done.

"All clean now… feel better, Ilyushka?"

Ilya nodded, leaning into Danya's touch. He was at peace. He could spend the rest of time in this tub, warm and cared for by the love of his life.

"Wanna do me next?" Danya whispered.

That brought Ilya back to reality. Danya had a lot of hair to clean, but Ilya loved admiring it. Would Danya let him dry and brush it? Would that be too much? Danya was hiding it under a knitted cap and letting it get ratty from working in the junk shop all day. Just once he'd love it to be completely perfect.

Ilya was thorough in cleaning Danya off, loosely setting his arms across his shoulders once he was done. Danya pressed their foreheads together, soft smile on his face. "You still haven't told me how I can pay you back."

Ilya hummed, eyes flicking upward as he ran through his options. "You can let me brush your hair and then fuck me into the mattress. How's that?"

The guffaw told Ilya plenty. "That's it? You're sure? Brushing my hair? Isn't that a favor for *me?*"

"No, you let it turn into a rat's nest so frequently and it makes me sad." Ilya couldn't help pouting about it.

"Yeah, all right. Come on then."

They got the tub drained and wrapped themselves in towels. Danya sat on the foot of the bed while Ilya grabbed a brush. He kneeled behind Danya, running through his hair with his fingers first after patting it dry. Danya grunted with every knot Ilya got stuck on, eventually huffing, "Think it's time to get that brush out, Ilyushka."

Ilya clucked his tongue. "And here I thought this was supposed to be for *my* enjoyment."

Still, he moved along, working meticulously to get through every tangle. Danya's hair practically glimmered in the low lamp light of the room, strands falling through Ilya's fingers like water. These were the silken threads he adored so much, that reminded him of the dawn.

"I do love your hair," Ilya sighed.

"Funny, I like yours too."

Ilya rolled his eyes and hooked his chin over Danya's shoulder. "I don't understand how... It's always a mess, no matter how I brush it."

"It's soft and fluffy... And it's cute when it hangs in your face. Especially when you're sweating." Danya crooned the last sentence, making Ilya roll his eyes again. Danya's appetite was healthy, to put it mildly.

"Well, why don't you get to work on that then, Danulyachka."

There wasn't a second of hesitation as Danya whirled around to pin Ilya to the bed, kissing him so hard he sank back into the comforter. Their fingers were laced together, Ilya's hands shoved against the pillows. Danya's wings encased them, trapping Ilya in a warm, feathery world with just the two of them.

Their hips ground together, Danya's cock resting along Ilya's inner thigh, permeating heat into the sensitive flesh. Ilya sighed as Danya's mouth trailed downward, sucking harsh marks into his skin, teeth scraping against the bruises. Ilya never would've expected an angel to be so *bitey*, but perhaps it was a leftover urge from his curse. Who knew what lingered still? Especially since Ilya was terrible at his job.

Danya pushed Ilya further up the bed as he worked down his body, biting all over his chest, nipping at his stomach, sucking more bruises into the valley of his hip. Ilya shivered as Danya's hot breath ghosted over his cock, twitching to life from all the attention. Danya avoided it, pulling a desperate whimper out of Ilya. His angel chuckled, running his tongue across the soft inner flesh of Ilya's thigh, making yet more marks.

"All mine," Danya whispered. "Only I know—"

Danya forced Ilya's thighs apart, finally mouthing along his length, tongue flicking across the head. Ilya's breathing came in faster, skin clinging to his ribs as his desperation grew. "Danya, please, I want more."

Danya purred back, "But I'm having so much fun."

"I told you to fuck me into the bed, now *hurry up* and *fuck me already—*"

The scrape of the glass bottle of oil on his night stand sent another shiver up Ilya's spine, reeling from anticipation. Danya coated himself generously, sitting up on his knees so Ilya had a clear view. He rubbed the excess against Ilya's hole, three fingers sliding in with ease. Maybe he should've been embarrassed that it was so easy now, but the speed helped when everything felt so urgent from Danya's incessant teasing.

"I never would've expected a priest to be so bratty in bed," Danya laughed.

Ilya's face burned, part embarrassment and part frustration. "Only because you love to draw it out so much! *Simpleton.*"

"Oh yes, please mouth off more! I love you being confident enough to assert yourself. Very sexy of you, in fact."

"I'm never sucking you again if you don't *quit and shove it in—*"

Ilya's words died in his throat, coming out as a garbled moan. Danya pressed in, sliding up to the hilt. His eyes turned up to the ceiling, trying to adjust to being full. He breathed in sharp and short when Danya began to move, brutal pace right off the bat. Their skin slapped together as Danya pounded into him, grinding over his spot with every thrust. The tips of his fingers prickled, nerves fraying at the edges. Danya grabbed for his wrists, pinning them above his head again. Ilya arched his spine, writhing under Danya to put on a show.

Danya let one foot hang off the bed, leveraging his height to adjust the angle he moved. A ragged moan leapt from the back of Ilya's throat, Danya mirroring the sound.

"Lot less mouthy now, Ilyushka."

"Can't think when you're this rough," Ilya gasped. "It's just good."

Danya seemed to take that as his cue to be even rougher. The grip on his wrists tightened just a fraction, ache spreading through his arms and sending a jolt of electricity through his groin. The bites returned as well, teeth digging into his translucent flesh. Ilya's head was in a fog of feeling, pathetic whimpers escaping his lips as he was overwhelmed. He must've had over a dozen marks all over his throat and shoulders, Danya claiming him over and over. Every new sting brought him closer to the edge, sent more heat flowing in his veins until they were white hot.

"I'm close," Ilya whined. "Danya–"

Danya grabbed Ilya's shoulders, pulling out enough that he could flip Ilya onto his stomach. He shoved back inside, forcing a cry out of his partner. Ilya clawed at the pillows desperately as Danya resumed his relentless pace. Danya grabbed a handful of his curls and yanked his head back, forcing his back to arch deep. Ilya's jaw hung slack as he gulped down air, the edges of his vision going fuzzy and dark. His thighs were quaking from the strain and a burn worked up his spine as heat worked its way down his groin. His cock was sandwiched between his stomach and the sheets, the added friction proving to be overwhelming.

His body clenched as he came, hips bucking from the effort. The world went dark for the briefest of moments, fading back to color just as quickly. Danya snarled and slammed into him one last time, spilling into him. Ilya shivered from the sensation, slick heat dripping down his thighs as Danya pulled out roughly.

Ilya collapsed against the bed, face planted into the pillows. Danya flopped next to him, staring at the ceiling as he panted to catch his breath. They didn't speak for a long moment, Ilya finally lifting his head to look over at Danya. Danya's eyes lazily rolled over in their sockets to look back at him, languid grin on his face.

"So how'd I do?"

Ilya huffed a laugh in reply. "I think I have been well and truly *fucked*."

"Good then?"

"Yes, you insufferable angel."

Danya chuckled and moved onto his side, encasing Ilya with a wing once more. Ilya's eyes fluttered shut and he snuggled Danya, hiding his face away against Danya's collarbones. A beat passed before Danya spoke, "Think it's gonna get crowded in the church tomorrow, Ilyushka. Probably the last quiet night we're gonna have for a while."

Ilya groaned at the reminder. So many people would demand Danya's attention, try to keep him to themselves. He knew Danya would come back to him, but the terror the one good thing he had in his life would be taken away held him all the same. What if the people kept them apart? What if the church came and whisked him off to the Capital as some sort of symbol? A storm of emotions roiled inside of him, clearing only when Danya kissed the top of his head.

"I can *hear* you overthinking, Lyubimi. Stop that."

"Or what?"

Danya gently grabbed Ilya's chin, tilting his head up so their eyes met. "There's that bratty mouth of yours again."

Ilya huffed at him. "You didn't answer my question."

"Or I'll rearrange the dishes in the cabinets."

Revulsion wracked his body, nostrils flaring as he inhaled a deep breath. A deep scowl carved itself into his face and he glared at Danya with everything he could muster. He was particular about everything in his life, Danya knew this. The meltdown this would bring on would be of legendary status.

"I hate you for even suggesting that," Ilya hissed.

"But it got you to stop worrying about whatever was on your mind, didn't it?"

Ilya huffed again, rolling over and pulling the covers over himself to block Danya off. He pulled the chain for the lamp, leaving them in complete darkness. Danya snickered and crawled under the covers beside Ilya, wrapping his arms around him in a warm, firm hold. Tension melted out of Ilya's body, sigh escaping through his nose.

Another beat of silence, then Danya asked, "Do you forgive me?"

"Yeah. I suppose."

A shiver ran through him when Danya kissed the back of his neck, holding on to him a bit tighter. Ilya listened to his breathing, slow and steady as sleep overtook his partner. He never knew that such a sound would be so important to him, but it was. Danya meant safety. He didn't have to keep wandering through the Eternal Night that was life; he had a bit of the Eternal Day here with him.

Still, it depressed him to know that tomorrow it would all go to shit.

17

December 30th, 1927

Ilya had been too anxious to sleep. He rose before dawn, gently prying himself out of Danya's grasp. He stretched his arms above his head and yawned, making his way back to the bathroom to clean up the mess from the night and get his vestments back. His neck prickled as he stepped out into the main part of the rectory, but he assumed it was more nervous energy. How could it not be?

He took his time cleaning off, rubbing the icy, winter morning water over his skin. Ilya enjoyed the living heat rock that was his partner, but sometimes the chill was better for clearing the mind. It wasn't fun, exactly, but Ilya felt like he could think straight now. He pulled on his vestments, careful and methodical, one of the most practiced actions of his life. He wasn't sure he'd be able to handle civilian clothing if the day ever came, not when this outfit was like a second skin.

Light was starting to peek over the mountains, turning into his favorite time of the day. He loved watching the sky fade through a rainbow of colors, from deep purple to that brilliant vermillion, to warm orange, pink, and then the blue of the day. It was that midpoint that most reminded him of Danya. Every time he witnessed the sky turning he imagined it was how the sky looked when Danya was born. The break of a new day, a fresh start, hope renewed after the long night had faded away.

That's what he'd done for Ilya. More metaphorically, but still. Velak might as well be a black hole for all the energy they sucked out of the world, but Danya had given him hope that life was still worth living.

A knock on the side window made him shout in surprise, clutching his chest and recoiling as he looked in the direction of the noise. Several faces were pressed against the glass, all people he didn't recognize. Ilya whipped his head around and noticed the other windows were crowded with people as well. He rushed to the front door to lock it in a panic, grateful for the timing as the knob rattled.

The bedroom door slammed open, crashing into the wall as Danya swept out of it in a fury. Even with the glass between them Ilya could hear the crowd gasp. Danya stepped in front of Ilya, great wings spreading open to block him from view.

"Apparently you'll need to close the curtains at night," Danya muttered, his ire turning upon the people as he shouted. "Go the fuck away! Come back for ceremony!"

Danya's feathers stood on edge in his anger, trying to make himself look bigger. Some of the strangers backed away from the windows, but another still rattled at the door.

"We deserve to see the angel you've been hiding!"

Another voice called, "Give him to us, he belongs to all of us!"

The world was spinning around Ilya, ears ringing. They were going to take Danya from him, he would be gone and Ilya would be left alone or killed or worse and everything would be wrong again.

Danya came to the door, pulling it open and grabbing the offending man by the back of his coat, lifting him clear off the ground. The man gagged from the force, the crowd around him gasping.

"Are you deaf, or do you have a death wish? I said go away!"

Danya bodily threw the man across the snowy lawn, nearly

sliding to the cliff's edge. There was a trench in the mud where the man's body had traveled, further evidence of Danya's strength. Once more Ilya was caught between terror and gratitude, deciding gratitude was more appropriate. Danya would never touch him that way, and this strange man could have harmed him. All signs pointed to the townsfolk being willing to attack and kill him, in fact. Memories of the mob who forced him into the woods resurfaced, nausea twisting in Ilya's gut. Would he have to fear for his life at every moment? What would happen to him if he ever had to be without Danya?

Danya kept beating his wings, shouting at the crowd until they dispersed and went elsewhere. Ilya collected himself long enough to lock the door to the rectory, hopefully preventing any more unwanted visitors. He shut all the curtains until Danya came back inside, pulling the curtains over the window in the door. They stood in darkness, Danya's golden freckles twinkling like stars. He reached for the lamp on the side table, pulling the chain to turn it on.

Ilya hugged himself, nails digging into his arms. This was a fear he hadn't known since childhood; wondering what innocuous move would set off the most violent reaction. There was a high possibility his mother would come today as well. She loved having reasons to berate him, and he wasn't sure he could face her. The last time he'd come across her at the market he'd clammed up and run away. He'd been lucky enough to hide in an alley until she gave up, too day drunk to put in a real effort to hunt him down.

There would be nowhere to hide here.

Warmth and the scent of cinnamon, tobacco, and linseed overwhelmed him. Two solid arms wrapped around him, fingers stroking through his mess of curls. Ilya pressed his face deeper against Danya's neck, inhaling a shuddering breath.

"They're going to kill me," Ilya croaked.

"I won't let them. If anybody touches a single hair on your head I'll throw them back down the hill. Or worse. Depends on who it is. Ask me what I wanna do to Ivan."

Ilya's laugh was brief and watery. "I can imagine a lot of things."

"I'd settle for breaking his nose if you let me. Even just a finger, a pinky. Something. If it's the last thing I ever do I want that rat's ass of a man to get what's coming to him." Danya's grip on Ilya went tighter. Not crushing, but even more protective.

"I think it would be very sexy of you to break his whole face, actually, Danylko."

"Sun's sake, don't tempt me. Think Mom would actually be upset with me if I did it unprompted."

Ilya lifted his head, placing a brief kiss on Danya's cheek. "I'm sure she'd forgive you. Knowing Ivan, he'll present you the opportunity to all by himself today."

Danya brushed Ilya's hair back out of his face, calloused thumb swiping across his cheek. Silence hung between them, and the longer it went on the more of Ilya's resolve melted away. His lip quivered, eyes stinging with oncoming tears. He buried his face against Danya's chest, sob bubbling out of mouth. Danya held him close, wings enveloping his body.

"Danya I hate it here– they won't let me be happy–"

Danya whispered back, "We could just leave. I could carry you and we could fly a million miles away from here."

Ilya sobbed again. "The Church would hunt us down to the end of our days. They'd excommunicate me, call me a deserter... We can't win."

Even if they wouldn't be persecuted, Ilya was terrified by the prospect of leaving. This had been his home for his entire life. He barely knew the world outside of it, everything he knew was here. He'd have to leave his church, his memories. His father's grave stood in the yard, and having to leave him behind would kill Ilya. He knew it was foolish, but it was so hard. It was complicated and difficult and he couldn't vocalize it because he knew it was hard to understand how illogical it was.

Ilya took his time crying against his angel instead of expressing his fears, clinging tight to him. It took a long moment, but eventually he'd calmed down, wiping at his eyes with a sleeve and trying to look presentable.

"I'm sure I look like shit," Ilya grumbled.

"You're always handsome to me," Danya whispered back. "But if anybody says anything about it I'll shut them up. My teeth are... unsatisfied."

That worried Ilya. He worried about the curse, if it had truly gone away, if it *could*. "Do you feel like you might revert?"

Danya licked his lips, unable to answer Ilya. The silence dragged on until Ilya sighed, going to start breakfast, cracking eggs into a cast iron pan. "It won't hurt my feelings, Danylko. I know I'm not good at my job... I'm sure some things linger."

"Don't say that, Ilyushka. I don't... I don't know. I know I'm not the same as I used to be. I know there's parts of me still missing... And parts of me that have been filled in by a void. I never used to be so angry... A curse powerful enough to change an angel has to be some of the greatest evil the Realm has to offer, doesn't it? I... Ilya, please don't blame yourself. This is on the man who hurt me, not you trying to fix it."

Ilya looked back at Danya, taking in the pain in his expression. How much did Danya remember? Ilya felt selfish making his pain the focus of their relationship. Danya had lost a lover, a mentor, his charge. His whole life had been taken from him, had been turned into a murderous beast. He'd bother Danya about it after ceremony. In the meantime he asked, "Do you know who it was?"

Danya shook his head, rubbing the heel of his palm against his forehead. "I can get glimpses of his face, but I was changing by the time I got a look. It's all a blur. I just remember being in pain. Emotional, physical... Everything hurt."

Ilya reached out for Danya's hand, entwining their fingers. "I'm sorry. You know you can tell me anything, right? I can be strong for you too."

Danya snorted, bringing Ilya's knuckles to his lips. "Yeah but you're not an immortal Sun being... It's my *job* to protect you. That's why I was made in the first place."

"And I'm a healer. It's *my* job to relieve you of what pains you. Even if it's memories."

That gave Danya pause, large, pupiless golden wells locking on with Ilya's burned out, hollow whites. They were both impossible men who had been hurt by so many things, trying to heal the other and find comfort in them. For a brief moment, Ilya's apprehension disappeared. Perhaps he was exactly the man Danya needed after all, just as Danya was the man for him.

Perhaps it was the intention of Danya's dear Mother, perhaps it was simply happenstance that bound them together. None of it mattered; what mattered was healing through one another. They would come out of this together, stronger together, happier together.

"You are my joy, Solnishko, and from the day we met, I made it my mission to care for you. That hasn't changed."

Danya pressed Ilya's hand to his cheek, holding it as if it was his most prized possession. Perhaps it was. "And I will keep you safe. No matter what happens. You are my charge now, and I won't fail you. I won't."

"I believe you."

They held onto each other for just a moment more, Danya finally parting to get changed. Ilya finished their breakfast, toasting bread to serve their eggs on. Any little thing to keep his mind off the lingering dread, the fear they would be swarmed and his life would be turned upside down.

Pandora's box had already been opened, though. He knew this. There was no putting those demons back, they were out in the world now. Nothing would ever be the same.

"Suppose we should light some candles for ceremony," Danya said upon his return.

Ilya grumbled through bites of egg and toast. "I was enjoying only having to do it for you. I've never had a full church in my life…"

"You'll get through it, Lyubimi. Then we'll have the rest of the day to ourselves."

The optimism was unwarranted, even if it was charming. "Unlikely. But let's get it over with."

A dull roar had developed beyond the door into the church. Ilya wished they'd had time to lock the front doors so they could set up in peace, but alas it would not be so.

"So… how should we do this? People will swarm to see you immediately I'm sure."

"I'll just let you lead the way. If they get rowdy I'll try and look big and scary or something. I'd be happy to toss people out by hand to make a point again too!"

Ilya pinched Danya's cheeks and cooed, "My big, scary angel man."

Danya scowled. His face flushed red from his embarrassment, but he didn't push Ilya's hand away.

"I have the cutest angel the Sun has ever made," Ilya continued. "They don't even know what you're really like."

Danya finally broke, huffing and brushing Ilya's hands away. "Well, hopefully *they* think I'm scary, or we'll have problems."

Ilya gave him one last quick kiss then grasped the doorknob. Anxiety dropped in his stomach like an anvil, sitting in the pit with a powerful weight. Danya touched his shoulder, and Ilya found the strength to open the door.

A hush fell over the church as he stepped out, Danya falling in step behind him. Ilya gazed out at the crowd, eyes crossing from how many people there were. Every pew was filled to the brim, many more standing in the aisles, and more still spilling out the front doors, clamoring to get a view. This couldn't just be people from Velak, surely some were here from Kursiya too. It was too soon for visitors from the Capital, but they'd be here soon enough.

Bile crawled up the back of Ilya's throat, acid licking his tongue as he swallowed it down. They both worked to light the candles around the altar, whispers among the crowd slowly returning. Ilya did his best to not hear any of it, taking his place behind the altar, Danya just off to his side behind him. He pulled out the great tome that was their gospel, panicking as he flipped through the pages. Shit, what lesson would he even teach from today?

Scarlet hung in his peripheral, and it became clear then. No better lesson than the hope of the dawn.

Ilya grabbed his book of hymns, telling everybody what page to turn to. He hoped the booklets left in the pews hadn't molded, but frankly he wouldn't be surprised if they were just frozen shut. They hadn't had time to start the fire behind the altar, and with the front door open, the freeze was obvious. Maybe next time they'd have help to at least close the doors.

Ilya signaled for the crowd to start the hymn, waiting a beat until joining. Danya's eyes bore holes into him the second he started; his cheeks warmed from it. He'd never sang in front of Danya, much too shy to do it in front of one person. This way his voice could be drowned out, the meek, scratchy sound lost in a flood of stronger voices. He'd grown up enjoying the hymns, but after his father's death, his mother would shout at him for making such terrible, shrieking noise. If she was in a particular mood, she might beat him for it, claiming he sounded too much like his father. On her worst days, she would choke him, wishing he'd stop breathing, accusing him of enjoying his father's death, of trying to take his place.

He'd lost much of his voice after that.

Even still, he could hear his voice echoing throughout the church. It had to be the acoustics of the building, carrying him above the rest. The building was much too large for its own good, an immodest spectacle as much as Ilya was. Especially now, having every possible seat filled, it was much too big. Ilya would not claim to be a fan of giving sermon to this many people, and he futilely hoped they would all see how bad of a job he did and not bother coming back, angel or no.

The song ended, a quiet applause going through the church. Behind him, Danya's hands clapped firmly. He barely caught the faintest whisper, "You sound beautiful."

Ilya swallowed hard. He refused to believe that. Danya was his partner; he was supposed to lie to him and inflate his ego.

He flipped through the tome again, settling on the proper part of the manuscript. He inhaled deep then began to read.

"In dawn we find the eternal gift that is the rising Sun. The Sun is eternal, and She will always be with us. She brings us life, warmth, and light. There is always hope in a new day, a new start. Dawn can be found at all points in our lives, marking new beginnings.

"Velak has come to know one of the Sun's greatest beings, that of an angel. He is the dawn itself. He is hope where this town only recently knew nothing but darkness, haunted by a creature of the endless night. He is a protector, with strength enough to shield us from harm.

"He is the most profound representation of the Sun's love for all the creatures that live under Her light. A perfect being."

The crowd murmured as he spoke, whispers of "finally!" passing through. Ilya glanced at Danya, the two of them exchanging a nod. Danya spread his wings in a great flourish, as wide as they'd go. They were a burst of light behind him, white hot fire that faded into rust colored embers. The morning light filled the room, feathers glittering under the rainbows of stained glass. Ilya regarded their majesty, resisting the urge to stroke his fingers across the surface. In a way it was a shame that he would be the only one to know how soft the feathers were.

Danya stepped in front of the altar, blocking Ilya from view. Ilya sighed in relief, sagging against the stone. "Thank you," he whispered to Danya.

A hand appeared behind Danya's back, Ilya taking it gratefully. Nobody could see them touching, it would be fine. He just needed this small thing, that was all. If worse came to worse, it could be passed off as a reassuring touch between friends. All would be well.

"So my mistake has hidden this creature from us all!" called a familiar voice.

Danya's feathers stood on end without hesitation, snarling under his breath as Ilya's blood ran cold. He knew that voice, knew what it was capable of. His body shook violently, fear wracking him in a way that even the pain of death at the hands of the drekavac hadn't. Ilya lost his grip on Danya's hand, gasping for air that wouldn't come. He held onto the stone of the altar desperately, watching the world spin around him.

She hadn't seen him yet, Danya wouldn't let her, but her frequent drunken stupors made her bold enough to rush at Danya anyway. A man in the crowd shouted, "Hey, you can't just approach a holy being that way!"

"The priest is my son and I'll do as I please!" Irina spit, kicking the pew as she passed. "You hid him from us, you absolute cretin! Out of my way, you traitor, show me that thing I birthed! He needs to be punished!"

Ilya caught a glimpse of his mother from behind Danya's feathers, her pale blonde hair a mess as ever, vomit stains down the front of her white and gold dress, the uniform of a priest's wife. Her black eyeshadow was smudged and melted into the creases of her lids, perhaps applied fresh days ago when she was sober enough to remember to retouch it. She was every bit as familiar as the day he left, given a few more wrinkles and some deep frown lines.

Drool pooled under his tongue, his stomach flipped, and the world still swayed around him. His body wanted to purge its fear, but Ilya couldn't allow himself to be embarrassed in front of so many people. He couldn't look like his mother. His body held so much shame, but that was a burden he refused to bear.

Adrenaline pulsed in his veins, telling him to run, to hide under the altar, to do anything, but he was frozen in place. So much for fight or flight.

Ilya could sense the heat of Danya's rage building, reaching for something at his hip that wasn't there. What had he tried to grab?

"You need to leave," Danya growled, "Right now."

"I'm his *mother*, you can't stop me even if you are an angel!"

The crowd roared in protest, some rising from the pews to grab for Irina and pull her back. She screamed in rage, kicking her feet and thrashing as she was pulled away. Danya stepped down from the altar, beating his wings to send a gust of wind out across the swarm of people, their agitation rising.

"Leave! All of you, now!" Danya's voice boomed through the chamber like thunder, louder than Ilya had ever heard him. He sounded unlike himself, an authority that was unfamiliar.

"You're a disgrace!" Irina screamed. "Pavel would've never stopped ceremony early! Useless child, pathetic boy! YOU CAN'T DO ANYTHING RIGHT!"

Danya surged forward, grabbing Irina by the front of her dress and lifting her above the crowds. They gasped in awe while Ilya tried to keep his vision focused. His mother was nothing more than a violent banshee writhing in Danya's grip. He carried her to the door, tossing her out into the snow, tumbling down the steep, snowy, muddy hill.

Danya turned upon the churchgoers, that commanding presence in his voice echoing across the nave. "Know this! Our great Mother, *my* Mother, placed me on this Earth to protect those she deems worthy, and I will not hesitate to do so! If you cannot behave as Her children, then you will not be welcome in this house of worship. Now leave, and think on what you can do to prove yourself to Her!"

The crowd jeered and complained, the voice of Ivan rising above them. "He must be a fake! That damned priest has tricked us to get in our good graces again! Liar! Get him!"

Ivan rushed from the group towards the altar. Ilya pulled himself away from the stone, stumbling back, trying to reach for the door to the rectory. It wouldn't matter, though; they'd tear him apart, they'd break down the door. Nowhere was safe.

Ilya had hardly taken a step back when a sick crunch rang out through the hall, sending the room silent. Danya stood in front of him, holding Ivan by the back of his head, which he had slammed into the stone. Blood pooled under Ivan's face, following the lines carved into the altar. Ilya stared at the mayor, the man who'd made it his mission to make his life a nightmare.

Danya yanked Ivan's head back, revealing the red mess that was his face. Ivan's nose was squashed flat against his face, several of his front teeth missing, his forehead and cheeks scraped up from the stone.

Danya leaned down to hiss directly in Ivan's ear, "I've had enough of you, *kozyol.* I'll say this one more time only. Get. Out. Don't ever come back here. Don't even *think* of it. If you were smart, you'd resign, but I know you're not, so just know that if you try to gang up on Ilya again, you're the first I'm looking for. Got it?"

Ivan groaned in response, spluttering blood on the altar and the front of Ilya's vestments. Ilya's skin prickled in disgust, hands itching to scrub his body clean. He wanted to claw his skin off, debating doing the same to Ivan for making such a mess. Nothing like one's own violently disproportionate neuroses to clear the mind.

"I will consider healing you if you leave and take all of your like-minded cronies with you. I won't ask for an apology, because you'd probably keel over and die for even considering it. Do we have a deal?"

Ivan nodded weakly, whimpering as Danya tightened the grip on his hair. Ilya decided it was answer enough, pressing two fingers to Ivan's forehead. The symbol of the Sun formed around his wrist, glowing bright and golden. He concentrated first on Ivan's nose, wincing from the cracking as it shifted back into place. His teeth slowly grew back in, though Ilya took no care to make sure they were as straight as before. Finally the wounds on his face closed, skin knitting together and leaving behind pale, shiny scars.

Ilya gasped for air as he pulled his hand back, sweat coating his brow. He was out of practice and Ivan's injuries were severe. Ivan didn't deserve it, but if it kept him from acting up again, so be it. He could show mercy if it guaranteed his safety.

Ivan's eyes locked with Ilya's, filled to the brim with terror.

Good.

Ivan yanked out of Danya's grasp, stumbling back to the churchgoers that retreated with him. "Good riddance, you freaks. The law will deal with you. I don't need to come back here to see your priest's neck in the noose. Go back to living in sin!"

Ilya managed to grab Danya's sleeve in time to prevent his surge forward. Ilya wasn't even remotely strong enough to hold him back, but Danya respected his wish for restraint. A deal was a deal, regardless of Ivan's threats.

"Not if I break your neck first!" Danya shouted. "My Mother will see you left in the Realm for the life of hate you lead!"

The people finally dispersed and left the church. Danya locked the main doors and rushed back to Ilya. Nausea gripped Ilya once the adrenaline coursing through his veins began to subside. Danya dragged him back into the rectory without a word, and once they'd passed the threshold, Ilya collapsed onto his hands and knees to spill his guts.

It had been half an hour of sheer terror gripping him. His body found release, tension melting out of his shoulders as he spit acid onto the floor. Danya kneeled beside him, rubbing the area between his shoulders. Ilya sat on his haunches once he'd finished, wiping at his mouth with a sleeve. Ivan had already got blood on it, however little. If he was already filthy it didn't matter, it would be the same to clean anyway.

Danya waited a beat and grabbed a towel from the kitchen, wiping up Ilya's sick. He set it aside, scooping Ilya into his arms and bringing him to bed, making sure he laid on his side. Danya sat next to him, stroking his forehead.

"What a twist of fate... Now you're caring for me," Ilya grumbled.

"I've always cared for you, Ilya."

Heat rose to his cheeks, thankfully for more pleasant reasons. Danya continued to soothe him, touch light. Ilya's embarrassment refused to subside. He was weak, letting his mother instill such fear in him after all these years, letting Ivan antagonize him as he had. Even if he'd stood up to him in this moment, Ilya knew Ivan would make good on his word. There would be an investigation, the Church would find him guilty of loving another man, and then he'd find a short drop and sudden stop.

"I hate everybody here," Danya hissed. "Especially Ivan and that woman. I'm sorry, Ilyushka..."

Ilya's eyes fluttered closed. He focused on Danya's touch, those broad, strong hands cupping his cheek. They would be his anchor point.

"I hate that you saw me like that. I'm a ridiculous child."

"Hard to be an adult when you get treated like that."

Ilya groaned, pressing his face into Danya's palm. As much as Danya had fought him, Ivan was right. It was the most awful ceremony anybody in town had been to, surely, even before his mother ruined everything. He was a sham of a priest. He'd never live up to his father's name; he'd conceded this long ago.

"Ilyushka," Danya whispered, "I can hear you thinking too hard again."

"No you can't," Ilya grumbled back. "Angels can't hear *shit*."

Danya scoffed, laying down and pulling Ilya's face into the crook of his neck. A pathetic whimper escaped Ilya, hiding away against Danya. He kissed Danya's pulse point, chest rumbling as he hummed.

"I think you should take it easy today," said Danya.

Ilya snorted. "You? Not wanting physical intimacy?"

"Think this is plenty physical intimacy, Lyubimi."

Ilya curled his body against Danya's. The slung arm and cage of feathers returned, sheltering Ilya from the world. Danya buried his nose in Ilya's curls. He breathed him in deep, letting out a dreamy sigh. Ilya was at peace.

"You're very cute like this, Ilyushka."

"I'm not cute. I'm a crabby hardass."

"Your ass is actually pretty soft last I checked."

Ilya snorted and gently smacked Danya's chest. "Fuck you."

"I thought I told you to take it easy!"

Ilya broke into a fit of giggles, rolling onto his back as he tried to get himself under control. He looked at Danya, cheeks growing warm again. Danya's grin was as bright as the Sun, golden eyes sparkling in the shaded room. His angel's beauty enraptured him. He was falling in love all over again.

Danya brushed Ilya's curls out of his eyes, kissing his forehead.

"Thank you for dealing with me," Ilya whispered. "Even when I'm a total disaster."

Danya scoffed again. "The only disaster is that sad excuse for a woman who claims to be your mother only when it's most advantageous to her. And who gets drunk at seven in the morning anyway? Gotta be fucking kidding me."

"This is late for her, believe it or not... I'm more surprised she called me her child. Most of the time I'm just a "thing" to her. Or "mistake", if you prefer. Can't remember the last time she used my name. But... I appreciate you not smashing her face on the altar."

"Mm. Well, hopefully a tumble down the hill will compel her to not return. It's not the least of what she deserves."

"I know, just... It's going to sound so stupid, but she's still my mother. A part of me still hopes that maybe one day she'll love me like she used to. That she'll still be my mother... I can't bring myself to hate her." Ilya paused and frowned, contemplating what he was saying. "I know that makes no sense."

"I don't think I have parents like humans do, being what I am, so I can't say I understand. I don't know that I can... but I trust you know your own mind. And... I guess it amazes me that despite everything, there's still even a scrap of hope in your heart for her. You have so much more love to give than anybody gives you credit for, you know that? That's what's so wonderful about you."

Ilya's voice was small as he spoke, "I don't know about that, Danylko."

"Yeah, well, I do. It's pretty clear everybody expects you to be a terrible person, a lazeabout. Hardly better than a murderer from how they talk about you... But you're not. Sometimes I worry that you've allowed yourself to agree with them."

Ilya stared down at Danya's chest. He couldn't meet his eyes anymore. He didn't want to tell his partner he was wrong, that everything he was saying was complete nonsense, so he went silent.

"Not many people would've healed a night creature," Danya whispered, lips nearly pressed to Ilya's ear so he couldn't keep trying to escape. "I think it takes a special kind of person to do something like that."

Ilya's eyes stung with tears that he fought to hold back. He rolled onto his side, trying to escape all the kindness Danya was drowning him in.

"You're better than all of them," Danya continued. "Despite what they think, despite what *you* think, you embody the ideals that you're meant to follow. I mean fuck, I'm an *angel* and you do a better job. You're so incredible, Ilyushka, and I fucking love every part of you, whether you like it or not."

Ilya choked on a sob, high-pitched and pathetic sound escaping from between his pressed lips. It was all too overwhelming, being showered in all these words. His shoulders ached from how tense they were, bodily refusing to take in everything his lover spoke. It was all too much.

A warm palm traveled down his back, settling on his hip. Danya wasn't forcing himself closer, but the heat kept Ilya grounded.

"I hate how much I fucking cry since I found you," Ilya confessed. "Fuck you."

"I love that you're willing to cry. I love that you don't hold back, I love that despite how everybody in town wants you to be you continue to be yourself. I love you, Ilya."

"Stop," Ilya choked, "Stop…"

Danya went silent, keeping his hand on Ilya as he kept crying. He'd never felt so much sincerity. He never imagined he could have a partner who accepted him as he was, for everything he was, who wouldn't change a thing.

Ilya rolled back to face Danya, grabbing his face to pull him into a kiss. He sobbed despite himself, Danya taking care to kiss the tears off his cheeks. Ilya hiccuped and sniffled, breath shaky as he tried to calm himself. He was disgusting. His mouth still tasted acrid and now there was snot running down the back of his throat.

Danya didn't press further, for which Ilya was relieved. It was hard to believe anything he'd said. Danya wouldn't lie to him, but the words couldn't reach him. His mind couldn't process them, no matter how much Danya insisted it to be the truth.

"I'm a mess," Ilya sobbed. "I hate this. You still want to kiss a dumb, snotty human man, you Sun forsaken bird brain?"

"*Yeah?* What kind of question is that?" Danya said it as though Ilya had asked him if the sky was blue.

To prove his point, Danya pinned Ilya to the bed by his shoulders, capturing his lips in a slow, deep kiss. The press of Danya's mouth was firm but not demanding. Warm, but not hot, not pushing too far. It wasn't asking any more of him, only showing affection.

They stayed like this for what felt like hours, rolling around in bed and doing nothing but kissing, touching each other, clothes still on. They were locked together in this moment of tenderness and Ilya's heart grew fonder with every passing moment.

Danya was on his back when Ilya finally broke the kiss, panting for air and pressing his face into Danya's shoulder.

"I love you too," Ilya mumbled. "I didn't say it earlier. But I love you too."

Danya rested his hands on the small of Ilya's back and nuzzled against his head. "You never have to say it back. I already know. I'll always know."

"How did I get so lucky to have you as the love of my life?"

"I could ask you the same question. Rest, Ilyushka. It's already been a long day."

Ilya sighed. "Yeah…"

He threw off his vestments and crawled under the covers with Danya, curling up against his body again.

This was where home would be. If the Church came for them, if town came for them, if the whole world decided it was against them. Danya was right where Ilya wanted to be.

18

February 26th, 1928

In the following weeks Ilya had to deal with yet more rumors about him and Danya, this time that they were involved with one another. They were less offensive this go around if only because they were true, but the terror of being found out was palpable, sticky on the back of his tongue. Ivan's shouting put them in a serious bind, whispers of reporting them passing through the town. The only sign that something was amiss was from that first day in the church. An angel too defensive of a supposed friend to be reasonable, Danya stumbling out of Ilya's bedroom, Ilya leaving his bedroom nude in the first place.

After that, they hardly so much as looked at each other in public. If they had to leave the house, they did so one at a time to avoid all temptations. No unconscious affections, no pet names, nothing. Ilya refused to tempt fate. For his part, Danya was also highly unwilling to risk his partner.

Ilya had been looked upon with contempt his whole life in Velak. It was hard to tell if there was any new and fresh animosity amongst the old standard. Danya could hardly leave to work in the shop without being swarmed. Berta was apparently incensed that he'd wanted to keep working, considering his status, but Danya insisted he'd be too bored otherwise. Eventually Berta appreciated the business; the trick of buying something in order to see a living angel did wonders for the shop.

There existed a tension between Danya and Berta. The same could be said for Ilya and Oyuna. Both women in their lives were important figures, people whom they trusted above all else. They had to remain secret, but having nobody else to talk to was wearing on both of their souls. They agreed to share with them, and only them. Ilya was ambivalent about Berta, but Danya insisted that she adored him, and was even coming to care for Ilya. He chose to believe her.

Oyuna had cared for Ilya his whole life. Beyond grandmother, she'd been more of a mother figure to him than his own. When he could finally manage to escape his mother's tirades, Oyuna was the first to give him a hot meal and ice his bruises. If there was anybody in town he cared about as much as Danya, it was her.

He had to tell her.

ILYA LABORED into the night making croissants from scratch, waking early to get them baked. While his partner had never been an early riser, he got up for the smell of fresh pastries. Ilya was moving them to a cooling rack when Danya emerged from the bedroom.

Danya was squinting to cope with the early morning light, coming over to Ilya and examining his work. Ilya's heart fluttered at the sight; a sleepy angel was something to behold.

Danya grumbled at him incoherently, making Ilya laugh. "Try again, Solnishko?"

"Not feeling like sunshine this early... But these smell really good. When can we have them?"

"They need to cool for another moment, forgive me."

Danya whined, head lolling around his shoulders in a fit. "Ilyushenka I'm hungry *now*..."

Ilya took Danya's chin between his thumb and forefinger, lifting his head to give him a quick kiss. "You're very cute when you're whiny."

Danya used a wing to smack Ilya's side and Ilya laughed again, devolving into a giggling fit. He squished Danya's cheeks between both of his hands, forcing Danya's lips to pucker and smooching them quickly. Ilya loved being the morning person in the relationship, seeing Danya this groggy and useless was endearing.

Danya grumbled against Ilya's mouth, shoving him back against the counter and kissing him deeper. Danya's hand settled on Ilya's hip, but he made no further moves. The morning sun was pouring into the kitchen, he was surrounded by the smell of baked goods, and his indescribably handsome partner was making out with him. This was the life he'd always dreamed of having made into reality.

It didn't get better than this.

Ilya lost track of how long they kissed, but his lips were swollen and puffy by the time Danya reached behind him to steal a croissant off the rack. Danya dashed away, wings flapping once more as he perched on the back of the couch with his prize. He stuffed his mouth with the pastry, groaning as he spilled flakes over everything.

Mouth full and speech muffled, Danya groaned, "Oh fuck, this is amazing."

"Danulyachka you are making a *mess*—"

"I'll clean it later, I promise. *You* eat now, you bird."

Ilya scoffed. "There's only one bird here. Or maybe you're more of a gargoyle, hunched over like that."

Danya shrugged, flapping his wings and sending the crumbs onto the floor. Ilya told himself that at least they'd be easier to sweep up. He distracted himself by making tea, biting into his own pastry while he waited for the water to boil.

"I don't know if I mentioned it," Ilya said, "But these are for Oyuna… I wanted to visit her today and tell her. I'm nervous but… I need to do this."

"I understand. I guess… I could tell Berta as well. Honestly, I think she already knows…"

"You know we can't be seen together right now, Danylko."

"Yes, but I can fly before we get into town. Nobody has to see us. We can just meet on the path back and talk about everything. Is that okay?"

It was hard to be okay with much of anything lately, but Berta meant the world to Danya. Telling her now or the next day wouldn't matter, the results would likely be the same.

The days were getting longer, but their world was as dark as midwinter. What would it hurt to find a light in all of this?

Ilya sighed. "All right. Let's go then, and make sure to lock up tight. Surprised nobody's tried to break in yet."

"After throwing people around that first day, they don't want to test me. I'm very willing to do more, by the way. I'm *over* this."

"Yes, well, let's hope it doesn't come to that." Ilya packed his croissants in a fabric lined basket, throwing in a jar of jam for good measure. It wasn't anything he'd made, for which he was disappointed in himself, but in his heart of hearts he doubted Oyuna would notice a difference.

Once they'd both gathered their things to be ready for the day, they locked up and began the tense, quiet journey into town. In spite of Ilya's worries, the path was pleasant. The snow had begun to melt away, the deciduous trees smattered through the woods forcing tiny, green leaves to line their branches. Spring was crawling its way back. He had to admit it was refreshing to see the Sun again.

While he was a priest of the *Eclipse*, the unity between Mother Sun and Father Moon, the Sun was his favorite celestial body. She had given Ilya the greatest gift of his life in the form of Danya. For that, he would spend all eternity in gratitude. One day when he could finally stand by Her side, he would be able to tell Her just how much Her incredible son meant to him.

Standing next to him, Ilya was curious if there were angels of the Moon as well, or if night creatures choked them out. The Moon did His best in the fight against the night, and many things did thrive in the dark, but He wouldn't be half the being without the light from the Sun. Perhaps angels were exclusively Her realm after all. He'd have to look into it when he had time; perhaps Oyuna would have some insight.

VISITING OYUNA WAS ALWAYS A TRIAL. Ilya adored her, but her proximity to his mother's house terrified him. After Danya threw her out of the church, the sickness that washed over him intensified. He paused just outside the alley to Oyuna's place, leaning against the building to stabilize himself. He clutched the basket of croissants to his chest as his body quaked.

After counting to ten at least a dozen times, Ilya finally found the courage to peek down the walkway. His mother wasn't usually awake this early, and that proved true still. Relief came in the form of his stomach untwisting. He stepped up to Oyuna's door as silent as he could, knocking gingerly.

Quick, pattering footsteps came from behind the door before it opened. Oyuna grinned and cheered, pulling Ilya into a hug. Her face was pressed into his sternum, which was awkward with his uniform, but it was brief.

"Father Sokolov, what a surprise! Come in, come in." She ushered him inside and to the kitchen, swiping his pastry basket to set on the table.

Ilya took care to wipe his boots at the door, then came to sit across from her at the table. "I hope you like the treats I brought. There should be jam too."

Oyuna carefully undid the cloth, gasping at the sight. She waddled off to grab utensils and plates, fine white china painted with pale pink roses and sage green leaves coiling around the rim. Ilya set a croissant on each of their plates and settled in, spreading jam across his and taking a bite. He was grateful they were still warm despite the long journey into town.

Oyuna hummed around her bite, nodding in approval. The apples of her cheeks were plump and tickled pink from how big the smile on her face was. Ilya's chest swelled with pride.

"I still remember everything you taught me, babushka," Ilya said. "Those came out of the oven just this morning. I hope you like them."

"Just incredible, Ilyushka. You should be proud of this batch. Did our new resident angel get to try any?"

"He did! He swiped the first one when they hadn't finished cooling. Temperature never seems to affect him much."

Oyuna gave a sage nod. "I see, I see. I regret not coming to see you both yet, but the shop has suddenly been so busy with so many visitors. I can't remember so many people ever being in this little town! But it's not every day a child of the Great Mother lives in your church, is it? And he's been under our noses this whole time! Why did you keep him hidden for so long?"

A sharp pain lanced through Ilya's heart, spreading through his arms. Oyuna had met Danya, had seen him just as he was starting to change. Surely she'd seen him around town after the fact too. He was constantly running errands after work, out in the open. The question hurt him in a way he couldn't describe. It was the kind of question he'd expect to hear from Ivan, not her.

"It wasn't intentional, I promise. I didn't know what he was until the wings sprouted from his back." Ilya wasn't sure what to think now. Could he trust Oyuna with the truth? Could he truly depend on her? No, she wouldn't forsake him this way. It was just an extreme situation. That was all.

"Mm, well, he didn't seem very angelic, did he? Always smoking and drinking with that Berta, tinkering with whozits and whatsits. Of course you didn't know. Though I won't claim to know how the Sun or Her children work, that's your realm of expertise, isn't it? But no matter! It's not often you find the courage to visit, young Ilya. May I ask for the reason?"

Ilya swallowed. He clenched a fist, nails digging into the mound of his hand. He could do this. He had to do this. "Well, I was actually going to ask you about him... I do wonder what She thought when She was making Danya. You might have heard about the... kerfuffle on that first day. He's protective of me, he says that was his job from before I found him."

Oyuna's eyes were already large and owlish behind her way-too-thick glasses, but they went even bigger in her surprise.

"Really? Do you know who it was he was protecting? Or what, perhaps, who knows what sacred artifacts lie hidden about the world. Though it must not be important enough if he hasn't gone back to do it yet. Or did he fail?" She paused when the words tumbled out of her mouth, clutching a hand to her chest. "Dear me, there I am making assumptions on the part of the Sun and Her children again. I'll have to come in later for repentance. I apologize for my verbosity, Father."

Ilya bit the inside of his cheek. He'd have time to explain everything to her later, he was sure. It was fine. "It's all right, babushka, no harm done. But back to the matter at hand, I... It's been nice, having him around. Less lonely. I'm complete."

"Yes, yes, you're always all alone there in your church, hardly even coming to town." Oyuna waved her hand at him, rolling her eyes. It was a conversation they'd had many times, and she didn't understand why he isolated himself from the rest of Velak. Never mind the fucking hill. "I don't know how you'll ever find a wife sequestering yourself away like that, young man, but I'm glad you finally have a friend."

Ilya only just managed to suppress a wince. He fidgeted with his hands under the table, worrying his fingers over his cuticles and pushing them back until they were raw. The sting kept him grounded.

He felt smaller than a mouse.

"I've never really been interested in women, you know this. Nobody in Velak really... suits me."

Oyuna nodded in affirmation. "That much is true, yes. You should go on a sabbatical to the Capital, find a nice girl who wants to get away from the city. There's bound to be enough satisfactory ones! I'm sure you'd get plenty of attention if you brought your angel friend with you too. Perhaps he could find a wife as well. Do angels even marry? I suppose I should look back at the scripture again..."

Ilya wasn't actually sure if angels married, something he may or may not have researched in the days since Danya had been realized, but it was beside the current point.

Where the collar of his vestments had once been a comfort, it suffocated him now. It was wrapped tight around his throat. He dipped two fingers under it, pulling it away from his pulse point, and still Ilya choked on air. She didn't understand.

But she *would* understand.

"Actually, Oyuna… I have someone. I'd been meaning to tell you for a while now, but I only found the heart to do it today."

Oyuna's face fell, shame in her expression. "Oh, my boy, my Ilyushka… I don't know why you felt like you had to hide her from me, but I assure you that your happiness means everything to me." She scooted her chair closer to him, smile brightening. "So tell me all about her! What's her name?"

Ilya wanted to vomit.

"It's Danya."

Acid licked at the back of his throat and bubbled in his stomach. He wanted to burst out of this house and toss himself off the cliff into the river gorge. This wasn't going how he wanted, he knew it already.

Oyuna's expression fell into absolute neutrality, betraying nothing and everything all at once. Ilya shattered into a thousand pieces from her silence, tensed his shoulders so she wouldn't see him shaking.

"Father Sokolov," not Ilyushka, not my boy, not even just Ilya, "I'm happy for you. You've always been a very sad, lonely boy."

He should be so lucky that this was her reply, all things considered. It wasn't hatred, she hadn't turned around and beat him to death with a rolling pin. It wasn't complete rejection either; he hadn't been asked to leave, never to see her again. She even said she was happy for him.

Then why was he so empty?

Ilya found the courage to croak out, "So you're okay with us?"

"I know you've been without a good male figure in your life since your father died, and your mother being the witch that she is certainly hasn't guided you," Oyuna said, tears wetting her eyes. "I'm very sorry you won't have any children of your own. I had hoped to help raise more grandchildren…"

Ilya's body was coiled tight like a spring, ready to snap at any second. There was too much tension, too much pain. He felt like an ant crushed under a thumb, nothing but a pile of viscera left under a massive weight. He desperately needed her approval, her love. If he didn't have Oyuna, what was he left with?

"Oyuna. Please. You approve of our relationship, yes?"

"I want you to be happy, Father Sokolov. That's all."

It shouldn't have come to this for Ilya to realize he was an orphan.

Yet here he was.

Ilya shoved his chair back and stormed out the door without another word. Oyuna didn't say a thing to him as he left, which made it all the worse.

DANYA WAS PERCHED HIGH in a tree, watching Ilya make his way into the town square, then disappear from view as he turned towards Oyuna's shop. He worried for Ilya. He always did, but there was a fresh nervous energy to the day that he couldn't place.

He heaved a beleaguered sigh, flapping his wings rapidly as he landed on the forest floor. Pine needles and dead growth from the winter crunched underfoot as he walked onto the path into town, trying to draw as little attention to himself as possible. Flying was so much faster and convenient. That said, when you had a horde of out-of-towners swarming you the second you landed because they could spot you from a mile away, it became a game of pros and cons. For how important today was, Danya decided being stealthy was the better approach.

He'd borrowed one of Ilya's cloaks, hoping he could sneak to the junk shop without being seen. There were some suspicious whispers, but he managed to dash in without notice.

The bell above the door jingled, signaling Berta, wherever she might be hidden. Danya stepped into the maze of stuffed shelves, tossing his hood back once the door had clicked shut again. "Babushka! I know it's my day off, but Ilya had business in town and I want to talk to you."

"Just a moment!" She called out to him from his workshop in the back. A metallic clang of bells came from the room, sounding an awful lot like the alarm clock he'd been repairing, which was already an uncommon find around here. He recalled one in Tatyana's shop, but she'd been ahead of the curve.

"You better not be breaking my shit you hag! I was going to use that!"

"Don't you start with me boy! You're lucky you make me so much money now!"

Danya chuckled as she stormed out into the front, eyes narrowed at him in suspicion. Berta was wiping her hands off on a rag, black grease staining the dingy gray cloth.

"Now why on Earth are you dressed like that, hm? Hiding from everybody?"

Danya guided her to the pile of milk crates in the back, pulling several out so they could sit. Danya patted the second pile and Berta did as instructed.

"I have something important to talk to you about, and I didn't want anybody bothering us. It's... I know it's fucking impossible for us to have a serious conversation, but I wanna try for this, okay?" Danya twisted his wrist inside his other hand, rubbing the skin as the air grew tense. Berta had a tough shell, but inside was soft and tender. They insulted one another and shouted, but at the end of the day they cared about one another. Berta would understand, he was positive.

Berta's back straightened, attentive as Danya spoke. "This must be serious if you're getting this bothered. Tell me then, what is it?"

Danya slammed his eyes shut, brow furrowed as he ruminated on how to say it all. He hadn't put much thought to it. Being blunt was probably for the best.

"Ilya and I are together. Romantically. We're... romantically involved. I love him. And I just... needed you to know that. Because I love you too." A pause, then he spluttered, "Not in the same way! Just... I know I have my Mother and all, but... if I have one on Earth, it's you. And I needed you to know about us."

Berta was stunned into silence, lips parted in shock. She closed her mouth, nodding and staring at the floor. She worried her lip, nodding several times before meeting Danya's eyes again. "I had a feeling. I heard the rumors about what happened on that first day at the church, but even how you moved around him in your home... It was too familiar. The way you've talked about him to me has been so fond. You'd get testy with me if I said a negative word after that night you met with his mother... I should've known."

Berta went silent again. Danya chewed over her words, trying to gauge how she felt. She wasn't yelling at him, she didn't seem any more distant. She seemed disappointed, maybe, but not with him, from what he could tell. That had to be a good sign, right?

"So... you're okay with it? You're not gonna try and have him hanged or some shit? Report me to the church or something?"

Berta was utterly scandalized, smacking his arm in her anger. "*Zhopa!* Do you not know me at all?"

Danya hissed at the smack, rubbing his arm to soothe the skin. "Answer the question then you insufferable old woman!"

"I love you like a son, you shitty brat of an angel!" She leapt off her pile of crates, moving into his space to glare at him even harder. "Nothing you say or do would ever make me love you less, Danya. You've been a bright light in this old woman's life. Life has been a nightmare since Andrei passed, and then you showed and woke me up. You've given me happiness I never thought I could have again. If you've found somebody who's making you happy in the same way, then Sun's sake, I'm glad."

It was Danya's turn to be stunned into silence. His vision blurred with tears and he cleared his throat. He hadn't been expecting sincerity like that from Berta, but it meant the world to him. "You don't mind that he's your least favorite person in town?"

Berta heaved a sigh. "You know I apologized and said I was wrong, and I stand by that. I saw how scared that boy was that me or Ivan would find him out, even with how clearly he wanted to be close to you. Does he love you as much as you love him?"

Danya nodded firmly. "Without a doubt in my mind. He kept trying to push me away at first, but it was because he felt unworthy. Ilya decided he wasn't worthy of love long ago... I had to force it out of him, but once he let go it was amazing. Every time I can make him smile, hear his laugh... Even the most lilting voice on the radio can't compare. But he could probably outsing some of them too.

"I didn't even know he could sing until that day at the church. Every time he comes out of his shell a little more, becomes more of who he really is, I just want to kiss him. He's surprised every time I do. I don't think he ever believed he'd find love, which is why I'm even more glad that I can give it to him. I owe him my life... I could spend the rest of his life devoted to him and it wouldn't be enough time."

Berta reached out to touch Danya's wings, smoothing the feathers. "I hadn't noticed how puffy you get when you're emotional, Danylko. You sound like my Andrei when we were young... If he treats you well, then I'm happy for you. And don't you go fucking things up, you understand me boy?"

Berta gasped in his ear as Danya hauled her into his arms, burying his face against her hair. "It means so much to me that you understand. I'm sure Ilya will be happy to have somebody else to talk to. I love you, Berta. If I fuck things up with him, you have permission to hit me with that fucking alarm clock."

"Damn straight." She pulled back from him, settling on her feet. She smoothed out Danya's feathers once more, patting his shoulder. "Now go enjoy your day off with him, would you?"

Danya laughed and wiped at his eyes. "Yeah, I will–"

A wave of energy rocked through him, as if he was feeling the anguish of a thousand people all at once. His heart began to race, pounding hard enough he could hear it his ears, could hear the rush of his blood thrum in his head. Something was wrong. Something was wrong with *Ilya*. He was in distress, and Danya had to find him *right now*. There was a pull in his mind, like a magnet to its match. He could sense where Ilya was, not too far off. He had to go *now*. Ilya was in so much stress Danya worried his life was in danger.

Berta's tiny voice cut through just enough. "Danya? What happened to your clothes?"

Danya blinked rapidly to break his focus for just a moment, looking down at himself.

Rather than the crimson pullover and khaki slacks he'd been wearing, bright silver armor lined with gold shone on his body. There was a weight on his wings, the tops of them covered in the same plates with gold edging. Large gauntlets ran up his arms, polished, cut rubies the size of an egg placed in the center. It was all bulky and inconvenient, but as he walked his movement wasn't impeded. Good then, it wouldn't slow him down.

"Danylko, is that a *sword?*"

Danya couldn't stay any longer. He rushed to the front of the shop, throwing the door open and launching himself into the sky. He spread his wings out wide, beating the air around him until he was high above the town, flying over every alley and walkway, following the pull he felt.

He found Ilya crumpled on the ground, cornered by his mother in a gap between some houses. Danya snarled as he watched Irina grab Ilya's hair to pull him up, fire burning through his chest and boiling his blood.

He'd had enough of this woman.

ILYA RUSHED OUT from Oyuna's porch, panic overtaking him. He blindly turned corner after corner, coming into a clearing surrounded by a group of houses. He slumped against the nearest one, sliding to the ground and clutching at his hood, pulling it over his face so he could hide, pretend that he was invisible for just a moment.

He had nothing left. Why was he still here? What was the point? Why wasn't he allowed to leave? He wanted to go anywhere else, somewhere new where the people only knew him as a priest and a healer who traveled with a beloved being of the Sun. If people didn't know him he could teach them, could start anew, could finally be himself. Maybe they'd even appreciate the work he did so he could take joy in it, could pursue deeper study because there would be a point to it all, could stop feeling so *fucking useless*.

He didn't mean to be different.

He just was.

Ilya hated crying so much. He was too soft, his heart so covered in bruises that even the smallest act ached a thousand times more. Injury upon injury to his mind, and this was the thing to finally break him. The one person in town he'd trusted above all else, and she'd betrayed him. That was all the hope he'd had left to give. It was gone now. He was nothing but a hollow shell, a husk of the man he was expected to be.

Ilya tilted his head up, letting his hood fall back to stare at the sky. The tears stopped as he retreated into himself, pulled back from the world around him. What if he just stayed here a while? Danya wouldn't have to know. He'd go home eventually, when it was too dark for people to notice, when he could be nothing but a ghost in the night. Truthfully, he'd died the day his father did. The first accusations began before his body even went cold. The child named Ilya had gone into the ground with Pavel Sokolov, never to be seen again.

His eyes were open but he focused on nothing. Every painful memory from the past decades came flooding in, every plea that fell on deaf ears. He spiraled and spiraled, descending into darkness. If this was what the Realm of Eternal Night looked like, then he'd already been here a long time. This was nothing new for him.

The kick to his ribs was unexpected. Ilya shouted in pain as he was knocked over into the snow and mud, coughing from the force. He looked up just in time to be kicked in the head. Stars burst in his vision, which then went black. He covered his head and tried to scramble to his feet, sliding around on the wet ground as he blindly searched for purchase.

"Who's there?" Ilya cried. "Why are you doing this?"

"How dare you come near me after humiliating me! In front of all those people!"

He should've known it was his mother. His worst fears were coming true.

Blow after blow landed upon him. A fist in his gut knocked the breath out of his lungs, launching him backwards onto the ground again. One, two, three more kicks to his ribs until Ilya rolled onto his stomach. He could hear the bone grinding in his ears as he tried to crawl away.

His vision began to fade back in, but it was too late. The shatter of glass came down on his head, more stars and darkness filling his head. Blood burst from the impact, running across his neck and over his forehead. Even with his eyes closed the world spun around him. He crumpled onto the ground again, fingers digging into the mud.

"Mama," he sobbed, "Please stop!"

Her sharp, talon-like nails scraped against his open scalp as she clutched a clump of his hair, yanking his head up and sending more hot blood down his face.

"How dare you call me that! You hide an angel from me? You evil brat, keeping his miracles all to yourself because you're still so selfish! I heard you walked around naked with him, I should've known you were a sick *freak*. You're going to corrupt him, just like the rest of this stupid place. I should've thrown you into the river when you were born!"

They were close enough to the cliff's edge that he could hear the river just in the distance. A cold fear gripped his body as his mother began to drag him through the mud toward the sound; she was going to kill him. She meant it this time.

A light as bright as the Sun filled his vision, clearing the darkness away. His mother screamed and let go of his hair, dropping him face-first back into the mud. Ilya fought a wave of nausea as he tried to shove his hands into the mud and push himself up. He looked up just in time to see Danya's back, his great fiery wings spread to their peak grandeur. He caught the gleam of silver and gold armor, sword strapped to his right hip, but the world was spinning and twisting too much for him to focus.

All he knew was that his shining savior had arrived.

19

Danya held Irina by the front of her sad excuse for a dress, pinning her to the nearest wall. He'd been strong, he knew this, but there was a new ease in his movement that made him feel *powerful*. This was his duty. This was what his Mother had sent him to do. He would defend his charge with his life, and that charge now was Ilya. He refused to let his second love die because of his failures again. No more.

Irina thrashed and screamed like a banshee. She clawed at his gauntlets like a rabid wolverine, eyes as wild as one. She kicked his chest, barely a tickle between his newfound strength and his armor.

"What will it take for you to leave him alone, Irina?" His voice was even despite his rage, impressing even himself. "Tell me. What's it going to take?"

"I want him to die! I'm going to kill him! Let me kill him!" She smashed her head back against the wood of the building behind her, kicking her legs out and aiming for his arm. Danya held firm, holding her as far away from his person as possible.

"If you try I'll drop you in the gorge myself. I don't know if anybody will notice, and who would miss you? But that's not my decision."

As much as Danya felt it would be easier for Irina to be permanently dealt with, he was positive that would shatter his relationship with Ilya forever. He wouldn't seriously harm her; not without permission, anyway.

He wanted her out of Ilya's life for good. He'd find a way to make it work.

Irina screamed again, "You wouldn't– not unless you're a demon, or a shitty angel!" Danya snorted. "The Great Mother will never take you back! I married her greatest servant, nobody loves Her more than me!"

Danya rolled his eyes. "Suppose I'm a shitty angel then, you hag of a woman."

Ilya groaned behind him and Danya turned to face him, an acidic mix of sadness and rage roiling in his stomach. Ilya looked unsteady on his feet, blood running down his face.

Danya changed his mind; he was going to destroy this woman. Just as soon as Ilya was safe, at least.

He let go of Irina, dropping her into the snow and mud so he could catch Ilya in his arms. He wrapped his wings around Ilya's body to block off any of Irina's further assaults, only the glow of his facial freckles to provide light in the cocoon of feathers and armor. With such an awful head injury, Ilya probably needed the darkness.

"I'm sorry Ilyushka," he whispered. "I should've just come with you."

Ilya groaned in return, tone indignant. Ilya didn't blame him, but Danya blamed himself. He knew how close Oyuna was to Irina. He didn't think.

A blow came to his left wing, Irina screaming as she tried to beat it with a fist. Danya lifted his head to scowl at her, light flaring around his head. She cried out in pain from the flash, clutching her eyes and curling in on herself. Smoke rose from under her fingers, a noxious smell filling the area. Ilya didn't seem bothered by it; maybe it was because his eyes had already been burned out.

"What did you do to me! Monster, you're a monster! You're a demon, a night creature, nothing but a farce!" Irina lashed out wildly with a hand while using the other to keep covering her eyes.

hoped nothing lingered. He didn't deserve for his awful mother to glean any satisfaction from further destroying his life.

Ilya was more than happy to get into bed when Danya guided him. Danya made him lay on his back, digging around for extra pillows to prop him up. Ilya smiled at him, eyes still unfocused.

"I probably have a concussion from that. Wake me every few hours to make sure I haven't died in my sleep, okay? I should be out of the woods in 24 hours."

Danya dragged a hand down his face but nodded. "Yeah. Yeah, okay. Do you need anything else?"

"Just sleep... Might want food later. Do you think you can manage that, Danulyachka?"

Danya hated that version of his name. Ilya only ever said it when he was annoyed or making fun of him. But if Ilya was well enough to tease him? Danya was thrilled to hear it. It was the finest music in the world to hear Ilya tease him. ·

Danya did make Ilya stroganoff, though. And he'd liked it.

Lovable ass.

Danya took hold of Ilya's hand, bringing his bruised knuckles to his lips, placing a soft kiss on the skin. "I will make sure it's edible, Ilyushenka. Please rest for me, okay?"

Ilya flashed another brief, soft smile, eyes fluttering closed after. Danya pulled the covers over him but kept hold of his hand. He watched Ilya's breathing like a hawk, well over an hour. He glanced at the clock, sighing as noon passed. He'd better start on food.

DANYA WAS ENTIRELY grateful that Ilya kept a tin box with recipe cards of all types. Some were hand written, both by Ilya and who Danya guessed was Oyuna, others were clipped from books and magazines, some even printed on postcards. He frantically looked between the cards and what ingredients they had on hand, deciding on the vegetable soup that Ilya made when he didn't want to go into town. It was simple to make (hard to fuck up) and wouldn't be too difficult for Ilya to get down.

He was in the middle of fighting with the onions he was attempting to dice when the telephone rang. The loud bell startled him just as he was starting his first cross cut, narrowly missing the tip of his finger. He set the knife aside and wiped his hands on a rag before picking up the receiver and holding it to his ear.

"Hello? Who's this?"

"Greetings. Is this Father Sokolov that I'm speaking to?"

Pain bloomed behind Danya's eyes from the sound of the man on the line. He knew this voice. Why did he know this voice? It couldn't be anything good if it was familiar to him. How in the world did he still have memories missing? What did this mean?

"No... no. This is his... assistant. I'm afraid he's indisposed with work in town at the moment. Can I take a message? Who am I speaking to?"

"Ah, my apologies sir, but a message would be acceptable." Danya scrambled just in time to grab a pencil and paper to take notes with. "My name is Nikolai, I am a Senior Hunter from our fair Church of the Eclipse. I've been sent to investigate the claims that an angel resides at the church in your dear town of Velak. I have been sent by Cardinal Vitaly if Father Sokolov would like to verify for himself.

"I don't wish to do any harm, simply to understand why we were not notified of this supposed angel, and why his behavior is so unusual. I'm sure he's told you tales of other angels sent by the Great Mother, their singular purpose in the world, but how brief and fleeting their visits are. That he supposedly hasn't returned to the Realm of Eternal Light is very curious!"

Danya rolled his eyes hard enough he was sure they'd pop out of his skull. He might pop them out and shove them in his ears himself to save his sanity. There had been enough people snooping around their home anyway, what was one more person in his business?

"I've seen this angel, yes, and he feels real to me at least. He's got wings and everything," Danya replied, trying to keep the disdain out of his voice. "What will you do if your investigation concludes the same? What could he be if he's not an angel?"

"Both good questions, young sir." Danya barely suppressed a

sneer about how much of a condescending ass this Nikolai was. "Well, if he's not an angel, it's a high possibility he's a vampire that's glamored the whole of the town. Perhaps a leshy as well, given Velak's proximity to the forests. It would be hard to say without closer examination. If it's true? We'd have to consider disciplining the dear Father for keeping this information back, but we'd likely have him and the angel transferred to the cathedral in the Capital.

"I understand the Father has asked for a transfer out of Velak, as I've been told, 86 times? As recently as a few months ago. I've been asked to verify these claims of abuse from the town personally and make a final judgment on the matter. As I said, if this creature is in fact an angel, as you've claimed, we'd want to transfer the Father to the Capital anyway. We'd be happy to permanently release him of his duties in Velak if the abuse claims are true as well."

Danya spoke without hesitation. "The things they've done to Ilya are nothing short of cruel. I've heard the way they talk about him, claiming he's a murderer because he couldn't heal his father's illness as a child. Just ask any of them, it's all any of them ever fucking talk about– Sorry, forget church people don't like swearing."

Nikolai was silent on the end of the line for a beat. Dread filled Danya, twisting his gut. Had he just ruined everything for Ilya?

"First name basis with the Father, I see. You must be very close."

Danya swallowed. "I consider him a very good friend. He helped me find work here after my life in Kursiya fell apart. He's a good priest, Mister Hunter, I promise you that. If you have to reprimand him for not reporting this angel to you, I understand, but know that if you bring him to the Capital, there will be no better example of what the Mother teaches than him."

Nikolai chuckled into Danya's ear, crackling with static. There was an air to the sound, a hint of knowing that set him on edge. Danya and his bird brain needed to shut up. He was going to get them into even deeper shit at this rate.

"I'm sure that will be the case. I feel you should know, I'm calling from Kelot. I believe it's a four day's ride from here to Velak, and this will be the last place with a telephone line to my knowledge.

I should get back on the road to meet my next destination by night-fall. Good day to you, Mister...?"

Danya stammered out, "Da...mitri... Dimitri. Good day, Hunter Nikolai."

Danya hung up the receiver to stop himself from further fucking up. He dragged his palm down his face, smacking his forehead several times. Stupid!

At least there was hope from this. Ilya would finally be allowed to leave without the risk of persecution and excommunication. That was all Danya wanted. If nothing else came from this, he hoped it was that.

Even still, the call hadn't felt right. There was an air of unease the whole time Nikolai had spoken, as if he'd already made his decision, as if Danya was foolish to expect anything but the worst. He knew this man's voice, knew it had to mean something. His head throbbed as he struggled to pull anything from the void in his mind, eyes slamming shut to remove sensory distractions. He caught flashes of memory, sensation.

Nikolai's shouting. Woodsmoke and the crackling of an enormous bonfire. A pain in his chest, burning and lodging itself deep into his flesh. The taste of ink at the back of his throat. The darkness of the woods and the Moonless night. That awful, terrible hunger that could never be satiated.

Nikoali had something to do with Tatyana's death. He could glean that much. Nikolai was there the night she died, when she was burned as a witch and a heretic. Danya couldn't piece together if Nikolai had ordered it or just carried it out, but it didn't matter. Nikolai was either a monster or had no problem taking orders from monsters. It was hard to decide which would be worse.

Once the onions had stopped assaulting his eyes so thoroughly, bumbling his way through the soup wasn't so bad. It wasn't exciting, but he and Ilya both needed less excitement in their lives right now. Danya looked at the hand-scrawled recipe card, grabbing a pen and crossing out the name, replacing it with the title 'Fuck It Soup'. Better.

He sat on the couch, glancing at the clock on the wall. It had only been two hours since Ilya had fallen asleep. Danya wouldn't wake him just yet. Unfortunately, that gave him too much time to think. He'd been fighting off the flashes of memory by cutting up every vegetable in the house, but now they couldn't be controlled.

Danya pressed the heels of his palms against his eyes and growled. Stars bloomed across his vision as he desperately fought the wave of sadness. What did Nikolai have to do with this? Why did his voice fill him with so much fucking *dread?*

The smell of firewood filled his nostrils again, screams ringing in his ears. Black eyes gleaming in the firelight, staring him down. Then there was pain, pain, pain, followed by fear. Flashes of Tatyana entered his mind. Her plans for the future, how she'd connect all of humanity with advanced communication devices, how she'd work with the growing interest in rail lines to make sure nobody would be isolated. He remembered a cardinal confessing the church was losing its grip, the people didn't go to church for worship anymore, too disillusioned with the disgusting displays of wealth and power. They had to take a firmer hold on people, punish them for overstepping their authority.

It was always about power. These men didn't speak for his Mother. Maybe they believed they did, but Danya knew his Mother would sooner have him strike down the pontiffs than let them oppress the common people. He would rather assist every man, woman, and otherwise in learning magic than let only a chosen few be given the gift. Maybe if the practice wasn't so isolated Ilya wouldn't have to be like this right now.

Then again, maybe if Danya wasn't anything more than a winged brute he could've just fixed it himself. He had no idea if he had magic of his own. Aside from the glowing and the flying, at least. And the magical armor now, he supposed. He had so much to learn about himself, and he couldn't remember if he knew it all to begin with. He tried to recall his first moments on earth, but it was hard. He just… existed. That was it. He came into existence and he knew everything that he was supposed to.

Danya sighed, digging around in his pockets for his clove cigarettes. Ilya was lenient about smoking if he was too stressed, and that was as true now as it ever was. He hadn't been this stressed since he tried to cook for Ilya to impress him. He took an enormous drag off the first cigarette, turning half of it to ash with one pull. He blew the smoke out of his nostrils, wishing he could breathe fire to match it. Maybe he could, for all he fucking knew anymore.

There was too much nervous energy in his system. Ilya's injuries, the ominous phone call and forthcoming visit, and every mistake he made that lead to Tatyana's death. He couldn't do this anymore.

Danya went to rummage in the bathroom, pulling a bottle of aspirin out of the medicine cabinet. He found a clean rag, breaking off a chunk of ice from the icebox to set inside of it as a cold compress, then went back to their bedroom.

Ilya was sleeping peacefully. Danya felt guilty having to wake him, even as instructed. He pulled the chair away from Ilya's desk and sat beside the bed, setting the medicine and ice on the night-stand. He took a moment to look him over, more swelling having appeared. He flapped his wings in frustration, feathers sticking out on end as he swallowed his rage.

Danya had a temper sometimes. He was sure part of it came with the territory of being a protector, but part of it had to be a lingering side effect of his curse. He didn't remember being this angry all the time. Trapped in the mind of the drekavac, all he knew was hunger and rage. He didn't even know what had made him so angry as a monster; everything and nothing. The light, the lack of food, all the people who got in his way.

Things before he was cursed came into focus now, but his time as a beast had always been clear in his mind. He remembered every day, every justification for his actions, slowly inking over the life he'd had.

He didn't want to trouble Ilya with it; there was too much guilt. Especially not now. Now was a *terrible* time for all of this to come up. Everything was happening too much. They'd only just managed to enjoy being together, and now a million and one immediate threats hung over their heads. Who said Danya had time to dump all of his trauma on his deeply traumatized love?

Definitely hypocritical of him, he knew that. They were both idiots. That's why they belonged together.

Once this was all over, once Ilya was able to leave and go some-where better, Danya would tell him. Then they'd have time to work it all out.

"You know how you give me guff for thinking too loud, Danulyachka?"

Danya jolted, cigarette nearly dropping from his lips onto the sheets. He sighed and slumped back in the chair, glancing down at Ilya and meeting his single eye.

"Don't you start. I'm taking care of *you* right now, Ilyushka."

Ilya waved him off, swallowing audibly. "It's the smoke. You don't do that inside unless you're about to lose it."

Danya sighed, smudging his cigarette out on the ceramic tray Ilya had put on the nightstand. "There's a lot happening right now, Lyubimi. You got a phone call while you were asleep."

Ilya seemed to be trying to make a face, but his face was too banged up to have any reasonable expression. That fiery hate bloomed in his chest, fingers prickling. The things he wished upon Irina weren't the least bit holy. Good thing Danya was a shitty angel anyway.

"What phone call?" Ilya asked. "Who was it?"

"A Hunter named Nikolai. Said he's going to be here in four days to *investigate* the claims that I'm an angel. Cardinal Vitaly sent him. They can both kiss my ass."

Ilya snorted, rolling his one good eye. "I know of Vitaly. He's a strange old man who likes to spend too much time looking at all the priests and nuns in training. If there's any silver lining to my father's death, it's that it took me away from the Capital before he had enough time to find me interesting."

Murder had entered Danya's heart the second he'd become the drekavac. He had no idea if it would ever leave. "Fucking great. Well, good thing the Cardinal fucking sucks because Nikolai is also a fucking creep and it makes sense they'd work together. He was there when Tatyana died. I don't know if he did it or was just there, or if he's the one that cursed me, but I don't fucking trust him. I don't like him coming here, I don't think anything good will come of it."

Danya fidgeted with his hands, pulling out a fresh cigarette. He didn't smoke it, but holding it between his fingers settled some of his agitation.

Ilya reached out to him, brushing the tips of his fingers against the back of Danya's hand. "Hush, Danya. You're on edge. Did he say anything else?"

Danya sighed, placing his cigarette in the ash tray so he could lay across Ilya's lap. He looked up at him through his lashes, eyes fluttering shut when Ilya's hand settled on his head. He took a deep breath, letting his energy settle. Ilya's hand migrated to the space on his back between his wings, forcing a groan out of him.

"Not now, Ilyushka—"

"But it made you relax. Now tell me the rest."

Danya grumbled back, "He said they'd investigate your transfer out of Velak and to the Capital. I don't think it's much better than here, but at least it's not here."

Ilya hummed in thought, stroking the nape of Danya's neck idly. "I'll admit that I don't think he's being honest about that, what with everything about this situation... I want to hope that maybe it'll turn out. I want to hope that we can go somewhere better."

"I know, Lyubimi. It'll be fine." It wouldn't be, but Ilya needed anything to look forward to right now. Having your own mother admit to wanting to murder you would take a lot to balance back out. Danya wasn't going to add to that pain right now.

Ilya started playing with his hair, the fire in Danya's chest cooling into embers. Ilya brought a calm to him unlike any other.

Ilya asked, "Did you manage dinner then?"

"Yeah. I renamed your recipe though. Wasn't apt enough."

"I fear what you decided on, but hopefully it'll give me a laugh some day. But, I think I could eat..."

Danya placed a gentle hand on Ilya's shoulder the second he tried getting out of bed, forcing him back. "No, you stay here. I brought some aspirin and a compress for you. Focus on that, I'll check on dinner. Not sure if it's done yet."

Ilya smiled at him, reaching for the compress to hold against his face. "You said four days for Nikolai to be here?"

"That's what he told me. Said he's in Kelot, wherever that is."

Ilya nodded. "Hopefully I won't be in as much of a state by the time he gets here. I doubt it will look very good though."

"Hey. It'll be evidence that you can't be safe here anymore. If something good comes out of this... This stupid bullshit, let it be that. I'll be right back, okay?"

Ilya nodded again. He looked exhausted, even with how little expression he could manage.

Four days. Four days until the world would be upended.

Danya would be ready.

20

March 2nd, 1928

Ilya loved Danya very much, but if he didn't let Ilya have his independence back he was liable to strangle him. Perhaps he'd make good on his past threat to put him into the soup; there was a metric ton of it in the icebox still, because Danya had made *more* in his unwavering panic.

By the blessing of the Great Mother Ilya had come out without a concussion or any lingering maladies. By the next day he had full clarity again. His head had a nasty bruise and had been swelling, but not because of any bleeds. The hair over his cut had started to come in without color, but that was nothing to cry about. His bruises had calmed, turning that sickly brown in between being purple and yellow.

Not to say he didn't have aches and pains. His ribs were awful, but the brunt of it had passed. Aspirin also helped.

Lots and lots of aspirin.

Still, Danya had hardly let him leave bed. Ilya understood, but he was champing at the bit the closer they got to Nikolai's visit. He'd called from Kursiya just yesterday; any moment now he could arrive and they hadn't so much as discussed their plan for how to handle it.

This morning Danya was trying to keep him in bed again, which was the final straw. Ilya was terrible at defending himself, and the anxiety of the day brought out the worst in him.

"He's coming today, Danya! There's no more time to rest, get off me."

Rarely did they use each other's standard names anymore, but Ilya was at his limit. He could provide no more affection when either a potential out or a potential threat were about to walk through the door.

Danya was dejected, but still determined. "Ilyushka, please, you're not well yet, the stupid Hunter can wait—"

"But I will not. Out of my way." Ilya pressed a hand to the center of Danya's chest, pressing him back. It was like shoving a solid brick wall. Danya did not budge when touched, but he did move back anyway. Ilya went over to the chiffonier to start gathering the pieces of his vestments, beginning the slow ritual of dressing himself. It was difficult with his ribs glowing in fiery pain, but he felt a little more human with the process.

"Lyubimi, I'm still worried about you. If something happens with him, you won't be at your full strength. How will you fight back?" Danya stepped behind him, placing a hand on the small of his back. Danya was determined, then.

Ilya paused as he pulled on the golden cuffs around his wrists, glancing at Danya over his shoulder. "It turns out my mother taught me one good thing in life, which was how to defend myself. You'll find my censer and all my incense in the sacristy. The brown bricks are the regular stuff, the yellow and black ones are... other things."

Danya's brows knit together as he tried to process what Ilya had just said to him, but nothing was coming. "Ilyushka, what the hell are you talking about?"

Ilya huffed back, "Poison incense, Danil. I'm not without defenses."

The sharp inhale through Danya's nose told Ilya he'd touched a nerve. Danya was already an informal diminutive of a name, but not once had Ilya called him anything but Danya or another sweet name. Ilya needed it to be clear how serious he was.

"What's with you right now?" Danya grabbed him by the shoulder and turned him around. Their faces were close, Danya's soft glowing eyes contorted by his confusion. "Ilya, why are you being like this to me?"

"Because I'm not kidding around, Danya! I love you and I appreciate your concern for me, but I'm not made of glass. We don't have the time for you to keep babying me. He's a *Senior* Hunter, which means he is very skilled, and very dangerous. If he had anything to do with Tatyana's death then that means he's willing to do terrible things. We don't even know to what *end*. I can't be locked in this room any longer while we have no plan."

Ilya broke out of Danya's grasp, pulling on the last of his accoutrement and heading into the kitchen. He was going to make something that wasn't just *Fuck It Soup*. Danya's feather-light steps followed behind him.

"Ilya, your mother beat you until you were nearly blind! She broke your ribs and tried to kick your head in! She was going to *kill you!* You're still injured, Sun's sake! How is it that you're supposed to be a healer and so shit at taking care of yourself?"

Ilya whirled around and snarled, "Go out back and ask my father if you're so curious! Now *drop it*. We have other things to worry about right now. For all we know he's going to march through that door and kill us both because he already knows who you are! Did you even think about that?"

Danya tossed his hands in the air, dragging them back through his hair to pull on it. "No, I didn't, because I was worried you were going to fucking *die!* Do you even understand, Ilya?" Danya grabbed Ilya by the shoulders again, giving him a brief but firm shake that made Ilya's ribs ache. "Tatyana died in front of me! That's what had to have happened, because what else would it be? You think I want to watch the other love of my life pass away too? Do you?"

Danya rattled him again, fingers digging into his arms with more strength than he probably knew. Ilya winced, trying and failing to jerk his body out of Danya's grasp. "Well I didn't die, okay? But I could if we don't know what the fuck we're doing! How are we going to handle this man you absolute fucking bird brain?"

Ilya did *not* expect Danya to pin him to the wall. A hiss of pain escaped his clenched teeth, immediately swallowed up by Danya's mouth hot on his. All of Danya was hot all the time, but the undercurrent of anger made it a sickly heat that threatened to burn him up. Ilya was so caught off guard he couldn't think to react, hands held half-clenched near Danya's face.

This was not a sweet kiss; this was not a desperate plea, this was pure force. Danya's teeth sunk into the soft flesh of his bottom lip, threatening to break skin and spill crimson. Ilya seethed from the pain, eyes watering until Danya pulled back.

Those golden eyes were glassy with unshed tears, deep pain etched onto his angel's face. Ilya was caught between anger and passion, entwining together in his chest. He wanted to get close to Danya again. To curse him out or kiss him, he couldn't decide. His heart pounded as he panted for air. He grabbed for the front of Danya's shirt, pulling him in again to force his own searing kiss onto him.

"I said I love you, you stupid angel," Ilya gasped. "I love you—"

"Funny way of showing it, you bastard human—"

"I'm sorry." Another gasp from Ilya, this time from Danya pulling his collar to bite at his throat. "Fuck, my ribs hurt so much, breathing is hard."

Danya scoffed. "That's what you get for not resting, shithead."

"Should we be doing this if you're so concerned about me?" Despite his words, Ilya made no attempts to shove Danya away again.

Danya paused, dragging his tongue over the spot he'd bit to soothe the skin. "Do you want to stop?"

"Yes and no," Ilya groaned back. "Yes because of my Sun forsaken ribs, no because I want you anyway."

A soft, warm sigh blew across his ear. Ilya shivered, groaning and clutching at his side. Danya stepped back from him, arms crossed. Ilya was still caught between anger and passion, but for slightly different reasons now. He narrowed his eyes and scowled.

"Did you do that to make a point, you damned angel?"

"Maybe." Danya flapped his wings irritably, the breeze sending Ilya's hair into his eyes. "Did it work?"

"If by 'work' you mean am I very hard and still angry at you, but mostly angry that my ribs hurt too much for you to fuck me, then yes, Danulyachka, it *worked* and I *hate* you."

Danya laughed at him and Ilya relished in the tension between them melting. Danya was too stubborn on most days and Ilya wasn't much better when he was wound up. This whole argument was stupid. Arguing at all was stupid. The fact that he could barely stand and *definitely* couldn't do anything with Danya was the *stupidest*.

Ilya brushed his hair out of the way and huffed, placing a hand on Danya's cheek. "Just… please. We have to make a good impression, either because we need him to not suspect you remember anything, or because this might be my only chance to leave Velak in peace. Do you understand?"

Danya leaned into Ilya's hand, turning his head to kiss the center of his palm. He nodded, beleaguered sigh blowing through his nose. "Still don't like it."

"I appreciate that you are my sworn protector, but know that I am still a capable man. Okay? I promise when drunk women aren't sneaking up on me after I've been emotionally devastated I can hold my own."

Danya grumbled into his hand, "You wouldn't have fought her even if you'd known she was coming."

"No. I don't think I would've had the heart. I'm glad you were there for me."

Ilya guided Danya into the kitchen, having him sit at the table. Ilya opened all the cupboards to check what they had. They were sparse for supplies, which made serving food to Nikolai difficult, but they could be presentable enough for the initial visit. Nikolai would likely stay at the inn back in town, if only to keep up pretenses. It would give them more time to plan properly. This whole situation had thrown him severely off balance.

Not helping was Danya lifting him by his armpits onto the

counter, turning him around so they were back at eye level. Ilya huffed and cast a glare at him. "What are you doing now?"

"This is gonna be our last moment alone for a long time... I just want to enjoy you for a little longer. Okay?"

"If Nikolai sees us it could blow up this whole operation, Danya."

"It'll be the afternoon when he arrives, that's always how long you take when you make the trip. You said you were frustrated anyway. Please?"

Ilya tried to protest, but the words died in his throat when Danya trailed gentle kisses across his jaw. Instead he nodded, soft sigh escaping his lips as Danya's pressed to his skin. Ilya lifted his hands, holding in them the air for an awkward moment before touching Danya's back. He rubbed the pads of his fingers against the base of Danya's wings, goosebumps covering his arms from the groan he got in return. Ilya hadn't deliberately touched Danya here much, but it seemed like the least strenuous way to bring him off now.

That hot mouth crashed against him again, teeth clacking from the sudden force. Danya nipped Ilya's lip, much gentler than earlier, rolling it between his teeth. Danya reached down, pushing aside the flap of fabric at the front of Ilya's vestments to unbutton his pants. Ilya gasped when Danya's warm hand wrapped around him, pulling his cock out into the open air to stroke him.

Their actions grew more and more frantic, kisses desperate while their pace became feverish. Danya's grip was firm around Ilya as he tugged him, thumb rubbing against the slit. Ilya moaned in his ear, trying to keep his back straight as he kept rubbing the base of Danya's wings.

"It's silly that this gets you off so much," Ilya said, voice rough with desire.

"Shut... Shut up–"

Danya rut against Ilya's thigh, pulling the collar of his vestments down to suck harsh bruises back into his skin. His old ones had just disappeared, but Danya wasn't one to leave him bare-skinned for long. This angel loved claiming his human, displaying all of his affections on Ilya's skin. Ilya didn't mind that he was so bitey; he liked being marked. Ilya tilted his head back to give Danya more room to work. Danya wrapped an arm around Ilya to keep his back straight, hand pressing into his hip as Ilya kept rubbing his wings.

"Fuck, I can't think straight with you doing that," Danya gasped.

Ilya laughed and replied, "Can you think gayly instead?"

Danya groaned again, batting Ilya in the head with a wing. Ilya laughed harder, whining between breaths as fresh pain lanced through his chest. If there was any tension between them still, Ilya had killed it with his lame joke. Danya made terrible jokes all the time; it was only fair he got one too.

Danya took both of their cocks in hand, grip tight to force them to grind against each other. Ilya dug his nails into Danya's back, pressing hard against the base of his wings to force another lewd noise out of his angel. Danya's breath came out as a shudder, swallowing audibly as he worked them.

Danya mouthed at Ilya's neck again, moving to his jaw, kissing his ear and breathing against it. "Close, Ilyushka. Are you?"

"Not as much. Think you're extra easy to please being touched this way," Ilya crooned back.

Danya huffed at him and Ilya stroked the fluffy, downy feathers a bit harder. Danya's whining moan was sharp and sudden, hot ropes splattering across Ilya's stomach. Danya let go of their cocks and panted for air, warm flush to his cheeks. He looked shy and positively run over. Ilya felt powerful.

"I guess back massages are dangerous territory," Ilya teased.

"You're a menace. I... shut up. I'm getting you back."

Ilya had never seen Danya so flustered. It was adorable. Anticipating how he'd make good on his threat was equally fun.

He did *not* expect to get lifted and promptly laid out on the kitchen table.

Ilya hissed in pain, face scrunching as he sucked in a breath. "Fuck that hurts– you're going to be the death of me, Danya–"

Danya yanked Ilya's pants under his ass, past his knees, and finally past his ankles. He tossed the heap of leather aside, forcing

Ilya's knees apart. Ilya's cock twitched as Danya loomed over him. He desperately wanted Danya inside him, but whatever healing his ribs had gone through would be undone in an instant. On top it all, this was the *kitchen table!*

"Danylko, we eat here! You'll shatter my ribs all over again!"

A playful smirk grew on Danya's face. "Lyubimi, you worry too much. I'm going to use the table as intended."

Ilya had barely opened his mouth to speak when Danya kneeled in front of him, pushing Ilya's thighs back and laving his tongue across his hole. A choked off gasp erupted from Ilya's throat, a combination of shock and pleasure. He was torn between keeping Danya in place and throwing him off.

"Wha— What the *fuck* is this?"

Danya chuckled, mouthing at Ilya's perineum. Ilya's toes curled and he worked a hand into Danya's hair, fingers wound tight in the crimson strands. He *wanted* to be horrified by what his angel was doing, where his *mouth was*, but unfortunately, that mouth was good at getting him to comply with a lot of things he wouldn't have considered.

"Don't tell me I already have to go back to asking you to not be weird, Ilyushka."

Ilya tilted his head forward to scowl at his partner. "*I'm* being weird, he says! *Cyka blyat*, Danulyachka!"

"I'll rinse my mouth out later if it makes you feel better."

Ilya was going to *smack* this man. "No!"

Danya let go of Ilya's thighs, leaning back on his haunches. "Do you want me to stop? I can suck you instead, if that's better…"

Ilya let his head fall back, glaring at the ceiling. Did he? It wasn't *bad*, but it was *so* different. He had so many unnamed neuroses he was fighting against at any given time, such as right now, but Danya clearly wanted to do this for him. If it wasn't bad and his partner wanted it, then maybe he could allow it just this once.

He was also terribly hard and wanted to finish before this Sun forsaken Hunter showed up.

Ilya sighed. "Fine. But if you get funny don't be surprised if I kick you in the head."

Danya leaned forward again, placing kisses along Ilya's inner thighs, swirling his tongue over the milky skin. He nibbled at a patch dangerously close to Ilya's cock, sucking and biting the skin until it went red. Ilya was throbbing from the attention, bemused by his partner's obsession with biting him.

"Always the teeth, Solnishko."

"Because you're *mine* and everybody should know it," Danya growled, diving back in and sucking on Ilya's hole again.

Ilya bit his lip and moaned, hooking an ankle around Danya's neck to force him close. Danya's tongue was warm and wet and soft, circling the ring of muscle. Ilya was a mess of soft, breathy sounds, grabbing at Danya's hair again for leverage. Danya groaned in response, dipping his tongue inside of Ilya once more. Ilya had to resist the urge to arch his back, gripping tight on Danya's locks instead.

"Grab as hard as you want," Danya rasped. "I want it."

That was a revelation that Ilya would pocket for later.

For the moment, he was in the throes of pleasure. Danya's tongue passed over that bundle of nerves just inside him. The noise that came out of Ilya was lewd, whiny, and incredibly embarrassing. He smacked his hands over his mouth in a feeble effort to recover his dignity, but Danya's chuckling told him it was too late.

"I knew you'd like this. Just wait until your ribs are healed, I'm going to ravish you so badly... I'll worship your ass every morning, day, and night—"

Ilya desperately hoped Danya made good on that threat.

He hoped they'd be safe enough for him to make good on that threat.

Danya kept licking, biting, and sucking on his skin, tongue running a stripe from his hole to the base of his cock. Ilya sucked in air through his stomach, skin sticking to his aching ribs as he gulped down breath. His head was in a fog, blood sparking with nerves and electricity. Heat coiled in his gut and worked down to his groin, threatening to send him over the edge. Sweat dripped down his back, the damp making his curls stick to his forehead. He was a disaster.

"Close, Solnishko— Please, Danya—"

Danya lifted his head to take Ilya's cock in his mouth, bobbing his head while crooking his fingers inside Ilya's ass. The pads of Danya's fingers rubbed against his spot, his mouth was hot and wet, and Ilya could hold back no more.

Ilya threw a hand over his eyes and cried out with his orgasm, his other hand yanking on Danya's hair. He spilled into Danya's mouth, shivering with every audible swallow. His angel groaned around him, vibrations humming in the base of his spine.

He slumped on the table, limbs tantamount to jelly. One leg still rested on Danya's shoulder, which Danya was happy to place gentle kisses along. When Ilya lifted his head to look at him, Danya was more smug than ever.

"Good?" Danya asked.

"Sun's sake, Danulyachka. Yes, it was. I love you and you've turned me into a lusting mess of a man, you insufferable bird brain."

Danya chuckled and kissed his knee. "Love you too, my favorite bratty slut priest."

Ilya was winding up to smack him until a knock on the kitchen door sent a chill through his body. He froze in place, heart pounding so hard he feared it would shatter his frail ribs. He let his head fall back, meeting the blacked-out, glassy eyes of one Senior Hunter. His skin was gray and ashen, hair black and cut short, and a hint of stubble on his broad face, cast in shadow by a wide brimmed black leather hat.

Ah. This was Nikolai.

Ilya wanted to die.

21

To say Ilya was shaking with terror was putting it mild. They'd fled into the bedroom in a flash to clean up. His heart threatened to shatter his ribs all over again with how hard it was pounding. His body shook so violently he couldn't find purchase on his pants to get them back on.

This was it. Everything was over. His life was over. He'd be excommunicated and they'd take Danya away from him and his best course of action would be to drop dead in the middle of the woods and rot.

Warm hands pressed into his cheeks, stilling him. The calloused thumbs brushed over his cheeks, a light scratch that centered him. "Ilyushen'ka. Look at me. I won't let anything happen to you, okay? Do you understand me? Never. I'll take us far away from here if I have to. I won't let him hurt you."

Ilya wanted to believe Danya so badly. He desperately needed it to be true, but Hunters were the most elite force the Church had against night creatures. A Senior Hunter surely knew how to handle a rogue angel. This was going to be terrible.

Ilya covered his mouth in a feeble gesture to hold back nausea.

Blessedly, nothing came out of him, but acid tickled the back of his throat all the same.

Danya sat him on the bed and helped him redress, cleaning up as best he could and setting Ilya's vestments straight again. The beaded chains of medallions on Ilya's clothes rattled with his fear. Danya swiftly tossed them back onto the blankets. Danya kneeled in front of Ilya, hands settled on his thighs, thumbs pressing into him once more. Always Danya's thumbs in his flesh, to claim possession or to soothe.

"Ilya. If he wanted to, he could've just killed us there. He clearly has an agenda, which means he needs us alive, and needs us to cooperate with him. It's not over yet. Okay?"

Ilya nodded dumbly. It made sense. If Nikolai's goal had been their deaths, catching them in a compromising act would've been the best opportunity. It would be fine for now.

"I still want to vomit," Ilya grumbled back. "But I guess we should face the music."

Nikolai was still waiting at the door when they left the room. Danya went to start the kettle while Ilya let Nikolai in.

"Hunter Nikolai," Ilya said, "I am unsure if there are enough apologies for what you've had to witness this morning, but please accept my humble offering, as well as, perhaps, some tea?"

He had no idea how to do this anymore. It had been decades since he'd been in the Capital, and just as long since he'd been face to face with a Hunter. Up close, Nikolai was as terrifying as he remembered the others being.

They looked like walking corpses, which was a lot coming from Ilya. All the warmth of life had been replaced by the inky, gray shadows of the Night. His movements were smooth and calculated, each heavy-booted footfall resonating through the room like thunder. The hairs on the back of Ilya's neck stood on edge, tension curling in the pit of his stomach. It was like the drekavac waiting to strike him from behind in the woods, all those months ago.

To Ilya's surprise, Nikolai laughed. "Two men on their kitchen table is hardly the worst thing I've ever seen, Father. One of the more pleasant things I've stumbled upon, actually."

Danya's head whipped around in surprise, and Ilya had to stop from mirroring the gesture. He expected to be admonished at least a little, called a sinner or a shame upon the Church's name for his deviancy, but Nikolai seemed to relish in it. There was a new unease bubbling in Ilya's gut, but he wasn't fearing for his life anymore. That *was* nice.

Ilya stepped aside to allow Nikolai into the rectory, leading him to the kitchen table before scowling and changing course for the living room couch. Nikolai chuckled behind him and the hairs on Ilya's arms stood up. He hated that sound already.

They sat at opposite ends, Nikolai letting his heavy work bag drop to the floor. It was enough heft to rattle the glasses in his cabinets. Ilya only barely caught Danya glaring at the back of Nikolai's head and hoped his own silent glare got his angel to behave.

"Well you've, ah... seen a bit of Danya for your investigation I suppose. I really must apologize again–"

Nikolai held up a hand to silence him. "Despite what the church claims publicly, two men together isn't unusual in the Capital. Truly, I can think of plenty of men, even amongst the council of Pontiffs, who'd love to have their way with you.... Perhaps myself included."

Nikolai's grin set Ilya's teeth on edge as acid flicked at his esophagus. There was something so vile about the public condemnation of people like them, but indulging in private as if it was nothing. Upholding purity amongst the common folk, and making exceptions for clergy. Ilya's fists clung tight to the edge of his vestments.

They both glanced up when Danya came over with teacups, doing his level best to loom over Nikolai. Danya's feathers stood on end in his silent rage, wings spread just enough so he appeared larger and more threatening. Ilya would be charmed by how bird-brained his angel was if not for their current circumstance.

"He's mine," Danya ground out, "But I'm sure there's plenty of other priests you can take advantage of."

Nikolai laughed and waved him off, taking his teacup and not bothering to meet Danya's eyes. "Only jokes among clergymen! I would never deign to impose, and certainly not over a *supposed angel*."

Danya's gaze flicked up to the ceiling briefly then returned to the side of Nikolai's head. If Ilya had to guess, Danya was hoping to fire beams of light from his eyes to make Nikolai's head burst like a grape.

"I'll admit I didn't expect you to, ah, share my proclivities, Hunter Nikolai. I expected to be excommunicated on the spot."

Nikolai chuckled over his tea and shook his head. "We treat our kind well, Father Sokolov, you don't need to worry. I imagine there must not be anybody else like you here in Velak, yes?"

"No. I wonder about the Mayor sometimes but... no." Ilya spotted Danya give him an incredulous look out of the corner of his eye, which he ignored. "I spent so long thinking I'd die alone... Then our Great Mother gifted me with a miracle, and one of Her own children at that. I feel very blessed to love and be loved by the divine itself."

Nikolai's smile continued to not reach his eyes. He sipped his tea and gave another nod, crossing one leg over the other. "It seems such a beautiful gift. A shame you didn't come to the Capital more, Father."

Danya walked behind Ilya, hands settling on Ilya's shoulders. "Well, I'm here with him now. He's my charge, and I will stay by his side. I will do *everything* to protect him from harm."

The unsaid threat hung in the air. Nikolai seemed perfectly unaffected. Danya's fingers dug into Ilya's shoulders for a brief moment, a warning that he was on edge and at his limit.

"You'll have to forgive Danya. I believe he's an angel of protection, and well... they are some of the fiercest warriors sent by our Sun. But you know this, of course, being an expert in all manners supernatural, Hunter Nikolai."

Nikolai shrugged. "Perhaps he is, perhaps not. I'd be very protective of my lover as well, either way."

Ilya's face was burning, partly from the embarrassment of being so open, and partly from frustration. His wings! Were out! And visible! What was so disputable about it all?

Even still, being open about his relationship with Danya felt strange. Wrong, in a way. He was so used to having to keep it secret, and Nikolai kept attempting to flirt with him in front of Danya. Everything about the day had been nauseating.

"I promise he's very much the angel he's rumored to be." Ilya kept his tone as neutral as he could manage, despite the anger gripping his throat. "You can ask all the townsfolk, they'll confirm."

"That was my plan, in fact! I'm sure I can learn a lot from your townsfolk, both about your *angel*, and about your situation here." Nikolai's smile was more genuine now, but he might as well have been spilling venom from his mouth for all he seemed to despise the both of them. Ilya didn't understand what Nikolai's agenda was, why he hadn't simply killed them in ambush when he had the chance.

Perhaps he really had been hoping to coerce Ilya into sleeping with him for their safety. Ilya weighed the option seriously in his mind as bile bubbled in his stomach yet again. Would it be worth it?

"I'm sure you'll learn a lot from the citizens of Velak. They're a… gossipy bunch," Ilya said, pausing at Danya's scoff behind him. "I'll admit there's not much room here in the rectory, but there is a sleeping area in the attic for you if you need."

"Unless I'm going to be sharing *your* bed it's best I get a room at the inn, Father. I'll return in the evening, if dinner is acceptable to you?"

Ilya could *hear* Danya's feathers standing on edge, saw the shadows of his wings spreading out of the corner of his eye. He sighed through his nose but gave Nikolai a welcoming smile. "It would. I'll have to make something special, it's not often I get such prestigious visitors as yourself, Senior Hunter."

They both rose from the couch so that Ilya could lead Nikolai back to the door. Danya remained behind Ilya, arms crossed as he seethed.

Nikolai brushed off the front of his coat and turned partway to look at the both of them. "Well, I shall see the both of you again soon enough."

Ilya nodded in return. "Of course. And I will… make serious consideration of your offer."

Danya inhaled sharply behind him. This damned angel was going to get them killed if he didn't *get his act together.*

Nikolai's eyes twinkled and another sickly grin spread across his face. "I appreciate the consideration, Father. And, my dear *angel*, consider sharing, won't you?"

Nikolai's back was to them by the time Danya had lunged forward, snarling as he slammed the door shut. He furiously dragged his nails back against his scalp, pulling at his hair in rage. "It's a good fucking thing he's not staying here or I'd have strangled him. I wish I could just turn back into the fucking drekavac and eat him. *Share?* Fuck *off!*"

Ilya sighed, approaching Danya to grab hold of his hands. As their fingers laced together all the tension melted off Danya, even his wings sagging to the floor. "Danylko. It's... something to consider, at least. I... I want us to be safe."

Danya hugged him tight, face pressed into his curls, feathery cage enveloping his body. "Please don't. Please... Don't sacrifice yourself more than you have. I can't take it, Ilya. I don't want him to use you like that."

Ilya sniffled, turning his face into the crook of Danya's neck. "I'm so tired, Danya. I just want to be at peace. If I do this, and we can leave? That has to be worth it, right?"

"He killed Tatyana, Ilya. He'll kill you too. I won't be able to live with myself if he hurts you. Please." Danya pulled back, cupping Ilya's face in his hands, calloused thumbs rubbing over pale cheeks. "I love you so much. You've been hurt enough already. I'd rather run and hide with you forever than live in peace knowing what you had to do to make it happen. I will fight for you every day, against any force they throw at us. Please."

Tears blurred Ilya's vision. Danya was willing to fight, but was Ilya? He hadn't known peace in over twenty years, could he stand being on the run from his own church for the rest of his life?

"I have a headache," Ilya finally sobbed, "And I don't know what to do."

Danya stroked Ilya's hair, sighing through his nose. "You don't have to decide on anything right now. We have the whole day, okay? Just… I don't want you to hurt yourself, Ilyushka. I love you."

"I love you too, Danylko. I'll think on it more… But I don't think I'll have the heart to give Nikolai what he wants. I've always been too much of a coward."

Danya pinched both of his cheeks, pulling at the skin gently. Ilya's face scrunched up in his irritation.

"Don't talk like that. I won't have you lying about my boyfriend, you hear me?"

Ilya batted Danya's hands away, huffing at him. "Now you stop that." He sighed, pressing his face to Danya's chest again. "Guess I'll just focus on dinner. See about stocking the sacristy so we can defend ourselves if it goes to shit."

"It'll be all right, Lyubimi. I won't let anything happen."

Ilya wanted to believe Danya, that it would all be okay.

But he couldn't lie to himself like that.

22

Ilya had banished Danya to the sacristy to collect their defenses and pack bags in case they needed to flee in a hurry. For his part, Ilya was doing his best to cobble together dinner. He decided on pirozhki; they didn't have much meat still, but plenty else to bulk them out, and plenty to make dough with. He stared out the window while he made the dough, eyes roaming over the graveyard. There were several lots that needed their headstones, but nobody had come up to order them, even still.

He got the pastries in the oven and dug through the pantry for other drinks to offer. All he had was a bottle of wine that was meant for ceremony. Ilya couldn't stand having it in the rectory, conjuring disgust every time he glanced at it in his hand. He looked back out at the graveyard, hesitating. Whatever happened tonight, it was probably his last chance to visit his father.

He had to speak to him before he left. So much had happened.

Fresh spring air filled his lungs when he stepped outside. The clouds blew by in the lazy breeze, still cool from the clinging winter. Ilya loved the change of the seasons. When the ice began to melt away, when the trees began to bud with new green life, when all the animals began to scurry around and roost once more. All came back to rejoice in the return of the Sun, to embrace her endless warmth. This was the true mark of a new year to him.

The graves were silent as always. Velak was painful in its lack of noise sometimes, but the graveyard held a gentle stillness. It was meditative rather than isolating, a small square of peace on top of a muddy beacon that loomed over town. There were pale green strands of grass attempting to break through the frozen earth; Ilya wished them the best of luck. He couldn't ever remember a time the yard had been carpeted green.

There were no signs of visitors as Ilya passed by the other stones; no flowers, no letters, no sentimental trinkets. He wasn't sure much would change after he left. He hoped the restless dead didn't feel forgotten and unloved.

Ilya tossed his cloak behind him and sat in front of a familiar stone. It was polished white marble carved in the shape of an angel, hands held together in prayer while perched atop an ornately carved plinth. Moss had overtaken the stone, green eating away at the pure white. Ilya had tried to clean it many times, but he didn't know these things. Nobody had wanted to take up the grave-keeper mantle, and the church hadn't sent anybody as a replacement.

And thus, his father's grave stood in disrepair.

"It's been a while, Papa," Ilya whispered. "I'm sorry it's taken me so long, but I've been busy. In a good way this time.

"I met somebody. I wonder what you'd think of him sometimes. I think you'd be awestruck, reverent even, since he's an angel. Literally! I still can't believe it either... but I worry you'd be sad, since he's a man. You were always open to everybody. You loved everyone and everything, no matter their faults or vices. You loved in spite of how painful it sometimes was... I wonder if you'd still love me. I like to tell myself you would.

"I love him more than I have words for. I don't know that I deserve him, or what I could've done to be granted this miracle. I don't know what he sees in me, what I do that gets him to stay. I wasn't even the person he was sent to look after! The Great Mother didn't choose me, and here I am with one of Her children, claiming him as my own… But he makes me happy. Happier than I've been since… before you left.

"Mama is still terrible to me. I'm sorry, Papa. She tried to kill me, you know… I know it would break your heart to see us like this. But you also know she's always been hard on me. I don't know if you ever tried hard enough to stop it… but I can never be near her again. There's a small, tiny chance I can leave Velak and be away from her… If I'm willing to sacrifice my dignity and person, I suppose. I don't know if I can do that… but I want to leave, Papa.

"But I'm scared to finally leave you behind. Forever. I haven't been able to heal since you left us, Papa. It's been so hard."

Ilya curled in on himself, face pressed into his hands. A lump formed in his throat, heart clenching as his shoulders wound tight. Leaving Velak meant so much to him. It was a pure freedom he'd never known, a chance to toss aside all the vile, hateful people who's only joy in life was to bring him misery.

It was also the only place he'd ever called home. His entire life had been here. His last living parent was here, his father was here, his church was here, his things and his routines. Having one small town as your entire universe was terrifying. The small glimpses of acceptance in the Capital, no matter how steeped in hypocrisy, enticed him. To know there were others like him, that he could be open in his love, that he could celebrate it for the joyous thing it was: enticing.

Opening up his world overwhelmed his senses, threatened to make him burst from the inside. He hoped it would all be worth it.

The sob he'd been holding at the back of his throat erupted from his lips, hot tears running down his cheeks. He lifted his head to gaze upon his father's headstone. He traced his fingers over the carvings, not yet overcome by nature.

Pavel Sokolov
1861 - 1897
Father, husband, priest.
Velak's greatest healer.

That was all Ilya had been left with. It made him angry that his father was nothing but six words. It was all about what he was to other people, not about who he was as a person. Nothing about his fountain of kindness, his love for all things, how he tried to see the best in everybody. No, this was a selfish stone, it was Velak remembering him for the favors he did.

Perhaps he'd be less angry if he'd ever been given a chance to mourn, if his father's undeniable skill hadn't been held over his head for so many years. Ilya had tried to learn, to improve his abilities, but it was no use. Nothing had ever been good enough.

Ilya choked on his next words, hiccuping from his mouth. "I'm sorry I'll have to leave you, Papa, but I can't stay here anymore. I can't. You know that. I can't be happy here. I've *never* been happy here. I'm going to take Danya with me and I'm going to find a new life. I can do it with him. I'm so, so sorry I have to leave you in this wretched place. I hope a life well-lived makes up for it."

His knees threatened to give when he stood, clinging to the wine bottle for dear life. Ilya propped himself up on Pavel Sokolov's headstone, a wave of vertigo thrumming in his head. The world spun and spun until finally Ilya found the strength to stand tall. He was leaving in whatever fashion it manifested. Nothing would ever be the same, but it was time to let go. He had to do this.

Ilya uncorked the bottle of wine, lifting it to the setting Sun. He stared at the dark liquid inside the green glass, heart pounding. This was the most heinous substance on earth, the thing that had destroyed his life and the lives of many in Velak. He wanted no more of it.

He took a sip, face scrunching from the bittersweet flavor. What did people even see in this stuff?

The rest he tipped onto the ground, splashing over his father's grave. One last drink before he left for good, before they would never see each other again. Ilya would be haunted no more, his father's spirit couldn't follow him wherever he was going. Soon Ilya would be free of all expectations. This was it.

He watched the dark red liquid puddle on the soil. It slowly, slowly receded into the earth. His eyes bore holes into the muddy spot until it disappeared, and for a bit longer still. The breeze started again, his vestments billowing in the wind, curls falling in front of his eyes.

Ilya craned his neck to stare at the sky. He admired the pink clouds scattered across the golden sky, slowly fading into the purple of night. The brightest stars were beginning to show, the faint cast of the moon rising above the mountains. Would the sky still look like this wherever he ended up? Would it be this clear? Would the Great Mother slowly fall behind the silhouetted mountains to cast the valley in shadow?

Fiery feathers encircled him, translucent and luminous in the last bit of sunlight. Ilya brushed his fingers across the surface, soft just like Danya's hair.

He leaned back, settling in Danya's arms when they wrapped around him. Despite his trepidations, at least in this moment, he was at peace. There was hope for the future, something to look forward to.

Ilya could let go now.

23

Their hands laced together as they walked back into the rectory. The silence between them stretched to a thread, strained and anxious, though not because of simmering anger. Danya wanted to speak. Ilya saw the muscles of Danya's throat shift and stiffen, words caught in a lump. Danya was handling him like fine china again, but he supposed the situation called for it. Ilya had no idea how much Danya overheard. Enough, it would seem.

Ilya pulled open the oven, holding his hand just above the metal grate to check the temperature. He moved his tray of pastries onto the rack, meeting his lover's golden gaze once the door shut. Danya stared back wordlessly, so Ilya set his timer. Danya's anxiety was making his *teeth* itch.

Ilya put one hand on the counter and another on his hip, frowning at his angel. "Danya if you don't speak I'm afraid I'll have to throw you into the oven as the second course."

Danya guffawed, tension melting off his body. "I probably taste like chicken."

Ilya snorted. "I wouldn't say that. Maybe a bit like gingerbread."

"Ilyushka!" Danya laughed at him, stepping up to kiss him,

gentle, careful still. "But okay, you caught me. I've been worried since Nikolai got here."

"You and me both." Ilya sighed and pinched the bridge of his nose, groaning in his exasperation. "I don't know what to even expect. If I say no to... to sleeping with him, what will happen next? Will he just kill us on the spot? Will he drag it out? I don't know."

"No, just... I remember everything now." Danya pressed his fingers to his temples briefly, wincing in pain before throwing his hands out in exasperation. "He was the one that cursed me. It was him. He shot me with something when I tried to save Tatyana. I keep seeing everything and it... it hurts, Ilya. I can't lose you too. Please don't... don't give him anything. He'll try to kill us anyway."

Danya couldn't look him in the eye. He worried his cuticles, jaw clenched so tight Ilya worried he'd shatter his own teeth. Ilya stepped close to him, taking Danya's hands into his own. He placed a gentle kiss on his cheek, resting his head on his angel's shoulder. Danya wrapped his wings around Ilya, a gentle warmth radiating off of his feathery shield.

"We'll have to fight him and run, Danya. He's strong and clever, but there are two of us. That has to count for something. If... If I leave my censer on the counter, I think we'll have a chance. Put some scarves on so we can cover our noses if I have to poison the rectory." Ilya lifted his head to meet Danya's glowing eyes, his brows furrowed in worry. Ilya rubbed the space between them with a thumb, only causing Danya to scrunch his face further. "And you have your fancy armor now. We won't be defenseless. If it goes to shit, grab me and we fly away."

Danya grumbled at him, blowing air out of his nose. "Yeah. Okay. I guess that's all we can do, isn't it? Hope he doesn't have too much of an upper hand. Just... wish I remembered how to fight properly. That's still eluding me."

Ilya placed his hands on Danya's chest, smoothing out the fabric of his cardigan. His thumb caught on a loose thread, making a mental note to repair it later. Not that it truly mattered right now, but pretending he'd have the chance to fix it brought him comfort.

"Well, you've managed so far just brute-forcing your way through things. I'm sure it'll be effective still."

"Hey now, you make me sound like a meathead." Danya pouted at him, lips pursed so perfectly Ilya couldn't help but kiss them. They were locked together like this, lips brushing together, teasing. There was an absence of heat in the action, not meant to spur each other on, only to be close and share affection, one final moment of peace in each other until it was ripped away.

Danya's sigh was long and beleaguered when they parted. Ilya felt much the same.

"Suppose we should face the music, Ilyushka."

"Suppose we should, Danylko."

Ilya found his thickest scarves, tying an ochre-colored one around Danya's neck. It complimented his warm toned features, like it was meant to be there. Good; they didn't need to draw suspicion. He tied a black scarf around his own neck, blending perfectly with his vestments. They were as ready as they could be.

"Why aren't we just running," Danya whispered. "What's stopping us?"

Ilya chewed his lip. He didn't have a good answer for that question, mulling on it as he checked the pirozhki. "I think we have too much pride. And perhaps a little revenge on the man who destroyed the life of the angel I care about and who holds so much power over others is in order. Trying to stop him from doing harm to others... It feels like my true duty to the Sun."

Danya snorted. "So we're too good of people for our own good because we actually listen to my Mother?"

Ilya smiled back at him. "I suppose we are."

THEY ACTED THE PART, pretending as though nothing was amiss. They all had a silent agreement to one last meal until the illusion of peace shattered. A light drizzle had started, the stubborn winter chill attempting to keep its grasp on the world. Ilya was filled with a sense of strength. They were doing the right thing in staying, in trying to fight this horrific force, hopeless as it might be.

Danya was an angel, and Ilya a priest. It was their duty to the Great Mother to cure this illness, to cut out the rot in the foundations. If their church had lost its way, they would tear it all down and begin anew.

They ate their pastries between quiet conversation, light topics to begin.

"Velak is a quaint little town, Father Sokolov, as are its people. I'm surprised you'd want to leave it," Nikolai said.

"I'm surprised they didn't have words with you about me," Ilya offered in return. "Danya can tell you when he first arrived, all they wanted to do was complain about me."

Danya rolled his eyes and bit his tongue, choosing to down the rest of his tea in lieu of a reply.

"Their tone suggested some feelings of resentment, but nothing out of the ordinary for a small town like this. The rural types don't know how good they have it, do they?" Nikolai chuckled and placed the last bite of his dinner in his mouth. The air in the room was sucked out: the last bits of their pretend decorum eroded with each crumb brushed off of Nikolai's uniform.

Ilya sipped his tea, leaving the last bites of his food on his plate, delaying the inevitable still. "No, I recall the Capital being quite loud and boisterous. Hard to find yourself there, easy to be drowned out and forgotten. I'm sure many have slipped through the cracks. It's hard to forget anybody here."

"Indeed... Now, I did conduct my investigation into our angel problem, and I'll say my findings are yet to be conclusive. I'll have to conduct a final examination, though all signs point to your *Danya* being such a divine creature." Nikolai said the name with such disdain. Ilya found it shameful for a church Hunter to despise a child of the Sun so deeply. Danya's feathers bristled ever so slightly, but Ilya was proud he managed to control himself. "A physical exam is the best thing, you understand as a healer I'm sure. If you wouldn't mind giving us some privacy later, Father Sokolov?"

Ilya and Danya both set their cups down. The ticking hands of the grandfather clock next to the fireplace echoed in the room. Just seconds until everything changed.

"Of course, Hunter Nikolai. Was there anything else you needed from me before I step out?" Despite his words, Ilya remained planted in his seat. His intentions were clear.

Nikolai smirked back at him, smug air permeating the room. "I'm curious if you'd given any thought to my proposal... I do think it would be a waste to not share in the touch of another man. I doubt a boy as pretty as yourself can be satisfied with just the one, surely."

Boy. He was 30 fucking years old. The assumption he was promiscuous for the face he was born with was equally absurd. *Stupid man.*

Danya's nails dug into the wood of the table, cracks forming under the tips of his fingers. For once Ilya's patience was equally thin.

Ilya flashed Nikolai the briefest smile in one last attempt to be amicable. "I've spent a considerable amount of time thinking on your proposal, Hunter Nikolai. You're correct I've not known the touch of another man before Danya, but unfortunately for you I've found his to be the only one here that I need. I'm afraid my dear guardian angel is also unwilling to share, which I'm sure you know.

"I am equally unwilling to sleep with a man who would use his modicum of power to extort sex from somebody lower rank than him. Holding my freedom hostage so you can find your pleasure is vile. I find you despicable, and I know when the time comes, the Night will welcome you into its bitter embrace."

Nikolai smiled at him. Once more it failed to reflect in his eyes. They were glassy black voids: nothing to hide, and nothing to show.

"Well. I can't say I'm surprised by your response, but I am very disappointed. I had thought you to be much more intelligent, Father. A shame to waste a body like yours."

"Sun's *sake*, would you shut the fuck *up* already?" Danya tossed his teacup aside, jumping to his feet and launching himself at Nikolai.

In a brilliant flash of light Danya's shining silver and gold armor formed to his body, ruby-crusted sword in hand. In as quick of a move, Nikolai pulled a chain from his belt. It was black cast iron, a large iron ball at the end that went hurtling towards Danya. The ball glanced off Danya's jaw just as he tackled Nikolai to the floor. There was no mistaking the sizzle of burning skin as the iron made contact with Danya's skin. Ilya caught a brief glimpse of the raw, smoking flesh before the two were rolling on the ground. Ilya leaped back as they crashed into the table, shattering a chair into splinters.

Ilya snatched his censer off the counter, stepping into the corner by the pantry to light the incense. He fumbled with the matches, keeping an eye on Nikolai and Danya to avoid their warpath. They were tangled up together, both using their supernatural strength to hold the other down. Danya's eyes burned gold while the veins around Nikolai's eyes feathered out in black, like ink in water.

Finally Ilya held his hands steady enough to strike a match, lighting the brick of sickly yellow incense. He pulled his scarf up as the marigold-colored fog spilled out of the pot. He swung it back and forth, quickly filling the room.

"Danya, scarf!" he shouted, swinging his censer towards the brawling men.

Danya did as instructed. Nikolai used the brief distraction to grab for the end of his chain weapon. With a flick of Nikolai's hand the chain was wrapping around Danya's bare wrist. Danya's skin smoked on contact, a cry of agony ripping from his throat. His sword clattered to the ground, narrowly missing Nikolai when it bounced off the wood. Danya snarled and tugged on the chain with all his strength. He yanked Nikolai to his feet, though the thin chain held strong. Danya launched his unhindered fist at Nikolai. Nikolai dipped out of its path just in time, uncoiling the chain of his weapon.

The ball struck Danya in the chest this time, enough force to send him flying back into the rectory door. It cracked on impact, Danya slumping against the wood.

Ilya was in a panic. He swung the incense around more and more, daring to step near Nikolai. The iron ball slammed into his ribs as Nikolai whirled on him. Ilya collapsed into a heap, censer clattering to the floor. He gasped for air, hands clutching desperately at his ribs, definitely rebroken.

A great cloud of yellow smoke erupted from the metal pot. The room was filled to the brim with a noxious haze. Nikolai's knees buckled, desperately clawing at his throat while he coughed and wheezed.

"What the fuck is this?" Nikolai spat. "You stupid fucking priest—"

Danya groaned behind them. He staggered to his feet, eyes filled to the brim with liquid gold, glowing with his rage. The whites were gone and fire began to lick up his palms, slowly clenching into fists. Nikolai turned just in time to have a set of hot knuckles make contact with his cheek. The Hunter howled in pain, the scent of more burning flesh filling the room. He coughed and heaved, clawing at his throat and then at the floor.

Ilya wheezed, wincing as pain shot through him with every breath. All that mattered was the incense was working and they'd be free to go soon enough. He watched as Danya loomed over Nikolai, admired the flames contained in his palms. What other abilities did Danya have just out of reach?

"Have you had enough yet, fucker?" Danya spat. "Will that be all? Am I angel enough for you? Has the helpless priest outsmarted you?"

Nikolai gasped for air, slamming a hand against the wood as he grabbed for something at his belt. The black veins around Nikolai's eyes filled with more and more ink, spidering across his neck and arms. He panted still, but had found the strength to act.

With his ribs the state they were, Ilya barely registered the pain that was a small crossbow bolt lodged in his neck. It burned like heat against skin after being stuck in the bitter cold, a white hot intensity that had you craving the chill once more. His nerves twitched and jolted and he writhed on the floor involuntarily, bile gathering at the back of his throat.

Ilya could swear he heard Danya screaming, saw his light go out, the gleam of his armor shatter into silver sparks to leave behind his regular clothes. It was the briefest of moments and all Nikolai needed. He whipped out his meteor hammer once more, wrapping it around Danya's body. He screamed again, thrashing against the cast iron and failing to break through.

Ilya lifted his hands, watching his veins pulse and go as black as Nikolai's. There were already patches of dark golden scales on his body. They itched terribly. 'Like a motherfucker', as Danya might put it. It was a funny way to say it.

It was also *a little* funny the drekavec would do him in after all.

He choked from a second bolt strike just beneath his right collarbone, more icy heat penetrating into him. Ilya rolled onto his side despite his pain, retching black bile onto the polished wooden floors.

A steel-toed boot made impact with his stomach, forcing even more to gush out of his mouth. More thick, gooey ink oozed out of his ears and his tear ducts, plugged his nose. He couldn't escape it.

"Father I really should thank you for doing whatever it was that restored our dear angel. The council of pontiffs have been furious at me for losing their prize, but they'll be thrilled to have Danil back in custody. He'll serve a greater purpose now, I promise." Nikolai grinned at him. Ilya couldn't decide if it was better or worse that it was an expression of genuine mirth this time.

Nikolai stomped over to his bag, pulling out much heavier iron chains. One side had spikes that Nikolai was all too happy to press into Danya's body. Ilya whimpered as Danya cried out in pain, smoke rising from every wound. He could hear the sizzle of liquid boiling over and over, wheat colored blood dripping from the chains.

"Solnishko," Ilya croaked. He reached out for Danya, fingers cracking when metal boot toes smashed into them. Ilya cried out once more, "Mercy—!"

The corners of his vision grew dark, the endless nausea and pain fading into an excruciating hunger. He felt so empty. He needed to fill the void.

"Go, Ilya! Get to the woods!"

Ilya. He was Ilya? Maybe. He needed to run. If he didn't find somewhere to hide before dawn, he would burn to ash. But he was so *hungry*. But he needed to go away.

Ilya scrambled to his feet, long black talons scratching the surface. He shoved through the door to the church? His church, maybe. This holy place that made his skin burn. His teeth ached, his brain stuck in a case two sizes too small that made his head throb. Shiny black feathers burst from his hands as he rushed outside, indigo ink dripping from the growth.

He avoided the always-muddy hill to crash into the trees. He was running, had to run far away. Who was he? It was hard to say. Somebody told him to run, somebody that cared about him. Who was that?

Did anybody care for him?

He ran on hands and feet? Legs now, carrying him for miles. One more head, then a second popped up beside him, long necked and without flesh on its face. It wore a crown of black feathers, long fangs glistening in the faint moonlight. Not a trace of humanity remained with him.

What was a human?

Why was he running? He couldn't even remember that anymore.

He came to a stop by a creek running down the hill. He panted for air, lapping water with his three heads, each desperate to drink their fill. It wouldn't satiate his urge to feed, but it would keep it in check for now.

He looked to the sky, at the thousands of… stars? In the sky. They were harsh on his eyes, emitting halos of light that blinded him. The great ball of silver was even worse, pain lancing through his head. All three heads hissed and turned their gazes down. He dove into the nearby thicket, fearing what the silver light would do to him. He dragged his talons over his bony face, hissing at every chirping bird and snapped twig. Everything was a threat, out to destroy him.

That's what he remembered. He was running from something that wanted to hurt him. What was it? It didn't matter. It could be anything, everything. He would kill it.

One of his heads alerted him to a soft, golden light in the distance. It bounced slightly, moving further away from him. This one didn't hurt to gaze at, was inviting him in.

He wanted it. He wanted it all to himself. The light hated him, wanted to hurt him, but he would hurt this light. He would consume it all for himself, and maybe then he would know satisfaction.

He began running, galloping on scaled, four-toed feet. His desperation overcame him, replaced only with an urge.

He would feast.

24

The agony of the iron chains piercing his flesh was nothing compared to watching the love of his life flee into the gaping, toothy maw of the pines. Danya could see the familiarity leaving Ilya's eyes second after second, barely more than a terrified animal. Watching Ilya's form twist away from his lovely human shape into a beast that would sooner eat him than kiss him.

Danya hung his head in shame, finally let the defeat wash over him. His head pounded as every memory returned, the look of terror on Tatyana's face as she told him to run, begged him to leave. The terror he felt at leaving her behind, morphing into base instinct that only told him there was danger behind him.

There would be no kindly priest to break Ilya's curse. Just an angel who had failed his duty. Twice.

Danya was a shit excuse for an angel. He had to be his Mother's least favorite son for how royally he kept fucking up.

Heavy boot falls rattled the floorboards next to him, chains shaking in kind and renewing his wounds. Smoke and the smell of cooked flesh filled his nostrils; he had no idea where Ilya got the cinnamon smell from, Danya thought he smelled like pure, rotting *death*.

Nikolai grabbed hold of Danya's chin, forcing his eyes upward. Nikolai's face was plastered with pure serenity, the first genuine smile Danya had seen from him. Nikolai was thrilled with what he'd done. Danya would fucking kill him the second this fucker slipped up.

Danya yanked his head out of Nikolai's leather-gloved grasp, snapping at the air where his hand had been. Dammit. "What do you even fucking *want?* All Ilya wanted was to leave, we could've been out of your hair. We would've fucked off into the woods and never come back."

Nikolai clucked his tongue, driving his fist into Danya's jaw. Danya snarled, feathers stood on edge and fire licking up his fists in his rage once again. Nikolai circled around him, keeping a wide berth. He examined Danya in silence, like a wolf watching its prey. Danya wished he could conjure the drekavac he had been so he could chew through Nikolai's stupid fucking ankles.

Nikolai paused in front of him and Danya made another lunge. Nikolai side-stepped out of the way with ease, watching in bemusement as Danya slammed into the floor. The spiked chains dug in deeper, more honey colored blood spilling. He hissed through his teeth, glaring at the hunter who now loomed over his body.

"Tsk, tsk, my little angel. You're much more violent than before. I suppose the night has crawled into you and left its mark, just as it did on me. On all of us…"

Danya attempted another lunge, earning a swift kick in the nose. The resounding crack rattled in his ears, more sticky, gooey blood dripping down his face. For all the pain he was in, it didn't matter anymore. He had nothing left to live for except to make Nikolai's life as horrific as possible. Until his last breath, he would make this man suffer in any manner he had power over.

"You're quite persistent. Hard to say if it's that sense of justice the Mother instills in you, or if you're simply an idiot. Perhaps both, if I were to be honest. Then again, blind justice is blind foolishness."

Danya spit at his feet, flecks of gold coating the black material of Nikolai's boots. "What's the point of all this shit? Why the grandstanding? You could've killed us at any time for all you prepared. Why keep me alive now?"

Nikolai's smug expression flickered only briefly, but it was enough to keep the fire in Danya's chest lit. "I'll admit to an error of judgment on my part. I assumed your Ilya would give in to his priestly, self-sacrificing ways and give me what I wanted first. What's life without a little fun, after all?"

Nikolai paused, watching Danya's movements. Danya would never admit that he was drained, fighting spirit dependent on pure adrenaline and hate. "Can't form a pattern," Danya spat. "Can't make it easy for you."

Nikolai rolled his eyes, squatting a few feet away from Danya. "Angels are all surprisingly easy to deal with. Very strong, yes, but naive to a fault. All it takes is a little ingenuity, and a little cast iron." Nikolai shoved at the chains, a new plume of putrid smoke rising from Danya's body. "Now, as for what I plan to do with you? Well… normally I might just kill you and dump you into the woods, but the church has a newfound purpose for you. It was a mistake to have cursed you in the first place… You've become such lovely material."

Danya's brows knit together as he tried to process what he heard. Materials? What the fuck did that mean? Nothing good, that much he knew.

Being hoisted to his feet meant yet another wave of pain lancing into his flesh. Every nerve was on fire, threatening to immolate him from inside out. His knees were like jelly, barely holding him up. If being dead weight is what it took to inconvenience Nikolai at this juncture, he'd do it.

"Time to go, little angel. You'll be made a spectacle one last time, I'm afraid, though you'll be reviled as you should have always been. What a shame you've brought on Her name."

Nikolai marched him first through the church. Ilya's church, his father's church. Danya's eyes rolled in his skull lazily, moving from the polished black marble floors to the carved, arched ceilings. The window in the roof let in only the silver light of the full Moon. Should he call the moon Father? Could he beg Him for aid in this time? He barely spoke with his Mother, though. If She wasn't listening, Danya doubted He was either.

Silence dragged between them as they began the final march down the muddy hill. Danya fucking hated this hill and the only silver lining to all of this was that he'd never have to see it again. As the earth squelched beneath their feet, Danya swore an oath to himself. The second he found an opportunity, even the most minute of slip-ups, he'd take his chance. He would bring down the wrath of all the Sun on those around him, they would be nothing but charred, blackened ash. He would be a supernova of energy. He would hold on to this as long as possible, and then he would break free.

And then he would find Ilya.

And then he would fix this.

And then he would have his love back.

The rattle of chains, the throbbing pain of the needle points jamming into his muscles, the unearthly smell of rot. It was an hour to walk into town until his feet found solid ground on the cobbles of the main square. Danya glanced over at the entrance to Berta's shop. The upstairs window glowed orange through the transparent curtains. She'd be going to bed soon.

Danya couldn't leave that hag without saying goodbye. No matter the circumstances.

He thrashed in Nikolai's grasp, snarling and hissing, putting on the biggest show he could. "Unhand me! Monster of a man, murderer!"

Nikolai remained undeterred, dragging Danya to the inn across from the town hall. A wooden cart with a cast iron cage was hitched to the entrance, two enormous black horses attached to it. They chuffed and knickered upon Nikolai's approach, stepping back from Danya as best they could.

Danya lunged at them, the horses screeching and rearing. Nikolai threw Danya to the ground, reaching out to calm the horse. It settled under his touch, panting hard in its fear. Distant echoes of doors opening and closing rang across Velak, people pouring into the streets to check the commotion. Danya spotted Berta in the distance, stepping into the crowd that formed around him and Nikolai.

Mayor Ivan stepped to the front, adjusting his glasses to examine Danya before approaching the cart. "Hunter Nikolai, what is the meaning of all this? Why is this angel in chains?"

Nikolai ignored Ivan, glancing out at the crowd. He spread his arms out, making direct eye contact with the men closest to the front. "And who among you would help me cage this demon? This foul beast of the night that has tricked all of you? He fooled your priest and killed him in cold blood! And he will do this to the rest of you!"

Gasps erupted from the group, whispers spreading between them. Danya heard talk of Ilya being a stupid child, of Danya's demonic influence explaining his deviancies. They questioned if Danya had been here all along, if he foolishly believed his grand schemes could come to fruition now. Oh, how glad they were that the great senior hunter had finally saved them from this curse!

Danya searched the crowd, meeting Berta's eyes just as a pack of men surrounded him. She looked sad, confusion and fear spread across her face. Danya let his rage slip for just a moment, chest aching in his sorrow. Berta had been his lifeline, had helped give him purpose alongside Ilya. She had changed her mind, had been willing to be better. She couldn't believe them, could she?

Once again, Danya was thrown onto a hard surface. The chains crushed against the wood, digging into his delicate wings. It was a wonder no chain had jammed into his spine; perhaps that was just his remaining bit of luck. The door of the cage slammed shut. Danya scrambled to his knees, looking out at the mob of Velak. He found Berta's tearful gaze, doubt clouding her.

"He tells lies," Danya shouted. "He cursed me, he cursed your priest, and he would see you all burn so he could hold power over you!"

Ivan approached then, hand slipping through the bars to grab at Danya's bonds. He pulled hard, slamming him against yet more cast iron. Danya cried out as flesh made contact, burning his cheek.

"It's funny," Ivan said. "I should be angry at you for being a freak and a murderer, but you did us all a favor. Now we can get a priest who's actually good for anything."

Danya glared at this wretched old man. All his time here and Ivan could never muster a single good word. He didn't even know what Ivan provided for his community, other than stoking hatred. He had made Ilya's life a living hell, from the second Ilya had taken him in. He recalled the day he'd found Ilya sobbing in the back of his church, embarrassed to be seen but too upset to stop. He recalled the way the citizens of Velak at large spoke about Ilya, how they had abused him all his life. Ivan was a symbol of Velak, of all the evil that Ilya had been made to endure for all these years.

Enough.

He used what little strength he had left to quickly lean back, lurching forward to slam Ivan's arm between his body and the bars. The bone crunched like gravel, eliciting an ear-piercing scream from Ivan. He slammed against Ivan's arm twice before Nikolai intervened. He shoved a pronged stick between the bars and against Danya's neck.

Searing jolts ran through his body, muscles spasming and contorting. The shock was enough for him to collapse to the floor and release the mayor, who swore and cried. The crowd jeered and shouted at him, throwing rocks at the cart the second Nikolai stepped away. Danya twitched against the boards, gasping for air. He had no idea what Nikolai had just done to him; it was similar to the pain that came when he touched a circuit with bare hands, concentrated right into his nerves.

His ears rang, heart beating out of time for just a moment. Despite how shit he was physically, his soul felt settled knowing he'd doled out even an ounce of the pain that Ilya had endured. Ilya would hate that he'd done it, had never approved of violence, but more's the pity. Ilya wasn't here right now, and Danya needed anything positive in his life.

He gathered his strength to shout after Ivan, quickly being carted away to be looked after. "It's a shame I never got to eat you! I would've been doing this town a favor! May you never recover!"

Nikolai whirled on the crowd, waving a hand in Danya's direction. "Do you see? Do you see what this demon has done to your dear mayor, the pain he's wished upon him? You're safe now from this foul creature! May you only know peace with our dear Mother from here."

The mob cheered, crowding the cart as Nikolai readied it for travel. There were so many people shouting at him, rattling the bars, grabbing at any part of them they could. He hissed when the stray hand of a blonde girl (Polina, wasn't it?) grabbed a handful of his feathers, yanking them free for herself.

"This man tricked me into being attracted to him! It was all a ruse so he could hide sleeping with Ilya!" Polina shouted.

"He touched my radio and fixed it, he's using night magic!"

"He changed the Father's heart to be attracted to him!"

The voice of Oyuna. If Ilya were around to hear it, he would be nothing but broken shards of an already shattered man.

The mob followed as Nikolai signaled for the horses to start moving. The cart rattled across the uneven cobbles, a new wave of ache digging into his body. He was so defeated. Eventually the people of Velak lost interest, hanging back to watch and scream from a distance. One last voice carried on the wind, the voice that broke him entirely.

"My boy! You're taking my boy!"

Danya's eyes slammed shut, biting his lip so hard it split. He wouldn't cry. He couldn't.

He was going to miss Berta so much.

Perhaps one day they could meet again. He hoped he wouldn't have to wait until his Mother called him home.

At last, the fire inside of Danya burned out. It was nothing but hazy coals, fighting to consume whatever it could until the light was snuffed. He was the ash at the bottom of a campfire, nothing but dust.

Danya had nothing left.

The stars above swirled in the sky, glittering cosmos that he had once called home. Flashes of Tatyana flooded his mind, all their time spent together. Things were simpler at the start. He knew his task, knew the joy of true love, knew the adventure of discovering what it meant to live. Tatyana had taught him every possibility she knew, taught him to know himself.

She would've loved Ilya. He knew that. Where Danya had failed to completely bring him out of his shell, he was positive Tatyana could have. Her energy was infectious.

He missed them both so much.

25

March 2nd, 1928

Danya found it weird they were still moving through the night. Light injured the drekavac; he could recall every burn from when he stayed out too long at night. Not only that, but they'd make easy pickings for bandits like this.

"Hey, fuckface, why the fuck haven't we stopped for the night already?"

Nikolai tsk'd at him, not bothering to give him even a glance. "You're very vulgar. Is the drekavac curse so effective? It's too bad you're more useful as materials. Studying you would be fascinating."

"Would you just answer the question?" Danya wasn't in a position to be making demands, but it was clear that Nikolai wasn't going to kill him. Might as well annoy him while he could.

And perhaps if Nikolai became angry enough to hurt him, he wouldn't mind. Punishment was all Danya felt he deserved in this moment.

Nikolai sighed irritably. "If you must know, it's for your benefit. Your little monster can only travel at night, as I'm sure you understand."

Danya wrinkled his nose and rolled his eyes to glare at Nikolai's back. "How could this *possibly* be to my benefit?"

Nikolai chuckled in such a condescending manner that Danya's blood turned to hot magma. He possessed all the fire and fury of the Sun, temper blazing out of control without his charge to ground him. Even if it cost him his life, the second he had a chance to break Nikolai in half, he would do it.

"He's going to want to feast on *your* flesh long before mine, little angel," Nikolai replied. "You're a source of light that doesn't hurt to simply look at. They hate the light. Why not attack the one source that won't hurt?"

Another derisive snort. Danya ground his teeth together so hard he could've worn them smooth. He'd let Ilya consume him. Never would he harm him, even as a monster. If Ilya happened to eat Nikolai after? A fucking win in Danya's book.

"You keep calling me material. What for?"

He'd gotten Nikolai talking. He had to keep him talking. If there was even a single chance to escape later, perhaps using Nikolai's ego against him would help.

"Did your dear Tatyana not tell you? Did you not ask why she was throwing her notes away?"

If Danya's veins were glowing with rage he wouldn't be the least bit surprised. He desperately needed to kill this fucking guy.

"I never doubted her intentions for a second."

Nikolai fully turned around in his seat to look at him, cold black eyes filled with an uneasy mirth. "Is that so? You were never curious why we came after her?"

"Because you're miserable misogynists who've become entirely misguided?"

Nikolai scoffed and turned back around. "She was helping us. She was going to get in your good graces and bring you to us to use."

Ice settled in his stomach for just a moment. "You're lying." Danya hated how his voice wavered.

Another condescending laugh. "Does it hurt that I told you

before she was ever going to? I doubt she ever admitted it to you anyway."

Danya was silent, hot tears gathered at the corners of his eyes. Nikolai had been gloating and telling the truth this whole time. Was there any good in him lying?

"What are you doing with angels?"

At this, Nikolai looked at him again. That serene, sickening smile was back on his face. "Creating better versions of yourselves, of course."

THE REST of the night was travelled in silence between them. Danya winced every time they hit a rock or dip in the road that made the cast iron sticking into his flesh reopen his wounds.

The clicking of horse hooves and the whir of birds and insects chirping in the woods made for decent enough white noise that he could doze. He looked to the sky as his eyelids grew heavy. The waxing crescent Moon had been blocked by the clouds. What little light had existed earlier in the evening had been snuffed out.

It had been raining a lot recently. Danya recalled a time as a drekavac when he was able to stay out long into the day thanks to the cloud cover. It had been painful still, but he wasn't burned.

Would Ilya be able to follow them in the day? The hunger would drive him, and if dying was no longer an obstacle, he would likely push through the pain.

Danya held this small bit of hope to his chest as his body finally gave in to exhaustion.

DESPITE HOW LATE HE SLEPT, Danya adored dawn time. Ilya woke then. In turn, Danya would wake to the smell of breakfast, the sight of his partner at peace in front of the stove. On rare occasions he'd even catch Ilya looking content, not a single wrinkle of worry on his face. He dreamed of the days when he'd always be that way.

The soft morning light would glow on his curls, outline every shape of Ilya's body so it was easier to admire. No matter how groggy and cranky he was, catching a glimpse of his partner's smile made it all the better. Ilya had told him that if Danya were any time of day, then it was the dawn. His hair was like the perfect sunrise.

Raindrops pattered on his cheeks and eyelids, forcing Danya to awake to a gray, sunless sky. His limbs flamed with pain, iron needles still dug into his flesh. He hissed through his teeth as Nikolai began to pull the wagon off the road.

It was difficult to not wish for death in this state.

Danya overheard the ground crunching while Nikolai made camp. It was a surprisingly modest tent when you considered how grandiose and immodest the church was in all things. He expected the tent to be gold leafed at this rate.

"So I get to stay in here then?" Danya called.

Nikolai snorted. "I would be a fool to give you even an inch, little angel."

"Oh, is that all you have? You wouldn't have been able to satisfy Ilya anyway." Danya knew what was coming, but he took sick pleasure in riling Nikolai enough to get a reaction so strong.

Nikolai grabbed at his chains through the bars, yanking Danya forward with enough force that his nose cracked on impact. Yet more golden blood spilled down his face. Danya's head spun, the space between his eyes burning with an intense ache.

Nikolai let go of him, heat radiating from his coals for eyes. Danya tilted his head back, letting blood gather at the back of his throat before he spat at the hunter. Golden speckles covered Nikolai's face.

Danya crooned, "Aw, look, we match now."

Nikolai was grinding his teeth so hard Danya was sure he could mill wheat between his molars. He wiped the golden blood away, hissing back, "If only I could let your pathetic little boyfriend eat you and be done with it."

Danya smiled at Nikolai's back until it was clear he wouldn't be getting another rise out of him. He turned his attention to the woods around them. His eyes scanned over every gnarled conifer, past every thorn bush, but nothing was revealed. Not a twig snapped, not a shadow too dark to be anything but a hidden monster. Nothing.

The faint flame of hope he'd held in his chest went out in a frail puff of smoke. He laid on his back again, watching the clouds roil and turn black above. Not even the sight of his mother to comfort him.

26

March 4th, 1928

The rain was constant. While Nikolai had his oiled coat and wide-brimmed hat to protect himself from the downpour, Danya remained exposed. It was nice to finally have all the dried, crusted blood from his various wounds cleaned, but it was beginning to wear on his soul. The fact that he couldn't pry his wings free to shield himself added to his misery.

He wasn't cold, exactly. He'd barely felt the chill of Velak's snowstorms, for all of Ilya's worried scolding. Still. Every drop that landed between his eyes was going to drive him to murder. He wanted to murder Nikolai anyway, but there was another veneer of rage on top of his existing anger.

The inky black of the night eventually gave way to the shadowy gray of the morning. Danya had already given up hope of spotting Ilya in the shadows. No beast would come to free him, either out of love or hunger. Any day now they'd return to the capitol, he would see those white marble pillars that dared reach up into the Sun's territory, and that would be it. The thing Tatyana had died for would come to pass. Ilya would be gone forever. He would still be a failure.

"So really. What are you going to do to me?" Danya asked.

"Oh? Are you being civil now?" Nikolai replied.

Danya scoffed. While he raged at the rain, the fire had been snuffed out of him days ago. He was nothing but cooling embers waiting to wither into dust. "From the sounds of it this is my last chance to find out what's going on."

"I don't see the point in telling you. You won't be aware of your fate when it's all said and done."

Danya listened to the horses clopping away in the mud. His jaw tensed as horrifying imagery flashed in his mind. Tatyana had been good with machinery, but her specialty had been communications. What could she possibly have had to do with these blasphemous works? What manner of monster would they force him to become this time?

"If I won't be aware then what's the fucking harm in telling me?"

Nikolai hummed in thought, clucking his tongue and then replying, "You'll become materials for a greater purpose. An angelic machine that obeys the commands of the church. The wings of angels are beautiful sights, but the new ones we've made for you and your siblings... Truly a picture of the divine. The glass is as marvelous as the Capitol cathedral.

"The common people are beginning to get out of order. They don't attend ceremony, they don't give to their churches. You saw in Velak, the disrespect Father Sokolov endured for years! The lack of gratitude! They think now that they can use their radios and their phones to reach each other they no longer need their church? It can't stand.

"You will become a new angel, a better version of yourself. One that keeps these *degenerates* in line. We will take our power back!"

"You're so full of shit."

Nikolai whirled around to glare at him, an intense gaze that Danya returned equally.

"You saw for yourself how those pitiful *villagers* behaved, how easily they gave into their hatred, and you tell me this?" Nikolai might as well have been spitting his words for how furious he was. Good thing Danya's face was already soaking wet.

"You're not better. You won't win. Control like yours only lasts for so long."

Nikolai stopped the cart, leaping from his seat to better face Danya in his cage. Danya barely masked the smirk attempting to creep onto his face.

"You–" Nikolai's thick finger pressed against the iron bars. "You, do not matter. You are a vessel for the machinery that your pompous, hedonistic, vapid, bitch ex-girlfriend helped us create. She was happy to betray you until you acted pathetic enough to charm her. She tried to hide all the evidence from you, tried to burn all of our plans, but it didn't matter. You're going to be a mindless beast once again, and she'll have died for nothing. You'll have failed in your duties *twice*. A truly pathetic example of an angel. Your Mother is surely ashamed of you."

Danya nearly missed the crunch of the undergrowth followed by the wet sound of a knife entering Nikolai's back. He let out a gasp, processing his injury for a brief moment. Black veins pulsed from his voided out eyes, teeth grit as Nikolai turned on his assailant.

Danya scrambled to his knees, glancing in every direction. He counted six men in dark clothes that approached them. Some had chains in hand, others had knives, one had a crossbow.

Nikolai had a bolt in his shoulder by the time he reached his crossbow, snarling as a bolt of his own pierced one of the men's chests. Danya's heart pounded, eyes darting every which way. The two men with chains rushed the wagon, smashing the lock to the cage with a mallet.

"Are you freeing me?" Danya's desperation was at its peak, but he'd take anything.

"Think we'll just turn you into the pontiffs ourselves," one of them replied.

They pulled on Danya's chains and dragged him out. He fell to the ground, hissing between his teeth from the force of spikes in his muscle. Smoke rose from the wounds again, golden blood burning across the blackened iron. He was sick to death of bleeding, and also very light-headed.

"You're coming with us pretty boy," one of the men growled.

Danya's vision spun when the two men dragged him back to his feet. Maybe if he vomited on their boots they'd leave him alone? This was a fucking mess. Oh well. His head already hurt.

Surprise, smashing his head into his captor's face didn't make it better. Thankfully, the man stumbled back into a nearby tree.

The other rushed up to him. "Stupid bird bitch!"

A hidden cattle hammer nearly missed Danya's skull. He backed into a different nearby tree deeper into the woods, spending the briefest moment catching his breath when his attacker came at him with another swing.

"Could you at least cut me out of these things before you cave in my skull? Shit!"

The commentary was not appreciated, it seemed. The other goon managed to get himself together, swinging the iron chain he held. Danya wasn't sure of his chances, but at least these men were likely more stupid. It was easier to escape stupid, unprepared men than the expertly trained hunter.

Danya hobbled away, trying to not slip in the mud. Always the *fucking* mud. The bandits chased him, boots splashing heavily. Unfamiliar cries of pain rang out behind them, each preceded by the whoosh of a crossbow. Nikolai was putting them out too easily; of course the monster hunter would find human men trivial.

Danya kept running, rain pouring down his face and into his eyes. He was exhausted and in pain, but he would keep running.

But the silence behind him gave him pause. He stumbled to a stop, glancing over his shoulder. All he could see were trees and rain. Out of the corner of his vision, the men chasing him ran along the path, shouting to each other. He couldn't make out their words. He assumed Nikolai had scared them straight, which was good for him. He could take his chance to escape, as futile as it might be.

The high, shrill hissing of a snake sent an icy spike through his chest. A warning. It grew until it sounded as if a dozen snakes were behind him. Danya turned just in time to witness the monster Ilya had become.

Talons raked across his chains, three bony faces snapping in his face. Danya threw his leg out, kicking Ilya in the stomach to keep him back. The center head whipped forward, fangs as long as cooking knives sinking into his calf. His veins burned white hot, hotter than his own fury.

"Son of a bitch!"

The bite was brief and failed to hit bone. Danya pretended to not see the gaping holes in his flesh and kicked Ilya once more with his uninjured leg. No time to worry, he needed to avoid dying.

He added enough force behind the strike to send this drekavac back a few feet, ribs cracking loud and clear. Ilya's shriek had his ears ringing, the rest of the forest deathly silent in response to his agony. The beast rolled into a tree, heads going limp on impact. Danya stumbled back, tears stinging his eyes.

This sucked shit. He didn't want to hurt Ilya. This was far and beyond failure in his duty, this was the opposite of his purpose. Why did he keep fucking up so badly? Maybe he needed Ilya to just kill him and get it over with.

"Ilyushka," Danya sobbed, "I'm sorry."

Danya planted his feet into the mud, bracing himself for whatever was to come. He would take his punishment. This is what he deserved.

Ilya got to his feet quickly, springing back up. His heads wheezed in unison, all trained on Danya. The visible dent in Ilya's chest made Danya nauseous. He stared at it while Ilya rushed him again, claws slashing through iron and skin. The metal went red hot, burning through his clothes. Danya twisted away on reflex, summoning the last ounce of his strength to try and break free.

If this was his last moment, he would embrace his former love one last time.

The chains fell in a heap at his feet. He spread his wings wide, still more pain working through him. Danya no longer remembered what it was like to be okay.

Ilya shrank back upon seeing Danya's wings spread, all three heads hissing and snapping at the air irritably. Danya let them relax, sagging so hard they dragged across the forest floor. He would pose no threat.

The drekavac tackled him to the ground, center head sinking its teeth into Danya's arm. Another head bit into his neck; he gagged from the force. His arms quaked, slowly reaching to touch Ilya. The feathers were soft, the iridescent scales smooth. It felt right that even as a monster, Ilya was beautiful.

"Ilya. It's me. I love you."

The corners of his vision were growing dark, body growing stiff. Danya summoned one final burst, lifting his wings to wrap around their bodies. One last protective, feathery cage, one last attempt to reach him. Ilya refused to let go, his last head sinking its teeth into his hip.

Danya turned his head, even as teeth tore deeper into him; he was used to that sensation. He placed a gentle kiss on the snout of the drekavac, of Ilya. Ilya's feathers stood on edge, grip faltering. Danya's own grasp was failing, heart pounding rapidly in its desperation to keep him alive.

The smell of burning hair invaded his nostrils before everything went black.

27

Ilya couldn't breathe. Not well, at least. The rain was freezing, each drop like an icy pellet slamming against his bare skin. The thing underneath him was warm, at least. Ilya blinked rain out of his eyes, lifting himself with his hands to see what the warmth was.

The figure was striking. A shock of scarlet hair, warm brown skin, golden freckles. Who could this be?

No. That was wrong. He knew this man. He loved this man. That much he knew.

The man had two deep, gory wounds on his neck that shone liquid gold. His lips were blue, skin gray, veins around his mouth and eyes inky black. This man was sick and Ilya loved him and wanted him to live.

Instinct told him to reach out with a hand, touch it to the beautiful man's cheek. Warm light emanated from his palm. He stroked his hand across the man's face, fingers gently curling into the beautiful strands of hair on his head. The visible veins retracted back into the skin, color returning to the ashen face, wounds closing. Ink leaked from his hand, slowly washing away with the rain.

Danya. This was Danya. The love of his life, the angelic warrior who he called protector and companion. He remembered now. How could he ever forget somebody so incredible? This champion of the Sun who cared for him, gave him hope unlike any he'd ever known? Danya, who had taught him he could still be happy, who taught him what real love was supposed to be like.

Danya.

A gloved hand dug into his curls, yanking him off of Danya's body and onto his feet. Ilya clawed at it in desperation, eyes flicking up to meet the cold gaze of another man. Red dripped from his leather coat, spatters of mud covering the worst of it. He let go of Ilya only to grab his wrist like a vice, threatening to break the delicate bone.

"I should have just fucking killed you," he hissed. "My ego, my mistake then. No matter. Just as your stupid angel was fixed, so too shall you be."

This was Nikolai. Unfortunately, he remembered that too. Nikolai had caused all of this misery, had made him a monster who hurt Danya, had made Danya a monster who hurt others, who obeyed his church without a single thought, who craved power above all else. Ilya remembered him now.

He made a feeble attempt to break out of Nikolai's grasp, his fist clenching tighter. Ilya's breathing grew strained again, fighting against the ache in his ribs. His head pounded as memories flooded back in crashing waves, every feeling, every thought that had been lost.

"If only your little protector bird had agreed to share, perhaps you would've seen reason and aligned with your church instead of becoming an *apostate!*"

Ilya spat in Nikolai's face. He hoped whatever poison had just been running through his teeth remained to send Nikolai to his grave. How *dare* he. Nikolai's glare was wild, inhuman in its rage. It was like staring into the eyes of the drekavac, all those months ago.

"There is only one blasphemer between us, hunter. She knows that."

"Take it to your grave then, you disgusting little priest."

Blood erupted in the back of Ilya's throat, searing agony at the side of his neck. The handle of a knife stuck out in his peripherals, choking off his air. His mouth was coated in the metallic, salty taste. He gurgled and gasped, coughing to keep from drowning on his own life force.

Nikolai removed the blade in a swift motion, a new spray of red, red as Danya's hair, red as the dawn sky, red that stained the very air around them in its amount. Ilya covered the wound with his hands, anything to stop the bleeding. Nikolai pushed him back into the mud, wind knocked out of Ilya's clogged lungs.

He aspirated, strength fading fast. He could only ask, *Why, Great Mother, can I save others, but I cannot save myself?*

His vision went white for a flash. For a moment, Ilya believed he was being drawn into the realm of light, but an unearthly screech, followed by the gray sky returning, corrected him.

"NO!"

It was as if thousands of voices spoke in unison, so loud it shook the wet ground beneath him. Ilya grit his teeth, trying to hold on, to understand what was happening. He watched Nikolai scream, palms going to his eyes as smoke rose from under his gloves. He clawed at his face, ashen hunter's skin turning angry pink as more burned away under his hands. It bubbled and boiled, blood popping from arteries to stain the raw flesh.

Nikolai dropped to his knees next to Ilya, another agonizing scream ripping from the back of his throat before collapsing in a heap.

Ilya gasped again and again, eyes darting around in fear. He couldn't breathe. His air was gone. This was it. He dropped his hands in his defeat.

The ground shook as a massive figure rushed to him. Ilya's eyes went wide, trying to take it all in. Alabaster flesh that twisted around a vertical mouth full of jagged teeth, like if the knot of a tree were filled with thorns. Dozens of red eyes that looked in every direction, some with more pupils than should be possible. Two golden rings floated around the creature's face, giving off a warm light that surprised him in its gentleness. Fiery wings sprouted from the head, back, and Sun knew what else.

"I've got you, Ilyushka," the voices said.

Danya.

Two long, claw-like fingers extended out from one of the angel's hands. Danya pressed them to Ilya's neck. If Ilya had air left he would scream his pain. His head pounded, body convulsing in one last, futile attempt to stay alive. Danya scooped him into his arms quickly, face down to the muddy floor of the woods. The familiar pounding of wings reverberated in his ears.

As the ground shrank beneath him, Ilya stopped feeling cold. His heart slowed in his ears, the thrum of his blood down to a trickle.

At least he'd saved Danya. At least, with his last, he'd managed to do good. Just this once.

ILYA OPENED HIS EYES. It was a shock to be greeted with gray sky again. The rain had lessened to a sprinkling, the lightest of drops hitting his forehead. The wind whipped by him, rustling the tall grass that surrounded him. His vision shifted, face pressed into Danya's warm chest.

He opened his mouth to speak, no sound coming out. His throat was on fire, scratched raw and open. Danya stroked his hair, gently shushing him.

"It's okay, Lyubimi." Danya's voice wavered, the most unsteady Ilya had ever heard it be. "I'm looking for a place for us. She told me. You just have to hold on for me, okay? She promised– Mama promised–"

Ilya tilted his head up, meeting the warm, glowing eyes of his beloved. Hot drops hit his forehead this time, tears streaming down Danya's cheeks. Ilya lifted a curled hand, moving shaking digits to grasp the damp, ratty, crimson threads that made up Danya's hair. From the moment the color had returned, all Ilya wanted was to reach out and feel it, to be close to Danya, to experience his warmth.

Danya was still as a statue while Ilya touched him. His hand moved to Danya's cheek, shaking thumb wiping away his tears.

Danya's warmth penetrated the chill of his body. A soft thing, a comfort. It never burned; it was a caress, an anchor point Ilya latched on to. As long as he felt that warmth, Danya was with him.

The warmth traveled down his wrist, relaxing his stiff fingers. Danya collapsed his hand on top of Ilya's, fingers curling around it. Ilya couldn't help his smile. Danya's thumb brushed over his knuckles, forcing Ilya's hand to stay against his skin. Ilya's skin was pale in comparison, but what little color he had was gone. It was as white as the mask of the drekavac.

There were so many things Ilya wished he could say. He wished he could tell Danya how much he meant, how grateful he was, how happy he'd been. How wonderful that these last few months had been so much better for his love. How wonderful that Danya had been kind, had changed the heart of at least one other.

He tried to speak, nothing but a wisp of air passing through his teeth.

This sucked.

Ilya choked on a sob, the pads of his fingers pressing into Danya's cheek. All he could taste was metal on his tongue. What a horrific thing to go out on. It had never occurred to him that his last taste would matter so much to him. He would've liked something else.

"You'll be okay Ilya," Danya whispered. "She promised. Hang on for me, okay? She promised."

Danya held him to his chest again. Ilya breathed in that spiced scent. The rain had washed away the clove cigarettes, but the sweet, cinnamon smell remained. At least his last scene was a good one.

Ilya cried still, though nothing fell from his eyes. He cried and cried, desperately clinging to the life he didn't have anymore, feeling too much like a scared child again. The child he'd stopped being the day his father died and left him the burden of all of Velak; the child that Oyuna had once adored as her own; the child that his mother had accused him of being.

In the end she had been right.

Ilya's grip faltered, hand dropping. His fingers tangled in

Danya's knotted hair as his body grew limp, the warmth disappearing. He was numb and scared and horrified to leave.

"Hang on for me Ilyushka." Danya's voice was so desperate, a soft echo in the back of his mind. "Hang on, please!"

And still, Ilya's grip failed him and the world went black again.

28

Unknown time, unknown place.

The squawk of a raven woke him. Ilya was warm again. This made sense to him. The Sun's paradise had to be warm, above all else. Surely it would be beauty incarnate, unlike anything on earth.

Would he get to see his father?

Would Danya have been called home to be with him?

His eyes stuck when he tried to open them. Ilya groaned as he rubbed at them, wiping the crust away. He blinked rapidly, blurred light filling his vision until clarity returned.

A white plaster ceiling not unlike the rectory stretched out above him. Much more mundane than he'd imagined the realm to be, if he was honest. He'd hoped for a few more handsome men.

Or even just one handsome angel. One who should've been called back, who was not in this bed next to him. Was he with Tatyana instead?

Ilya pushed himself up, glancing at the space beside him. The covers were mussed, which suggested *someone* had been sleeping next to him. His head pounded as it flooded with too many thoughts and worries all at once. He rubbed at his eyes again with the heels of his palms, hissing through his teeth. He blinked and looked around, taking in the sights.

The walls were more white plaster, dark wooden beams holding everything together. The floor was made of flat, dark gray stone tiles. In several places the stone was shattered or missing, grass and flowers and vines crawling up from the exposed earth. Dry leaves covered the floor in front of the bed. Ilya trained his eyes upward.

There was a gaping hole in the ceiling, branches of a tree smashing through. Several large ravens perched on them, beady black eyes staring Ilya down. One cawed at him, head tilting in its curiosity. It didn't seem to be afraid of him, and thankfully wasn't aggressive. Ilya blinked in surprise, doing his best to absorb everything.

He wasn't dead. He couldn't be, at least, because his idea of paradise certainly didn't involve broken surroundings and *more birds*. The one with the dirty mouth was enough.

Ilya pulled himself out of bed, glancing down at his clothes. He was relieved to be clothed, considering how he last remembered his state of being. They were plain black pajamas not unlike the ones he used to wear. They were standard church issue, and not a fussy affair. It was comforting to have something so familiar.

His heart ached. Danya had dressed him while he had been out. He'd wanted Ilya to be comfortable. His eyes stung; Danya cared for him so much.

It was a selfish relief that Danya hadn't been called home. He was sure Tatyana missed him, but Ilya needed him here. Very badly.

Now, why did Danya bring him to a run down, filthy room? He should know better.

A raven bawked at him, drawing his attention back to the tree. When he stepped up to it, the raven beat its wings and yelled at him again. Despite his better judgment, Ilya held his hand out, clucking his tongue. The raven's feathers puffed up, staring at his fingers. Ilya couldn't help but laugh; it looked the same as when Danya was irritated.

"You're both little bird brains, aren't you?" Ilya cooed. He reached out, stroking a finger along the raven's beak. He kept his movement slow, careful. The bird settled, eyes closing as Ilya kept petting it. "You are a little bird brain... that's why you're both cute."

The raven perked up after a moment, gently gnawing on Ilya's nail before flying into the branches. He'd never had pets; maybe these wouldn't be so bad. The ravens at his old church had done well to keep the place pest free so long as he threw out seed for them. Perhaps in time he'd earn these birds' trust as well.

He opened the door to the room, greeted by a sight that had him reconsidering his "alive" status. It was a grand room that stretched two stories tall. In the center stood an enormous deciduous tree, perhaps an oak based on the shape of the leaves. Its branches crowded into the roof of the building, light leaking through the holes it created. Painted paper flags adorned the trunk, long faded with time. Encircled around it were also a set of stairs, plain boards that had been nailed into the tree. It was hard to say if Danya had done that or they were here when he found it.

Immediately in front of the room was a grand fireplace ringed by rotting couches and plush chairs. Across from that was another room, a front entrance of double doors, and what seemed to be a check in desk. He supposed a fancy old hotel wasn't the worst place he could've been brought.

Ilya stepped toward the tree, glancing around still. A bathroom lay next to the bedroom he'd come out of, and next to that was a kitchen and dining room. There was even a library in the corner. Once he was at the base of the stairs at the tree he could spot a set of double stairs that lead to the second floor, though they had caved in long ago.

Ilya wrinkled his nose. Surely Danya would've been able to manufacture better stairs than *boards nailed into a tree*. Though he supposed when you could fly, stairs hardly mattered.

Ilya stood before said stairs, tentatively stepping onto the first board. It seemed to be well embedded, though it creaked under his weight. He grimaced. Did he want to risk this?

"Danya? Danylko?"

He listened carefully, but no response came. Was he out?

Ilya sighed, carefully stepping onto the next plank. He took them one at a time, hoping they would hold with every step he climbed higher. He kept a hand firmly on the tree, trying his best to not think about the lack of railing and the high possibility he could simply fall to his death. What a waste that would be.

Finally he made it to the second floor. Where the lower level was overgrown but in otherwise good shape, this floor was a mess. Dust and litter were strewn about the halls. Several doors from the old guest rooms had been knocked in, making a wide entrance to a chaotic space of even more junk. It reminded him of Berta's shop, something that brought both fondness and terror.

A pattern of crackles and flashes from the corner of his vision caught his attention. The noise and light happened in even intervals; Danya must be welding. He'd borne witness to the task a few times when his church had been renovated, but it had been years since. It came as no surprise that Danya had gotten himself into welding, but it was also giving him far too much power. He'd worry about whatever mad science Danya would get up to later.

Ilya paused in the doorway, peeking into the room. Walls from at least two rooms on either side of this one had been knocked out to make a larger workshop space, though the rubble didn't seem to have been well cleaned. Danya stood hunched over a metal table, shoulders wound tight in his concentration.

Ilya stepped forward, foot crunching over crumbled brick. He swore from the pain in his sole, gasping as the full force of Danya's angelic power shoved him bodily back into the tree. It knocked the breath out of him, wheezing as the bark dug into his back. He glanced down at his assailant, golden eyes meeting his gaze. Those eyes went wide, a look of disbelief spreading across Danya's face. The arm that had Ilya pinned relaxed, falling to Danya's side.

"Danylko," Ilya wheezed, "It's just me."

A soft gasp burst from Danya's lips. Danya's hands pressed to Ilya's cheeks, rubbing his thumbs across the apples. His grip was firm, as if clinging to Ilya for dear life. Ilya placed his hands on top of Danya's, taking gentle hold of his wrists.

"Solnishko. Are you okay?"

Fat tears rolled down his angel's cheeks in waves. Every blink brought more moisture. Danya's lower lip quivered, biting it to keep it in place. Danya's brows knit together, his eyes slammed shut, and finally a sob escaped the back of his throat. Danya forced himself to look at Ilya again, eyes glassy with tears that refused to stop. Ilya moved his hands to Danya's cheeks, mirroring his touch, so that he could try to wipe his face clear.

"Danya... I'm here. I love you. I'm here."

Danya's face screwed up again, the sobbing uncontrollable now. Not once had Ilya ever seen Danya like this.

Danya wrapped his arms around Ilya, dragging him to the floor with his weight. Ilya winced as his back scraped against the tree, settling on the precarious floorboards surrounding it. Danya's arms wrapped around Ilya's waist as he buried his face into his lover's stomach. His angel refused to speak a word, could only cry and hold on to him with every ounce of strength he could muster.

Ilya held his hands in the air awkwardly for a brief moment. One hand came to rest on the crown of Danya's head, fingers brushing through those brilliant scarlet locks. Danya whimpered, leaning into his touch. Ilya placed his other hand on the side of Danya's head, Danya pillowing his cheek into Ilya's palm. Danya continued to sob as Ilya stroked his hair, though the action did seem to soothe him.

When Danya's sobs softened into sniffling cries, Ilya sang to him. His voice was low as he sang a church hymn. It was one Danya had mentioned liking the first time Ilya had sung for his angel. It was a lullaby to soothe an anguished man, one who still refused to speak. Ilya's throat lit aflame with the effort, but he pressed on until finally Danya was silent.

Gently, he lifted Danya's head for their eyes to meet once more. Golden pools of light were rimmed in red, cheeks flushed from crying. Not once had Danya ever cried in front of him; that had been Ilya's job. His heart shattered into a million pieces thinking he had even a hand in his lover's tears.

"I prayed to Her," Danya croaked, "Every day. I begged. I told

Her I couldn't fail again. I couldn't lose my love a second time. I begged for her to save your life, and She did. But then you fell asleep again. And didn't wake up."

Danya paused as a fresh wave of tears overtook him. He hiccuped and gasped, breath coming in shaky as he tried to calm himself enough to keep speaking.

"I thought I was being punished. That She was keeping you alive but not awake so I would suffer with my failures." He hiccuped again, sitting up enough to bury his face into Ilya's collarbone, trying to breathe in his scent. Ilya went back to stroking his head. "But you're awake. You're okay. She wasn't mad at me... She wasn't. Mama... Mama fixed you. She fixed you and She's not mad at me!"

Danya broke once again, fingers digging into Ilya's vestments as cries of anguish escaped him over and over again. Ilya's chest wound tight, hands aching with familiar shame. Danya kept his emotions close to his chest, preferring to focus on Ilya's. Ilya was stupidfor being blind to them for so long.

"You're not a failure, Solnishko. I'm here. She loves you. She loves us all, but of course She loves one of her children most of all. You're Her son. Danya... Danylko... I'm okay. You'll be okay too. We will be okay."

Danya didn't seem to hear him, quietly sobbing against Ilya's neck. Ilya held him close, Danya practically crawling into his lap, curled up in the fetal position in his arms. Danya's great feathery wings cradled them both, a shield from the world around them. The only thing that existed here in this space was him and Danya. They were together.

When his back began to ache, Ilya gently woke Danya from his exhausted slumber. He rubbed at his eyes, sniffling as they both got to their feet.

"I'm sorry," Danya whispered.

"Hush." Ilya leaned up, placing a peck on Danya's lips. "Don't apologize to me again. Kiss me, you silly angel. Show me your love."

Danya needed no further prompting. He picked Ilya up, holding him tight before their lips met again. There was no heat behind it, no feverish physical wanton need. There was desire, but it was more a craving for affection. Danya was so careful with him, tenderly kissing Ilya, remapping his mouth. Their tongues slid together, Danya tasting every inch he could get. Still, they made no moves to go further. All they had between them was kisses and gasping breath.

For a moment Danya broke the kiss to speak. "I kissed you every morning you were asleep. I felt like I didn't deserve it... That I didn't have a right to touch you. But I wanted you to feel loved, even if you were in the realm between. I had to make sure you felt it. I needed you to know how much I loved you, Ilyushka. My Ilya..."

Ilya's eyes stung with tears this time. He knew Danya loved him, saw it in every action he made, every breath he took, but hearing it from Danya's lips to his ears was nearly too much.

Gently, Ilya moved Danya back. He smoothed out his lover's hair, frowning at every knot he passed over. He'd fix that. For now, he had questions.

"How long was I out?"

Danya's face crumpled, head turning down. Ilya wished Danya wasn't so ashamed.

"Six months."

Ilya froze. He had been expecting a few days, perhaps a few weeks at most. Half of the year?

"Oh, Danylko, I'm so sorry." Ilya pulled him in for another kiss, relishing in the touch. Danya whimpered, sniffling desperately to hold back from crying again. "I'm so sorry, Solnishko. I've left you for far too long."

Danya shook his head. "Doesn't matter. Just needed you here. Now you're here. S'all I wanted."

Danya's voice was strained, Ilya could see the muscles of his throat wound tight. He ran his fingers over the warm skin, soft light emanating from his touch. Danya wasn't injured, and he couldn't heal wounds of the mind, but he could try to help his partner relax.

A sigh escaped Danya's lips, a release of tension held too long. Good.

"Thanks, Ilyushka…"

Ilya felt light, despite everything. He and Danya were reunited, they were in a safe place. They could finally spend time together. They could be as open as they wanted here. No more fear. No more hateful townsfolk to call them useless, to tell lies about them. It was all gone.

"How did you find this place? It's so strange."

Danya pulled back, holding his hand out for Ilya. Their fingers laced together and Danya began to lead him back down the stairs.

"Mother told me. Not with words, just… pointed me in the right direction. Nobody's come to bother us so far, and fucking good riddance. We're in the middle of nowhere and the rest of the area around here hasn't been touched in probably years. I… I tried to work on things some, but…"

Ilya squeezed Danya's hand tight. "Give me a few days to become neurotic enough and I'll have everything fixed in no time."

Danya huffed a laugh, shaking his head. "I'm glad it already feels enough like home that you'd want to do that."

"Of course it does. You're here with me."

They paused on the stairs, Danya looking back at him. His brows were knit, eyes glassy once more.

"Danya," Ilya continued, "We could be living in a hole in the ground and I'd be happy, so long as you were in it next to me. I'll be with you until my last if I can help it."

Danya panted quietly, forcing more tears back down. "You mean it?"

"Always, Danya."

Danya went back to leading him down the stairs, clearing his throat before speaking again. "You'll like it here. Kitchen's huge, plenty of rooms to turn into whatever you want. Library's big, maybe something new for you to read. Got a whole fucking bar to ourselves, but I hid all the booze in the cellar for you. Wasn't sure how you'd feel about it… There's even a chapel room. Not gonna be like your church. Pretty plain as far as Eclipse churches I've seen"

Ilya smiled, moving his thumb across the top of Danya's hand.

"I think plain suits me anyway. I don't suppose I could trouble you to put some damn railings on these stairs though?"

"Ha! Fine. I'm sure I can work something out. Plenty to salvage from the area."

THE CHAPEL WAS in fact plain compared to his church at home. No, not home. Just Velak.

It was more like the rectory than anything else. It couldn't have been bigger than a classroom, only three rows of pews before the altar. There was no skylight, no confessional, and not a slab of marble in sight. A black rug trimmed in gold ran down the center aisle and onto the predella. He was happy the stained glass remained, three windows crammed together behind the altar and five more on the right-side wall.

He did miss some of the grandeur of his Father's church. He'd grown up admiring its beauty, excited to inherit it one day. Despite all he'd endured, he'd still held a fondness for that building.

This was a more modest place of worship, a temporary home away from home for weary travelers. He would allow himself permanence here. He would make do.

Ilya wandered forward, brushing dust off of the pews as he went. He glanced behind the altar, relief at finding an old uniform tucked away. Ilya turned his head when Danya sighed.

"Do you really have to wear that again? It looks stuffier than your last set."

Ilya snorted. "I want to. I'm probably excommunicated by now, but... it matters to me. You understand, yes? This is... These clothes are who I am."

Danya softened, nodding in affirmation. "As long as I still get to take you out of them every so often."

"Every day if you like, Danylko."

Danya whistled in approval, grin spreading across his face. "That's all I need to hear."

Ilya rolled his eyes, but he was relieved. That Danya was

returning to his crass sense of humor meant the world right now. If Ilya had truly been gone for months, being able to return to old banter must be a comfort. He would do anything to help heal Danya's heart, including endure a few jokes, as he always would.

DANYA BROUGHT them back to what Ilya presumed was their bedroom. The ravens bawked and fluttered down from the ceiling, staring at the both of them.

"I see this place came with friends," Ilya said. "You didn't kick them out?"

Danya shrugged. "They were here first. Seems rude to just kick them out. We have an arrangement."

"And what could you possibly have arranged with a flock of carrion birds?"

"Well, I feed them my leftovers and whatever seeds I can get my hands on. They eat all the fucking mice and warn me when people get too close. Sometimes bring me screws and bolts too."

Ilya scoffed and shook his head. Bird brains, all of them. "And do they wake you constantly, being in the bedroom like this?"

Danya approached one of the birds, gently stroking its head. The raven bowed its body to accommodate him, head tilting this way and that.

"Ilya. Love you. Ilya!" The raven called, throat rising and falling as it vocalized. It stared directly at Ilya.

Danya ducked his head. "They might've picked up a thing or two…"

"Enough they recognize me… Smart thing. Smarter than your bird-brained intruder, yes?" Ilya reached out to stroke this raven's beak as well, earning himself a strange purring sort of sound. Danya huffed beside him.

"Smarter than me, anyway."

Danya pulled Ilya in, arms wrapped tight. His wings spread out, wrapping them in a feathery cage. Ilya spotted the scar across the center, feathers not quite grown in. Ilya wasn't sure what had happened before he changed back, and he also wasn't sure Danya would share. Maybe one day.

He was enveloped by the scent of cinnamon, tobacco, and cloves. There was a layer of mechanical grease and linseed oil underneath, all familiar to him. This was where he wanted to exist.

"Is this the part where you drag me to bed, Danulyachka?" He kept his tone light, teasing. Danya kept his emotions close to his chest; it was hard to tell how raw he was feeling at any time. Danya had spent so many months comforting him, protecting him. Ilya would return the favor now.

Danya's laugh was watery. Perhaps still too raw.

"I want to, but also don't. I don't know. I just... wanna touch you right now. Am I making sense?"

Ilya pulled back to look Danya in the eyes. He rubbed his thumb across the apple of Danya's cheek, holding his jaw with a ghost-light touch.

"We can do that. You need a nap, Solnishko."

"You just woke up..."

"Doctor's orders, Danylko. No arguing."

Danya rubbed at his eyes, sniffling loud. "Fuck, even having you mother hen me again gets me."

Ilya guided him back to their bed. He helped Danya carefully strip out of his clothes, earning a few more cheeky remarks. Ilya did the same, leaving only bare skin. They faced each other as they laid down. Danya's hands roamed, moving over Ilya's face, his neck, fingers tracing the line of his collarbones and clavicle. They didn't wander much lower than his chest.

"It doesn't feel real. I thought... I just..."

Ilya pulled Danya's hand to his lips, kissing along the scarred knuckles. "I'm here, Danya. I love you. I won't be leaving any time soon."

"I... I need to thank my Mother."

"We can do it together. Later. Rest, my darling, stubborn angel. We will have tomorrow together again."

Ilya held Danya's face, gently using his thumbs to force the lids of his eyes to close. Danya smiled, short chuckle blowing out of his nose. He seemed to settle after that. Ilya watched him carefully, relieved as Danya's features softened with sleep. Ilya let his eyes fall closed again after. Despite being asleep for what was apparently six months, he was exhausted.

He supposed coming back from the dead was always going to be tiring.

29

September 12th, 1928

The leaves had begun to turn on the oaks surrounding their home, green slowly bleeding into shades of yellow and orange. The breeze was cool enough to make his hands stiff, but not the biting ice of winter. Not yet. They stood in the front yard of the old hotel next to a mossy statue of a raven, hands linked. Ilya had lit the last brick of incense he could find in the chapel, though he feared it would blow out with the wind. His eyes were closed, turned down toward the yellowing grass beneath their feet, sandalwood wafting in the air.

"We thank you, O Great Mother, for your blessings. Your light, your warmth, and the life you have provided us. For the life you gave your son, who in turn saved mine. For saving my life for his sake, for the love you have for him. We thank you for looking after his past love in your realm and keeping her safe in your care. Your love is real, and it is meaningful. It is felt, and we will endeavor to hold up your ideals.

"Thank you, Mother Sun, for blessing me with the love of your child. I will endeavor to keep him safe, as he keeps me safe. Until my last breath, I will love him. Your favor will not go without repayment in every action of my life."

Danya squeezed his hands briefly before letting go. The shift of fabric and crunch of the grass underfoot made Ilya open his eyes.

Danya was down on one knee. In his hand was an earring, one of Danya's own feathers linked to the end of a gold chain. It glittered in the low afternoon light, the last hints of summer until The Mother faded for the year. It was the same day Ilya had gone into the woods beyond the edge of Velak, the day his life had changed forever.

Ilya sobbed. The emotion came immediately, with incredible force. He doubled over, hand to his chest. He wanted to say so much, but the tears wouldn't stop.

"Ilya Pavlovich Sokolov. Ilyushka. Lyubimi..." Danya's voice wavered, nerves peaking. Ilya had no idea why he was even a little bit scared; he should know the answer already. "Ilya. Please... would you marry me?"

"Yes," Ilya choked out. Danya placed the feather earring in Ilya's palm. Ilya wrapped his fists around it, careful to not split the vane. Danya rose up, wrapping his hands around Ilya's.

"Dear Mother... Thank you for giving me a second chance. Thank you for loving me, and allowing me to keep loving this mortal man. I can never repay the debt I owe you, though I know you will never ask anything of me. I will work with him to spread your message, to fight those who would claim to love you while doing harm.

"Dear Ilya... I love you more than my own life. You saved me from a world of darkness, of pain and endless hunger. You restored me with your love, your faith in me. Despite all of *your* pain, all of your hardship, you did not let it harden your heart. Thank you for allowing me into it, despite your fears. I promise... You'll never regret saving that beast in the woods. Until your last breath, until mine, until the day we are called home. I love you."

Ilya kissed him hard, holding Danya tight. Danya wrapped his wings around them, light spilling through the translucent feathers. Ilya was surrounded by warmth and soft, golden light. He was home. This was where he was meant to be all along. Never in his life did he think he could have this, yet here he was. He was free of Velak, free of his prison of a church, free of judgment. He had a husband. He had a new home of his own. They loved each other.

They were free. And they would fight all who would threaten to take it away.

ONCE THEY SET their matching feather earrings on the nightstand, all bets were off. Danya was doing his level best to rip Ilya out of his vestments without actually tearing fabric. Ilya fumbled with the snaps on the back of Danya's shirt. They were a tangle of limbs and clothing haphazardly tossed aside before lips crashed together. Their mouths moved feverishly, unable to bear with parting. When they were bare, Danya shoved Ilya back onto the bed. He crawled over him, kissing Ilya into the pillows.

Ilya tangled his fingers in Danya's hair, pulling ever so slightly to spur him on. Danya groaned deep in his throat, the sound reverberating through Ilya's chest. Danya kissed down to his throat, sucking hard on the skin to make it bloom red under his teeth. Ilya whimpered, cock throbbing to life from the attention. In his mind it hadn't been long since last they were together, but his body craved touch like it was starving.

Danya made every mark he could, growling under his breath, "All mine."

"All yours," Ilya gasped.

He wrapped his arms around Danya's head, holding on to his hair again as he moved lower. Danya's lips and tongue trailed down and down, stopping at the dip in his hips. Danya gripped them hard, thumbs pressed into the pale, translucent flesh that purpled immediately. Ilya had missed this, the markings, the strength and pain that lit his blood on fire. Danya had him body and soul.

Lips wrapped around his cock, more heat, soft tongue flicking across the head. Ilya shivered and reached to grab the pillows above his head, nails digging into the fabric. He gulped down air, sucking it in through his belly, skin sticking to his ribs. Danya relented after just a moment, leaving Ilya hard and wanting.

Danya sat up on his knees, his own hardness hanging dark and heavy between his thighs. Ilya's mouth watered, his heart pounded. He needed Danya more than ever.

Danya grabbed oil from their nightstand and in one more swift motion, he was coated. His cock glistened in the low light of the room, Ilya's hunger only growing. Danya's fingers lowered and Ilya parted his thighs. He reached under his knees to spread himself wide, shivering as the warmed oil was spread over his hole. Fingers slipped in, spreading the slickness. Already Ilya felt filthy.

Ilya hissed, "Hurry—"

"So greedy, even on our wedding day," Danya crooned back.

Danya pulled his fingers out, taking hold of himself to press against Ilya's entrance. Ilya sucked air through his teeth. He wasn't used to this anymore, but the sting only spurred him on. He panted as Danya pressed in, shivering when their hips pressed flush together as he bottomed out. Ilya was full, Danya's heat pouring into his core. He felt every throb and pulse of Danya's cock, how it pressed against his spot. He'd needed this.

"You're tight all over again, Ilyushka— I'll go slow."

"Not too slow, Danylko."

Danya licked his teeth as he grinned, pulling out fractionally. He slammed back into Ilya, making him cry out. Danya's pace built up, steady and even. Ilya gasped and whined with each thrust, nerves lighting on fire, fingers prickling. He kept his arms hooked under his knees, looking up at Danya. Danya pressed their foreheads together, red strands of hair sticking to Ilya's sweat-soaked skin.

"Faster, Danya. Please."

Ilya's wish was Danya's command. He pounded into Ilya, relentless in his pace. Their skin slapped together wet and loud, Ilya shouting with each thrust.

"Oh Danya— Danya, please—"

"I've missed this so much," Danya growled. "Say the word and I'll fucking wreck you."

"Do it."

Danya kissed him hard, tongue forcing its way past his teeth to lick along every surface, to force more feeling into Ilya. Ilya let him, let him do whatever he pleased. He knew nothing but pleasure, Danya's ferocity bringing him to the edge. Danya grabbed hold of Ilya's knees, pinning them back so Ilya was bent nearly in half. Ilya instead wrapped his arms around Danya, nails scratching along his back, fingers digging into the base of his wings.

Danya's hips stuttered, sharp moan directly in Ilya's ear.

"Damn it Ilyushka— I don't wanna finish yet."

"But I'm close, Danya. Let's, together—"

Danya moved faster still, Ilya throwing his head back and shouting. Danya bit at his exposed throat, marking more pale flesh. Ilya kept rubbing at Danya's wings, relishing in the soft, fluffy feathers. Danya whined once again, biting into Ilya's shoulder as hard as he could.

"Ah fuck— Danya!"

Ilya's body was wound tight as a spring, head in a fog. His muscles flexed, pleasure bursting forth in his veins as he came. He splashed hot on his stomach in ropes, shiver moving down his spine.

Danya kept slamming into him for just a few moments more before he finished as well, spilling deep inside of him. Ilya gasped as heat filled his gut, the all-too-familiar feeling sending another wave of pleasure through him. Danya made a mess of him; he loved being a mess.

Ilya let his arms go loose, flopping back on the bed. Danya released his knees, propping himself up on his hands. They both gulped down air, Danya's sweat dripping down onto Ilya's chest. Danya grunted as he began to pull out of Ilya, both moaning as slick spilled out of his hole and down his thighs.

"You're my perfect, slutty little priest, Ilyushka."

Ilya rolled his eyes and smacked Danya's chest. "So crass, even on our wedding day."

Danya barked a laugh, falling onto his back beside Ilya. "You'd hate it if I changed."

Ilya snorted. "I would..." He glanced over to Danya. His

husband. His partner for the rest of his life. He wouldn't change a single thing about his beloved angel.

"So what now, Ilya?"

"Well, a bath probably."

"I mean, besides that. What are we doing? We haven't had a chance to talk about it but... Nikolai said some concerning things. I'm worried people are in trouble and the church has gone power mad. They're... doing things to my siblings."

Ilya knit his brows together, deep frown carving into his features. "They defile Her name to justify their greed... We saw it with how Nikolai spoke to me. The rules don't have to apply to them... I can't stand for it."

Danya moved onto his side, hand splaying out on Ilya's chest. "So what do we do?"

Ilya stared at the ceiling for a long while. Danya traced the tender bruises in his skin, waiting patiently.

"I think... we gather what resources we can, we get ourselves together, and then we go and stop them where we can. We're only two... but maybe if we can help the smaller towns and villages, we can encourage enough of them to stand up. But I can't sit and do nothing. I'm probably excommunicated, they're lying and saying you're a demon. We have nothing to lose anymore."

"I'm happy to knock out the teeth of every smug motherfucker who acts like that Nikolai piece of shit did. I am your sword, Ilya. Point me where I should go."

Ilya leaned over to kiss him, dreamy sigh escaping him. "Then, my beloved angel, let us protect the weak and vanquish evil. Together."

"Together."

ART CREDITS

Public domain works by the following artists, in order of first appearance:

Max Klinger. Part I: Night. *Im Walde.*

Charles Meryon. Chapter 1. *Gallery, Nôtre-Dame Cathedral, Paris.*

Ivan Shiskin. Chapter 2. *Cave in Caves and Volcanoes*; Chapter 4. *The Backyard*; Chapter 6. *Thaw*; Part III: Day. *Oak Grove*; Chapter 23. *Winter Moonlight Night*; Chapter 27. *Rain in the Oak Forest*; Chapter 25. *Twilight*. Chapter 28. *Hut in the Forest*; Chapter 29. *Clouds Over the Grove.*

Isaac Levitan. Chapter 3. *First Green of May*; Chapter 9. *Small Village Under the Snow*; Chapter 17. *Quiet Cloister*; Chapter 20. *Sketch for Eternal Rest*; Chapter 21. *Study for Monastery Gate and Wall.*

Ilya Repin. Chapter 5. *At Dominic's*; Interlude 1. *Study for Scene from a Ballet*; Chapter 24. *The Taking of Christ into Custody.*

Aleksey Savrasov. Chapter 7. *Thaw*; Chapter 11. *The Rooks Have Come Back*; Chapter 18. *Ukranian landscape;* Chapter 22. *Tomb of Alexander Pushkin in Svyatogorsky monastery.*

Giovanni Battista Piranesi. Chapter 8. *Interior view of St. Peter's Basilica in the Vatican, from Vedute di Roma;* Interlude: Tatyana. *Two churches near Trajan's column, S. Maria di Loreto and Santissimo Nome di Maria.*

Eugène Cicéri. Chapter 10. *Winter Scene with Two Men.*

Johann Ludwig Ernst Morgenstern. Chapter 12. *Church Interior.*

Giuseppe Cades. Chapter 13. *Blessed Francis Venimbeni Celebrating Mass for souls in Purgatory.*

Giuseppe Galli Bibiena. Chapter 14. *Framed Design for an Altar.*

Vasily Polenov. Interlude 2. *Fire in a Dry Cobra.*

Julius Kronberg. Chapter 15. *Eros and the Goddess of Destiny.*

Henry Scott Tuke. Chapter 16. *Boys Bathing.*

Gustave Dore. Chapter 19. *An Angel Appears to Balaam.*

Kitagawa Utamaro. Chapter 26. *Hebi and Tokage from Ehon Mushi Erami.*

ACKNOWLEDGMENTS

It's hard to know where to even begin with an acknowledgments section, because there are so many people who helped me get here. Let me try to be as thorough as possible.

Let me first start by shouting out Print Run podcast, without which I wouldn't have even known where to begin with my publishing journey in any fashion. While I ultimately decided not to go trad, the wisdom there helped me make the best decision for myself and my book.

Similar shoutout to Publishing Rodeo podcast, which filled me (and continues to fill me) with such dread it tipped me over into doing the damn thing myself. I don't think that was the intent, but thanks anyway!

Special thank you to Rio for being the only person who read this at the alpha stage right after NaNoWriMo. You put up with so much and I am so grateful. I hope you read and enjoyed this version too.

Similar thank you to Stephanie (aka Qwordy) for being my first beta reader and champion. Your friendship and community has been invaluable. I don't think I would've ever got this damn book done without your writing sprints. I am also glad to finally have somebody to watch Eurovision with so my other friends can know peace.

My Angel Wranglers. I would've been out to sea without you and your continued friendship and support. I'm so happy to call all of you friends. I treasure each and every one of you. Rafa, Tyler, Morgan, Rae, Cas, Auré, Quinn, Alex, Dorian, Danni, Frey, Wren, Em, and Angie. There aren't enough words to describe what I feel

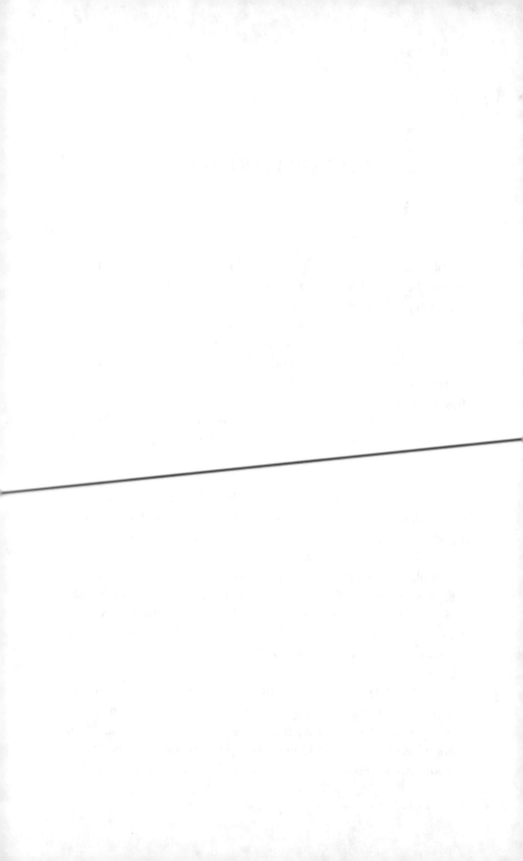

for all of you. We put together a whole anthology on a whim and loved and trusted each other enough to put in the work to make it happen. You've been some of my biggest, continued support, using your successes to uplift me and everybody else in the group. I hope now I'll be able to do the same for the rest of you. It would take many lifetimes to pay back even an ounce of what I owe you all. Thank you.

To my Loons. We met because of a silly podcast and because I asked too many damn questions at Office Hours, but I'm so happy I met you all. Even if Slack (Boomer Discord) gives me a headache.

To Eli, who has said and will continue to have to say that my writing is good and is worthy of being published. My friends are supposed to blow smoke up my ass, you understand, but especially the best friend I have. Thank you for putting up with me and for championing my work despite my best efforts, lmao. I fear it will happen again.

To my cover artist Soren, who did such and incredible job to bring this book to life. I knew you were the right fit from the moment I finally laid eyes on your work, and you lived up to every hope and dream I could've possibly had. Thank you!

To my editor Quinn, for ironing out this mess of a book. May you continue to trip up on my Americanisms in future books and other works we do together. Your kind but thoughtful and thorough critiques have made this story better.

To Monster Manor, which has brought me so many more friends and fellow authors than I could've ever expected. You're all wonderful, and the community you've created is one I couldn't be separate from. I promise you there is more angel fucking to be had from me.

Also thanks to the dickhead that I spite wrote this book because of, I guess. If you hadn't been such an asshole I don't think I would've gotten through the first draft of this. Continue to suck away from me.

Finally, to you, if you read all of this! I hope you loved the story, and thank you for your support of my writing journey. I hope you'll stick with me!

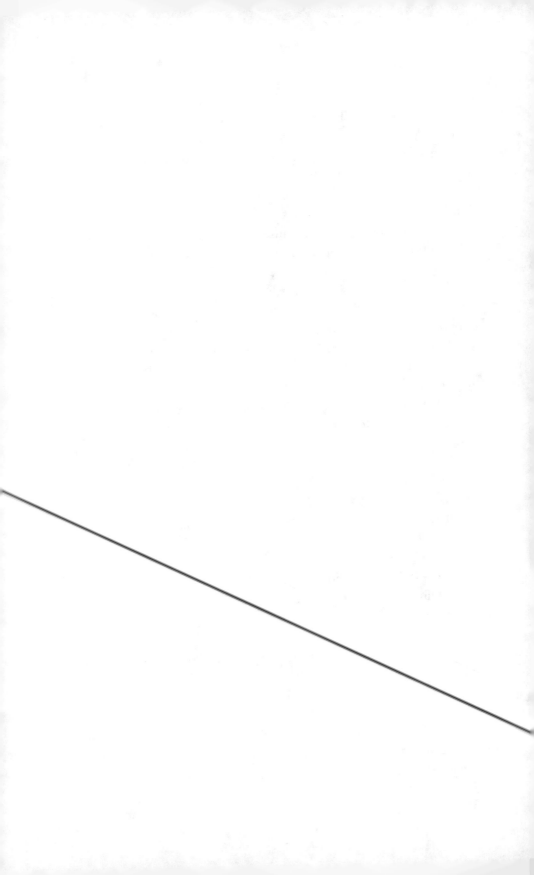

ABOUT THE AUTHOR

Ian Haramaki is an emerging author of queer fiction of all types. He has a short story entitled **Resta Con Me** within *Devout: An Anthology of Angels*. When not writing he is drawing very vibrant dinosaurs to hawk at fan conventions across the country. Maybe you can find him at a show near you.

twitter.com/cometkins

tiktok.com/@cometkinsart

goodreads.com/cometkins

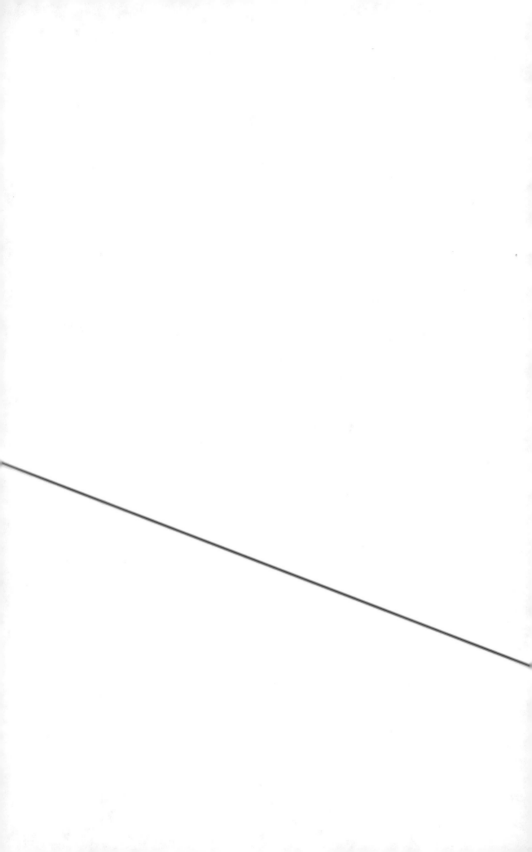

Printed in the USA
CPSIA information can be obtained
at www.ICGtesting.com
LVHW080256091123
763416LV00003B/3